THE BOOK OF DEVILS

THE BOOK OF DEVILS

BY

ROD VICK

www.penmorepress.com

ISBN:-13: 978-1-957851-90-7(Paperback)
ISBN:-13: 978-1-957851-89-1(e-book)

BISAC Subject Headings:

FIC031070 / FICTION / Thrillers / Supernatural
FIC009030 / FICTION / Fantasy / Historical
FIC028080 / FICTION / Time Travel

Edited by Chris Wozney
Emilia Rakić PR. Emily's World of Design

Address all correspondence to:
Penmore Press LLC
920 N Javelina Pl
Tucson AZ 85748

DEDICATION

To Dorothy Haslam, the kindest woman in town.

To my father, the storyteller, and my mother, the smartest person I've ever known.

ACKNOWLEDGEMENTS

I would like to thank the following amazing individuals for their editorial assistance and advice, which I relied upon extensively in completing rewrites: Larry Berg, Tom Kornkven, and Shawn Verdoni. I would also like to thank My Lovely Wife Marsha for her editorial input, although she is always far too kind.

In addition, I wish to thank Michael James and the good people at Penmore Press for their efforts in bringing *The Book of Devils* to life. Thank you to Chris Wozney, book editor, for the kind and essential feedback.

Finally, it is always important for an author to have certain friends who are so devoted and positive that even if he published ten years' worth of grocery lists in hardcover, they would slap him on the back, say kind things, and encourage him to even greater achievements. For me, that group includes David Boebel, Jerry Anich, Bruce Lammers, Michelle Lammers, Ted Bachhuber, Becky Bachhuber, Linda Stahlhut, Chris Ponder, Joe Rice, Carol Fickau, Chuck Becker, Nancy Dearborn, and Erin Everett.

PROLOGUE: CHICAGO

She was gone when he woke. Not long. His t-shirt was still warm where her head had rested against his stomach.

Mason Crockett sat up on the sofa, ran his hand through a tangle of rust-tinged curls, swiveled slowly right, then left, searching for the remote, switching off the TV. He had dozed off halfway through *Notorious*. It had always been one of his favorite films—partly because he loved Hitchcock, mostly because he crushed badly on Ingrid Bergman. They had watched *Casablanca* before that.

He smiled wanly.

They. He and Ricky Crowe. The young woman who had wanted no part of him. But they had survived—everything. And tonight had been the first time she had let her guard down.

Too much, maybe? Too soon? He knew Ricky was not exactly a people person. Prior to her sister's death, most of her free hours had been spent in her apartment, immersed in online role-playing games. Not a movie fan, she hadn't recognized the witty lines he had quoted from popular films. Crockett had figured it might take her a while to come around to the classics. And after all that had happened in Egypt and Ireland—and before that, Alabama—she could be forgiven for having some trust issues. She had been brutalized and betrayed in savage and heartbreaking ways.

Or had their budding intimacy simply been too awkward? He wasn't exactly Bogie or Cary Grant.

He stood then, quickly, slid to the window, wondering if he would catch her moving away down the sidewalk. He could still rush down the stairs, out into the night—How late was it?—and call after her. She'd turn, perhaps with some hesitation. He'd jog up, take her hand, smile, and in that smile, she'd know how he felt. He'd draw her back up the stairs and...

But the sidewalk was empty. As if captioning the lonely circle of streetlight half a block away, the words of Rick Blaine from the earlier film played in his head. *Where I'm going, you can't follow. What I've got to do, you can't be any part of.*

He felt a tugging at his core, as if his heart were a small boat taking on the darkest waters of the soul. He wanted her here tonight, in his small, cluttered, second-floor Chicago apartment. Needed her in a way he had never needed before. Already they had shared so much. She had saved his life at An Tsuil, the crumbling Irish monastery known as *The Eye of God*. And perhaps by the grace of that God, she had survived her own injuries and brushes with death.

All to defeat a great evil.

Now, it was done.

The struggle, the impossible challenges, their nearness to death, time and time again, it had forged a bond between them. But their closeness was more than the result of sharing experiences that had brought them both to the razor edge of mortality. Something that neither of them had expected, something that seemed to germinate at the atomic level had connected them.

Crockett sighed, picked up a mostly empty beer bottle from the floor next to the sofa, swigged the dregs. Life was funny. He had worked with Ricky's twin sister, Sasha, and for years had harbored a not-so-secret crush. A crush that had gone nowhere. He had been firmly ensconced in Sasha's friend zone. When he had met Ricky just weeks ago, she had not initially appealed to him at all. Sasha had been an outgoing, auburn-haired beauty with the brain of a climate scientist. What a contrast to Ricky, the introverted, college dropout with goth-black hair and an eight-inch scar down the left side of her face.

But now Sasha was dead, killed by foot soldiers of the soulless shrew they had vanquished at An Tsuil. And Crockett could not stop thinking about Ricky. This change of heart was not simply because Sasha was gone. In Ricky, he had discovered a beautiful, irreverent, courageous soul.

He took out his phone, looked at the time. Almost two in the morning. He frowned, tapped away.

HEY U DIDNT HAVE TO LEAVE. PLS COME BACK

He sent it, wondered for a moment if he would sound desperate, needy. Then, suddenly, he didn't care. All he cared about was having Ricky there, right now, tonight. He went to the window, stared down at the sporadically lit sidewalk, his heart full, his eyes glistening.

She would come. They had saved the world together. Now they were safe.

Ricky Crowe would come.

PART ONE

WHATEVER NIGHTMARES MIGHT COME

CHAPTER 1

Under blisteringly blue skies, she moved out of the gentle surf and wove an unhurried path through the glistening, tanned bodies reclining on blankets and under umbrellas and nylon sun shells dotting the white sand. In a black bikini, she was slender, and while not quite as tan as many of the others with whom she shared the beach, she was no longer as milk pale as she had been when she had left Chicago a year earlier. She had let her hair grow since rhen, down past her shoulders so that the original auburn had replaced the midnight dye job. Although it was plastered wet to her just now, when dry, it would be a tangle of gentle curls.

Yet, the longer curls could not fully conceal the thin scar down the left side of her face. That and the black patch over her left eye always drew a few furtive glances. She could imagine the questions as surely as if she were a mind reader. *What's her story? Accident? A fight? Yeah, she's lean and muscular. Maybe her eye is fine and she's just going for a look.* Then they would turn their gazes back to the sea or their partners or the slices of lime in their Coronas.

There had been another scar, below her left breast from a bullet she had taken at the monastery An Tsuil. A bullet that should have killed her. She ran her fingertips over the area as she walked. Now, a year later, not a trace. Unblemished perfection. If only the scar on her face would heal so completely. Or her eye. But those injuries had happened before her great folly.

In the past year, she had visited a dozen beaches. Ipanema, Cancun, Follonica, Mykonos, and elsewhere. Now she was in Aruba. And she was a year older, twenty-seven, although she wondered whether marking such milestones mattered anymore.

What mattered to Ricky Crowe was staying on the move. No friendships. No relationships. Just live like you had all the time in the world. Until it drove you mad.

And keep looking over your shoulder.

When she and Mason had returned from Ireland and the deadly confrontation with evil at An Tsuil, Crockett had celebrated the fact that the cult of Cessair had been broken, its leader and her army dead, its assets frozen, its followers in disarray, and the object of their obsession, the so-called Scroll of Life and Death, destroyed. Swept into the same vicious sea that had claimed Cessair herself.

But while cult leaders could be removed, the cults themselves were more difficult to kill.

Ricky stopped, felt the weight of sun and heat, looked back at the sea from which she had emerged. This friendly sea connected to other seas from which flowed memories of deceit, pain, and death. A distant sea held the body of her murdered sister Sasha. At least that was the theory. No one knew for sure, but it was assumed she had perished with Cessair's assassins when their plane exploded and plunged into the Greenland Sea not far from the Zackenberg research outpost more than a year ago.

Another sea held the mortal shell of Leo Brenner, the former head of the Habitat and Atmosphere Research Project Foundation–HARP–where Sasha had worked. Leo had been a friend who had saved Crockett and Ricky twice, although it was his betrayal—after being tricked and seduced by the power-mad Cessair—that had placed their lives in danger. In the end, he had paid for his sins by perishing along with Cessair in roiling waters half a world away.

Brenner's words returned to her daily as she soberly assessed her options. It was he who had warned that cults often persevered after suffering defeats. If Doomsday fails to arrive on the date named by a group of True Believers, no problem. Just a minor misreading of the stars. Here's the new date. If the Omnipotent Leader is deposed, defeated, or slain, no problem. The snake grows a new head. Or perhaps several. If the goal of the mob is refuted by cold, hard evidence, no problem. They simply rearrange the facts to conform to their warped vision of reality.

In a world of clear-eyed reasoning, following the defeat of Cessair's zealots, Ricky Crowe would face no demons other than the ones that lived within her. In the real world—a world where splinter cults, conspiracists, and fanatics flourished—she remained in great danger.

She stepped under the awning of the beachside bar, ordered a Coke. So many stops since leaving Chicago. She had gone to Crockett's that last night not to say goodbye. Well, not in so many words. That sort of thing would have been awkward at best, possibly ugly. She could not have expected him to understand her leaving. Not unless she revealed all of her secrets, but doing so might put Crockett in someone's crosshairs. So she had gone simply to see him one more time. But she had stayed too long. It had been so good, enjoying the warmth, the human touch as the old movies played. And if she was honest, she had wanted to stay; but Ricky understood that she could not gamble her survival on the toss of emotional dice. And the danger she faced could not be allowed to threaten anyone she cared for.

After leaving Chicago, where she still had the apartment that she had shared with her sister, Ricky had fallen hard. Leaving had torn at her soul in a way she had not expected, as had the bleakness she was certain would define her future. Years earlier, Sasha had taken her in and helped her get clean after Ricky had been nearly lost to alcohol and brokenness. Until her sister's death and the frenetic events that had followed, that apartment had been her sanctuary. Her sister's love had kept the world's evil at bay. Now, on the run and in despair, she had returned to drink. The hell she faced was too much. She would always be alone. Always be without real friends. Always be hunted for what she might know.

Or might be.

Always.

The alcohol had numbed her in those first months. Seeking human connection, she had entertained many partners, men and women.

Trying to fill the void.

Trying to deal with the anxiety of a life on the run.

Trying to feel normal.

But the encounters weren't real or meaningful. Pathetic imitations of things she really desired. The people and relationships? Disposable. After a night, a week, a month, she would be gone. No explanation.

Ricky had once called Cessair a monster. But what was *she*? Like a vampire, she tried to draw a kind of sustenance from those who were truly alive. And like a vampire, despite these intimate encounters with strangers, Ricky would never be one of them. She would only grow more monstrous and dangerous to those near her the longer she stayed.

The Scroll of Life and Death had guaranteed that.

Then, nine months ago, she had stopped. No alcohol. No lovers. There had to be another way.

The Coke arrived.

"The pretty lady drinks alone again today," said the smiling, brown-skinned bartender. "This proves that men are fools."

"I can give you a hundred examples of why men are fools," said Ricky in reply. "For instance, flattering ugly women in order to earn better tips."

The bartender did not flinch. "You are referring to your scar?"

"I'm not referring to my toenail fungus."

The bartender laughed. "I like you! But what is a scar? Your American Liberty Bell has a scar, yes? But no one says, 'This is an ugly thing!' In fact, the scar has made it more beloved, more memorable."

"Yeah, well, there's also the eye."

Now the bartender shrugged. "Our scars, blemishes, tattoos, injuries, these are merely curiosities on the road map of our lives. How boring if there are no points of interest along the way."

Ricky smiled. "I'm starting to like you, too. Even though you're full of shit."

This brought another laugh from the bartender. "You have got it right! There is much shit on the road map of my life!"

He gave her an affectionate wave and moved to refill the glass of another customer. Turning back toward the ocean, Ricky took a long sip. As she did, her thoughts traveled back to Chicago.

At first, she had believed Crockett. Or had wanted to. It was over. There was no threat from Cessair's followers. Now, she wondered if Crockett really believed that, or whether it was just something he was willing to say to make sure she would stay in Chicago and try to live a normal life, whatever that meant.

However, if she stayed, it was inevitable that Crockett would learn her secret.

That knowledge would make him vulnerable. She might manage to keep it from him for a few years, but cult splinter groups would suspect, and they might see harming Crockett as a way of getting to her.

Ricky could not allow that.

Even if she and Crockett defied the odds and no cult members *ever* appeared to threaten their idyllic existence, a day would come when she would have to protect Crockett from what *she* was destined to become.

And so she had left, traveling in ways that were difficult to track. Even so, within a few months, she had seen signs that her fears were warranted. A woman's gaze lingering too long on her from a nearby table at a sidewalk café. A man in the shadows outside her hotel, gone when she looked again. A hotel maid casually mentioning that someone had come looking for her. A car following her cab; a generous tip had convinced her driver to lose him.

She knew there was a chance that she was being paranoid, that these incidents might have commonplace or even innocent explanations that had nothing to do with her, aside from perhaps a morbid fascination with her mutilated face. But when she and Crockett had pursued Cessair, it was their paranoia that had helped keep them alive.

So she kept moving. Perhaps she would come up with a better plan, eventually. Meanwhile, Aruba was nice. Yet... She had arrived only two days ago. Already, she felt alone. And loneliness led her to play the what-if game, to imagine an alternate scenario that denied the dangerous realities.

What if I had stayed? she wondered, replaying that night in Chicago with Crockett for the thousandth time. Or if he had come with her. Oh, to have him here now in this place of warmth and white sand and a cool room where the shades could be pulled shut. Yet, she understood this to be a fantasy. She knew how it would have played out.

It was better this way. Or, she wondered, was this simply a lie she told herself to make the days bearable? They had both felt the connection. In the weeks after her disappearance, Crockett had doubtlessly suffered mightily. But that suffering was a grain of sand compared to what he would surely have endured in the decades ahead had she remained in Chicago.

What of her own suffering? Would a time ever come when, surrounded by happy people, walking barefoot across warm sands, and bathed in the gentle beat of bossa nova, she would truly feel content?

She stepped away from the bar, strolled past more sunbathers, then through the iron gate that separated her lodgings from the public beach. A dozen brightly-painted bungalows faced a small pool, beside which empty chaise lounges currently reposed. Each bungalow was a separate little unit decorated in an island motif. More like hotel rooms with king beds, baths, and kitchenettes than cottages. Hers was number nine.

Ricky tapped in the four-digit code, opened the door, slipped inside, leaned back against it, closed her eyes. After the searing sun, the cool darkness of her room felt good, bringing the ghost of a smile. Yet, there was something a moment later. Something almost heard. Something almost smelled. Something almost felt.

Her eyes flew open. Only darkness. Yet, she knew.

I'm not alone.

CHAPTER 2

Her windowless prison seemed to be a subterranean room. No sound penetrated the mildewed, block wall, and the floor felt clammy. She had no recollection of arriving here. Maybe they had used chloroform on her. Or jabbed her with a needle. She supposed someone could have even knocked her over the head. One minute she had been standing in her bungalow, and the next thing she remembered was waking, shackled to the wall, her head thick and achy, her mouth like cotton. She still wore the bikini. As far as she could tell, she had not been violated.

How long she had been unconscious, Ricky had no way of knowing. Earlier, a man had opened the wooden door to the room and looked in on her. He appeared to be an islander, dressed in long shorts and a tank top, tattoos down his right arm. Since then, there had been no one.

Iron bands half an inch thick encircled her wrists, secured by a bolt and a lock. To remove them would require both a key and a ratchet wrench. A thick chain connected these bracelets to an iron plate in the block wall behind her, where each was secured by four bolts that looked like they might defy budging even if a wrench materialized in her hand. The chain was long enough to just allow her to sit on the damp, cold floor. Her ankles were unbound, not that it made any difference. No tape had been placed over her mouth, bolstering the notion that the cell was probably underground in a place where shouting would do her no good. Since few homes here had basements, she guessed this was a commercial building.

A covered, five-gallon utility bucket sat to her left. Her toilet, from its stained appearance. An LED light was installed flush against the ceiling, although the switch for this must have been outside the room. No doubt some sort of sound-deadening foam lined the space between the hidden joists above. The room was empty of other items or adornment, except for stains and scrapes on the floor and walls that suggested the grim purposes for which it had previously been used. Ricky suspected human trafficking. Briefly, she considered that as a reason for her abduction. However, there were prettier girls on the beach. Girls who were not missing an eye, whose looks were not ruined by an eight-inch facial scar.

No. This was about her involvement with Cessair and the scroll.

They were fools. There was nothing she could do for them.

As if this thought were a summoning incantation, the wooden door swung open on screeching hinges, and three men stepped into the room. One was the dark-skinned man she had seen an hour earlier. The second, Caucasian, looked like a bodybuilder and wore stained cargo pants and a short-sleeved, flower-print shirt whose party theme seemed to mock the current circumstances. The third was in his sixties, short, stocky, with a mustache. He wore shorts with deck shoes and white, calf-high socks along with a short-sleeve shirt whose vintage and food stains were a cry for help from the nursing home dining hall. He seemed to be the leader, or at least the mouthpiece.

Deck Shoes offered a grandfatherly smile. "You can call me Bob."

Ricky said nothing. Her eyes traveled from him to the other two, radiating silent hatred.

Bob nodded to one of the men. "Hermes!"

The dark-skinned man instantly moved forward, and before Ricky could process and react, pinned her right leg to the concrete floor.

"Josiah!"

The other man moved out from the doorway, and over Hermes' shoulder, Ricky now saw that he carried a crowbar. She had barely time to scream "No!" before he swung it like he was trying to kill a snake, crushing her shin.

The pain was startling in its intensity. A tortured scream exploded from her, seeming to shake the walls of the dungeon. Hermes and Josiah moved away, and several minutes passed before Ricky had quieted to a softly whimpering heap. Her lower leg was bent at a sickening angle, the shin clearly fractured. While the bone was not visible, the violence of the crowbar had broken the skin as well, creating an ugly gash.

Bob took a step closer, removed a handkerchief from his shirt pocket, wiped beads of sweat from his forehead. Then he smiled again. "You had the scroll. Some said it was destroyed. Maybe it was. Maybe not. Wouldn't it have been just the thing to say it was gone, but for you and your friends to hide it away somewhere?"

Ricky gritted her teeth, tried to ignore the pain. "It...went into the fucking sea."

Bob nodded. "Like I said, maybe it did, maybe it didn't. Let's say for a minute you're telling the truth. Then it's gone. But you seen it. So you got two chances here. You either tell us where it is, or you tell us what's on it. Or Josiah will break something else. And he'll keep breaking bones until you tell us everything."

"There's nothing," said Ricky, gasping. "There's nothing for me to tell you." She gritted her teeth again. "The scroll is gone. And I couldn't read...I couldn't read it. It was all hieroglyphics. Ancient fucking Egyptian."

Bob glanced to his henchmen again, gave them a nod. Swiftly, they repeated their violence on her left leg. The pain shot through Ricky at what seemed a magnitude increase of ten.

"I know you suffered a lot to...*eliminate* the unfortunate Cessair. Maybe you're used to it. The pain. And you think perhaps your initial silence will cause us to stop, to abandon you as a lost cause. But that won't happen, Miss Crowe. I think you're lying, and unless you tell us the truth, we will proceed. And I will tell you that we have instruments of pain that will make you beg for the sweet mercy of Josiah's crowbar!"

Ricky did not want to give them the satisfaction of seeing her tears, but she could not help it. The combination of excruciating pain and abject hopelessness reduced her to a blubbering heap of bruised flesh. It seemed she had bawled without interruption for several minutes before she noticed that no one was speaking. She attempted to blink away her tears. The three men stood there, staring. She followed their gaze to her legs.

She flexed her calf muscles carefully, noticed that the lower legs were straightened once again. The gashes on both shins had closed as if they had been healing for weeks. The pain was mostly gone.

Hermes took a step backwards. "Voodoo!"

Bob put a hand on his forearm, shook his head slowly. "No, not voodoo."

Hermes continued to stare, wide-eyed. The shin scars were now hardly visible. "Then...the scroll?"

Bob nodded, unable to look away. "She's immortal!"

***

They had spent several minutes inspecting her like adolescents held spellbound by a roadkill cat. Finger pointing, eyes bulging, whispered amazement. Her hopelessly shattered shins had healed in minutes. Bob had smiled. After that, they left her alone.

Although she was grateful to be rid of them for the moment, Ricky believed that whatever they were planning for her would be even worse than she had already suffered at their hands.

And she cursed loudly, knowing she had brought this upon herself.

Just over a year ago, Sasha had been part of a research team at Zackenberg Ecological Research Operations—ZERO Station—in Greenland, along with other climate scientists. In five thousand-year-old ice, they had discovered a parchment map that had quickly attracted members of the ancient Cult of Cessair. The cult had murdered all the researchers, but before she died, Sasha was able to get the map to Ricky, who enlisted the help of Leo Brenner, Sasha's employer, and others at HARP Foundation. Together, they hoped to beat the cult to the hiding place of the Scroll of Life and Death, which was the prize the map promised.

The Cult of Cessair had sought the map for millennia. They believed the Scroll of Life and Death could bestow immortality. They were willing to do anything, risk anything to obtain it.

Ever the skeptic, Ricky had not believed in the powers of the scroll. What she believed was that it was a near worthless, five thousand-year-old artifact pursued by misguided fanatics. But Brenner had sown doubt. He had become infatuated with the murderous Cessair, had sworn that the woman had used the scroll to make *herself* immortal. Ricky was unconvinced. Perhaps Leo had been tricked. And if it was all a charade, was it really worth risking their lives to pursue mass-murdering fanatics?

On the other hand, if the scroll was genuine, that sort of power in Cessair's hands would put the whole world in danger.

With their lives and perhaps the fate of seven billion people on the line, the stakes had been high. Ricky had needed to know. After her team had tracked down the scroll, she had performed the ritual of the elements—earth, water, wind and fire, using the translation provided to her by a young mystic, Luja Issa. Incredibly, the incantation had set in motion a *fifth* element, which Luja had called *akash*. Some defined this as energy or spirit or even magic. Whatever it might be, it had indeed made Ricky immortal. In doing so, it also confirmed that Cessair was no addled fanatic tilting at windmills. She was an eternal, five thousand-year-old sociopath.

It also confirmed that if Cessair got her hands on the scroll, she might indeed possess the power to seize the world by its throat. That meant she needed to be stopped. To do so required that they confront Cessair and perform a variation of the original ritual, returning her to her mortal state after fifty centuries as a kind of demi-god. And then, at the next sunrise, Cessair would die.

Because that was the catch. The immortality offered by the Scroll of Life and Death was all or nothing. If you chose to return the gift, a swift death followed.

Of course, one could choose to remain immortal. Yet, as the centuries fell away, perpetual life might become more of a curse than a blessing. Friends, family and lovers would age, die. And that heart-wrenching cycle would repeat, endlessly. Indeed, long-term relationships would be impossible. Even after a decade or two, when only one of the partners was observed to be aging, there would be problems. It was possible that others would consider the possessor of eternal youth a monster. Lovers and friends might turn away in revulsion. After all, wasn't such magic an affront to God? And what heart—even an immortal one—could endure the repeated rejection of those who had been most dear? What mind could deal with the knowledge that, eventually, even the last of the human species would suffer extinction, and even later, all life? What mind would not collapse upon itself as the reality was amplified, century after century, millennium after millennium, that one's life would continue even a million years after the sun expanded to burn the earth to a cinder?

On the other hand, how difficult would it be for one in perfect health to use the ritual to undo the curse, knowing that she would crumble to dust with the next sunrise? And if a supreme deity existed, when the time came, how would one's Maker react to one who had long overstayed her earthly welcome, whose hubris had led her to dare to defy nature?

And to the myriad additional sins that now must be weighed?

If only Ricky had been more patient, more trusting of Luja's words.

While the transformation had helped her to survive the struggle against Cessair's minions, the reality was that there was no do-over. She was screwed. Either live forever and watch everyone around you—everyone you cared for—turn to dust generation after generation, or undo the incantation and die when the sun rose on a new day.

Her captor, Bob, might be part of the Cult of Cessair. Or he might be an imitator or wannabe or just some sick, evil bastard. There were lots of little splinter groups that had germinated in the months after Cessair's death. The one difference? Cessair had been immortal, and consequently had been able to command the loyalty of a vast network of spies, assassins, tech geeks, and many respected professionals. She had accumulated this power incrementally over the course of centuries. In recent years, she had become the head of a global antiquities recovery foundation, TROVE, that returned lost treasures to museums and was respected within the archaeology community. It had been a brilliant and elaborate cover that allowed her people access to almost any ancient ruin or historical site—which usually meant any site where they expected to also find clues that would bring them closer to the scroll.

As ruthless and single-minded as the current class of fanatics was, none were united by that kind of power or bankrolled by that kind of money. And although this likely limited their reach, they were still dangerous.

As Ricky's current situation clearly illustrated.

What made them more dangerous still was that none of them considered the ramifications: that immortality carried with it horrors one could hardly imagine. When fifty thousand years had passed, would the immortals find themselves alone in an inhospitable place that bore no resemblance to the world in which they had been born? Would they long for death, or even then, would they be unable to utter the incantation?

No. No one thought of these things. All they thought of was cheating death in ways that would allow them to enrich themselves. The world could be a very profitable place if you could take risks and not worry about knives or bullets.

The screaming of the hinges interrupted her thoughts. Bob and his lackeys stepped back into the cell. Only Bob came forward, hands together in front of him as in prayer, a smile on his face.

"You've given us something to think about," said Bob.

Ricky offered a derisive pebble of laughter. "Bet it'll be just like watching a Mensa meeting."

Bob smiled as if suppressing a laugh. "Usually the first shin loosens the tongue. We broke both of yours...temporarily." He smirked, coughed into a balled fist. "So maybe you're exceptionally tough. Or maybe you're telling the truth. Maybe after you performed the ritual, the scroll was destroyed. And maybe you really don't know what it said."

"So you're kind of fucked, I guess," said Ricky, offering a malicious smile.

"Or are we?" Bob turned for a brief glance at his companions, who remained silent, then stepped closer. Ricky kicked at him savagely, and with a hand motion, he signaled

Josiah to hold her feet. Then Bob stepped close again, carefully reached a forefinger toward her face, ran it along the eight-inch scar. He used the finger to push up the eye patch, exposing the empty pocket beneath. If not for the shackles restraining her wrists, she would have snapped his neck. He studied the old injury with a sympathetic expression, let the patch fall back into place, backed away. Josiah released her legs.

"The scroll," said Bob, "it did not restore the eye."

"That's not how it works," said Ricky, her voice almost a growl. "Whatever you are when you do the incantation, that's what you are forever. Which means if *you* do it, you'll be a syphilitic gargoyle with halitosis in perpetuity. Tough break."

Bob seemed amused rather than insulted. "Were you such a tough talker before you became immortal?"

"I hated talking to anybody before I became immortal," said Ricky. "And you've reminded me why."

Bob smiled, gave a small bow. "Well, you'll have to excuse us. We have to pick up a few supplies."

Ricky could not imagine what "supplies" might improve their situation. "The only supplies that are going to help you sick assholes live longer are whole grains and green vegetables."

Bob's cheek twitched. "Maybe. But we're going to try a little science experiment."

Ricky suddenly felt queasy. She could not be killed, but there were still terrible things that could be done to her.

"No sarcastic remark?" asked Bob, seeing that his words had hit their mark.

Ricky struggled against her shackles, a useless exercise. "What kind of experiment?"

"You're going to donate a little blood. Out of your veins, into ours."

She understood. They were hoping that a transfusion would result in immortality. Ricky doubted it would work. However, if it did, they would keep her here in chains forever. They might use her not only for their own needs, but could sell her blood to select clients who would pay a king's ransom for immortality. Or they could dole out immortality selectively, as Cessair had planned to do, creating the kind of army that could indeed enslave humanity.

"It won't work," said Ricky bitterly.

"I'm guessing you don't know that for certain," said Bob. "But if you're right, well, as I mentioned, we have many methods of torture more unpleasant than the crowbar. And because you're immortal, we don't have to worry about being too rough. You'll end up begging us to listen to you."

Ricky shook her head. "I already told you all I know."

"We'll certainly employ every technique at our disposal to ensure that this is true," Bob said brightly. "We will be most thorough. It is a good thing this cell is soundproof." He grinned, raised both eyebrows as if sharing a naughty secret.

"Sick bastards!"

"But, if we conclude, after all the sweat and blood and screaming, that you really do know nothing, then we will eliminate you."

"Fuck you!" shouted Ricky. "I'm immortal, remember?"

Bob smiled indulgently. "It's true. We can't kill you. We could, however, chain you to several hundred pounds of scrap iron and sink you a mile offshore. How many centuries would you lie there in the slime, still alive in some fashion, before the chains rusted away and freed you? Into what sort of madness might you descend?"

"Wait!" said Josiah, a big hand on Bob's shoulder. "If she don't talk, then we got nuthin'?"

"Patience, my friend," said Bob, soothingly. "Her blood, remember? And if that doesn't work, she has friends whose shins won't heal who might have the answers we seek."

A cold sweat broke out on Ricky's forehead. "Fuck you!" she shouted again, but Bob had already turned to go. She continued to rain vulgarities upon them as they locked the wooden door behind them and for several minutes after the sounds of their footsteps had disappeared.

CHAPTER 3

When she was alone again and no longer had the need to summon hatred to demonstrate her bravado, Ricky began to shiver. Then she screamed, louder, searing, soul-ripping screams, and then louder still. She wondered if she were in shock or maybe going mad, for as she screamed, into her head popped an odd memory. A story she had read in school, "The Cask of Amontillado," where the vengeful Montresor chains the drunken Fortunato to a wall in the catacombs beneath Montresor's villa. When Fortunato realizes he is doomed, he screams. But the niche where he is imprisoned is so deep underground that no one can possibly hear, and so Montresor screams along with him, urging him on, inviting him to scream louder still. For Fortunato, this had the effect of heightening the horror of it all, underscoring that no rescue was possible, that nothing in all the world could be done to prevent or forestall his fate. For Ricky, the effect of her own screams was much the same.

Eventually, she grew exhausted and sobbed the ugliest of tears. Even this could not be sustained indefinitely, and she grew silent. As the grim minutes passed, fear bred anger and resolve. Before she had become immortal, Ricky had been trapped in an Egyptian mastaba and an Irish passage tomb, in both cases buried beneath tons of stone and earth. Yet, she had found a way out, even though she had not possessed a thread of hope. Perhaps there was a way out of this prison as well.

But, she reminded herself, in those earlier instances, Crockett and others had been with her. Here, she was alone.

Think!

There had to be a way. Her mind would not concede the possibility of failure, the possibility that she might—as Bob had threatened—be chained to an anchor at the bottom of the sea for centuries in some fugue state or, worse, fully aware.

She took several deep breaths, examined her surroundings again. Iron wrist bracelets, thick chains, dense block walls, no windows. Ricky's heart leaped as she saw the crowbar had been left behind, abandoned on the floor in their haste to leave. Almost as quickly, her enthusiasm faded as she realized that the tool was well out of her reach. And even if she could have reached it, she doubted she would have been able to use it to pry the bolts out of the wall. They were too solid and there was no raised edge under which to insert the end of the crowbar.

She sat, stretched her legs, which were completely healed. An examination of the ceiling yielded nothing. Even if she had sufficient chain length and turned the utility bucket upside down to stand on it, there were no pipes, no electrical conduit, no ductwork, not even a rusty nail.

How soon before they're back?

She lurched against her restraints, knowing that they would not break, loosen, or show weakness of any kind. Even so, there was nothing else to do. The thick iron bracelets cut painfully into the wide heel of her hand but would go no farther. She felt angry, disgusted even with herself for surviving against a truly clever, superhuman adversary like Cessair, only to be taken out by Bob, who looked like he should be filming PSAs for colonoscopies. What good was it to be immortal if you could be chained up like a dog?

She pulled against the chains again. She had no key. The only way those iron bracelets were coming off was if her hands suddenly shrunk to the size of a five-year-old's.

She gave a sobbing laugh, imagining herself with tiny hands. She laughed again, harder, and then her laughter raggedly degenerated into tears.

I am going mad.

A moment later, Ricky gasped at a sickening thought.

An awful idea. But in her current situation, there were no ideas that weren't awful.

Josiah had broken both her shins with the crowbar. But they had healed. If she broke the bones in her hands, she could slide off the iron bracelets. In short order, they would heal, too.

She could not afford to wait, to build up her courage. The pain would be savage, perhaps worse than the shins. But she had to do it now. If, in fact, she could do it at all.

Rick pushed away from the wall as far as the chains allowed, gritted her teeth, clenched shut her eye.

"Fuck! Fuck! Fuck! Fuck!"

She slowly moved her left arm toward the wall, then brought it back as hard as she could, throwing her whole weight into it. A paroxysm of pain exploded up her arm, and despite her efforts to prevent it, a rasping cry escaped.

But she knew if she stopped, she would be done. The temptation to rationalize defeat and avoid the pain would be too great. She repeated the motion, again and again like a frantic wolf, caught in a staked trap as wildfire approached, a crazed animal trying to gnaw off its own leg. Again and again she repeated the motion. There seemed to be no hand anymore, only pain. In desperation, she used her legs to push against the wall as well—more leverage. Spatters of blood sprayed, speckling her forearm, her torso and the floor.

She was incapable of holding any ideas in her mind, nor any words except two: *Don't stop!*

Skin was gouged away by the iron bracelets. Joints dislocated. Bones splintered and snapped. Her hand, fanlike and dexterous, collapsed in upon itself like a building consumed by fierce fire from within. And then, aided by the lubricating effect of her blood, what remained of her hand slipped through the ring.

She gasped as if suppressing a scream, something whose sound and timbre seemed equal parts gratitude and horror. What hung limply at the end of her left arm resembled the bloodied claw of a dead sparrow. She tore her gaze away from the sight, sobbed in earnest for a few seconds, and then readied herself.

One down, one to go.

***

Josiah Villieu slouched in his leather recliner, although it wasn't real leather. Some sort of vinyl look-alike. And the dark-brown vinyl wasn't in very good shape anymore. There were numerous holes in the seat area from years of car keys and who knew what else being ground into the upholstery. The arms were slashed and punctured and stained as well. But it still pushed back into a reclining position, and the footrest still swung up into place. Upholstered recliners were a rarity in Caribbean climates, and so he supposed it had come from the lobby of one of the hotels where American tourists would be used to such comforts. Josiah had found it abandoned on the side of the road, several miles away, soaked following an afternoon rainstorm. Who knew how many days it had sat there or whether it had fallen off the back of a truck or been stolen. He had brought it back to the garage, let it dry for a week. A damned comfortable chair if he said so himself. Better than sitting for hours on the folding chairs that Bob had given them, waiting for whatever "merchandise" was being dropped off or collected.

Sometimes it was automobile parts. Or mobile phones. Or guns. Sometimes it was the kind of merchandise that needed to be kept in the cell below.

Bob handled all the details. Josiah didn't know the man's deep history, but he had cobbled together a flimsy backstory from things Bob had said while sober, things Bob had said while drunk, conversations Josiah had surreptitiously overheard, and rumors.

Bob was—or had been—an American citizen, but had chosen to hurriedly relocate here twenty-two years ago under a new identity (no one knew his real name) to avoid prosecution for acts committed with a twelve-year-old girl. He had lampreyed himself to Big Henry, owner of the garage business, doing the jobs Big Henry didn't want to touch. He'd been diligent and loyal and knew where all the secrets were hidden, so when Big Henry had died of a massive heart attack at age thirty-seven—likely cocaine-induced—Bob had taken over, dealing with the same shady sleazeballs as had his predecessor.

The centerpiece of the operation was the garage, a single concrete block building with two metal retractable doors at the front. The door on the east side was tall enough to allow commercial trucks to load or unload. Inside, half a dozen fifty-five-gallon metal barrels rested against one wall. Josiah and his chair occupied the center of the garage's west side, along with three metal folding chairs, a card table, a half-size refrigerator, and a forty-two-inch flat panel TV connected to a DVD player. In the back corner were two doors, one leading to a toilet, the other to a closet-sized office space with a small desk upon which rested a closed laptop. Just to the left of the office, three-foot lengths of two-by-twelve boards covered a six-foot long opening in the floor that might have been mistaken for a grease pit. However, the boards concealed steps leading to the lower level, which featured two anterooms and the third room designated as a holding cell.

Josiah erupted in laughter, his eyes riveted on the TV screen where *Talladega Nights* was playing. "Shake and bake! Those fuckers are hilarious!" he said to no one.

The garage serviced no vehicles, yet it had been operating continuously for more than twenty years. Neighbors ignored the comings and goings of its customers, probably figuring it was safer to do so. Police never searched the premises, for operators gave them no reason to. Trucks coming and going was no crime, and the solidly-built structure allowed for no concerning sounds to escape. Most importantly, in more than twenty years, no one who had spent a night or more in the underground room had voiced a complaint about the accommodations. Once you were in the underground holding cell, there was no hope. You would eventually leave in the back of a van or truck, and what remained of your life would be spent in a hell of drugs and forced sex acts. Or, if someone simply wanted you gone, you would leave in other, unspeakably gruesome ways.

No trucks were making deliveries on this day; for Josiah, the duty was easy. Bob and Hermes were out picking up the medical supplies necessary to draw the woman's blood. At first, Josiah had thought Bob was just another crazy American obsessed with youth and beauty. All the talk about immortality, and the crazy online groups he communed with in the cramped office. Josiah remembered how excited the older man had gotten a year ago about something that happened at some science outpost in Norway or Greenland or somewhere. Then this girl had shown up, and Bob was like a madman. Josiah had done what he was told, not because he believed any of the magic baloney, but because Bob was the boss and paid him well. Then he'd seen the girl heal. It was like he'd seen in that Indiana Jones movie where he pours the Grail water on his father's wound and, hallelujah, it's gone! Only this was no movie. And it got him thinking about living forever, no more worries, and how great it would be. And now maybe in just a few hours or days, he'd be immortal, just like the girl. People could shoot at him, knife him, throw him off a cliff. It wouldn't matter. He could do whatever he wanted, though maybe he'd have to go away so no one would try and put him in a cage like they did with the girl.

He had to admit, though, to a certain uneasiness about it. Hermes had referred to it as "voodoo" earlier when they had all watched the girl's leg heal. Despite his general disbelief in the occult, it had scared him a little. His departed mother had been very religious. Just thinking about her now compelled Josiah to make the sign of the cross. She had maintained that messing with the dark magic could put your soul at risk. Was this that kind of magic?

On the other hand, if he could never die, why should he worry whether his soul was white as snow or stained scarlet, as he had heard the nuns say? He had certainly done much while in Bob's employ that would put him on the road to hell. The trafficking of drugs. Helping to make sure certain liabilities disappeared— after being tortured to the point where they begged for death. Providing a holding site for young women and children destined for lives as sex slaves and worse. Josiah had had his way with many, for what did it matter, really? They were already doomed. Their fates were decided. It was no worse than throwing a rock to break the window of a condemned house.

On the TV screen, cars raced around the track in ways that they probably wouldn't in a real NASCAR race. "Shake and bake!" he shouted again, right in time with the actors.

Of course, many of those who had passed through the garage had deserved their fate. Those would surely not count against him, he reasoned–assuming his mother was right about heaven and hell. Still, there doubtlessly remained considerable stains on Josiah's own soul that could not be scrubbed away with a few dozen Our Fathers or Hail Marys. But this woman's blood, it could make that point moot. Instead of thirty or forty years, if he was lucky, until he stood, shamefaced, before his

Maker, waiting for the terrible, inevitable, eternal condemnation—tormented forever by hideous demons which might peel his skin, or fill his stomach with maggots that would consume him from the inside out, or set him afire—instead of that grim future, he would be truly free. Never a thought of death or punishment. A life where he could do whatever pleased him with whomever he wished.

Josiah laughed again. This had to be one of the top ten movies of all time. Should have won an Oscar, but he knew that all of that was fixed. He heard a noise. Maybe Hermes and Bob were back. He shifted his weight, ready to scoot the chair into an upright position, when he was startled by a figure suddenly looming over him.

It was the girl. And she was holding the crowbar.

"Shake and bake this, motherfucker!" The crowbar came down.

***

Ricky had to will herself to stop swinging the crowbar. There was no reason to continue. There had been no reason to continue a dozen swings ago.

After freeing her right hand, Ricky had waited until it was usable again, then had jammed the end of the crowbar between the door and its frame, splintering the wood and allowing it to swing open. If her screams could not be heard from above, she knew the sounds of her escape would not alert whoever had been left on watch. Outside, she had discovered two rooms similar in size to her cell. One was empty except for half a dozen wooden pallets. The other contained boxes of what appeared to be knock-off handbags and basketball shoes. She had carefully ascended the steps, pushed away a couple of the boards that concealed them, and realized for the first time that she had been beneath a garage. She took several minutes to study the layout, to make sure the only person there was Josiah.

Then she had stealthily emerged. Thinking that escape was impossible for her, Josiah had not been the most attentive jailer.

And now he was hamburger.

She knew she should leave now. Run. Get far away. Keep a lower profile. Try to disappear.

Immortality. Yeah, it's great.

Cessair was dead, but there were still bands of fanatics out there who suspected she knew things. And now they would probably believe that her blood was the elixir of life.

Bob and Hermes were evil but insignificant men. Human scum. If she ran, she would never see them again.

But she wasn't going to run. Not yet.

***

The two men returned half an hour later, chuckling over some shared joke, yet puzzled that Josiah had opened the large garage door. They became deadly serious, and Bob drew his gun when they realized Josiah wasn't enjoying *Talladega Nights* as much as usual.

"Jesus!" said Bob, wide-eyed, scanning the garage, his pistol in the ready position, held with two hands. They had only been able to recognize Josiah by his tats. Bob's hands shook slightly as his eyes went to the covered stairwell. The floor planks were in place over the opening, as he had left them. That meant the girl likely was still down there. This might have been a hit by competitors who failed to realize what valuable commodity was secured below. Josiah wasn't much of a loss. Muscle was easy to find, and cheap. As long as they still had the girl, they still had everything.

They could live forever.

She's got to be there!

He silently vowed that, if one of their enemies had taken her, they would not rest until she was reclaimed. There would be no negotiating. And much blood would flow. He had begun to contemplate life as an immortal. What a burden would be lifted if death was no longer possible. He was no Bible thumper, but Bob acknowledged the possibility that whatever came after this life might be influenced by whatever saintly achievements or sinful transgressions had characterized his human journey. He had no desire to be reborn as a cockroach or salamander or worse, and his resume suggested there was no reasonable hope for anything better.

She's still here. I know it. She has to be.

Moving to the covered stairs, Hermes removed three boards and the two men descended slowly, as Ricky had hoped, no doubt wondering whether those who had ambushed Josiah were waiting for them, if they might be walking into a trap. As soon as they disappeared, Ricky darted out from the toilet, quietly replaced the three boards in the grooves atop the pit that brought them level with the concrete floor. Then she laid a longer board lengthwise over all of them.

She suspected Bob and Hermes would clear the first room quickly, but they would be more cautious about the second. They would see that the door to the cell–the third room–was broken, but they would still need to move slowly, not knowing what waited for them inside. She might have thirty seconds. She dashed to the brown creeper van parked just outside, throwing herself into the driver's seat, hoping that the set of keys she had removed from Josiah's pocket was a second set for this vehicle.

She smiled when it started. She quickly pulled forward until the right front tire rested on the long board pressing down onto the short lengths concealing the stairway, making it impossible to lift any of the boards beneath, trapping the two men below. She exited the van, let the motor run, lowered the garage door. Almost immediately there were footsteps on the stairs, then pounding on the underside of the boards.

"Hey! What the hell!"

Bob's muffled voice bellowed from below, realizing he was trapped, not sounding so smug now.

Ricky called from across the building. "Hey, Bob! Sorry, but it looks like that immortality thing isn't going to work out!"

"You goddamn bitch! You—"

"You're going to have to speak up!" shouted Ricky. "I can't hear you so well over the sound of the van!"

"When we get done with you, you're going to wish..." Bob stopped, likely connecting the dots, realizing what was to come. The running vehicle in a closed garage. The carbon monoxide that would build up, eventually find its way to the lower level. "Shit! Goddamn it, let us out of here! Shit!"

Hermes' fists joined Bob's as the two cursed and grunted. But there was no way they were going to lift two tons of cargo van. She was sure their protests would get more desperate, eventually collapse into pitiful begging. Then things would get real quiet.

And she would not be around to hear it. The bastards deserved this. How many young women had they raped and allowed to be sold into sexual bondage? How many murders had they abetted? They could burn in hell. She had a few bucks she had taken from Josiah and a green windbreaker she had found on a hook in the toilet. That would get her back to her bungalow. And then she would go.

But where?

CHAPTER 4

Mason Crockett unlocked the door to unit D, the second-floor apartment he shared with no one. He was beat. Didn't feel like cooking. It looked like he'd be Doordashing wings again tonight.

His responsibilities at the HARP Foundation had become more substantial in the past year, understandable considering the death of its founder, Leo Brenner. His gut still clenched when he thought of Leo, how much he had liked and admired the man. The pleasant memories were always darkened by the inevitable thoughts of those last moments there on the cliff at An Tsuil.

Crockett grabbed a beer from the fridge, flopped onto his sofa, tapped on the TV with his remote. It was September, so there would be a ball game on. He wouldn't have to think too hard to enjoy the Cubbies or whoever was playing. A quick swig, then he got up and opened both of the windows facing the front. Upper sixties, nice breeze. He called in the wings order, returned to the sofa. A news program droned away. He barely registered it.

Damn, he missed her.

He would have bet the farm on Ricky coming back. They were a team. More than that, they were...*more* than that. Cessair was gone. They had a chance to make their lives whatever they wished. If she had expressed a desire for them to set up housekeeping in a grass hut in some remote jungle, he would have been online in an instant ordering a loincloth. Why the hell had she disappeared? Had his show of affection frightened her off? That might warrant her ghosting his calls or texting him to cool it. It wouldn't warrant leaving Chicago without a word. And she had deactivated her phone. She might be anywhere in the world.

Why?

Seven o'clock. The news program had ended, a few commercials had flashed by, and now the game was set to begin. Cubbies and Brewers. The wings arrived at 7:40, top of the third, score 1-1. As he did at the start of every game, no matter who was playing, he recalled his own days playing ball. Not the pros, but a little college ball. It had brought him to Chicago from Charlotte, and that move had changed his life.

Stop thinking. Enjoy the game.

Five minutes later, a knock on his door. Dr. Thomas Campion stood in the hallway.

Campion, in his sixties and author of several respected books on cults, had accompanied Crockett, Ricky and Brenner on their search for the Scroll of Life and Death. He had not emerged from the journey unscathed. Campion had broken his leg in Egypt and a couple of ribs in Germany. His knowledge of cults, including the Cult of Cessair, as well as the ancient cultures that had spawned them, had proved invaluable in their hunt. Crockett had talked with him frequently during the past year, had met with him occasionally for coffee or a beer. However, Campion had never dropped by without calling first.

Crockett ushered the man inside. "Doc, good to see you! This is sort of a surprise, but I've got plenty of wings, and it looks like the Cubbies just scored another run."

Campion, dressed in jeans and a royal blue windbreaker over a Northwestern University long-sleeve t-shirt, settled onto the sofa, eyeing the box of wings. "They do look good. Maybe just one."

Crockett passed him a napkin. Campion smiled, accepted it, pushed his wire-rim glasses up onto the bridge of his nose.

"I apologize for not checking before dropping by."

Crockett waved it off, muted the TV's sound. "Door's always open for you, Doc. This a social call?"

Campion finished off the wing, wiped the tips of his fingers on the napkin. "I don't know exactly how to begin."

Crockett knew that Campion never spoke frivolously, but his tone here carried a hint of foreboding. "Sounds serious. Are you okay, Doc?"

"Good, good, although the leg hurts whenever a storm rolls in. But that's beside the point. I came here tonight because I heard something. Came across it online, actually. You know the sort of sites I shadow." He grinned conspiratorially. "Anyway, I didn't want to talk about it over the phone."

Crockett shifted on the sofa. "Doc, now you're kind of scaring me."

Campion nodded solemnly. "I apologize for this cloak-and-dagger approach, but you may thank me after you've heard what I have to say."

"Sure, Doc. Go on."

The older man took a deep breath. "You're probably aware that I'm always doing research for that next book or academic article. In the process, I find my way to many arcane and obscure websites, as well as chat rooms, message boards, and discussions that aren't always easy to access. And that's by design. While talk about the Scroll of Life and Death has been rare this past year, once in a while, something pops up. Usually, baseless conspiracy stuff. Gone just as quickly. Lately, though, there's been a bit more interest."

"Do you think it's something we should be concerned about?" asked Crockett, polishing off wings as he listened. "Do...do you think it has something to do with Ricky?"

Campion hesitated, looking at his hands before he continued. "Mason, I know Ricky's disappearance has been difficult for you."

Crockett nodded, then looked up in alarm. "My God! Did you read something? Is she all right?"

Campion patted the air to settle his young friend. "Here's what I know. As I mentioned, there's been an uptick in interest in the scroll. A couple of small groups have pushed rumors that those of us who were at An Tsuil may have hidden it away. When that sort of thing starts getting repeated more frequently, it's disturbing, of course. And because Ricky has disappeared—a fact these groups are well aware of—much of the discussion centers on her as the likely possessor of the scroll. Or, if not its possessor, at least having knowledge of what it contains."

"They're destined for disappointment," said Crockett. "Neither of us knows the recipes for those elixirs from hell."

"Well, here's where it gets interesting. And scary. On one of the sites, they were talking about a tip that led several of the fanatics to capture the Grey Witch."

Crocket scrunched up his face in confusion. "I don't get it."

Campion bit his lower lip. "It's a code name. The Grey Witches or Grey Sisters were characters in Greek mythology. They shared one eye, which they passed between them. They used their gift of second sight to guide Perseus to the tools he would need to kill the Gorgon Medusa."

Crockett's eyes grew wide as he understood. The Grey Witch nickname was a cruel reference to the fact that Ricky had only one eye, yet they believed she could lead them to a gift even greater than those bestowed on Perseus. "No! Jesus! Are you saying some group of lunatics captured Ricky? Hell no!"

"It's okay," said Campion, attempting to calm his friend. "Or perhaps 'okay' isn't the best choice of words. Let's just say there appears to have been a favorable outcome for Ricky. The discussion was actually full of mockery for the men who captured her. It seems she escaped, and it didn't go too well for her captors."

"Thank God!" Crocket breathed a relieved sigh. Then the guarded look returned. "What do you mean that it didn't go too well for her captors?"

"The discussion was riddled with insults. Remarks about the captors' low intelligence. Lots of Darwin Award references. I—I think Ricky might have had to...*eliminate* them in order to escape."

They both sat silently for a minute, considering this.

"That assumes these events actually occurred," noted Campion. "With these cults, you sometimes hear stories that have little to no basis in fact. For instance, one report said that Ricky's captors wanted to drink her blood."

Crockett grimaced. "That's disgusting. Why in the world would they want to do that?"

Campion shrugged. "Perhaps they thought she had already used the scroll and was immortal... and that her blood could make them immortal, too."

The younger man snuck a glance at the TV, shook his head. "That's crazy. Cessair shot her at An Tsuil. Ricky almost died."

Campion stared straight ahead, his eyes slightly out of focus. "Almost."

Crockett picked up on the flatness in his tone. "Right. Lucky the bullet missed the vital stuff. That's what the doctor said."

"As I recall, she didn't allow the Dublin medical staff to do much of an examination. They noted the exit wound, the meager amount of bleeding. Bandaged her up, gave her a Tetanus shot, and told her to have someone look at it for infection when she got home in a few days."

The tone of Campion's inquiry alarmed Crockett. "I sense you're trying to get at something here, Doc, but I'm a little too thick to see it."

Campion offered a gentle smile. "Please don't be upset. But bear with me. Some of these little things seemed...*odd* at the time, and as I've considered them more and more in the ensuing months, other oddities have asserted themselves as well."

"What sort of oddities are we talking about?"

"Well... Ricky survived the gunshot wound. Not a grazing of the arm, or some such thing. A shot to the torso. And then a fall to the stone floor below the balcony. How far? Ten feet? Twelve? Very little bleeding, despite being hit right beneath the heart. But a minute later, she's on her feet, thinking clearly, devising a plan to defeat Cessair. No concussion either! Miraculous! No symptoms of shock!"

Crockett opened his mouth to speak but said nothing. He had indeed considered her luck and resilience miraculous at the time.

"And what about her climb across the cliff behind An Tsuil?" Campion continued. "Even with the fate of the world in the balance, not to mention your life, it would take an extraordinarily brave person to make that climb. One slip would have meant a hundred-foot drop into a rocky surf. Or consider that while tied to a chair, she tipped herself off An Tsuil's balcony onto the narrow, rocky edge of the cliff. And again, no broken bones. No gaping wounds. Leo fell that same distance and broke his back."

Crockett felt as if the curtain in a heretofore familiar room was being pulled back to reveal a window on the world he had never seen before. "Are you suggesting..."

Campion cut him off. "I'm not *suggesting* anything. I'm *saying* Ricky is immortal."

For several minutes, Crockett did not respond. He chugged the remainder of his beer, went to the kitchen, came back with another, guzzled half of it.

On one hand, it was impossible. Ricky had been as frightened and vulnerable at An Tsuil as everyone else. Or had she? He wondered now, for the first time, whether he would have been brave enough to inch across the cliff below the abbey if their situations had been reversed and Ricky had been a prisoner. Of course, if *he* had been immortal, that would have changed everything.

Suddenly, other things began to make more sense.

"She... she disappeared with the bag containing the scroll one afternoon when we were hiding out at her grandmother's house in Dublin," said Crockett, as if in a trance. "I didn't know where she had gone. Was worried sick. Later that day I found her in The Red Crow, a pub, drunk and busting up the place, like she was feeling all sorry for herself. At the time, I thought she must have been thinking about her sister. About Sasha."

"I'd guess she was mad at herself and the eternal consequences of her decision," said Campion. "She must have performed the ritual just before that."

Crocket lowered his head, tore at his hair. "But why? Why would she do it?"

"Could be anger over what Cessair's people had done to her in Germany," suggested Campion. "When emotions run high, we don't always make the best decisions. Maybe she wanted to become immortal to try and level the playing field. However, Ricky was a skeptic. I'd guess she wanted to test the scroll. If I'd been in her position, that certainly would have crossed my mind. Maybe she didn't believe it could really do what they said it could. And if it had been a fraud, why risk your life on Cessair?"

It seemed so clear to Crockett now. Once Ricky had realized she had lost her mortality, she had imploded. The only way back from that promised a quick death.

"In the Red Crow that night... she was having a breakdown, I guess."

"Yes, that seems an apt way to describe it."

"But," said Crockett, "she got past it. She went after Cessair."

Campion smiled kindly. "She went after you."

Crockett felt his face warm, but he also recognized the truth of Campion's statement and had trouble holding back a sob. After a few moments, he continued. "On... on the last night I saw her... here, in my apartment... we talked about immortality. What a curse it was. Living forever, watching your friends grow old and die. The one you loved. And the only way you could put an end to it was..."

"By ending your own perfectly healthy life," said Campion, finishing the thought.

"That's why she left," said Crockett, suddenly understanding. "She didn't want to watch us all grow old and die."

"And," said Campion, "didn't want to lead you where you couldn't follow. If she had followed her heart, struck up a relationship with you, how fair to you would that be in ten years? Twenty? Thirty? With her still young, and only death to change that."

Tears slid down Crockett's face. "Oh God! And death might never be an option! Without the recipe for the poison elixir, she'll literally live forever! She'll go mad!"

"Or she'll find another way."

"What do you mean?"

"The scroll has been destroyed, yes. But if Ricky truly wished to regain her mortality in some grand but misguided gesture she thought would end the danger to us, there is one other option."

"What is it?" asked Crockett.

"Not what. Who."

***

Thomas Campion sat in the back of an Uber, returning to his Chicago townhouse in the Gold Coast neighborhood. Telling Crockett what he had learned online had been a heart-wrenching task, but he needed to know. If Ricky was indeed immortal and others were searching for her, they might come after Crockett as well, wondering whether he had knowledge of Ricky's whereabouts. In light of these realities, the two of them had decided it was wise to employ some basic precautions. That was why Campion had gone to Crockett's apartment rather than sharing his discovery over the phone. While it was unlikely that someone had been able to upload a spy app into either of their devices, they had both been targeted sufficiently by Cessair and her goons to know that one should never underestimate the resourcefulness of psychopaths.

Yes, Cessair was gone. Most of her goons as well. And her assets had been frozen. Campion doubted there was another equally well-financed cult organization devoted to finding the scroll or unlocking its secrets. Yet, smaller groups and even individuals could still be dangerous.

"Keep your head up," Crockett had told him as he was preparing to leave. Then Crockett had wrapped him in a hug. "And keep your eyes moving. Call me if you get a bad feeling about anything."

Campion intended to do just that. He had been writing about cults for thirty-five years. While some were benign—if misguided—groups, others were ruthless and too far down the rabbit hole to reason with. He had almost died twice at the hands of Cessair's cult lackeys in Egypt and Germany. He did not intend to give them a third opportunity here in Chicago. This was his home turf. His building had security people on duty around the clock. And he had purchased a little insurance several months ago to guarantee his safety between his ride and the building. He patted the 9mm Glock G43 in his shoulder holster.

The taxi pulled under his building's awning. The doorman, Reg, escorted him to the front of the building, opened the secure door.

"Have a nice evening, Dr. Campion," said Reg with a smile.

Campion waved, moving toward the elevators. "You as well, Reg."

The ride to the nineteenth floor was smooth and swift. He moved confidently to unit 1904, tapped in the digital code for the bolt, then used his key for the main lock. As he stepped inside, the motion-activated entry hallway light came on. He pulled the door shut, setting both locks behind him.

The apartment was very nice, modern yet filled with classic touches, comfortable furniture and full bookshelves. The lake was several blocks to the east, but the view was nonetheless spectacular from his balcony. His writing desk faced the sliding glass door that accessed the balcony, but he was in the wrong frame of mind to write tonight. A cup of tea, and then bed.

If sleep would come.

He imagined he would try to sleep, then get up twenty minutes later, sit himself down at his desk, begin scouring the usual sites for clues as to Ricky's whereabouts. Maybe there was some way they could help her. There had to be.

Campion moved to the bedroom, kicked off his shoes and donned a pair of corduroy slippers. He undid the holster, set it and the Glock on his nightstand. As he sat on the edge of the bed, he worried about Crockett. The young man lived in a second-floor walk-up. No security people at the doors. Any delivery person or individual posing as one could easily be buzzed in. Crockett had, on his advice, replaced the locking bolt on his apartment door, but how much protection would that really offer against enemies who were highly motivated and well-armed?

He chuckled to himself. Even here on the nineteenth floor, wasn't security more an illusion than a fact? He enjoyed imagining his home to be impregnable, but knew every fortress had its weaknesses. He thought of the doorman, Reg. Campion would stop occasionally on his way in or out, and the two of them would talk about their lives, families, the prospects for the Bears this season. And he always included a nice bonus for Reg at Christmas. But the great human flaw, starting with the story about the apple in the garden, was temptation. And as tempting as knowledge could be, power and money seemed virtually irresistible. Campion wondered how much would need to be offered before Reg or one of the other doormen or security personnel would put their job in jeopardy? Or perhaps he was merely being cynical. Maybe the truth was that they could not be bought. Men and women of principles did exist, after all.

Rising, he moved to the kitchen, filled the teapot, set it to boil. Perhaps this was a good night to treat himself, to shake himself out of a mood. A little ginger tea with honey sounded good.

When he turned from the stove, two men stood facing him perhaps eight feet away. He blinked several times, certain that he must be having some sort of episode. But the men remained no matter how many times he tried to blink them away. How had they moved about so quietly?

He began to tremble uncontrollably.

CHAPTER 5

The storefront business was located on a Dublin side street, a mix of shops and walk-up apartments. One of these stood out because it was a single story and because its brick exterior had been painted purple.

It stood out for other reasons as well, such as the green plants in pots on the sidewalk in front, pressed up against the large window, around which a variety of strange symbols had been painted. The bevy of sparkling crystals dangling from threads or slim chains inside. The hand-painted sign hanging from an iron arm over the door:

MADAME LUJA
Spiritual Guidance
Readings

Scents, some as familiar as Earl Grey, some as mysterious as the Far East greeted those who ventured inside, where they would find a small, round, wooden table, around which rested five mismatched chairs. A saffron-colored lump of wax the size of a batch of bread dough from which an inch of charred wick protruded had melted onto the table's center. More charms and symbols hung by threads or tarnished chains from the ceiling, and a blue sofa rested against the right-hand wall, above which were shelves overflowing with well-loved books. Brass figurines, clay pots, walking sticks, oil lamps and other treasures cluttered the left-hand wall, some on shelves that were simply planks supported by concrete blocks. Overseeing it all was a glowing, painted golden cat's eye, rising like a sun on the deep blue back wall. A doorway opened off the left side of this wall, and through it strode Madame Luja.

She glided to the table, struck a match, lit the candle, rubbed her hands together and shivered. Luja had felt uneasy for days. However, she could not identify precisely what it was that should give her such a feeling. Only that darkness was associated with it. And the girl, Ricky Crowe.

Luja had expected this. It was only a matter of time.

Ricky and the man, Crockett, had been drawn to her just over a year earlier. They had come seeking a translator. Having heard that Luja had attended Cairo University, they had hoped she might put them in touch with someone who understood ancient Egyptian. As it had turned out, Luja herself was such a person.

This had shocked both Ricky and Crockett. Her youth, no doubt. A willowy, dark-skinned, twenty-four-year-old when they had probably expected some shriveled, wizened, octogenarian crone. With no other options, they had trusted her, and Luja had revealed the ancient document's secrets. They had called it the Scroll of Life and Death, an apt name as it turned out.

Earth, water, air and fire, plus one recipe for a life elixir, another for death.

An evil thing.

However, Ricky and Crockett had needed it to stop an even greater evil. They had succeeded. If only Ricky had been more trusting, more patient, less impulsive.

With the life elixir, the scroll ritual made one immortal. With the death elixir, it immediately killed those who were mortal and canceled the gift in those who had previously been made immortal. And for those whose immortality was forfeited, death would follow at sunrise. However, it was not only individuals who could be harmed by the ritual. If one wished, its powers could be used to lay waste to entire populations.

The scroll was gone now. At least in its physical form.

Even so, Crockett had understood that Luja would remember everything on the scroll. A year ago, he had asked Luja what she would do with that information.

"Take it to my grave," Luja had responded.

At the time, that had seemed ironclad. Crockett and Ricky would destroy the scroll once their mission was finished, and Luja would never discuss it with a soul, never attempt to use the mystical powers. What had been written on the parchment would die with her when the Universe saw fit to recall her to the place where stardust is born.

But in the ensuing year, other troubling likelihoods had occurred to Luja. One of these was that even without Cessair, there would be some who continued to seek the scroll and the promise of immortality. Although they would hear that the scroll had been destroyed, they might not believe this, might decide it a deception maliciously circulated to keep the truth from deserving free-thinkers such as themselves. Or they might believe Crockett and Ricky had kept the scroll for their own purposes, which would mean targets on their backs. Even if the evil ones had concluded the scroll really had been destroyed, they might suspect that Crockett and Ricky knew what had been written upon it.

And it was almost certain that Luja's role would, at some point, be intimated. Which meant they would come for her, too.

Luja told herself that this did not matter. Whether the Universe had planned a long or short existence for her in this world was of little consequence. What mattered was that no one used the power of the scroll. Even though Luja recalled every word, she would hold strong against any torture the seekers might employ. Even if it led to her death.

That was what she told herself. But Luja knew these self-assurances might turn out to be hollow. She was young, strong, but she was also a student of history and human nature. Fear, want, ignorance, temptation. These could turn angels to devils. They could corrupt the human heart and unleash an unlimited capacity for cruelty. Cult mentality had, throughout the ages, led the devout to sacrifice their brothers and sisters on the altar, sell them on the auction block, load them into boxcars headed for furnaces. She hardly cared to think what the seekers might do to her in their fevered quest for immortality, and despite her resolve and good intentions, she acknowledged the possibility that, with all hope exhausted and wracked with pain that crushed both body and soul, she might reveal what the scroll said.

The uneasiness of the past few days had all but confirmed her fears. The darkness was coming. It was near. Then, today, at 6:00 p.m., she had known it was time to light the candle that sat in the middle of her table.

An hour later, the bell tinkled cheerily over her shop door. Luja, cup of tea in hand, stepped through the doorway from her back room, took a moment to assess her visitor.

"Hello, Ricky."

***

She could easily be mistaken for a homeless person. Long, uncombed hair. Jeans and a plain white t-shirt, both of which looked like they had not been washed in a month. A tattered leather jacket with blood stains on the left arm. Whereas immortality had made Cessair a queen, Ricky Crowe looked the part of a peasant who slept in ditches. To Luja, this was a good sign. Cessair had not hesitated to crush innocents and sinners alike beneath her boots during her climb to the throne. Perhaps the curse of immortality had not stolen Ricky's soul. Not yet.

"I—I didn't know where to go."

Luja set the tea at the table and invited Ricky to sit. When she did, Luja excused herself, retreated through the door in the back wall, emerged a minute later with a second cup. She joined Ricky at the table.

"I think you *did* know where to go."

Ricky said nothing, took a sip of tea. Then a longer drink. A third swallow loosened her tongue.

"I'm lost."

"You're here," replied Luja. "I expected to see you again someday."

"I can never be who I was."

"None of us can."

Ricky sipped silently for a bit.

"The past year has not been easy for you," said Luja, as if she knew this for a fact—though it would not have taken a fortune teller to guess this from Ricky's current, unkempt state. However, her implication was that Ricky's difficulties extended far beyond the physical.

Ricky nodded, and out it came. She told Luja why she had left Chicago, where her travels had taken her since then, how alone she felt—always. And hopeless. And afraid, either that she would hurt others without intending to by getting too close, or afraid she would be physically hurt by those who still hungered for immortality. She told Luja about Bob and what she had done since then.

"First, I just needed to get far away. Sasha had a savings account. After she was murdered, the money went to me. I've used a lot of it. But I had enough cash to get off the island—secretly. I knew I could make a lot of money if I wished to use my immortality for that purpose. It would have been easy to coerce people into doing awful things that would have made me a fortune. But I didn't want to do that. I *couldn't* do that."

Luja offered a gentle smile. "You have just described the single greatest difference between you and Cessair."

"I tried to get to Miami." She shook her head. "I had to get off the island. Stowed away on a container ship to Spain. Hitchhiked. Slept under bridges and behind dumpsters. Tried to save my money for when I really needed it. And I didn't want to go on the grid to withdraw more. Didn't want anyone to follow me."

"You did not want anyone to follow you *here*," said Luja, emphasizing the last word.

Ricky nodded.

"But you needed to come here," added Luja. "Because I know what was on the scroll."

Slowly, Ricky nodded again.

Luja stared across the table. "It must be awful, what you feel. But I cannot do what you want me to do."

Ricky's gaze met Luja's. "Y-you know?"

Luja answered gently. "Anyone could guess."

Ricky's features contorted in desperation. "You have to help me!"

"I will not help you to die."

"You have to!" cried Ricky. "You're the only one who knows what is in the poison elixir. If you don't help me, what's in store for me is worse than death. You know it's true!"

"Go and live a good life," said Luja. "Come back to me in thirty years. After saving the world from Cessair, you do not deserve to have your life cut so short."

"What if something happens in the next thirty years?" asked Ricky. "You could be run down as you step off the curb. Or get pneumonia and die. Or have a stroke. Then there would be no one who could save me from... forever."

Luja said nothing to this.

Ricky shook her head in disbelief. "You can't possibly know what the future holds for you. How could you leave me with no options?"

Luja locked eyes with her, reached across the table and grasped Ricky's left hand firmly. "I give you my promise. I will never leave you without hope. Do you believe me?"

Ricky held her gaze for several seconds, then nodded.

"But what about Aruba? Was Bob right? Can my blood make others immortal?"

"That is a problem," said Luja.

Ricky's breath caught. "You mean it's true?"

"What I mean is that it doesn't matter if it's true. If this evil man in Aruba believed it was so, other evil men and women will think the same thoughts. And they will look for you."

Ricky recalled Dr. Campion's and Leo's warnings about cults, how the facts would not matter to them. Whatever "truth" they worshipped would emerge unscathed even in the face of overwhelming evidence.

"If there are more like Bob, they'll look for Crockett, too," said Ricky, covering her face with her hands, sliding them up into her hair.

Luja nodded. "It is very likely. Desperate souls will imagine Crockett knows what was on the scroll. And maybe they will think this of Dr. Campion, too."

"And you."

Luja met her gaze. "And me. Yes, we are all in danger. It is only a matter of time before some of these people trace you to me."

A tear slid down Ricky's cheek. "Oh, Luja, I'm so sorry! God, I wish I could just undo everything!"

Luja reached across the table again, squeezed Ricky's hand. "It was necessary to stop Cessair. I would do it again. In an instant."

"But don't you see? That's why we have to use the power of the scroll. You must mix the poison elixir. And I must perform the ritual. If these fanatics learn that I am dead—really dead—

maybe they'll believe the scroll was a hoax. Maybe it'll stop most of them from coming after the rest of you!"

"No," said Luja resolutely. "I will not make a human sacrifice of you."

Ricky's jaw clenched. "Then we will all die. Or live the rest of our lives in hiding."

Luja sighed wearily. "Why would the fanatics believe you were really dead?"

"What?"

"Many believe you have lied about the destruction of the scroll. And many would doubtlessly believe your death to be a lie. They would continue to pursue you and possibly your friends, believing always that you were in hiding rather than really gone."

"Shit!" She realized the likely truth in Luja's prediction. "There's no way out of this. No way for me to shake this supernatural curse."

Luja looked up at the unpainted wooden ceiling above the table, and as she did so, a circle of crystals dangling above them from thin chains swayed and sparkled, reflecting the candlelight, although Ricky had felt no breeze in the eerily still room. Luja retained this posture as she spoke.

"What defeats magic?"

Ricky floundered. "What? Um... I don't know. Reality?"

"You better than anyone know that magic *is* a reality."

Ricky recalled the discussions where it had been pointed out that every modern scientific concept had, at one time, been regarded either as impossible or as witchcraft. Yesterday's magic was today's vaccine, power source, or physics lesson. She grunted a spot of laughter.

"Better magic."

Luja lowered her gaze to Ricky.

"Perhaps. So, we need to find some better magic."

***

After the teacups emptied, were refilled, then emptied again, Luja had asked if Ricky had a place to stay.

"Maybe."

Shivering beneath a cold half moon, she now missed Luja's cozy oasis and its steaming tea. But she had needed space to think, decide what her next move would be and how it might affect Luja, Crockett, Campion and others. Although she had spent the first eight years of her life in Dublin, Ricky currently knew no one except Luja. Yet, she wondered whether there still might be a refuge into which she could retreat.

A year ago, she and Crockett had walked to Luja's shop from her Grandma Neve's apartment above a liquor store. Now she stood again on the sidewalk, staring up at the darkened windows on the second floor. The liquor store that occupied the ground level was closed at this hour and would not open again until 10:30 tomorrow morning. Ricky wondered whether the flat had been repaired and rented out to new tenants after her grandmother's death. Since she had no desire to barge in on a sleeping couple, she walked the short distance to the end of the block and came up behind the building. Not a trace of light. Curtains were drawn across only one window. And one of the back windows was boarded up with a sheet of plywood. A year later, and it seemed no one was living there.

But how to get in?

She recalled there was a fire escape several buildings down that she had used when cutting across the flat rooftops to escape from Cessair's thugs. She could return to the roof of her grandmother's former apartment and possibly climb down to one of the windows, which would be easy enough to break. However, she decided to try one other option first.

She returned to the front of the building, glancing up and down the quiet street for any signs of activity. The entrance to the apartment was through a door just to the left of the liquor store's big front window. A small bulb with a glass shield that gave it an antique carriage house look was mounted to the right of the door above eye level. Grandma Neve had always kept a spare key in this, which could be accessed by lifting the glass. Maybe no one had checked. Maybe no one but Neve had known about it. Small chance that it might still be there, but it would certainly make Ricky's life a lot easier tonight if it was.

She lifted the glass, reached. The key was there.

Thanks, Grandma. A lump formed in her throat. She quickly unlocked the door, stepped inside, taking the key with her, and locked the door behind her.

A small window near the top of the stairs provided just enough illumination so that she could see to climb. Had there been more light, the view would have been unremarkable. Bare wood walls with exposed studs, hooks for coats near the top, lots of spider webs.

At the top of the stairs was a landing and the entrance door on the right. However, Ricky could see it was not the same door that she and Sasha had rapped their tiny fists against so many times when they had visited as children. Ricky had horrible, vivid memories of the older door being smashed to bits last year by the thugs who had killed her grandmother. The new door looked like it had probably been reclaimed from some building demolition, but it was solid, and it had a new lockset. Ricky's key did not work.

"Damn it!"

She said it louder than she had intended, but after a moment of regret, she realized no one would have heard her. Gregor, the owner of the liquor store, lived elsewhere. She supposed she could just stretch out on the landing and sleep. This was a safe place. She had slept in worse. Even those who had studied the events connected to An Tsuil and the scroll would hardly expect her to return to this place, since her grandmother was gone.

And what if she got inside? She might find no greater comfort. After the trashing of the apartment, Gregor might have had all the junk and her grandmother's belongings hauled away. Instead of beds with soft mattresses, there might only be bare, wooden floors.

Yet, the small chance that there could be a mattress and the relief it would bring moved Ricky to wrack her brain. Cessair's goons had broken down the old door. Perhaps she could break through this one. If she was unsuccessful, she could always revert to Plan B, going across rooftops and trying to bust through a window.

She threw her shoulder against the door. It did not budge. She thrust against it again, this time harder. Still no movement. A third time. A fourth. She uttered a low growl of frustration.

Her vision were more accustomed to the low light now, and she twisted around, looking for something on the landing that she could use to beat against the door. Nothing.

Placing her hands against the opposite wall, Ricky gave the door a hard mule kick with her right foot. She repeated this two, three, four times. Then she switched to the left. After two kicks, she was startled to hear movement.

Someone was on the other side.

She felt the electric shock of panic. The scrape of metal against metal indicated the bolt was being slid free. There was no time to run.

The door opened.

"Jesus!"

Mason Crockett stood in the doorway.

So unexpected was this occurrence that both were rendered incapable of speech or movement for a moment. Ricky found her voice first.

"What? How?"

Crockett's eyes grew wide, moving up, then down, assessing her, taking her in. Then he leaped over the threshold and gathered her in like a drowning victim. After a moment, she returned the embrace.

They moved clumsily into the apartment, disengaged, and Ricky shut and locked the door.

"What the hell?"

Crockett smiled. "Good to see you, too."

She couldn't match her emotions with what she was seeing. Things were different, wrong. It was impossible that Crockett should be here, a phenomenon completely out of place, like finding herself in that Salvador Dali painting of a ship with giant butterflies for sails. Yet, here he was, wearing jeans and a button-down white shirt with rolled-up sleeves. Ricky shook her head, looked around the apartment. Crockett followed her gaze.

"Yeah, it's not quite the same as when Neve was here."

Her throat tightened again as she took inventory. The hallway led to a small kitchen. The refrigerator and stove were both gone, likely because they had been peppered with bullet holes. The shattered table was gone as well. All the wood splinters and mess had been cleaned up. The doors had been removed from the few cupboards, probably because they had been riddled as well. A couple of mugs and half a dozen tins of food were visible on the otherwise empty shelves. Cans of paint and painting supplies sat on the floor where the refrigerator had stood.

"Looks like Gregor is trying to put the place back together on his own, little by little," said Crockett. "There's electricity, but probably better if we don't turn on a light."

Ricky seemed to float into the first of the bedrooms, the one that had belonged to her grandmother. The last place Ricky had seen her. After Ricky had discovered Grandma Neve dead from a gunshot wound in the closet downstairs in Gregor's office, she had carried her up the back stairs, placed her gently on the bed, left a note for the Garda before she went after the murdering bastards. She shuddered. The bed had been disassembled, its headboard leaning against the wall, the mattress and box spring gone. The room was empty of all else but had been freshly painted.

"Why are you here?" Ricky asked as they moved into the small living room. A padded chair rested against the far wall, an end table next to it, a lamp atop this. A braided rug was rolled up and leaning against a wall. The rest—Neve's computer, her plants, her scarves—gone.

Now it was Crockett who struggled to answer. "Ricky, Doc is dead."

She gasped. "Campion?"

Crockett nodded. "They—they made it look like suicide. Threw him off his balcony! Left a note on his computer."

Ricky gritted her teeth, tried to hold back tears. Here was more blood on her hands. She had failed Neve and had stood helpless while Leo had put himself in harm's way. Now Campion.

"It's my fault. They're looking for me."

Crockett stepped in front of her. "They're looking for all of us! Doc came to my place the night it happened. He'd been scouting the message boards these shitheads frequented. There was renewed interest in the scroll. Some of these crazies don't believe it was destroyed. He... he wanted us to be careful." He decided to omit the part about Ricky's recent abduction sparking the renewed interest.

"How did they get to him?" asked Ricky, staring at nothing on the opposite wall. "Didn't he live in a..."

"A goddamn fortress," said Crockett. "Maybe a big bribe to someone. Maybe someone clever enough to defeat all the alarm systems. Jesus, it's awful! I had to warn you."

Ricky turned to him. "How could you possibly know where I would be? How?"

Crockett's eyes sought the floor for a moment, but then he locked onto Ricky. "I know why you left Chicago."

Ricky was silent for a beat before responding. "It was your shitty taste in movies."

Crockett allowed himself a grim smile.

"Look, I know now what you did. The immortality ritual. I... I don't know why."

Ricky turned away. "I had to know. If the scroll was nothing, I didn't want anyone to have to face Cessair's death squad. Especially me."

Crockett sighed, shook his head. "The ritual...it was too big a risk."

"Yeah, as it turns out, it was a pretty shitty idea. But at the time, there weren't a lot of other options. I suppose I could have just run away, but that didn't seem like much of a long-range solution." She considered the irony of this comment, considering how she had spent the past year. On the other hand, the situations were different. A year ago, running away would have been surrendering her friends to evil rather than trying to protect them from it.

"We would have figured it out."

"Yeah? Well, if what we would have figured out suddenly comes to you, let me know right away so I can feel even worse."

Crockett bit his lip, stared at the floor for a minute. "You took off in Chicago because you didn't want people to get hurt."

"Is that what I did?"

"Didn't want to get close to anybody. Keep moving. No relationships."

"Wow, did you pick up a psychology degree in the past year?"

"It's what Doc thought, and I think he was right," said Crockett. "And now I'm scared to death about what you've got planned next."

"It's none of your business."

Crockett stepped to within a foot of her. Ricky's took a step back, startled. "Goddammit, Ricky, how can you say it's none of my business? How many times did we almost die together? How many times did you save my worthless ass or put yourself in danger? How many nights did I lie beside you on that shitty little mattress, unable to think of anything but how goddamn close you were and how..."

He left the sentence unfinished. After a moment's pause, Ricky lunged forward, grabbing his head roughly with both hands, pulling him into a hard kiss. Instantly, his hands were on her hips, pulling her close. Her hands moved beneath his shirt as he undid the buttons, pushing it up, over his head. They stumbled backward a few steps to the room they had shared a year ago. It was mostly empty, the bed frame disassembled and leaning against the wall, the only other remaining furniture a tiny bedside stand and the ugly table lamp she had hated. However, the old mattress rested on its side against the wall. With one hand, Crockett tipped it and it thudded onto the wooden floor. With the other, he undid her bra. She lowered herself onto her back on the mattress and he pulled off her jeans. Then he shrugged off his own, standing there in the altogether.

Ricky chuckled and Crockett paused, confused.

"Still going commando, I see." She smiled.

Crockett returned the smile, and then they moved together.

***

"I love baseball," said Crockett as they lay together in the dark. Somehow, he was now wearing a Chicago Cubs cap. "But that was way better."

"You are such a stupid, stupid man."

Crockett smiled at this. For a long while, they were quiet. Then Ricky spoke.

"How?"

"Beet juice. Vitamin E. Lots of oysters. Some yoga."

She punched him in the side. "You idiot! How did you know I'd come here? And how did you get in?"

"Ow!" Crockett grinned, idly twirled a lock of her hair around his index finger. "Doc knew you didn't want the nut cases to come after us. He figured you'd try to make yourself mortal again. He was on to what you were thinking; that once you died, the culties might think the scroll was bogus after all. Or at least that you and your pals had no knowledge of it. So they'd stop pursuing the rest of us. But to die, you had to go to the only one who could help you perform the ritual. And that was Luja. So I figured you'd come to Ireland once you escaped from the baddies in Aruba."

"Wait, how did you know about Aruba?"

"Doc caught some online discussions about it. He finds—" Crocket paused, remembering that Campion was dead. "He had a way of finding cult shit online that would blow your mind."

"Bastards, every one of them!"

"Like I said, I figured you would come to Ireland. And since you didn't know many people on the Emerald Isle, it occurred to me you might come to Neve's old place if it was still vacant."

"You're just Sherlock fucking Holmes," said Ricky. "But this apartment. How'd you get in? I didn't see any smashed windows."

He smiled. "Waited until the liquor store was kind of busy. Walked in, started looking at bottles. While Gregor was helping another customer, I slipped out the back door into the stairwell, the one next to Gregor's office. Came up the stairs. Door was unlocked. Gregor probably figured he had missed seeing me leave—if he noticed me at all."

"Still the luckiest sonofabitch alive."

"I was tonight."

She met his gaze, kissed him deeply, moved a hand purposefully between his legs. Then they were together again.

Afterwards, they fell asleep for a bit. When he woke, Crockett's watch showed two in the morning. He noticed Ricky was awake as well.

"God, I'm starving!" She realized she had not eaten since yesterday morning.

"Hang on!" said Crockett, bouncing up, disappearing into the living room, and returning a moment later with a McDonald's bag in one hand and a canvas painter's drop cloth trailing from the other. He handed the bag to her as he settled back onto the mattress, pulling the drop cloth over them like a blanket. "Lots of leftover fries. I was too anxious to eat much."

"You came all the way to Ireland and you're eating McDonald's?"

"Didn't come for the food."

"They're cold," she complained, but they were also delicious, and she devoured them as if they were appetizers from a five-star restaurant.

"Next time, we'll order room service," said Crockett.

She tried to hide a smile. It physically pained her to think how she had missed that Carolina drawl in the past year. Now it played in her ears again. Her smile faded. *Humans love, the gods laugh.*

"If I remember, Gregor usually showed up around nine to stock shelves and do his bookkeeping. If we're going to use the toilet or shower, we need to do it before. He'll definitely hear."

Ricky sat up. "I'm going to shower now. One less thing to bother with later."

"There's a hand towel in the bathroom that I think Gregor must have left for daily use. You're welcome to it. I noticed a couple of ratty towels with dried paint on them in the kitchen. I can use one of those."

"I'll remember that when I write my YELP review."

Crockett laughed, leaned in, kissed her warmly. "What now?"

"I'm not sure," said Ricky. "Nothing's really changed."

"Except that you just set off more fireworks here than on Chinese New Year! Twice!"

Ricky shook her head. "Those bastards killed Campion. I won't let them hurt you. Or Luja. Or anyone."

"There has to be some other way than you giving up your life," said Crockett. "You don't even know if that will convince the nutjobs of anything. And...and Jesus, there has to be some kind of antidote to the scroll's magic. There has to be! That Egyptian sorcerer can't be the only guy in history who ever tapped into that hocus pocus."

Ricky grew thoughtful as she considered this. "Honestly... Luja said something similar. She asked me what could defeat magic. She said better magic."

"Better magic? Hot damn, I'm all for that. Did she have a spell in mind?"

Ricky shook her head.

"If she had, I wouldn't have been surprised," said Crockett. "Luja is one amazing woman. Too bad we can't just wipe the board clean of this whole mess. But you can't go back and undo your mistakes."

Crockett reached out a hand. Ricky took it. He pulled her over and, in an instant, they were tangled once again.

Afterwards, she retrieved her clothing from the various places it had been tossed en route to the mattress and went to the bathroom. She filled the tub, settled in, scrubbed weeks' worth of travel away, washed her hair, dried off as best she could with the modest towel. Then she dressed and returned to the bedroom.

Crockett was asleep.

The bath had refreshed her. But the warm water and steam had also relaxed her and allowed for a mental focus that often eluded her when she was in fight or flight mode. She had thought again of Luja's words, defeating magic with "better magic." Crockett had added another piece of the puzzle. There had to be others than the Egyptian sorcerer who had found ways to get the elements to dance in arcane and curious ways. She thought again of *Lebor Gabála Érenn*, known in English as *The Book of Invasions*, an apocryphal history of Ireland. While much of the book was certainly fiction, they had discovered a bit of truth in the tale of Cessair and her dark magic. What if there were other stories that served as thin veils concealing powerful truths?

Too bad we can't just wipe the board clean of this whole mess, Crockett had said. *But you can't go back and undo your mistakes.*

Then again, maybe you could.

***

Crockett woke hours later. Light streamed through the curtainless windows. The place beside him on the mattress was empty, cold. Ricky's clothes were gone. He called out.

"Ricky!"

No response.

Well shit.

CHAPTER 6

I've got a job to do, too. Where I'm going, you can't follow. What I've got to do, you can't be any part of.

Ricky grunted. *Stupid movie.*

If Ricky's theory was right, then she definitely had to separate from Crockett.

And she had to talk to Luja again. Ricky would need her help. The news of Campion's death had convinced Ricky that there was no time to lose. Anyone associated with her and the scroll was in great danger.

She had no phone, had gotten rid of hers when she left Chicago. Even if she'd had one, she had no idea what Luja's number might be—or whether the mystic even carried a phone. The shop was her only connection to the fortune teller.

Would Luja be there now, she wondered? Ricky had observed the woman retreating through a doorway into a back area of her shop to brew a cup of tea. However, Ricky was unsure whether this was where Luja lived, or whether it simply contained her office. If Luja kept an apartment elsewhere, then Ricky would have to wait until she arrived to open the shop.

She needed better magic. She needed it badly.

She retraced her steps to Luja's shop.

The sun crept above the horizon as Ricky arrived. The street was empty at this hour. She felt there was no point trying the front door, since the place would not open for another three hours. However, Luja might be inside. To check, Ricky made her way to the back alley. Luja's was the only one-story building on the block, so it was easy to pick out even from the rear. She recalled Luja's Volvo from a year ago and saw it resting just behind the building. This increased the odds that Luja lived there. On the other hand, maybe she had come in early today. Or perhaps the car no longer ran and had been sitting behind the shop for months, waiting for whatever came next.

As she tried to play detective, it occurred to her that there were many other reasons the car might be parked behind the shop at such an early hour. Not all of them were benign or innocent in nature. As a result, Ricky felt compelled to approach with caution.

The back of the building was unpainted, century-old, cream-colored brick. Three rusty, fifty-five-gallon drums sat in back of the building. One had its top removed and was filled with rainwater. Upon the other two rested several boards, forming a shelf that supported an odd assortment of clay pots bursting with herbs. There were no windows, although a faded sign six-feet high painted onto the brick advertised that, in its pre-Luja days, the building had been home to Mama Maeve's Café. A face cord of neatly stacked firewood covered by a tarp hid the bottom portion of this mural. Three concrete steps led up to a single, windowless, wooden door. Even from a distance, Ricky could see the fresh wood splinters near the lock.

It had started already. Someone had come for Luja.

Her heart bucked wildly. Had culties taken Luja, hoping that her memories would allow them to perform the immortality ritual? Had they tortured Luja until she confessed the scroll's secrets, then killed her? But Luja was strong-willed, resolute. She had said she would take the secret to her grave. Yet, could anyone really keep that promise under the sort of extreme tortures the most twisted human minds could devise? If Luja was inside right now, suffering, Ricky wanted to help her. However, without knowing what was behind the door, she could not simply open it. Although Ricky was immortal, she could still be captured and tortured herself, as the episode with Bob had reminded her.

Think!

She returned to the street and stealthily approached the front of the shop. Her grandmother had kept a hidden spare key. Perhaps Luja had as well. Crouching as she passed the large front window, Ricky saw the soft glow of light from the back room. She knelt in front of the door, lifted up the small, straw mat.

No key.

Her gaze traveled around the door, looking for another possible hiding place. On a whim, she tried the knob. It turned and the door opened a crack. Luja was too trusting. Almost too late, Ricky remembered the bell, reached up and held the clapper as she carefully pushed open the door just enough to let herself slip inside. Then she closed it, moved a few steps forward to crouch behind the séance table. A man's muffled voice carried from the back room.

Now she was inside, but she had no idea what to do. Without a phone, she couldn't call the Garda. Ricky looked around the room for something she might use as a weapon. She doubted crystals and candles would do much good against the firearms that Luja's captors would almost certainly possess.

Some of that Better Magic would be really handy right now.

The man's voice in the back room was louder now. Ricky drifted silently as a ghost to the beaded doorway leading to the back of the shop, leaned around the corner to get a look. She found a narrow kitchen, spotlessly clean, with older stainless appliances consistent with the building's former use as a café. A ceramic tea kettle sat on a burner, though it appeared to be off. No light was on, but illumination spilled in from an open doorway on her right, accompanied by a man's voice.

"C'mon, luv! We don't need to be doin' this. Just tell us what we want, and we'll be off."

His request was met with silence. Then Ricky heard a violent slap. Luja did not cry out, but it was certain she had been the recipient. It took all of Ricky's self-control to keep from roaring into the room to clench her fingers around the neck of Luja's assailant. Instead, she inched her way soundlessly through the kitchen, hoping that no one in the adjacent room had a sudden urge for tea.

"Give 'er another go," said the man who had spoken previously, as Ricky arrived at the doorway. Carefully, she peered around the jamb into what had probably once been the café's storage room and office. Now, it appeared to be Luja's home. A bed sat on the right, its headboard against the outside wall. Next to this was a small, squarish, iron wood stove, a modest stack of firewood beside it. A small, barred window set high on the wall provided sufficient light for their current business. A circular rug of braided rags covered the center of the floor, and a small table, a comfortable chair, and a wooden bookshelf stood at the left. Luja sat in a plain wooden chair at the center of the rug, her hands and ankles bound by zip ties. Two men with unkempt, shoulder-length hair flanked her, one blond in a leather jacket, the other dark-haired and wearing natty fleece. Glimpses of holsters beneath their outer wear confirmed they were armed. So was the third man, another blond with an ivory sweater and black windbreaker, his pistol drawn and pointed absently at the floor near Luja. In response to his command, the two lifted Luja off the chair, tipped her backwards and upside down, and submerged her head completely in a utility bucket filled with water.

The man holding the gun laughed, and Ricky fought the urge to run to Luja's aid. Their intent was not to kill Luja—she hoped. They wanted to terrify her, get her to tell them about the scroll. Thirty seconds passed. Forty. Fifty. A large bubble broke the surface of the water. At a nod from the third man, the other two lifted Luja's head out of the bucket. She gasped once, twice, her long, elaborately braided hair soaking, shedding water onto the rug. However, she did not cry out, look at the man with the gun, or say a word.

"Nothing yet, luv?" After a moment, he twirled his index finger. "Again!"

Ricky had no idea how long Luja would last. She would never tell them what they wanted. And even if she did, they would not leave Luja alive. Ricky looked around the kitchen for a weapon. She knew there must be knives, but hunting for them would create noise, and even if she found something long and frighteningly sharp, she would probably be able to wound just one of the men before the others overpowered her. Only a small paring knife rested in the stained ceramic sink and, feeling that it was better than nothing, Ricky pocketed it. Once again, immortality seemed to offer her no advantage. Or did it? She recalled having this same thought in Aruba, and a solution had ultimately presented itself.

She glanced around the kitchen again. Battered pots. Jars of dried fruits and mushrooms. More candles. Canisters of oil for the lamps in the front room. Boxes of exotic teas.

An idea came to her, perhaps worse than her previous escape plan, but she had no time for better. She grabbed the two canisters of lamp oil and a box of wooden kitchen matches from the counter. Ducking into the front room, she opened one of the bottles, sloshed the oil on the floor in the doorway into the kitchen, splashing it around the door frame and onto the back wall. She flicked a match into this and it caught immediately.

Ricky wasted no time admiring her work, rushing out the front door and around to the back of the building. There, she yanked away the tarp and pulled several split logs from the bottom of the pile, causing it to tumble sideways onto the back steps. In an instant, she sloshed oil onto this as well and ignited it. Because the back door opened outward, the heavy, flaming pile of firewood would render it impossible to push the door open.

Without hesitating, she immersed the tarp in the rainwater drum, then raced around to come through the front door. Those in the back room were certainly aware that the old, dry building was now on fire. They were also likely aware that they could not exit through the back. But the kitchen area and the back wall of the main room were now so consumed by flames, that they could not exit in this direction, either. Even now, they would be choking on smoke.

Ricky acted swiftly, wrapping the sopping tarp around her shoulders. Then she dashed into the smoke-and-flame-filled kitchen, crashing first into the sink, then the stove, then the refrigerator, the searing pain unbearable. The knowledge that this could not kill her was the only thing keeping her going. A weak glow ahead had to be the back room, and she plunged through. Luja's three captors hardly noticed her as all three struggled against the back door. As they pushed, a sliver of daylight would appear, along with tongues of flame which drove them back. They had apparently decided that the blast furnace kitchen was impassable, and so the back door was the hill they had chosen to die on.

Ricky paid them no mind, throwing the tarp over Luja's head.

"No!" cried Luja, her eyes wide, before they were covered by the tarp. Then Ricky bent, clasped her hands around Luja's waist, and lifted her over a shoulder. She ran through the kitchen, the smoke stinging her eye so badly that she relied mostly upon her memory of where the doorway was. It took mere seconds, yet, the pain was worse than even the shattering of her shins.

Just keep going! One foot in front of the other.

Moments later, they sat on the sidewalk, tossing off the smoldering tarp. Both coughed wretchedly. The shop was now completely consumed, the heat so intense that they needed to move several buildings away. Sirens sounded in the distance.

"Thank you," said Luja hoarsely after a wretched fit of coughing. "You did not have to do that." She hacked several more times. Then her eyes widened. "Your skin!"

Ricky looked. Her legs and arms were sooty and covered in blackened scabs, but even now the scabs were falling off, replaced by healthy flesh.

A man and woman jogged toward them from the south. "Are you all right?" asked the man.

"I think so," said Ricky, wheezing. She took a moment to catch her breath, which came easier with each inhale. The middle-aged woman, her jet-black hair tied back, helped Luja sit up. What Ricky saw next startled her, as the woman, kneeling behind the mystic, jabbed something into Luja's arm that made her grimace.

"What?" cried Ricky, but before she could react, a strong arm restrained her, and she felt a prick in her own arm. Moments later, everything faded away.

***

Crockett cursed himself. Had he been naïve to believe that he and Ricky would be together now? That they had been destined to be joined by romance and circumstance? Maybe he had been a fool. Had he really thought that after helping each other through whatever nightmares might come, that one day, they would reach that happy, golden land where they would have a cute house with a green yard where he could wave to her from his riding lawnmower, and she could wave in return from the back door while holding a freshly baked pie in her other hand? He clenched his fists. Sure, it wasn't ever going to go down quite like that. But their intimacy had seemed to suggest a future of some sort. Instead, she had disappeared while he slept. Just like Chicago.

It angered and confused him. She had clearly enjoyed the sex, as had he. And as they had held each other, if he had misread her feelings for him, she was one hell of an actress. She had disappeared the first time to try and protect him from *her*. But now he knew her secret. Was her leaving this time the same sort of sacrifice?

And their intimacy, had it been merely a kind of participation trophy? Oh, the poor guy, such a pathetic case. Why not throw him a crumb? No, she wasn't that cynical or cruel. He knew her better than that.

Or—he shivered at the thought—was it a goodbye gesture? Not just a prelude to disappearing, but a doomed soul facing the executioner, blowing a kiss to a lover in the watching mob. Despite everything Ricky had said about finding stronger magic, was she hoping Luja would make her mortal and allow her to die a real death with the next sunrise?

He now threw himself out of bed, pulled on his clothes. He had to get to Luja's, had to stop her. Assuming that was Ricky's destination. Was he overreacting? Maybe she had just gone out for a jog, like she had done some mornings last year when, to avoid Cessair's wrath, they had sequestered at Neve's. Or maybe she had gone to pick up coffee and scones. He realized he was starving.

But no. He knew where she was going.

Crockett strode through the kitchen, into the narrow hallway, pulled open the door to the stairwell. Two men that did not look like they were peddling religious pamphlets stood two-thirds of the way up the steps. Their eyes met Crockett's, and then everyone was on the move. Crockett sprinted back through the kitchen, found the back stairway that led down to the liquor store and Gregor's office. Racing down these in three bounds, he ignored the doors on either side and bolted straight ahead to the exit opening to the alley. He unlocked it, slipped the security bolt, burst outside and was slammed sideways against the building and then onto the ground.

They had him.

CHAPTER 7

She woke as if from a long nap. Her first impression was of sitting in a comfortable recliner. In the background, a pleasant hum like a vacuum cleaner being run in the room next door. But there was also an acrid, smoky smell, and this hurried her toward focus.

She saw now that Luja sat two seats away from her, awake.

"I am so sorry that this has happened to you."

Ricky moved her head slowly. "We're...we're on a plane."

"A private helicopter," Luja corrected her. "I woke only a short while ago. Thank you again for your courage at my shop. But...you would be free now if you had let things take their course."

The interior of the helicopter seemed as comfortable as the jet in which she had traveled to Egypt with Leo, Crockett and Campion, although the seat arrangements were somewhat different. To her immediate right was a large window built into an exit door that blended into the helicopter's interior wall. An empty seat was on her left, then the aisle, and then Luja's single seat beside another large window. They faced the back of the aircraft, where three additional seats faced them, empty at the moment. She sensed movement and heard low voices from behind her, but found her arms and legs had been secured to the seat in such a way that she could not turn around. Even if she attempted to turn only her head, the high seat back blocked her vision.

"Why the hell are we on a plane...on a helicopter?" said Ricky, still trying to jettison some of the fogginess.

The details came back. There had been men—awful men—torturing Luja. Then she and Luja had been on the sidewalk. Then there was a man and a woman. Were they in league with those assaulting Luja? If so, and their intent was to resume the extraction of information, what was the purpose of the helicopter? Surely there were other tortures that didn't require a costly and time-consuming flight to who knows where. She looked out the window. The sun seemed to indicate midday. But was it the same day?

"I have spoken to no one, but I have heard others moving around, heard voices," said Luja, who was also restrained.

The muffled sounds became footsteps, and a Schwarzenegger clone with a crew cut, wearing loose-fitting tactical pants and a black t-shirt that might have been painted on, approached from the direction of the cockpit, saw that Ricky was awake, turned and disappeared behind the high-back seats again. Moments later, he returned, followed by another, older man.

"I see you're awake," said the second man brightly, settling himself slowly into the middle seat across from the two women. He appeared to be about eighty, with a deeply-tanned, wind-weathered face, a hatchet nose, a whitening mustache with thick, matching eyebrows, and thin wisps of hair protruding irreverently from beneath a New York Yankees baseball cap. He stood five-foot-six at best and could have been a body double for Danny DeVito, sporting dress pants, a navy polo that fit tightly over his midsection, and a cream-colored sports coat.

"Cult parasite!" grunted Ricky, her lip curled, her one good eye radiating hatred.

The man appeared surprised, his mouth dropping open for a moment before he recovered. "I'm a little shocked. I thought you'd both be grateful that we got you away from there. Another minute and the Garda would have arrived, and you'd have had to answer a lot of difficult questions. Probably would have been detained. And if not, the buddies of those creeps you toasted would probably have grabbed you."

Ricky felt a stab of shock. "So you're telling us you're not with those bastards?"

The man shook his head. "Not at all. Forgive my poor manners. I know who you both are. My name is Xander Tessero." He leaned forward in his seat in a polite bow. In response, Ricky spat on the floor. Tessero's eyes widened in surprise.

"I hope you'll forgive *my* poor manners," said Ricky in a mocking tone, "but it's hard to feel all comfy and friendly after being roofied and loaded onto a chopper. Helicopter or windowless creeper van, you're the same guy—just with deeper pockets."

"And these," added Luja, testing her restraints. "We are detained against our wishes."

"Again, forgive me," said Tessero, "but I believe you'll understand as I explain. And this isn't just any 'chopper,' mind you. It's a Eurocopter EC175. Fast as a bullet train, with seats as comfortable as a private jet! But what sold me was the cutting-edge noise reduction technology. It's as easy for us to have a conversation as if we were flying first class from Dublin to Paris. And, flying by helicopter has a few advantages. We don't need a runway, so we can bypass airports, which comes in handy in some delicate situations."

"I would assume the kidnapping of two women would qualify as a 'delicate situation'," responded Luja.

"As I said before, I believe you'll understand as I explain."

"Great, then unfasten these goddamn restraints," snapped Ricky. "We're in a helicopter! No one's going anywhere!"

"All in good time," said Tessero calmly. "But for the moment, I hope you're both well enough. Any lingering effects of the drugs should dissipate in short order. May I offer you something to drink? Our bar is well stocked, though perhaps until you're feeling one hundred percent, nothing stronger than sparkling water."

Ricky sneered. "Is this the good cop-bad cop part? If we don't tell the nice old man the secret to immortality, then the human bank vault in the seat up front goes all MMA on us until we whimper that we've had enough?"

This prompted a surprised bark of laughter from Tessero. "Miss Crowe, you misjudge my intentions. I have no interest in the secret of immortality."

No one said anything for a couple beats. Ricky heard movement behind them accompanied by muffled grunts. Luja broke the silence.

"It would seem quite a coincidence that you rescue us from those who are seeking that secret, that you then hold us captive, yet have no interest in it yourselves."

Tessero cleared his throat. "Let me explain. To put it succinctly, I want to undo all the evil that Cessair has done."

After an awkward silence, Ricky laughed. "Yeah, well take it from me. There are some things that just can't be undone."

Tessero smiled. "I disagree. When you've lived as long as I have, you find that fewer and fewer things are impossible. I own a global technology company and have become far wealthier than I have any right to be. But I'm not a happy man."

"Try ice cream," said Ricky bitterly.

"Forty-some years ago, I was a young man in my early thirties," continued Tessero, ignoring Ricky's comment. "I was married. A beautiful woman, kind, generous. She was an art teacher. One of those saints that always has kids hanging around her classroom. They loved her. A friend of mine introduced us. I thought he was crazy for doing so. I was just getting started with some business deals, putting in sixty to seventy hours a week. We couldn't have been more different.

But somehow, Henna and I clicked. We tied the knot six months later. And before too long, we had a couple of little ones of our own. Joey and Elizabeth. Libby, we called her."

He paused here and seemed to struggle to hold it together. It took him a minute before he could continue.

"We weren't wealthy at the start. But I made a lot of the right moves, and even after we were well beyond comfortable, Henna kept teaching. It was her passion. Along with Joey and Libby, that is. She was completely unpretentious. No one who just met her would have suspected she was married to one of the world's richest men."

Ricky had no idea why she should find any of this important. She wondered if the old guy was just rambling. She supposed that if you had $500 million in your pocket, the helicopter dealers would hand you the keys even if your mental ladder had lost a few of its higher rungs.

"But everyone has their weaknesses," he continued. "Henna was a collector. Ancient art. Vases, small statues—stone, clay, bronze, wood. She displayed them throughout the house on shelves and pedestals. She had an eye for decorating—of course she did, with her art background—and so it all looked very classy and beautiful." He paused here again, and his face darkened. "But someone came looking for one of the pieces."

Ricky suddenly understood the connection.

"Cessair," she said, almost a whisper.

"For five thousand years, Cessair had searched for the scroll containing the ritual for eternal life. You know this well, of course. Her cult had no doubt run into hundreds of dead ends and false leads. Henna and I had never heard of her group. It's not like they advertised themselves. Typically, they were deep underground. But they would surface occasionally when they believed they had discovered a clue that would bring them closer to the scroll. This was how they came into our lives."

He paused here, looked out the window to his left, took a moment before continuing.

"Apparently a legend suggested there were three scattered and hidden artifacts that, when combined, would reveal the scroll's location. Because of the fragility of the original artifacts, the clue would be copied onto a new item every thousand years or so, and the old one destroyed. From wood to clay to bronze and so forth. And so it was that Henna, in her collecting, had unwittingly come into possession of a bronze bowl with strange symbols, very old. She had no idea what they meant, but the cult had tracked it to her and were certain it was one of their three artifacts. It was all bullshit, of course. The whole story about the artifacts, that is. It wasn't until that business at Zackenberg that a legitimate trail to the scroll emerged. But as you're likely aware, to cults and zealots, facts don't matter. They believed the bronze bowl would lead them to their prize. Propelled by the fever of their own delusions, they came for it. I was halfway around the world on business at the time."

Tessero paused again, but instead of tears, the memory seemed this time to give him strength.

"She fought like a lioness. Not to protect the bowl. She would have given that to the bastards in an instant. But the soulless sons of bitches wanted to eliminate any witnesses as well."

Ricky nodded. Just like Zackenberg, where her sister, Sasha, was one of a dozen climate researchers killed by the same nest of vipers in order to conceal news of the artifacts discovered in five thousand-year-old ice.

"And the worst of it? They didn't have to kill the children. Joey was four, Libby was six. They were asleep in their rooms upstairs." Now a tear did slide down his cheek. "But before they finished their awful business, three cult members lay dead on the stairs to the upper level and in the bedroom hallway. The security cameras showed six approaching the residence before video was disabled. The police report indicated that, based on blood trails, a fourth killer was likely badly wounded and helped from the premises by the remaining two.”

Luja spoke quietly. “Your Henna...she was very courageous. A loving parent.”

Tessero nodded. “Forty years has not dimmed my love for her. Nor my anger over what Cessair’s thugs did.”

“I’m sorry, but...” Ricky struggled for the right words, plunged ahead. “But your goddamned grief and your bottomless bank account don’t give you the right to abduct people! And another thing: The scroll ritual can’t bring people back from the dead, if that’s what you’re thinking.”

“No. That is not what I was thinking.”

Ricky looked to Luja, then back to Tessero. “Then what?”

Tessero held her gaze with cold, unwavering eyes. “I mean to kill Cessair!”

Again, the sound of movement from behind, which was quickly quelled. For a long moment, Ricky said nothing, wondering if she had misheard. Her mouth moved soundlessly as she searched for an appropriate response. It was Luja who spoke.

“Mr. Tessero, please pardon me. But Cessair has been dead for a year.”

Tessero’s gaze was resolute. “I want to undo all the evil that Cessair did. All of it. To kill her before she has the chance to use the scroll ritual to become immortal.”

“But she did that ritual five thousand years ago,” countered Ricky. “There’s no way to keep that from happening. It’s impossible.”

Tessero smiled darkly, but his gaze remained fixed.

“Did you really think the magic of the scroll was the only magic in the universe?”

Ricky blinked, uncomprehending. “I don’t understand what you’re getting at. Are...are you suggesting that we can cast some sort of spell here in this century that will make Cessair drop dead five thousand years ago?"

"Not exactly," said Tessero. "In the decades since my family was murdered, I've become somewhat obsessed with revenge. You might even say it's a madness. And perhaps you would be right. Yet, the senselessness of my family's deaths tore at me. Perhaps this is exacerbated by the fact that there seemed to be no recourse within the legal systems of the world. Cessair and her people were as elusive as ghosts. So I began my own crusade. My business holdings are solid and don't require much input on my part. I have more money than I'll ever need. So I've had time to devote to my obsession. For decades, Cessair searched relentlessly for the scroll. And I was searching for Cessair, but always several steps behind. I eventually learned that she had adopted the Rio Armstrong identity, but that didn't answer how I would make her pay for the lives of my wife and children. Then you came along."

"Cessair is dead," said Luja. "But the scales of justice are not balanced."

"Not by a long shot," said Tessero. "But I knew they wouldn't be even if I had gotten to the scroll first and had been able to use it to drain the life from that monster. There could be no balance or peace without my Henna and our children."

Luja's gaze was dark, piercing. "So you turned to magic."

"Some might say I turned to science," said Tessero. "Isn't all magic eventually found to have its roots in science?"

Ricky recalled Luja and Campion entertaining similar theories about the scroll. "Earth, air, fire and water. The four elements of the world according to many ancient cultures. Together, they can sometimes be used to activate a fifth element."

"Akash," said Luja. "The spirit."

"We know the power of these elements can be unleashed, thanks to what we have seen with the scroll," said Tessero. "And because I knew that killing Cessair wouldn't bring back my family, I immersed myself in the study of any kind of science or mythology that dealt with movement through time."

"Time travel?" Ricky was stunned. She suddenly understood the man's intent, and this brought a bit of involuntary laughter. "You can't be serious! Are you really suggesting that one could travel back in time forty years to save your wife and children from Cessair?"

Tessero smiled feebly. "You're not thinking big enough. I'm suggesting traveling back five thousand years to kill Cessair before she became immortal."

"What the...Jesus!" Ricky rolled her eye, struggled against her restraints. "You're loony tunes! That's impossible."

"Perhaps not," said Tessero. "Have either of you heard of John Wheeler?"

Ricky shook her head.

"American physicist," said Luja. "Was given the National Medal of Science, among many other awards."

Ricky gave her a hard, disbelieving look. "Do you have any idea how much money you could make if you auditioned for *Jeopardy!*?"

"That's right," said Tessero, beaming now at Luja. "And most importantly for our purposes, Wheeler came up with the One Electron Theory."

"Which means?"

"Everything in every time is one," said Luja.

"Let me explain," said Tessero. "You know what electrons are, right?"

Ricky felt her ears warm. "They're the little electrical particles that whiz around atoms."

"Right," nodded Tessero. "And so Wheeler got to thinking. Why is every electron in the universe exactly the same? They all have the same charge—negative—and they all have exactly the same mass. Exactly! Yet, they wouldn't need to. So Wheeler came up with a theory. What if they're all exactly the same because they're all the *same electron* being bounced forward and backward through time an infinite number of times? This made him wonder whether this might also be true with protons, neutrons and other subatomic particles. And if particles can move forward or backward in time, why can't groups of particles? Objects? Even people? Under the right circumstances, of course."

They were silent for a few moments.

Ricky looked to Luja, eyebrow raised. "This is legit? A real scientific theory?"

Luja nodded. "A theory, yes."

"Maybe you're just some crazy rich guy with a helicopter," said Ricky, returning her attention to Tessero, wary but suddenly intrigued. "But let's pretend for a moment that you know what you're talking about. Where do *we* come in?" She indicated herself and Luja. "Why do you need us? Just go back in time and whack Cessair yourself."

"Look at me," said Tessero. "I'm no action hero."

"And we are?" asked Ricky.

Tessero fixed his gaze on her, smiled. "From what I hear, you scaled a cliff to save your friend. And didn't you just pull another friend here out of a burning building?"

Ricky was about to protest, but she had cheated death so many times in the past year, she felt it would be futile to argue the point.

"You two *know* Cessair. You *know* the legend. You *know* what she's capable of. And Luja knows the language."

"I can translate written text," said Luja. "That is not the same as being able to speak it."

"I have people who can help with that. In a month, you'll be speaking the language well enough to get by."

Luja shook her head. "Even if this is so, it would be dangerous to move the pieces on the chessboard of time."

Tessero frowned. "More dangerous than the chaos and death Cessair caused over the last five millennia?"

"If we accept that you are right," said Luja, "and we could somehow change the past, on the one hand, many lives might be saved. Thousands over the course of five thousand years, perhaps. Or would time attempt to protect itself from any interference? Small deviations, yes, but no change in the overall?"

Ricky had not considered this.

"It is called the self-healing time travel theory," Luja continued. "For instance, I might travel back in time to assassinate Hitler before his rise to power in Germany. But another cruel dictator arises in his place, and so while the details are different, the overall results are quite similar."

Tessero said nothing to this, and Luja continued.

"Or, by our interference, would we start a tiny chain reaction that, over the course of five thousand years, would lead to something unimaginable? A worse nightmare?"

"'A Sound of Thunder'," said Ricky.

Luja appeared puzzled.

"Did I find a *Jeopardy!* question you couldn't answer?"

"In *Jeopardy!*, one is given the answer. It is the question that must be supplied."

Ricky executed another eye roll. "Whatever. 'A Sound of Thunder' is a short story by Ray Bradbury, about time travel. A guy goes back a couple million years, steps on a single butterfly. That minor event slightly alters other almost undetectable things, which change other minor things which, over the course of millions of years, lead to dramatic changes. When he returns to the present, the U.S. is a totalitarian dictatorship."

Luja nodded. "That is precisely what I meant. Could we justify the risk? Right now, there are only a handful of people whose lives might be in danger. Dare we jeopardize the lives of millions?"

"You risk the lives of millions as long as you live!" said Tessero darkly, pointing a gnarled finger at Luja. "Do you really believe that no one could pry the secrets of the scroll out of *you*? There are methods you cannot even begin to imagine."

"You will forgive my skepticism," said Luja, "but it is difficult to reconcile your supposedly noble intentions with the fact that we have been drugged, held against our will, and are being taken somewhere we have not consented to go."

"Would you have come with me if I had wandered up to you on the street and asked you politely?" No one said anything. "Of course you wouldn't. Based on what I've seen and heard, you probably would have kicked me in the balls and disappeared. And I spent a lot of time and money tracking you down in the first place."

"That's bullshit logic!" said Ricky. "Every authoritarian or madman believes the end justifies the means."

"You may see the logic in my methods when you hear everything," replied Tessero.

"If we agree to help you—and I am asking this only to gain a greater understanding of the whole—what happens next?" asked Luja.

"We are currently on our way to Egypt, a land you both have some familiarity with already. We'll need to make several refueling stops along the way. Then begins the process of preparing you for your journey. We have put together maps and virtual models of what the area may have looked like five thousand years ago. Where possible, you'll walk the same land, although in its modern form. You'll be tutored in customs and mannerisms. And, of course, in the language. We'll also have to make some cosmetic changes to Miss Crowe, whose very Irish appearance might draw suspicion in ancient Egypt. Once you arrive in the past, you will familiarize yourself with the area, find Cessair, familiarize yourself with her routine, and devise a plan to get her alone so that you can kill her."

"What happens if we tell you to go screw yourself?"

Tessero smiled. "You won't."

His certainty on the matter frightened Ricky. "Oh yeah? Why's that?"

"Think about it," explained Tessero, leaning closer. "All the lives Cessair snuffed out through the centuries—they will now live! There will never have been a cult of Cessair! Your friends, Leo Brenner and Dr. Thomas Campion, alive! And Cessair has hit you close to home, Miss Crowe. What would you give to have your left eye back? With no cult of Cessair, you never go to Egypt or Germany! And best of all? Your grandmother, alive! Your sister, alive!"

Ricky felt suddenly lightheaded. Was there even a small chance that this madman was on to something? She had mocked his fantastic plan, but she had seen magic already that was no less incredible than travel through time. To have her Grandma Neve alive again. And Sasha. The idea that even a tiny chance existed slammed her with a wave of emotion.

"I see your perspective has shifted slightly," said Tessero. "Perhaps I can nudge you over the edge."

Tessero nodded to someone in the seats behind the two women, and Ricky heard movement and scuffling sounds.

"What are you doing?" asked Ricky, suddenly worried.

Tessero said nothing, but the ponytailed woman who had injected Luja on the sidewalk in Dublin stepped from behind, sat in the seat across from Luja.

"Hey, it's Nurse Ratched," snarled Ricky. "Thanks, but no more jabs for me, bitch."

The woman only smirked as if she possessed knowledge that repelled any sting such sarcasm might generate.

Moments later, there came a ripping sound from behind, like duct tape being torn away. Then a familiar southern accent chilled Ricky.

"Damn, that hurt! Shit! This is the last time I fly coach!"

One of Tessero's goons now ushered Crockett roughly up the aisle and thrust him into the seat across from Ricky. She saw that his wrists were zip tied behind him.

Crockett smiled at her. "Looks like I've just been bumped up to first class. Hi, beautiful!"

Ricky's heartbeat accelerated to Maserati, and she tore at her bindings with little effect. "You dumb shit! Can't I leave you alone for one morning without you getting yourself captured by asshole psychopaths?"

"They made me an offer I couldn't refuse. It sounds like we're heading back to the land of the Pharaohs."

"Yeah, apparently," replied Ricky, a sick feeling growing deep in her gut. She turned to Tessero. "Why? You didn't need to bring him along."

"But I think I did," said Tessero serenely. "You see, it is very important that this mission not fail."

At a hand signal, Tessero's big goon reappeared, hoisted Crockett out of his seat and backed into the aisle. Crockett grunted and struggled, his feet barely touching the ground.

"Stop it!" shouted Ricky.

Oblivious to her cries, the ponytail woman stood, moved to the hatch beside Ricky, unfastened the safety latches and slid it open. She gave Ricky a malicious wink, then stepped out of the way. Ricky saw Crockett's eyes go wide as he realized what was intended.

"Oh Jesus! God, no! We can talk! No!"

Ricky screamed. "No! No! I'll do whatever..."

But the goon had already heaved Crockett out the open hatchway. Ricky screamed again as ponytail slid the hatch shut and reset the safety latches. The woman paused in front of Ricky on her way back to her seat and spoke gently in a British accent, offering a Nurse Ratched quote from the film *One Flew Over the Cuckoo's Nest*: "'You are under the jurisdiction of me'."

Ricky screamed and threw herself maniacally against her restraints, which held fast. Tessero remained in his seat, no more disturbed by events than if he had been watching a nature video on public television. "You goddamn psycho! You bastard! My God, what the hell!" Gradually, she realized that even if she succeeded in escaping, there was nothing she could do. She melted into loud, wracking sobbing.

"You did not have to do that," Luja said to Tessero, her voice catching. "Just the threat and she would have agreed to help."

"Perhaps," said Tessero. "But I would always worry that you were scheming some plan to free Mr. Crockett and yourselves. Or that you would simply refuse to go through with the plan. Now, I *know* you will. Because in doing so, Mr. Crockett will live."

Ricky's tear-ruined face raised slightly. Tessero continued.

"If you kill Cessair, my family lives, too. There's no cult. And I don't devote my life to revenge. You and Mr. Crockett never come to Ireland. And he is never thrown out of a helicopter into the ocean from an altitude of nearly two miles."

Ricky's breaths came deeply, quickly. "I'm going to kill you."

Tessero smiled. "That may be so. But first, you're going to help me. And once the world is set right, with your grandmother, sister and Mr. Crockett alive, you may want to thank me instead."

CHAPTER 8

When Ricky woke, she found herself in a comfortable bed in a darkened room. A noise had awakened her. Not in the room. Something outside. Machine noises. As her thoughts coalesced, she uttered a loud sob, then punched her pillow several times. She followed this with a string of blistering curses

She realized, of course, that cursing in a darkened room would not put her fingers around the neck of anyone from whom she wished to exact payment for Crockett's murder.

"Hello?" She swung her legs off the bed. "What the hell is this? Where the hell am I? Luja?"

To her right she could see a dull outline of light around blackout curtains. She stood onto the hard floor, took a few steps, steadied herself, and pushed the curtain aside. Through a window in front of vertical iron bars, she observed a wide compound with several date palms, as well as a patio table with umbrella and chairs. A high, brick wall stood about one hundred feet away. A gap in the wall was fitted with a twelve-foot metal door that had generated the mechanical sounds that had nudged her awake. It was being raised now to allow a truck to enter, a light in a panel next to the door blinking green. The packed earth between the wall and the building was lit by bright lights.

A fucking prison.

But not a legit prison. The workmanship did not seem institutional in quality. Sure, there were bars on the window, but the overall look was more like a compound that had been built years ago as a residence for someone seeking privacy. The current owner had remodeled with his own dark purposes in mind. She guessed that the rolling metal door in the wall was a recent addition that had replaced an attractive wrought iron gate. The new door offered no view of the outside. And it allowed no outsiders to view whatever atrocities might be occurring inside.

She let the curtain fall closed. She could see the outlines of the bed, made her way around it and found a light switch next to the door. Two lights embedded in the ceiling illuminated the room and, at the ceiling's center, a black, plastic dome the size of a softball.

Surveillance.

The floor was wood, or perhaps bamboo or some composite textured to look like wood. A small, oval rug rested next to the bed. The wallpaper pattern was wheat, and several tasteful landscapes hung from the walls, none of which seemed to represent any location in Egypt. A blond wood dresser stood across from the foot of the bed, and an open door to the left revealed a closet. A look into one of the drawers revealed t-shirts, slacks and underthings, all black. She noticed that she was still wearing her smoky clothes from the fire at Luja's shop.

Ricky expected the exit door to be locked, but it opened onto a larger room containing a sofa, two upholstered chairs, and a wooden table with two kitchen-style chairs. There did not appear to be a kitchen, but there was a simple refrigerator and a shelf supporting a small microwave oven. As she finished her assessment, the closed door on the far side of the room opened and Luja stepped out. She said nothing but moved across the common area to join Ricky. When she arrived, she leaned to Ricky's right ear and whispered.

"They may be listening."

Ricky nodded, pointed to a black dome in the center of the common room's ceiling. She went to her knees and motioned

Luja to do the same, facing her. Ricky draped her arms across Luja's shoulders, and Luja mirrored her action, and then the two dipped their heads together so that their faces were hidden behind their arms. Their voices were barely audible.

"Where is this?" asked Ricky.

"It is impossible to know. But I would guess somewhere outside of the city. The walls are high. From the outside, this compound might be mistaken for an estate rather than a prison."

"Which city?"

"I do not know. Shabramont? Giza? Tessero only said that we would be in the same area where Cessair had once walked."

"We have to get out of here!"

Luja was silent for a moment. "Do you think that is possible?"

"It's got to be. And I'm going to kill that bastard!"

"Sh!" Luja cautioned her gently. "So you do not believe in the magic that could bring back Crockett and your sister?"

Tears suddenly streamed down Ricky's face, dropped the short distance from her chin to the floor. "It doesn't matter what I believe. Oh, God!" Her body shook, wracked now by sobs she made no effort to hide. It took several minutes for them to subside. She didn't know whether Tessero was crazy or not. The chance that one could travel into the past, kill Cessair, and possibly return her sister and Crockett—among many others— was slim, yet the notion was intoxicating. Even if the chance was one in a million, to see them again, shouldn't she take it? Yet, she shook her head.

"We can't. We just can't. There's too great a chance that we could set terrible changes in motion. We might save a million while killing or destroying the lives of billions."

Luja nodded lightly. "I agree. As much as I know it hurts you, I am glad you feel that way."

"So what do we do?"

"We watch, we wait, we plan."

The sound of a lock being thrown brought both women to their feet. Ponytail stepped into the room. Ricky screamed and charged toward the woman, only to be stopped by a big hand swatting the side of her head. It belonged to the Schwarzenegger clone who had heaved Crockett out of the helicopter. She bounced to her feet and charged him. He swatted her again, then deftly swung her around as if she were a marionette and he the puppeteer, twisting an arm so far up her back that she could no longer move without feeling excruciating pain. "Mr. Tessero will see you now," said ponytail, and then the clone walked her out of the room.

They stepped through the doorway and into a hospital-efficient hallway that dead-ended thirty feet to their right at a windowless, doorless wall. To the left, the hallway led perhaps twenty feet to a door with a large window fitted with fire-rated, wired glass. In addition to the door to their shared room, three other windowless doors flanked the passage.

The man led them to the windowed door. An electric buzz confirmed that locks had been deactivated, and he ushered the two women through. They now stood in a room containing two long tables and half a dozen padded folding chairs. On the wall to the left hung an electronic whiteboard. They crossed through this room and passed through another secure door, this one windowless. Beyond was a featureless vestibule with one door on each of its four walls. They continued through the door straight ahead.

The room they now entered was a departure from the institutional grays and tans of the previous areas. At the center rested a pedestal-style oak table complete with candelabra, set for dinner. The walls were wood-paneled and hung with paintings of vibrant landscapes. Vases and carvings rested on shelves and several pedestals. A large, oval rug covered most of the floor.

Ricky wondered whether they were to be fed, but their guide steered them toward an elaborately trimmed golden door on the wall to their right. The woman spoke into a handheld. "We're here." A light on an electronic keypad blinked green to the sound of a bolt sliding open. Grabbing the handle, she pushed the door, and they entered a room as luxuriously decorated as the last, this one an office, apparently.

Behind a partner's desk that seemed, to Ricky, on a par with the legendary Resolute Desk from the White House, sat Tessero. A well-muscled thug loomed less than a yard from his left elbow. The ponytail bitch cruised around the desk and stood to his right. A couple feet in front of the desk on the right stood one more thug bodyguard. Their guide took his own place at the left front side of the desk. Ricky noticed there were no windows in the room, but lush, painted landscapes hung from the walls in ornate, lighted frames. A single closed door was set into the left wall just behind the desk.

"Welcome," said Tessero to Ricky and Luja, who still stood just inside the room. "This is my desert retreat. Not far from El-Hawamdeyya. It has served many purposes over the years, but I've tried to give it a few homey touches as well. However, I'm being rude. Let's have some introductions. You've met Chandon and Miss Allison, both of whom you will remember from our trip here. I'd also like to introduce Masud and Felix."

Masud, who wore cargos and a black t-shirt, had the complexion of a native Egyptian, dark eyes and a strong chin that made Ricky think of Omar Sharif. Felix had a different accent, possibly Greek, with long, braided hair and a loosely buttoned tan field shirt with rolled up sleeves. But Chandon, who was just a few steps ahead on her left, bore the full force of Ricky's hateful stare. It was Chandon who had thrown Crockett from the plane and who had beaten Ricky into submission minutes ago before hauling her off to Tessero's inner sanctum.

"I hope you have found your accommodations comfortable enough."

Ricky grunted, took a step forward. "You roofied us, abducted us against our will, and we woke up in strange beds. Yeah, feeling like a date-rape victim is so comfy."

Tessero smiled indulgently. "Well, we shall have to try and do better." Then his eyes narrowed in surprise. "Are you bleeding?"

Ricky felt the side of her face. At the corner of her mouth, she detected a bit of dried blood. Her body had already healed the initial damage.

"It's nothing. I just beat the shit out of your neanderthal's hand with my face to show him who was the boss."

Tessero seemed at a loss for a moment, but then cleared his throat and continued. "This will be your home for a while. It's where you'll do your training. And to make you feel more at home, in a few minutes, we will adjourn to the dining room, and you will enjoy a delicious meal prepared by Mido, my chef."

Ricky took a couple more steps forward. "So you treat us to a nice meal and that makes it all better? You're looking more like a date rapist every minute. Go fuck yourself, shithead! You killed Crockett!"

"And as I explained to you, we can bring him back."

"You don't know that!" snarled Ricky.

"I'm betting everything on it! That's how sure I am! And in the end, not only will everyone you love be restored to you, but all of Cessair's evils will be erased from the world."

Ricky took another step, now standing just a few feet from the front of the desk.

"You're the evil I'd like to erase from the world!"

Tessero laughed. "Evil?" He passed his hands over the desk, indicating a half dozen brass, crystal, and onyx paperweights or trophies affixed with metallic plates. "I've been recognized for my charitable donations worldwide! I've been a champion for the downtrodden!"

Luja spoke. "A thousand charitable acts does not constitute permission for even a single great sin."

"Sin?" Tessero smiled. "From Isaiah: 'Though your sins be as scarlet, they will be as white as snow.' Your journey into the past will wipe away those sins, restore goodness. My sin will no longer exist, and Cessair will receive her just punishment without first reveling in five thousand years of reward. Surely there must be something that can be done to move us past this...shortsightedness."

Ricky was now directly in front of the desk. She looked down, her eye catching on a Lucite square about four inches on a side. She picked it up, read aloud the attached brass plate: "Humanitarian Award presented to Xander Tessero by The Bess L. Winger Society." She smiled wearily.

"One of my proudest moments," said Tessero, weaving his fingers together over his chest.

Suddenly, Ricky's countenance darkened. She gripped the cube tighter and, with a cobra-like swiftness that surprised everyone, struck to her left, using the heavy crystal cube as a weapon, catching Chandon completely off-guard. His hands swung up with athletic efficiency, yet he was not in time to prevent the initial blow from the sharp corner of the cube, which opened a deep gash in his forehead. One of his hands went to the wound and he tried to fend off his attacker with the other, but Ricky was again too quick, this time striking an eye. Then there was no stopping her, and the cube came down again and again, her strong arms as swift and regular as the pistons on a Formula I engine, the product of years of morning boxing practice at the gym near her apartment, the storm driving Chandon to the floor. So intense was Ricky's rage that there were no tears, even though with every swing of the cube, she thought of Crockett.

Chandon had been still for several minutes. Blood spattered the floor and Ricky. She noticed that Tessero had not ordered the three remaining thugs to intervene. She stood. The look on Tessero's face was one of wizened amusement, almost as if he had expected her attack. She tossed the bloodied cube and it clattered onto his desk.

"When's dinner, you soulless piece of shit? I'm starving."

Tessero smiled. "Splendid. Let's eat. Miss Allison, have Deke clean up in here."

Allison nodded and exited the room, her narrow gaze on Ricky set at loathing. Felix moved to Tessero's side while Masud stepped forward with a nod, indicating that Ricky and Luja should turn toward the door. Before she turned, Ricky glared at Tessero.

"You didn't seem too bothered by Chandon," said Ricky, still breathing heavily. "Well, you should be. Because someday, you and I are going to be on the same side of the desk."

***

Ricky had no concept of time in this place, only that it was still night when Felix returned them to their "suite," as Tessero had called it. Her own skin spattered with drying blood, she had eaten ravenously as Tessero had prattled on about their training, surrounded by his thugs. Luja had tried to reason with him.

"Diseases mutate over time. Let us say you can do what you say. What if we carry a virus five thousand years back in time and release it into a world where immune systems are unprepared for it? Look at the near extinction-level results of European colonizers encountering indigenous people in the Americas. They brought smallpox, flu, measles and more, which killed ninety percent of the native people, who had never experienced these illnesses before."

Tessero had waved off her concerns cavalierly. "I've got medical people, and we've gone over this. We'll be inoculating the hell out of you. On top of that, my people have constructed a small room, an ozone chamber, if you will. It was quite easy to do. A simple ozone generator can decontaminate an entire house in a couple of hours. An hour before your departure, you will breathe oxygen through a mask while the ozone eliminates more than ninety-nine percent of any contaminants you might carry."

Ricky, on the other hand, believed Tessero was beyond reasoning, his mind as singularly fixated on the notion of traveling back in time as Cessair's Alchemy cult had been of achieving immortality. Doc Campion—her sadness renewed every time she thought of the kind, brilliant man, now dead at the hands of zealots like these—had warned that, whether their goal was real or the product of diseased imaginations, cult fanatics were equally dangerous. The powers of the scroll ritual had turned out to be real. So there was room in the world for magic, or at least the manipulation of phenomena—the five ancient elements—that would appear to be magical. But even if they acknowledged that wildly improbable marvels were possible under the right circumstances, the sort of time travel that Tessero hoped to achieve still seemed like madness.

"Language tutoring begins tomorrow. They aren't going to be speaking English in ancient Memphis, you know. And culture and customs. You'll need to be familiar with it all so you don't stand out. And we'll measure you for clothes, which you'll then learn to make yourselves, sewing by hand, from materials we provide."

Tessero had seemed to view the project as a kind of legitimate scientific effort, like planning a mission to Mars. Ricky, conversely, knew every minute would be a kind of torture, laboring under the weight of shackles and watchful eyes of enemies who had killed her friends. But for now, she would play along. As Luja had said, "We watch, we wait, we plan."

Before he had returned them to their quarters, Ricky had asked, "Are we bugged? Cameras? Listening devices?"

After a pause, Tessero had nodded. "Of course. There is too much riding on our mission to take chances."

It made Ricky wonder what other unfortunate souls had been imprisoned in these rooms. And what sick pleasure their jailers had taken in monitoring the cameras.

There had been little enough to say upon returning to their suite. But going to sleep right away seemed like a kind of surrender to Tessero's will.

"I'm sorry if I shocked you tonight when I..." She imagined Luja knew she was referring to her vicious assault on the late Chandon.

"Sometimes, justice must find men like these through avenging angels," said Luja.

Ricky did not feel like an angel.

"And Tessero allowed you to do it," added Luja. "He seemed to even take pleasure in it."

Not as much pleasure as I took, Ricky thought. "I noticed that, too."

"Perhaps it was a calculated gesture," said Luja. "A gesture or... a perverse ploy to plant a seed. Soften your resistance to cooperation with his grand project."

Ricky half-turned toward the ceiling, shouted to the surveillance devices. "Hear that, Tessero? We're on to you!" Luja looked shocked when Ricky returned her gaze to her. "Relax. I figured he or his pissants could hear us anyway, so fuck it."

She was about to excuse herself for bed—there was no point in remaining awake when any conversation could be overheard, and who knew what workload Tessero had in store for them tomorrow? Then Luja walked past her into the kitchenette. She opened the simple white refrigerator.

"Plastic water bottles and protein bars."

"I should have brought back a doggie bag from dinner," said Ricky.

Luja next opened the two cupboards, both of which were empty except for two plastic drinking cups, two hot beverage cups, a plastic container of instant coffee, and a package of teabags. She took down one of the cups, filled it with water at the small sink, and set it into the small, countertop microwave, setting the time for ninety seconds. As the microwave's fan hummed defiantly, Luja motioned Ricky to the refrigerator.

"Come take a look."

Ricky had no desire to stare at water bottles, but the look on Luja's face suggested she had something else in mind. She joined the fortune teller at the refrigerator, and Luja motioned for her to bend so that both women's heads were almost inside the box. Then Luja spoke just loud enough to be heard in spite of the microwave.

"We probably have about sixty seconds left. They can't see our faces or hear us. If we are careful, we can talk."

Ricky smiled, grateful for Luja's resourcefulness. "Tomorrow, we start looking for ways out of here. Weak spots."

Luja nodded. "And mind their routines. We must look for when they change watch. Whether people are in certain places at certain times of the day."

"And even though I hate to say it, we need to cooperate. Maybe they'll lower their defenses if they think we've bought into it."

The microwave dinged.

Ricky straightened up, spoke in a normal voice. "Well, I'm going to ask whether Tessero will pony up for something other than water in that fridge. The sonofabitch keeps a pretty bare cupboard for a billionaire." She looked toward the ceiling. "How about some Coca Cola?"

Her question was met with silence. She turned to Luja, who was steeping her tea, jabbed a thumb toward her room, and moments later, disappeared behind the closed door. For several minutes, Ricky stared at nothing, then returned to the kitchenette, grabbed a wooden chair and carried it into her bedroom. She positioned it beneath the black surveillance dome, climbed atop the chair, and punched the dome, shattering the tough plastic cover. Her knuckles bled, but she ignored this, grabbing wires and tiny plastic and metal apparatus and yanking it free. She then stepped to the floor, swept the chair with her as she exited her room and crossed to Luja's. Luja was lying on her bed, staring at the ceiling, her tea on a bedside table when Ricky barged in. Surprised, she popped into a sitting position as Ricky placed the chair beneath the surveillance dome in Luja's room and repeated her vandalism.

"Sleep well," said Ricky, turning and closing Luja's door behind her.

***

They established a routine in that first week. Breakfast would be waiting for them in the common room of their quarters after a gentle tone from hidden speakers woke them. Sometimes the breakfast would be familiar dishes like scrambled eggs or oatmeal with fruit. Other times it would be local dishes like ful: fava beans cooked in oil and salt, garlic, lemon and tahini sauce, served with sliced, hard-boiled egg. Then they went to the "classroom," the area with the whiteboard and table.

Tessero appeared only at the dinner meal. On the second day, he said nothing about Ricky's destruction of the surveillance devices in the bedrooms. When Ricky and Luja returned to their rooms after supper, Miss Allison and Felix now serving as escorts, they noticed that the domes had been repaired. Ricky wasted no time in bashing the two new bedroom domes into pieces and useless tangles of wires. On the evening of the third day when they returned to find the domes again repaired, Ricky bashed them again. Then she went to the common room and spoke to the ceiling.

"We can keep doing this every day until Amazon runs out of spy cams to ship to you! Or you goddamn perverts can give us a break and at least let us sleep without being watched!"

At the end of the fourth day, she and Luja observed that the smashed domes had not been repaired.

Ricky smiled. So it *was* possible to thwart Tessero. A small victory, but enough small victories might create an opportunity of some sort.

Their daily routine in the so-called classroom would begin with two hours of learning the language of ancient Egypt. Their instructor seemed ancient himself, a dark-skinned man, Mr. Fathi, skinny with a protruding, bowling ball-sized belly who always wore a blue dress shirt with rolled up sleeves and a brown tie. Luja suspected he was a retired professor from one of the universities whose pension was being pleasantly augmented by Tessero in return for language and history lessons and his absolute discretion with respect to the activities within the compound.

"You seem like a nice man," Ricky had said to Mr. Fathi, twenty minutes into their first day of instruction. "Tonight, why don't you contact the police and tell them that there are two young women being held prisoner here."

Mr. Fathi had frowned but had replied reasonably as if addressing a six-year-old. "Because I don't wish to be fed to the crocodiles."

While Mr. Fathi's pragmatism disappointed Ricky, she was impressed by his knowledge and patience—though of his two students, Luja clearly required far less of the latter, picking up concepts effortlessly. This did not surprise Ricky, since Luja was from Egypt and had already studied the ancient languages to an extent. She recalled learning some of Luja's history when she and Crockett first brought the scroll for translation. Luja had developed a meth addiction and dropped out of college at nineteen. A friend had guided her through recovery using calming teas, lots of meditation, and some New Age mysticism that had never been fully explained to them. Luja's curiosity about the mystic elements of her own miraculous recovery had spawned an interest in alternative religions, dead languages, arcane history, and unexplainable phenomena. This thirst had been difficult to quench, for by Ricky's estimation, her friend possessed a top-tier intellect. Consequently, Luja devoured everything Mr. Fathi said.

"Keep in mind, chickens, that we do not know the exact sounds or pronunciations of many of the old words or symbols," Mr. Fathi had told them, always referring to the two of them together as chickens, for some reason, usually using English, sometimes forgetting and using the Arabic *dajaj.* "There are no recordings. No pronunciation guides. Decades of research have given us some answers, but we cannot be one hundred percent certain. When you reach your destination, speak sparingly and listen much so that you can learn how they say things."

Mr. Fathi had obviously been briefed on the plan, or at least that portion of it that involved traveling to Egypt five thousand years in the past. Ricky asked him about that, too, during their first class together.

"Do you really believe we're going to be able to travel backward in time?"

Mr. Fathi had frowned again. "I will believe whatever will prevent me from being fed to the crocodiles."

After their language sessions, they would typically have an exercise break for half an hour. Often, this meant walking laps around the large house, which gave them an opportunity to study it and the property. Ricky noticed right away that there were no traffic sounds or conversations filtering in from outside. Occasionally, they would hear the rumble of a large truck, but little else. There must be a highway, but the compound must be some distance from other buildings, they reasoned. The brick wall surrounded their prison on all four sides but allowed for a wide sand-and-gravel setback to the house. The wall was tall enough that scaling it would be out of the question without a ladder or grappling hook. Aside from the picnic table and chairs she had earlier observed, the yard was empty.

The long, oddly-shaped house was blockish with a satellite dish perched on the flat roof. Two SUVs typically parked upon the packed sand-and-gravel near the house, probably for the thugs to use for errands. Mr. Fathi parked his green Suzuki Mehran near them. When he left for the day, he would pull close to the metal gate, which would rise noisily, clicking up inch by inch until it was high enough for him to pass beneath. Then it would click back to the ground, leaving no gap. Ricky and Luja were never outside during this time. A single-car garage with a closed door was attached to the west end of the building, presumably for Tessero's personal vehicle.

On their walks, they also spotted multiple cameras that seemed to cover most of the yard. If they left the building from any side, they would be observed. Felix accompanied them on these walks, trailing about ten feet behind. Four other thugs also stepped outside during these outings but assumed fixed positions. If Ricky or Luja made a run for the wall or tried to surprise Felix, the other guards most certainly would sprint to his defense. Based on snippets of overheard conversation, Ricky believed that Miss Allison monitored the spy cams from the security control room during the exercise breaks. Once the outings concluded, everyone went back inside the house, leaving the courtyard empty.

Upon returning from their walks, for the next hour and a half, Mr. Fathi would teach them about the culture and habits of the ancient Egyptians. "You chickens are fortunate," he had told them during that first week. "Women in ancient Egypt had rights nearly identical to men."

Ricky had replied to this glibly. "Were women held against their will in fortified compounds and forced to listen to lectures that were drier than a mummy's nutsack, or is that a more recent manifestation of equal rights?"

Mr. Fathi had stared at her over his eyeglasses, unamused, prior to continuing. "You will be journeying to the Late Predynastic or the Early Dynastic period."

"What does that even mean?" Ricky had asked, glaring.

"Prior to about 3,000 B.C., Egypt had several kings who controlled at least three different regions along the Nile," said Luja, who Ricky guessed could give Mr. Fathi a run for his money regarding certain aspects of Egyptian culture and history. "When the various kingdoms were united under one ruler, it was referred to as a dynasty. The First Dynasty may have begun sometime between 3,300 B.C. and 2,900 B.C., but it is difficult to fix an exact date."

"Egyptian society was quite stratified," Mr. Fathi had continued, nodding in appreciation at his star pupil. "Before the unifying pharaoh dynasties, there was the local king, of course. Then there was a nobility made up of the king's officers, scribes and governors. Most of the population was peasantry, typically farmers. Some held other jobs, such as bakers or carpenters. There were slaves, too, but they were usually criminals, enemies captured in war, and foreigners." He turned to Luja. "Because of your knowledge of the language, you will be masquerading as a scribe." His eyes found Ricky. "You will travel with her as her servant. Your name will be Panya. Luja will be called Meryt. You should get used to these names."

Ricky had opened her mouth to respond, then thought better of it.

A short lunch usually followed. Their meals had almost immediately begun transitioning to the types of foods they were certain to encounter at their destination: grains and vegetables with little meat. Ricky's had also featured a little, yellow pill.

"It will gradually darken your skin tone," Tessero had explained. "We don't want you to stand out too much. With your Celtic looks, you'd be like the one scoop of vanilla ice cream in the chocolate shop."

"What about my eye?" Ricky had asked, pointing to her patch. "Won't that stand out?"

Tessero wrinkled his nose. "What, you think nobody ever had accidents in ancient Egypt? Being scarred or crippled to some extent was not uncommon. Life was dangerous, and medical knowledge scarce. Average lifespan for men was twenty-five. Women, a bit more. But we'll get you a patch that looks more appropriate to the time period."

"You've thought of everything, haven't you?"

Tessero smiled. "I know you mean that derisively, but I have tried to be thorough. Attention to details is often the difference between success and failure. It is ultimately why Cessair failed. She neglected to think of the consequences of her actions."

"I don't think Cessair cared what consequences people suffered as a result of her actions," said Ricky.

"I am not speaking of consequences to others," said Tessero. "She had built herself an incredible empire, was respected around the globe as Rio Armstrong, but she was obsessed with the scroll. For five thousand years she chased it so that she could use it to make her immortality impossible to undo. She did not think of *those* consequences. Of never, ever being able to die, even after the rest of one's entire species has gone extinct, like the last dodo. What it might do to the human mind, life lived ten thousand years. A million. More! It is frightening and horrifying. Had Cessair thought of these ultimate consequences, she would have concluded that even meeting one's maker with blood on one's hands is preferable to immortality that cannot be undone." For the first time, Ricky felt a flash of respect for Tessero. Unlike nearly everybody else, he understood the horror. But the moment passed. She and Luja were still prisoners. Crocket was still dead. This insane idea that was Tessero's obsession had taken the form of a prison.

In the afternoon, they would study maps and geography, guessing that Tessero's experts had created models that approximated what the area had been like five thousand years ago. After an hour break where Miss Allison—chaperoned by four of Tessero's thugs—drilled them in agility and conditioning so they could face whatever physical challenges might lie ahead, they returned to the classroom to work on stitching their own clothing from coarse linen and weaving sandals and bags from papyrus reeds.

Later, they would receive another language lesson, and then Mr. Fathi would lead them to the dining room. The routine here was almost military in its rigidness. Luja would move to the left side of the table, while Ricky would follow behind Mr. Fathi to the right. The two were never allowed to sit beside each other during dinner. The golden door to the office was several feet behind Ricky's chair. When Mr. Fathi reached Ricky's chair, he would stop and remain standing until Tessero appeared from within his inner sanctum. Ricky would wait, often impatiently, behind him. Then, Tessero would accompany Mr. Fathi to his car, receiving a daily report on his pupils' progress. Ricky and Luja would sit, watched over by Felix and Miss Allison, until Tessero returned. Then the meal would be served.

One evening, after two weeks of captivity, as they waited for Tessero to return to the dining room, Ricky pointed her chin toward Miss Allison. "So are you some sort of cockney prostitute or what?"

Allison smiled as if humoring a slow child, but in her eyes, Ricky recognized primal hatred, which was the precise reaction she had hoped for. "I know you think you're being clever, dear, but your vulgarity merely makes you an embarrassment when you're in a room full of adults."

"I'm just trying to figure out what you're doing here if you're not the oral entertainment committee for these gentlemen. I mean, with being party to kidnapping and accessory to murder and all of the rest, it's pretty clear you have no moral compass. And you can't be very smart if you haven't already realized that this bullshit enterprise is doomed to failure."

"She's the head of security of this *bullshit enterprise*," said Tessero, barging back into the room. "Miss Allison is former MI6, which should add a bit of gravitas to her credentials."

"Ooh, Mercenary Barbie! Although in the end, that's just another kind of prostitution, right?"

"Enough!" he shouted with real authority. Instead of taking his seat beside Allison, he continued around the table to his office door. "Come!" he said, bending to the keypad and then pushing open the door. "I think it's time you see this."

After a moment's hesitation, Ricky stood, and Luja moved around the table. With a gesture, Tessero ushered them into his office. Allison and Felix moved to follow, but Tessero raised a hand to stop them. Ricky could see this infuriated Allison, and so she gave her a wink.

"Xander," Allison protested, "this not a good—"

Tessero silenced her with a look, closing the door behind him. He turned to face the women and found Ricky smiling.

"Pretty ballsy move, Tessero," said Ricky, her eye narrowing on him. "Your hired muscle is on the other side of the door. And you and I are on the same side of the desk."

Tessero at first seemed not to understand the significance of this remark, but then he chuckled with far more confidence than she would have expected. "Tell you what. If you're going to kill me, wait until after I've shown you something. Something the others' eyes aren't intended to see."

Ricky told herself that she had no interest in anything that Tessero had to show her. He was evil. What he had done to Crockett rendered him unredeemable. Yet, her hands were at her sides rather than around his neck.

Something the others' eyes aren't intended to see. He had her attention.

He walked stiffly to the wall on their left, stepped up to a mill-with-waterwheel landscape and tugged the right edge of the frame until it popped away from the wall. The picture swung outward on hinges, and behind was a wall safe with a keypad.

Tessero turned to them. "I'll ask you to face away for only a moment."

Ricky rolled her eye, but she and Luja turned. Tessero tapped in a code. They heard a click, and then he bid them turn around again. The safe hung open, and in Tessero's hands—upon which he now wore white gloves—was an old, care-worn book. He walked to his desk, set the book down, then returned, offering each of them a pair of white gloves.

"To protect our treasures," he explained. Then he led them to the desk and pointed ceremoniously to the manuscript. "*Cín Dromma Snechtai.*"

To her surprise, the name clicked immediately with Ricky. "The lost manuscript."

Tessero nodded, beamed, as if equally proud of his find and impressed by Ricky's knowledge.

"Celtic, by the sound," said Luja, as she and Ricky slipped on the gloves. "You are familiar with it?"

Ricky offered a small nod. An ardent reader, her interest in Celtic history and mythology had ignited during the first eight years of her life. After her father was killed in a factory accident, their mother had moved to Chicago with the two girls. While Sasha had seemed to flourish in this new environment, making easy friends, graduating with honors, and conducting climate science research with the prestigious HARP Foundation, Ricky had floundered. After being raped at age thirteen, a hideous betrayal that had also left her with the eight-inch facial scar, she'd descended into alcoholism. She'd begun to struggle in school and later dropped out of college, hiding away, playing online games with strangers, and immersing herself even more fervently in the study of Celtic myth.

She had tended toward those myths that were darkest.

Her sister's death had forced her to confront the world head-on, and although it had healed some parts of her, the odyssey of pursuing the scroll had gifted her with additional scars.

"This isn't the original manuscript," noted Ricky, pointing to Tessero's treasure. "The original was lost, hence the name. No one knows where it is, or whether it was destroyed. But the original was around long enough so that its stories were re-told in other later manuscripts. Monks attempted to duplicate the original. This one's quite old, by the look."

"All true," agreed Tessero. "As you found in your dealings with Cessair, Ireland holds much mystery and, it would seem, for lack of a more appropriate word, magic."

"The monks, they wrote down these stories in about the seventh or eighth century," said Ricky, gesturing toward the book. "The tales were first told much earlier. Possibly millennia."

Luja considered this. "All right. Why is this book important?"

"*Immram Brain*," said Tessero with a smirk, his eyes on Ricky. "You know it, don't you?"

"*The Voyage of Bran.*"

Tessero's smile broadened. "Do you wish to tell the story?"

If Tessero thought that flattering her for her knowledge of Celtic myth would earn a sliver of loyalty, he was, she decided, delusional. However, given the opportunity, her passion for the old tales was difficult to curb.

"An *immram* is a voyage story. *Brain* is Old Irish for Bran. The hero of the story is Bran mac Feabhail, He was out walking, heard music and fell asleep. When he woke, a woman carrying a branch with white blossoms told him to take a crew and journey by sea at night to the Otherworld, hanging nine lamps from the masts of his ship. He and his crew spent a year in the Otherworld enjoying the local cuisine and women, but eventually, they grew homesick. However, when Bran returned home, hundreds of years had passed. No one he knew was still alive, and the people in his land only knew him from legends of a long-ago hero."

"So, it would seem he traveled through time," said Luja. "What is the Otherworld?"

"Some suggest it's a land of the afterlife, equivalent to the Underworld in the myths of the Greeks and Romans," said Tessero. "But others view it more like another dimension."

"Perhaps like stepping into another time period," suggested Luja. "And the branch with white blossoms?"

"The woman visitor told Bran that the branch was from the Otherworld," noted Ricky. "That branch must be a necessary part of it."

"It is indeed," affirmed Tessero. "A traveler must have something from the place you wish to go. Which is why we're in Egypt. We needed something from Cessair's time."

"But," objected Luja, "just having such an item would not transport us into the past. Even if we went by boat, like Bran. There must be more to it than that."

"Correct," said Tessero. "Think about the story. What else is going on?"

"The nine lamps," said Luja.

Tessero nodded. "Good."

"And Bran heard music," said Ricky. "That might be part of it."

"Why?" asked Tessero, although Ricky was certain he already knew the answers to all of these questions.

Ricky shook her head.

"Music has always been a powerful force," said Luja. "My knowledge of Celtic mythology is limited. But look at the tale of Orpheus from the Greek. The sweet chords from his lyre lulled the vicious, three-headed dog Cerberus to sleep and allowed Orpheus himself to enter the Underworld."

Tessero nodded, but Ricky knew the answer he sought was not in the Greek, but rather in the Celtic tales.

"The Dagda!" she said suddenly.

Tessero clapped his hands together, barely able to suppress a grin. "Why?"

"He was one of the chief gods in Celtic mythology."

"Don't sell him short," said the old man. "He was a king!"

'Of the Tuatha dé Danann," continued Ricky. "A supernatural race that is said to have existed thousands of years ago. He controlled the seasons...which is a way of saying he controlled *time*."

"How did he do this?"

Ricky squinted in concentration. "Uh...the harp! One of his most powerful magical possessions was a harp. When he played it, he put the seasons in order."

Tessero coughed. "That's right. By playing the right sequence of notes, one can control one's place within the seasons. Rearrange time, so to speak."

"Another question," said Luja. "You mentioned nine lanterns on the boat. Why nine?"

"Nine was the most magical number in Celtic myth," said Tessero. "Power and perfection."

Ricky stiffened as she understood. "What you're describing means the secret is the five elements, just like the Scroll of Life and Death. Only instead of immortality, in this case they unleash a different kind of magic."

Luja's eyes widened. "The white blossoms that were given to Bran."

"From the earth," noted Ricky, nodding.

"Travel by boat."

Ricky nodded more vigorously. "Water."

"The music Bran heard."

"Air. And the nine lamps were the fire element."

"All combining to bring akash—the spirit!" concluded Luja.

"Of course, of course," agreed Tessero. "That's a very simple, a very symbolic way to look at the process. What really appears to happen is that the proper notes vibrate the membrane that separates one point in time from another. Do you remember my previous mention of Wheeler's theory of subatomic particles traveling through time?"

They nodded.

"What may allow them to do this is the fact that those particles mimic the particular sonic sequences of the Dagda's harp. Or perhaps it would be more accurate to say that the Dagda's harp mimicked the sonic sequences of our electrons."

Ricky's mouth dropped open. "Are you suggesting that subatomic particles make sounds?"

"Scientists have already established this," said Tessero. "Swedish university researchers found that any subatomic activity causes a hum that's almost impossibly faint and twenty octaves higher than the highest note on a piano. Inaudible to the human ear."

"Let us say you are right about this," said Luja. "How would one ever know what notes to play?"

Tessero smiled, raised an eyebrow toward Ricky. "Since you're familiar with the Dagda, I assume you're also familiar with the Fomóirians."

"According to the legends, they were creepy warrior monsters," said Ricky.

"That's right," said Tessero. "Very dangerous, but clever enough to steal the Dagda's harp and discover its secrets."

Ricky gave Tessero a skeptical look. "That's not in *Lebor Gabála Érenn*," she said, referring once again to the apocryphal history of Ireland she had depended on to learn about Cessair.

"No," agreed Tessero. "It's not. It's from a less well-known account, *Lebor nan Diabhal. The Book of Devils*."

It was rare when Ricky encountered a source of Irish history or mythology with which she was unfamiliar. However, she had never heard of this one. Tessero continued.

"You see, the legend stated that only the Dagda could play his own harp. Others had tried, but...nothing. No sound. Or at least none they could detect. Of course, for vibrating the dimensional barriers, the harp produced notes dozens of octaves beyond human hearing. But there was enough animal in the Fomóiri that *they* could detect some of it, sort of like a dog whistle. And not all of them were brutes. Some of them even intermarried with the Tuatha Dé Danann, the supernatural race that spawned the Dagda. A few of their clever fellows worked out a formula for, as they say, arranging the seasons, and so gave us a time travel symphony."

"But," Luja began, her expression confused, "the name of the book. If it was the work of ancient Celtic people, they did not know of Satan. Did they even have a word for *devil*?"

"No, it makes sense!" said Ricky. "In the old legends, the Fomóiri leader was Balor, who is considered a Satan figure. He wouldn't have been called Satan at that time, or been referred to as a devil. That wasn't part of the early Celts' language. But the legends were eventually written down by Christian monks who settled in Ireland and Scotland, and in translating and adapting the tales, would have referred to devils and Satan."

Luja appeared alarmed by this revelation. "If this is true, then such monsters would be wreaking havoc throughout the ages!"

Tessero's expression became serious. "Let us just say that, although the Fomóiri were clever, they also possessed an animal impulsiveness that ultimately led to their undoing."

Ricky thought this over. "Kind of like...someone who knows nothing about jet planes, but somehow figures out how to get one in the air, and then says, 'Now what?'"

"A fairly appropriate metaphor," said Tessero. "Because of their brashness, their impulsiveness, their lust for power, they unleashed forces they were unprepared to deal with. Of course, we will have an advantage that will hopefully prevent us from... crashing the plane, so to speak. We have the benefit of the scientific method."

Ricky blinked. "Wait, does that mean you've tried it? Time travel?"

"Well, I haven't personally," admitted Tessero. "But we've had several test subjects verify what the Fomóiri learned."

Luja shook her head. "Why has no one done this before?"

"A number of reasons, I'd say," he replied. "First, most people regard these Irish legends as fairy tales. A grave mistake, as we've seen with Cessair's five thousand-year reign of terror, a reign made possible by the magic of the Scroll of Life and Death. Second, very few know of *Lebor nan Diabhal, The Book of Devils*. And even if someone were to know of it and believe it, what are the chances that any of those would have the financial resources to recreate the Dagda's harp, an instrument that produces notes so far beyond the audible range?"

"I guess that begs the question of why you are the exception to all of those cases," said Ricky.

"You already know the answer to that," said Tessero. "I have revenge as a motive, and I have plenty of money to fuel my quest along whatever path must be taken. And since Cessair's evil came about as the result of a powerful magic, I know that magic is real, and that true revenge would require magic."

These revelations were mind-bending to Ricky. *Better magic.* Was this the sort of opportunity Luja had meant? Or was it a power better left alone?

Luja also seemed dazed by this information. "You say you have recreated the Dagda's harp?"

Tessero raised a finger as if to say *Wait!* Then he tottered back to the wall safe, returning a few moments later, out of breath, with a small, black jewelry box appropriate in size for a brooch. Inside was a polished, flattish, perfectly round black stone slightly larger than an Oreo cookie.

With a modest flourish, Tessero announced, "The Dogwhistle. The traveler blows into it like a pitch pipe. Once the Fomóiri supplied us with the tones necessary, the airways and holes were cut by laser. Can be carried in a pocket. Please don't touch."

Ricky could hardly believe that such a tiny item could possess the power to bend time. Then again, she thought of the scroll that had granted her immortality, scrawled on goatskin.

"If you're not just bullshitting us, this is...this is beyond amazing." She wanted to hate, to think only of the pleasure she would experience in bringing Tessero to a painful end. But Crockett, her sister, Dr. Campion, her Grandma Neve. Their faces raced through her mind before she could apply the brakes once again. *No! This is wrong!* As tempting as it was, they could not yield to it. And simply showing them a polished stone with tiny holes drilled into it didn't prove anything. "You said you had used the scientific method. But you haven't traveled personally."

Tessero shook his head. "No. Others have, not I."

"Who? I mean, can we talk to them?"

"It was none of the men who are currently working here," said Tessero. "So I'm afraid that won't be possible. However, you'll see the results for yourself soon enough."

He replaced the book and jewelry box in the safe, escorted them out of the office and back to the dinner table. As they rejoined Felix and Allison, Tessero laughed quietly.

"What's so funny?" asked Ricky as the food was brought to the table.

"It's nothing." Then he relented. "I guess my little talk must have impressed you."

"What makes you say that."

His smile broadened. "You forgot to kill me."

CHAPTER 9

A storm swept through the following day, and so they exercised in the classroom under the watchful eye of Felix, who in lieu of walking led them in calisthenics, yoga and rope jumping.

"Your boss should join us," said Ricky to Felix, who occasionally smiled at a snide remark, attempted to make conversation about the weather, or flirted with Luja, who offered him no encouragement whatsoever. "Tessero doesn't look like he's done a pushup in forty years."

Felix positioned himself for the next stretch, which the other two imitated. "You are funny, Ricky Crowe. I like you. And your beautiful friend, who will have nothing to do with me."

He slow-counted to thirty, and then they relaxed prior to changing positions.

"But you don't like us enough to leave the front door unlocked tonight, right?" asked Ricky.

Felix wagged his finger playfully. "Ah, you know I cannot do that."

"Crocodiles, right?"

Felix seemed to not understand. They held the new position as Felix began another slow count.

Later that day, in the classroom, Mr. Fathi zeroed in on their destination.

"Mr. Tessero says you will be arriving in Tarkhan."

"Why Tarkhan?" asked Ricky. "Why not Memphis or Giza?"

"I am only told Tarkhan," said Mr. Fathi brusquely. "I am not told the why. But Tarkhan is not far from either of those. It is perhaps fifty kilometers south of Saqqara."

This gave Ricky some idea of location, since they had visited Saqqara during her last trip to Egypt—a trip she hardly cared to remember. It was there that she, Crockett, Leo Brenner and Campion had first looked for the Scroll of Life and Death, where she had met Cessair, where Brenner had betrayed them, and where they had been buried alive in a mastaba. Now, she was the only one of that group who remained.

But you can bring them back! All of them! the voice in her head cooed. She silently willed the voice to fuck off.

"The Saqqara of five thousand years ago is very different from the Saqqara of today," said Mr. Fathi, as if reading at least some of her thoughts. "The step pyramid of Djoser, the oldest of all the pyramids, was not built yet. And Giza. When you arrive, the Great Pyramids will not yet have risen, not for another five hundred years. The ruler of the region will be Shendjw, sometimes referred to as Crocodile."

This time, it was Luja who spoke. "How can you be sure of that? Five thousand years ago is a time of great mystery. Scholars describe a transition between many rulers and tribes to a more unified Egypt under a single dynasty. But exactly when this occurred over a period of several hundred years is difficult to say. And even more mysterious is the pharaoh known as Crocodile. So little is known. Some say he did not exist."

Mr. Fathi let out a patient sigh. "I am required to instruct you as Mr. Tessero has directed me. I believe he has information that may be unique in nature."

Recalling her conversation with Tessero, Ricky wondered whether the "unique" information he possessed had been gathered by the men who had experimented with his Dogwhistle. Again, she was sucked in by the tremendous research and educational value that such a tool could provide for the world. And, again, she remembered the incredible danger. Once more, she thought of Bradbury's cautionary tale and wondered whether Tessero's experiments had already created subtle or not-so-subtle changes in the world's timeline.

How would she know? What if, a month ago, there had been no cancer in the world? Ever. What if it simply hadn't existed? Then, three weeks ago, Tessero had sent his beta testers five thousand years into the past. What if they had accidentally carried with them some microbe or virus that subtly altered the DNA of the ancient Egyptians, eventually altering nearly all human DNA so that, two thousand years down the line, cancer is widespread across the planet? And for those in the present, since history had been altered before they were born–Ricky and Luja included–they would have no memory of a time when there was no cancer, because in the changed timeline, it had always existed.

Unless we were the ones doing the changing, we would never know.

But she realized this sort of what-if thinking was about as productive as lying awake at two in the morning, wondering whether an asteroid might someday slam into the earth.

Perhaps sensing the growing anxiety in his time travelers in training, after dinner, Tessero, Allison, and Masud escorted Ricky and Luja to a room accessed off the security control center. Inside was a small swimming pool over which a very large wire cage had been built.

Ricky uttered a single laugh. "If that's a rat trap, Tessero, I don't think all of your guys are going to fit inside."

"It's a Faraday Cage," said Masud, the first sentence she had heard him utter.

"A Faraday Cage?"

"It's a metal cage that blocks electrical fields," said Masud. "In this case, potential fields from the insi—"

"I know what a goddamn Faraday Cage is!" Ricky snapped.

"To be truthful, I have no idea whether the cage is necessary," admitted Tessero. "It was a precaution against sending the entire compound back in time."

Floating in the pool, although anchored and tethered securely so as to be stationary, was a raft of cedar planks atop large, foam floats. Six-foot poles along three sides of the raft supported nine oil lamps.

A bit different than the time machine H.G. Wells imagined, thought Ricky.

"As you can see, we have the water, the fire, the Dogwhistle will supply the air, and I have a little artifact from Cessair's time that we will use for earth," said Tessero proudly.

"How does it work?" asked Ricky. "Is there a switch to flick or something?"

Allison failed to completely stifle a laugh. She spoke to Tessero. "Xander, are you sure this one is bright enough to be sent on such an important mission? But then, she's only going to be playing the part of a servant, so I suppose that won't be much of a reach."

"Better an unwilling servant than a willing slave," responded Ricky, her eyes dark and narrow. She wondered whether Masud would come to Allison's defense, but he stood there as if admiring a Dali in an art gallery.

"No switch," said Tessero, ignoring the bickering. "The music begins the journey."

"I really wish we could have spoken to some of your beta testers," said Luja. "Just to see what it was like. I think we would feel so much better prepared."

Tessero cleared his throat. "As I said earlier, none of them are here at the compound."

"Didn't you take video of the process?" asked Ricky. "Or of your interviews with them upon their return?"

"Unfortunately, there are no videos for you to see," replied Tessero, sounding, it seemed to Ricky, more evasive than matter-of-fact.

Ricky shook her head, laughed humorlessly. "You did all that research, you created this whole goddamned facility, you conducted experiments that have immense scientific significance, and you took no videos?"

Allison's voice was thick with loathing. "As if you're qualified to have any sort of opinion on matters of science!"

"How fucking qualified do you have to be, bitch, to know this sort of thing should be archived? Jesus, time travel is bigger than the moon landing! How stupid would it have been for Neil Armstrong to forget the cameras at home?"

"That's enough, you two!" shouted Tessero. "Like it or not, we cannot make the documentation you seek magically appear!"

"Yeah, because there's no such thing as magic," sneered Ricky.

Allison's voice was a growl. "Get rid of her, Xander! She won't cooperate! She'll ruin everything!"

"It's too late for that!" he replied. "And she will do what needs to be done. She's just trying to get under your skin!"

Ricky opened her mouth to reply with another caustic remark she knew would spike Allison's blood pressure, but Luja's hand on her forearm stopped her. "I think we have seen enough for today."

They were swiftly returned to their rooms where Ricky fell into a foul mood. "I hate that bitch!"

"Your animosity is justified," said Luja gently. Then she pulled Ricky into a hug and whispered. "There is a better chance they will become complacent and careless if we play the game."

Ricky grunted. "I know, it's just..." She thought of Crockett, of the smile Allison had worn when opening the helicopter's side hatch.

"I know," whispered Luja. And Ricky was sure that she did know.

The following day as they strolled circles around the compound in the ninety-plus degree heat, they noticed that Felix seemed agitated.

"Staring at my ass starting to get to you?" asked Ricky over her shoulder.

Felix averted his eyes without answering.

Ricky spoke to Luja, but loudly enough for Felix to hear. "Go figure. Some days, you can't shut the guy up."

At supper, Felix stood in his usual place several steps behind Luja with his back to the wall as they waited for Tessero to return from seeing off Mr. Fathi. As was the case that afternoon, something seemed to be bothering the guard.

"Jesus, Felix, all day long you've been looking like you're next in line at the amateur circumcision clinic," said Ricky.

When they returned to their quarters for the evening, Luja pulled Ricky into her room. "Something is wrong."

"Yeah, like this whole goddamn plan."

Luja raised a hand as if to suggest silence, then moved around the room, searching. Ricky understood that she wished to talk without fear of being overheard. The overhead surveillance device still hung broken and unrepaired, and so she joined Luja in sweeping the rest of the room. Even after finding nothing, they spoke in low voices, sitting on the bed with foreheads touching.

"Felix knows something. He seems...worried."

Ricky snorted. "Maybe he got himself in hot water with Tessero."

"Or perhaps there has been some problem with Tessero's arrangements. You seemed to hit a nerve when you asked about talking to those who had used the Dogwhistle or why Tessero had no video."

"Yeah, there's definitely something he's hiding. But..."

"But?"

"If he had discovered his time travel process didn't work, there would be no point in going ahead with things. But he's not pulling the plug."

"Yes. And Mr. Fathi hinted that Tessero had unique information about the Tarkhan of five thousand years ago. The mission of his first travelers may have been to assure that we would reach the right destination."

"Maybe some of Tessero's guys were killed by people in Tarkhan who believed they were evil spirits."

"But would Tessero keep that information from us?" asked Luja. "More likely, I would think he would use it as an illustration of the caution we must exercise so that we do not stand out."

They sat silently for a bit. Then Luja resumed.

"Perhaps there were problems. Perhaps Tessero's people came back...changed."

"That's a disturbing thought. Like what? Three eyes, or something?"

Luja sighed. "It is impossible to know. But...there is yet another explanation."

"I hope it's better than returning to the present as some sort of mutant."

"Tessero is motivated by revenge," Luja reminded her. "His mind is fouled by his anger. He does not see the potential harm. He believes all of his actions are justified by the good he might do. It is what the philosophers call a form of consequentialism. A thing is right based on what its consequences are. There is no ethical dilemma if one lies, cheats, steals, kills, if the result saves a person's life or feeds the hungry."

"So?"

"Perhaps there are no films because Tessero wants no record of what he is doing. Cessair's death will be a good consequence. After that, he destroys everything so that no one can ever travel through time again to undo what he has done or cause harm."

"Does he really strike you as the sort of guy who's going to do that?" asked Ricky. *"I have the power to change history! But don't worry. One and done!"*

Luja shook her head gently. "It is hard to imagine anyone turning their back on such power."

***

"After your arrival, it will be a short journey to Tarkhan by foot," said Mr. Fathi during their instruction the following day. The large white screen showed a rough map of what Tarkhan may have looked like five thousand years ago. "Bear in mind that roads in this time will be quite different."

"No express lanes?" asked Ricky without the energy required to break a smile. Mr. Fathi continued unperturbed.

"There were no wheeled carts. The way will most likely be narrow, so don't expect lovely parallel ruts. Remember, the wheel did not come to Egypt for another thirteen centuries. Because there was no need to consider wheels, the trail could go over difficult terrain and through narrow places. Care must be taken not to injure yourselves. On the other hand, some routes along the river might be gentler, but you must watch for *timsah.*"

Ricky raised an eyebrow. *"Timsah?"*

"Crocodiles," said Mr. Fathi. He tapped away on his laptop and, a moment later, a photo of a croc appeared on the white screen beside them. "And there may be some wider paths that were intended for sleds. But stones for construction were often transported by barge. Much easier."

"When we reach Tarkhan, will we beg lodging from a farmer or shopkeeper?" asked Luja.

"That is one possibility, although you will have coins to pay your way. They will be duplicates of what the people of Tarkhan knew at the time, although a bit nicer in quality, due to our production abilities compared to those of five thousand years ago. But they're made of the same material, and the merchants of Tarkhan will not turn them away. You could also stay in a tavern."

"Ancient Egypt had taverns?" asked Ricky.

"You won't find them with the same frequency that you would in Chi-ca-go," said Mr. Fathi. making her former city of residence sound like a dreaded disease. "But they existed. The Egyptians enjoyed each others' company just as we do, or any other culture. And a big part of the Egyptian culture was beer. So when my three *aldajaj* arrive in Tarkhan, it would be wise to seek out—"

"You said three," said Ricky with a smile. "Your three *aldajaj*. Your three chickens."

Mr. Fathi nodded. "And so it will be." Then he coughed a tiny laugh. "You didn't think that Mr. Tessero was going to send the two of you to Tarkhan without a chaperone, did you?"

"What the hell are you talking about?"

"The two of you are well-informed about Cessair, and so your task will be to gain her confidence and determine how and when to...do what must be done."

"We know that," said Ricky irritably. "And then we find and destroy the scroll."

"That task is reserved for someone with a somewhat different skill set," said Mr. Fathi. "Someone who has been training for this event much longer." When the look on Ricky's face registered surprise, Mr. Fathi gazed at her over the tops of his glasses. "You didn't think you were the only ones preparing for this, did you? Or that Mr. Tessero would put the means of time travel into *your* hands?"

"So Tessero is coming with us?"

Mr. Fathi frowned. "Mr. Tessero is a very old man. He is not a candidate for adventuring."

"Who then?"

"Miss Allison will be accompanying you."

"No!" Ricky sprang from her seat. "Not that bitch!"

"I assure you, Miss Allison will do a fine job," said Mr. Fathi, attempting to calm her. "In her months of instruction, she was an absolutely superb student."

"She'll make a superb corpse!"

Luja placed a hand on Ricky's arm, attempted to calm her friend. "We can talk of this later."

Ricky spoke through gritted teeth. "Fine. I'm sure there are a million ways to die in ancient Egypt."

"If that is meant as a reference to Miss Allison, I'm afraid that would be a horrible idea," said Mr. Fathi.

"And why is that? Who's going to stop me? Anyone who gives a rat's ass will be five thousand years away. And she deserves it. She helped murder Crockett."

"Be that as it may, if you kill Miss Allison upon your arrival in Predynastic Egypt, her part of the mission will go unfinished. This may thwart your plan to change the future."

Ricky scoffed. "Then I'll wait until after she destroys the scroll."

"Then how will you return to this time period? Miss Allison will control your means of travel through time. You will be stranded in the past."

She felt herself growing angrier. "You've got it all figured out, don't you? Well, when we get rid of Cessair and eighty-six that scroll, there will probably be some changes that send ripples down through the timeline. What if one of those little ripples results in your parents never meeting and so you never exist? Did you think about that?"

Mr. Fathi nodded pensively. "Since we cannot know for certain what form all of the changes might take, it is equally possible that I *will* be born, but that my DNA will be subtly altered by centuries of additions or subtractions to my family tree. And so instead of a bedraggled academician with what your culture refers to as a dad bod, I will possess the boyish good looks and the sardonic wit of Ramy Youssef."

For several moments, Ricky simply stared. Before she could respond, Mr. Fathi continued.

"See? For me, the glass is half full."

CHAPTER 10

A day later, as they made loops around the building for exercise time, Felix's mood seemed no better. Luja whispered her concerns to Ricky as they powered along ten feet in front of their overseer.

"I am worried about him. I miss the kindness. The humor. His…"

"Flirtiness?"

It was the first time Ricky had seen Luja embarrassed. "Well, yes, I miss that, too." She lowered her voice another notch. "I am not made of stone. He is an attractive man. But…"

"Yeah. Kind of tough to rationalize hooking up with a guy who works for a kidnapper and murderer."

"You are right. Yet, it is impossible not to like him."

"You two should not be whispering so much!" shouted Felix gruffly.

Luja frowned. "Except for maybe today."

"Maybe his football team lost and he had a lot of dough on the game. I'll see if I can loosen him up." Ricky looked back over her shoulder.

"Only a couple more days. Are you going to miss us, Felix?"

Felix said nothing.

That worked well. She tried again.

"Maybe if you ask Tessero real nice, he'll let you come along."

Still silence.

"Nice shirt, but Luja prefers when you wear the tight tees."

Luja's eyes went wide and she whispered fiercely. "What are you doing? Why did you say that?"

"I'm trying to get a reaction."

As they passed one of the sentries and rounded a corner of the building, Felix increased his pace so that he came within a foot of the two women. Then he whispered.

"Wherever Mr. Tessero sends you, stay there. Do not come back."

This stunned Ricky, and she could see the confusion on Luja's face as well.

"What do you mean?"

"You will die if you come back."

Ricky wanted to know more, but they had rounded the next corner, which brought them closer to another sentry and the cameras. Felix fell back before the sentry could observe his closeness, and it was another half minute before they were out of earshot.

"But why would Tessero kill us if we do as he asks?"

Felix whispered again. "He won't. But you can only go one way."

This time, Luja replied. "Tessero said that he had tested the Dogwhistle. That men had come back, proving that it worked."

"The other night, I heard them talking. Arguing. Miss Allison was upset."

"Probably had something to do with our little spat," said Ricky with a grin.

"She says you are a fuck-up. That you will not kill Cessair."

Ricky grunted. "She obviously has no idea how much I hate Cessair. Because of her, I've lost everything."

Again they moved apart, waited for another dead zone.

"Your questions about why there was no film, it bothered them," Felix continued. "But they lied. They did not want you to know about it. They say there *was* film, but no one will ever see it."

"Did they say why?" asked Luja.

They needed to separate and smile again before Felix could give his answer.

"It works if you go," said Felix. "But if you come back, you come apart."

"Come apart?"

"The men who Mr. Tessero sent, they came back all right," said Felix. "They were all happy. And amazed at what they had seen or done in the past. But then, after just a minute or two, they would get blurry. Like you were looking at them through a thick lens. And they stopped laughing and it was like little specks floating off them like dust and then disappearing, and in another minute, they were nothing."

Ricky's face went slack. "Shit." The enormity of this revelation stole her breath.

They remained silent until they had passed the next sentry. Felix remained ten feet back.

"Cassandra," said Luja.

"Who?" asked Ricky.

"From the ancient city of Troy. Apollo gave her the power of foresight. She always knew what the future held. But it was fated that no one would ever listen to her. She warned the Trojans about the wooden horse."

Rick offered her a blank look. "What does Cassandra have to do with anything?"

Luja sighed. "The name just popped into my head. It reminded me. Throughout mythology, whenever a bit of magic is given to mortals by the gods, it seems there's always a catch. Yes, you can have the gift of prophecy. But your warnings will carry no weight. Yes, you can become immortal, but you can't give it up. Yes, you can use the time travel power of the Dagda. But it's a one-way trip."

"If I ever get a chance to stand before these gods, I'm going to have a lot of questions."

"Do you think Felix could be lying?" asked Luja. "Perhaps Tessero told him to say these things."

"Why would Tessero do that? He needs our cooperation, and that sort of news is going to have the opposite effect. I'm feeling ninety percent less cooperative right now than I was ten minutes ago. And I wasn't feeling very cooperative then."

"So you believe Felix was telling the truth?"

"I believe we have to get out of here."

***

Ricky found it difficult to concentrate on Mr. Fathi's instruction in the afternoon. Even Luja appeared more distracted than usual.

Felix's confessions had yielded at least two disturbing facts, assuming that he could be trusted. First, that travel through time using the power of the five elements was possible. Tessero hadn't exaggerated his claims. Up to this point, her concern had been what course to take when Tessero's efforts failed to deposit them in 3,000 B.C. That scenario had been confusing and frightening enough. Now, they were forced to consider the terrifying possibility that his efforts might succeed.

And success would mean contending with a second disturbing fact: that they would either dematerialize upon returning to the present, or that they would be forced to remain in Predynastic Egypt.

No fucking way!

"Why are you telling us this?" Luja had whispered to Felix as they had finished their outdoor rounds earlier in the day.

Felix had smiled for the benefit of the cameras. "You deserve to know the truth. You deserve a chance to live, even if it is in a strange place."

It was also clear to Ricky that, with respect to Luja, Felix had a little case of Reverse Stockholm Syndrome.

126

"Jesus, if Tessero finds out you told us..." Ricky let the thought hang.

Felix had chuckled. "They know I am a joker. That I talk nonsense for your amusement. That's what they will think this is. They know that I speak, but not what I say."

When she and Luja were alone later, Ricky had initially proposed confronting Tessero. Luja had pointed out that this would point the finger at Felix as the most likely person to have revealed the truth. And confronting Tessero, she realized, would do them little good. They were prisoners, and with Tessero's ample manpower, could be forced to do whatever he wished.

Yet, one massive red flag suggested that they still did not know everything about Tessero's plans.

Miss Allison.

Why was she accompanying them voluntarily into the distant past if there was no hope for return? Had Felix lied to them? Had he misheard? Or were there factors at play of which he was unaware? Miss Allison might have her own agenda– might be planning to use the scroll to make herself immortal. But surely Tessero had considered this. To send Miss Allison on this journey meant that she had earned an enormous amount of trust. There was something that Ricky was not seeing.

"Miss Crowe," said Mr. Fathi sharply, bringing her back into the moment. "You should be studying the topography map of Meydum, not Dahshur."

Ricky considered him with a slack expression. "You're nuts if you think we're going to remember all of this."

"I don't. I merely hope you remember enough to survive."

To survive. Then Mr. Fathi wasn't in on the finer details of the plan, didn't realize that his *chickens* were preparing for a one-way trip with disintegration as a reward upon their return. Or perhaps he did, and he had meant that he hoped they survived long enough to kill Cessair.

"Let me pose a hypothetical to you," said Ricky, suddenly a bit more motivated.

Mr. Fathi half-closed one eye, considering her, it seemed, with both mild amusement and suspicion. "A hypothetical. This should be interesting."

"You mentioned survival. Could we? I mean, for how long? Could we live there if something happened and we had to?"

Mr. Fathi seemed surprised to be the recipient of a serious inquiry and gave the matter some thought.

"The language might be your greatest difficulty," he explained. "Diet would create problems for someone dropped into the culture without preparation, but you both have been transitioned to the food of that period, so it shouldn't rip your digestive systems apart. You'll stand a better chance of surviving diseases that would kill the ancients because of the vaccinations we've given you. And even with the language, because you would be immersed in the culture, it would present less of a problem over time. And you could explain away some of your difficulties with the language by noting that you hailed from far lands. Of course, the longer you remained in this environment, the more you would need to embrace its economic realities."

"You mean work for a living."

Mr. Fathi nodded. "Five thousand years ago, the Egyptians did not use money as we do today. Bartering was common. Trading goods. For instance, Luja might receive grain or beer in exchange for her services as a scribe or physician. And this was just at the point where we start seeing small, metal rings of gold, copper or silver being traded for baked goods, medicines, threads and so forth. As I mentioned previously, Mr. Tessero will be sending some of these with you, but not an endless supply. The old writings refer to them, after translation, as dbn. Remember that the written language of the ancient Egyptians is an abjad language—all consonants with no vowels. In modern times, we've substituted vowel sounds of our own, and refer to them as debens."

If it came to that, living in ancient Egypt seemed preferable to having one's atoms scattered across all the dimensions of infinite time, Ricky thought. If, indeed, her immortal atoms would scatter. It was unknown whether the magic of the scroll was greater than the magic of the Dagda's harp. However, even if immortality would allow her to return to the present, Ricky knew Luja possessed no such advantage, and she could not leave her friend in ancient Egypt on her own.

"So we could make it?"

Mr. Fathi tilted his head from side to side as if the idea were not completely crazy. "Egypt was a place where women were accorded many rights. Of course, there were dangers as well. Thieves and highwaymen. And women without protection were sometimes taken as slaves and concubines. But if one lived in such a way as to not draw undue attention to oneself, observed the local customs, and gained the trust of one's neighbors, it could be done."

Ricky nodded, buoyed marginally by Mr. Fathi's assessment. Then the old teacher spoke again.

"Of course, you two are nowhere near ready enough for something like that. It would take months of preparation, at the very least."

Later, as they took their seats in the dining room for the evening meal, Ricky noticed that Masud stood at the wall behind Luja instead of Felix.

"Are you lost?" asked Ricky. Masud said nothing, but something in his bearing sent a shiver down her spine, and she saw from the look on Luja's face that she was shaken as well.

Tessero arrived a couple of minutes later with Allison, and as they sat, Ricky asked point blank.

"Where's Felix?"

"He was needed elsewhere this evening."

It was possible that this was true. It was also possible that Tessero was being purposely evasive, that Felix's absence was directly related to their conversation in the yard earlier. However, if Felix was merely off on some errand for Tessero, then they could not mention that they were aware of the fatal issues surrounding time travel. Ricky decided to go in another direction.

"Look, we've spent the last few weeks learning all about the place we're supposed to go, but very little about what we do once we get there."

As she spoke, the food was brought. Tonight was gazelle cooked with onions and celery, served with a thick, cloudy "beer" created by allowing crumbled bread to ferment in water. Another attempt to acclimate their guts to the foods they might find in the Egypt of antiquity.

"We will get to that," said Tessero, again, she thought, too evasively. It was the same tone he had used when talking about the lack of time travel documentation. "You will learn Cessair's routine, gain her trust, and then do what must be done. It is difficult to develop a specific plan when we don't know the exact circumstances you will find yourselves in. Ninety-nine percent of your strategy will be formulated after you arrive. We've already schooled you in poisons and the most vulnerable points in the human anatomy. Much will depend on getting Cessair to trust you and lower her guard."

"See, I'm still trying to wrap my head around all of this," said Ricky. "How are we going to make sure we end up in Cessair's time period?"

Tessero chewed a slice of gazelle, washed it down with a gulp of the beer, and explained. "After several years of searching, I came into possession of shards of a pot from the tomb of a minor governor who died during the time Cessair frequented Tarkhan. You will recall the branch with the white petals? Well, these shards will be your 'branch.' The item from your destination in the past. When the Dogwhistle is sounded, with the shards in your possession,you will arrive in the right place."

Ricky shook her head. "But see, that doesn't quite do it. Cessair's actual date of birth and the time she spent in Egypt aren't mentioned in *Lebor Gabála Érenn*. And Cessair never mentioned it to any of us, either. She might have been there in 3000 B.C. But it could have been 3300. Or 2800. Unless your pot shards say 'Property of Cessair' on them, you could miss her by ten years, two hundred, five hundred! You're just guessing!"

She half expected Allison to jump in to say something like "Don't you ever shut up?" But the bitch was uncharacteristically quiet, and her expression suggested she was even mildly amused by the conversation.

Tessero smiled. "Let me assure you that I am not simply guessing. Not on something this important."

He would say no more on the subject, and Ricky wondered whether the men he had previously sent through time had been able to confirm Cessair's location before they had disappeared into the ether. Unless Tessero revealed this, her concerns remained unsatisfied. "We need to know more than the language and the landmarks. Even if we arrive in Cessair's time, how will we find her?"

"It depends on the time of the year," said Tessero. "In ancient times, Egyptians divided their year into three seasons. Peret, which we would call winter, ran roughly from January to early May. Then came Shemu—summer—from May to September. This was when the snows melted in the mountains in Nigeria and the rains would come, gradually causing the Nile to rise and flood. After that, Akhet, the time of flooding, which brings us back to January. Since it is September now in our time, you should arrive at the beginning of Akhet. Cessair will be just returning from the journey to beg her grandfather for a place on the ark."

Ricky was quite familiar with the rebuff that had pushed Cessair toward the dark side. It was all in *Lebor Gabála Érenn*. The Celtic legend said that she was a step-granddaughter of Noah and, although she had gone to live in Egypt, she had heard the warnings of a coming flood. Something much bigger than the seasonal flooding.

Traveling to the land of the Hatti, she begged her grandfather for a place on the grand boat he was building. However, Noah knew that Cessair had come under the influence of a powerful sorcerer in Egypt and feared the evil that she might bring onto the ark: the Scroll of Life and Death. He sent her away, and so Cessair resolved to sail to Ireland, which the Egyptian sorcerer believed to be uninhabited. As a result, he had concluded that God would not flood the island, since, if there were no people, there was no sin there.

She had taken the scroll with her, intending to create an immortal army and have her revenge on an unsympathetic world, free from punishment, even from God. But the scroll had been hidden away from her. She searched for centuries. Then, last year, Crockett, Brenner and Campion had scuttled her plans—with help from Luja.

However, when Cessair had described her ascension to super villain to Ricky and the others, there had been no specific dates and only general locations.

"I don't understand how you could know this," probed Ricky, shaking her head, realizing that she had hardly touched her food.

"That can all be explained in due time," said Tessero, who had finished his meal and now stood to leave. "We've only a few more days. Be especially attentive to Mr. Fathi." Then he strode to his office door and disappeared behind it.

Ricky noticed that Luja's meal had gone mostly untouched as well. As if reading each other's minds, the two stood. Allison, who wore a very slight smile, remained seated, but now spoke her first words since the meal had started.

"Not much of an appetite tonight?"

Neither woman replied.

"You might enjoy tomorrow's supper better," Allison continued. "Crocodile. Some people don't like it, but I believe you'll find the taste...familiar!"

It took but a moment for Ricky to understand the subtext. She saw that Luja was ashen-faced. Her own stomach was suddenly queasy, but her anger blotted out all other sensations. She dove onto the tabletop in the direction of Allison, but Masud was fast, twisting her right arm behind her and mashing her face into the linen.

Luja's voice came from behind. "Ricky, don't!"

"Let me go!"

"Not until you get a grip!"

Allison's laughter made Ricky struggle anew. "You're dead!"

Masud wrenched Ricky off the table, barked at Luja to follow, and then heaved her through the doors that led back to her suite. Once locked inside and unrestrained by Masud, Ricky exploded.

"Sons of bitches! Sons of bitches! They killed Felix! They fed him to...to..." She grabbed one of the kitchen chairs and smashed it against the wall until it was kindling. Luja watched morosely as Ricky picked up one of the broken chair legs and beat several deep dents into the refrigerator door. Then, realizing the futility of her efforts, she sank to her knees. "And that sadistic bitch enjoyed it! Just like she did with Crockett! We have to get out of here!"

Luja went to her knees beside her, grabbed Ricky by the wrist, pulled her close and spoke in a soothing tone. "It will be all right." Then, very quietly, she mouthed the words.

"I have a plan."

CHAPTER 11

The routine of dinner was always the same. Every day, after their instruction, they would be escorted to the oak table in the dining room, where Luja and Ricky would be seated across from each other. One of Tessero's human testosterone bags—formerly Felix, now Masud—would stand watch, guarding the door that led to the front entryway. Tessero would appear through his office door and receive his daily report from Mr. Fathi on his pupils' progress as he walked the old teacher to his car. They knew the meeting was over when they heard Mr. Fathi's Mehran start up, then the clank-clank-clank of the metal gate.

But today was different.

"Wait!" shouted Ricky as Tessero emerged from his office and greeted Mr. Fathi. All eyes turned to her. "We need to talk, Tessero!"

Tessero frowned. "We can talk over dinner as soon as I—"

"No!" Ricky's voice reverberated throughout the room. "Now! No more lies! We know you fed Felix to the crocodiles!"

Mr. Fathi's eyes went wide.

Tessero put a hand on Mr. Fathi's shoulder to try and resume his path toward the exit. "We can talk in a minute. I really must—"

"Now or we're done!"

Allison stood, oozing hatred at Ricky while speaking to Tessero. "You see? I warned you! She'll ruin everything!"

"Yes, everything will be ruined," said Luja. "You may force us to leap to the time before the pyramids, but we will do nothing to make your plan succeed. In fact, we will do everything we can to make it fail!"

Tessero's face had grown darker, almost purple, and it was clear he was barely keeping his anger in check. "What is it you want?"

"The truth!" cried Ricky. "If we're going to risk our lives, you owe us that much."

For a moment, Tessero hesitated, his expression uncertain. Then it hardened. "Yes! I had Felix killed."

Although Ricky had known this, hearing Tessero say it aloud was like a gut punch.

"Did he speak the truth to us?" asked Luja. "If we travel into the past, will we die if we attempt to return to the present?"

Tessero glowered at her. "Yes! There, you have the truth! Are you satisfied?"

He moved to guide Mr. Fathi again, but Ricky spoke.

"No! No, we're not satisfied! What if you're lying?"

"Why would I lie about that?"

"To keep us from trying to return. If we thought we would die, we wouldn't want to. Maybe you had Felix tell us that lie to help you tie up a couple of loose ends. We'd be two problems that you'd managed to hide fifty centuries away."

"That's ridiculous!" They saw that Tessero was fidgeting as if he were standing on an anthill. His daily routine had been upset, and it was driving him mad.

"Prove it!" cried Luja. "Felix said there were films!"

"After dinner, we can—"

"Now, or fuck your plan!"

Tessero clenched his jaw, exhaled loudly through his nostrils. Then he turned to Mr. Fathi. "If you don't mind, please wait here. This should only take a few minutes. Then you can give me the day's report."

Mr. Fathi gave a curt bow. "Er, of course. No trouble. None at all."

"Xander, bind her in chains!" roared Miss Allison. "We can bury her in the desert where she'll never be found! The other one can be made to cooperate! The plan can succeed with just us two!"

Tessero raised a hand, his palm extending toward Miss Allison. "Enough." Then he gestured to Masud, who ushered Luja around the table. Tessero unlocked his office and, moments later, Luja, Ricky, Tessero, and Masud stood inside.

Part one of Luja's plan had required two things to occur. They had to get Tessero to bring them into his office. And they had to make sure Mr. Fathi did not leave. Not right away.

They had recognized the weak link in their prison was Mr. Fathi. He passed through the gates every day at the same time. In, out. It was the consistency that marked their schedule and defined Tessero's actions that they hoped would free them.

Tessero went to his wall safe again, Masud at his side. He had the others, including Masud, turn away. Ricky and Luja moved to the left side of Tessero's desk and faced a large, wall-mounted monitor. Tessero returned with a compact external drive. He stood on the right side of his desk, gave the drive to Masud, who plugged it into the computer and began tapping. A few moments later, the large monitor lit up blue. Masud rose, handed a remote device to Tessero. Following a few taps, a video began to play.

The scene was the pool chamber Tessero had shown them. The camera appeared to be mounted stationary, showing the cage and the empty floating platform within. Ricky did not recognize the voice of the man doing the narration.

"OW-17-J, Alpha group expected return: sixty seconds. Predynastic excursion to Tarkhan, test only. Subject: Jibril Maloof, age twenty-seven. Subject: Arif Ali, age thirty-three. Forty-five seconds."

The countdown continued. Ricky could not look away and had to keep reminding herself of their plan. When the countdown reached zero, the flames in the nine lanterns flickered as if a strong wind had blown through the chamber. A few individuals off camera could be heard remarking how they had just felt their ears pop. And there on the raft stood two men who appeared out of nowhere. One moment the raft had been empty. The next, there they were. A cheer went up from what seemed half a dozen voices off camera. The names of the two men were shouted—*"Jibril is the man," "King Arif!"*—and the dark-skinned time travelers themselves raised fists in triumph. One was tall, slender and bald. The other was shorter, well-muscled, and wore a black wig that would have allowed him to fit in while visiting Tarkhan. The narrator's voice returned.

"Alpha group looking good. We have a successful return! Okay, we will get you out of there in a minute. How do you feel? Any unusual symptoms?"

"Feeling stoked!" said the tall one, who did a little dance around the edges of the raft. Several of the crew off camera shouted encouragement. One asked what it was like. *"It—it is hard to describe. It was like here, but...alive!"*

"The women left nothing to the imagination!" said the shorter one, grinning broadly. *"I almost stayed!"*

The others laughed. The tall one did a final dance whirl and sat down roughly on the raft, wiping his brow with the back of his wrist.

"Jibril? You good, man?"

Jibril gave a thumbs up. *"Yeah, man. Just a little dizzy is all."*

A moment later, Arif went down on his hands and knees. *"Whoa! Shit, man!"*

"Hey, what's going on out there?"

Concerned chatter from the group. Then terrified shouts as the two men seemed to blur and grit flaked off of them like pepper or ash in a gentle breeze.

"Get medical down there now!"

Three men rushed onto the gangway connecting to the raft, but by the time they reached the cage, the two men were gone.

Tessero stopped the video.

"That was horrible." Luja shivered, took an unsteady step toward Tessero's desk and supported herself by placing her hands atop his high-back office chair.

Tessero eyed them both. "Now you have the truth. Yes, when you travel to the past, you must live in ancient Egypt. But you will live. And because of your actions, your friends and thousands of others will live."

Ricky looked at the floor. "We have to talk about this."

"After we eat. Mr. Fathi is waiting and—"

"Send him on his way! The two of you can talk tomorrow!"

Here was the second part of Luja's plan, which depended on Tessero deciding that their need to discuss their fate was of greater urgency than Mr. Fathi's progress report. After several moments' hesitation, Tessero nodded to Masud, who opened the office door and informed the old teacher that he should go. Pulling himself back inside, he shut the door and resumed his place beside Tessero.

"What we saw on the video...this is what happened every time?" asked Luja

Tessero pointed to the blue screen. "What you saw was our first attempt. But yes. Ninety-nine seconds. Every time." He shook his head. "If that's not enough to make you believe in a higher power..."

"What do you mean?" asked Ricky.

"Remember, nine was a sacred number to the ancient Celts and Egyptians."

"But isn't a second just a random amount of time?" She was stalling. Waiting to hear the sound that would put in motion the next stage of their plan.

Tessero smiled. "One would have thought so. The modern concept of one second wasn't developed until about 1,000 A.D. by al-Biruni of Persia. By the 1600s, that second was being used to mark times in mechanical clocks. Using astronomical tables to determine the precise length of what they termed the ephemeris second, modern scientists created the incredibly accurate atomic clock. Later, they found they could more accurately measure by hitting the electron of a cesium atom with a laser and counting the number of times it flipped in the course of one ephemeris second."

"And?"

"Approximately nine billion times. There's that number nine again. The ancients were on to something, it seems. But in our tests, with only ninety-nine seconds for us to determine what our travelers had learned, our debriefings with our subsequent time travelers had to be handled quickly. We needed to know if it was Cessair's time."

Ricky strained to listen. *Where is it? Did we miss it?*

Luja stared at Tessero in horrid fascination. "After the terrible results of your first experiment, you sent *more* men? Who would agree to such a thing?"

"I don't think Tessero asked for volunteers from among those who had seen the results," said Ricky darkly. "Probably new recruits who he attracted with promises of a big payday."

"Yes, well, their sacrifices will make a great difference," said Tessero in defense.

"Sacrifices made unwillingly are immoral," said Luja.

And then Ricky heard what she had been listening for: the distant clank-clank-clank of the gate rising in the courtyard as Mr. Fathi prepared to leave.

Their days at the compound had revealed that they could hear the gate outside when it started to rise. Ricky had been awakened by it on her first night there. She had also seen it rise from her room several times when Tessero's goons had taken out one of the SUVs for supplies. At the first dull clank, she had noticed the gate was less than three inches off the ground. Under half a foot at the second. Three inches give or take each dull clank. It had seemed like it might be important to know that at some point.

She also recalled her first visit to Tessero's office. Yes, she had been angry. But she had also desperately tried to see everything. Was there anything here that could help her now? Or later? She tried to remember where each piece of furniture sat, what items were left out on Tessero's desk, what artwork adorned the walls or rested on shelves? Were there any objects that could be used as weapons?

And she had noticed a couple of type E electrical outlets, their recessed circular design different from the standard in America, but the function the same. One of them was set in the wall to the right of where they stood now. It had seemed like it might be important to know that at some point.

They were about to find out. For their escape plan, everything up to this point had been fairly easy to predict. Almost everything from this moment forward would be guesswork. They hoped they had guessed right.

As the clanking began, Ricky reached into a pocket and removed a three-inch length of wire she had bent into a U-shape, coated except for where she had removed half an inch of the insulation from each end. She had torn this wire fragment from the ruined surveillance dome in her bedroom days earlier. Now she lunged and jammed the wire into the two holes of the outlet. Sparks flew and the room went dark.

"What the fuck?" Masud took a step forward in the dark, reached for Luja, but she had tipped over Tessero's chair in the space between the desk and the room's back wall as soon as the room went black. They heard Masud's grunt as he encountered the obstacle. But they listened no more, for they were already on the move to the door near the back of Tessero's desk, easy to find in the dark since it was just a couple feet behind where they had been standing.

Now they would see if they had been right with their first real gamble. If not, their plan was busted. They had guessed the door would be unlocked from Tessero's side. A quick twist of the handle confirmed this, and then they were through, shutting the door behind them.

They knew they had only seconds. The darkened room and the chair would not slow Masud for long. He would have a flashlight or a light on his mobile and would be through the door any moment.

From what they knew of Tessero's office, of the location of the garage, and of the look of the building from their walks outside, they had hoped Tessero's door would lead to a dedicated hallway designed to let him move unobstructed, undetected and safely from office to vehicle. It was too dark to see anything in this passage, but the direction in which they ran suggested their guess about this had also been right. In moments they emerged into the closed, single car garage.

Tessero's car, however, was not what they sought. Mr. Fathi's little vehicle would now be sitting in front of the metal gate, blocking the way. And the gate would be stopped after just four clicks, if Ricky had counted correctly, leaving a one-foot opening at the bottom. This was the most important guess of all. In fact, it was not so much a guess as a prayer. If the gate got its power from the same circuit that powered Tessero's office, then the gate was stopped now. If they were wrong, then the gate had been opened, Mr. Fathi had driven out, and now it was closed again, leaving them trapped.

Emerging from a side door into the heat and afternoon sunlight, the two women saw that the gate was exactly as they had hoped. They would be able to slip underneath. Tessero's goons would be too big and would be trapped on the inside of the compound until power was restored and Mr. Fathi's car was moved. They hoped this would require several minutes, time to flag down a car or truck or zero in on a nearby residence from which they might call for help. Or maybe there was someplace to hide. Any chance was better than being trapped inside the compound.

Ricky's hopes surged as it became apparent that Tessero's men did not yet seem to grasp what was occurring, and most had returned inside to try and assist with the power outage and missing women. When Ricky and Luja raced past the remaining two, there was a moment's hesitation before the men understood the impossible thing that had just occurred. And Ricky knew that this hesitation offered them just enough time to reach the gate and slip underneath.

A gasping sob exploded from Ricky. *Hell! We did it!*

As they passed Mr. Fathi's car, the driver's side door swung open and Mr. Fathi lurched out unexpectedly, his briefcase spilling open, hemorrhaging papers, notebooks, pencils, and flash drives onto the gravel, his arms wrapping around Luja's legs just below the knees, dragging her to the ground. *"Al timsah! Al timsah!"*

Ricky skidded to a halt.

"Go! Go!" cried Luja, but even if Ricky had wanted to continue without her friend, her hesitation had been costly. A body slammed into her, taking her to the ground on her stomach, only inches away from Luja.

"You goddamned, one-eyed freak!" The voice of her captor belonged to Allison, who put her weight on Ricky and struggled to wrench her left right arm up behind her. "I'm going to make you wish you were in hell with your pathetic boyfriend!"

Ricky clenched her teeth, pawed the ground with her free hand, her fingers closing on one of Fathi's spilled pencils. She caught Allison off balance, swung around unexpectedly, and drove the pencil deep into the woman's right eye.

"Join the one-eyed freak club, bitch!"

Allison convulsed, pitched face-down onto the ground, driving the pencil deep. She continued to spasm as the two thugs fell upon Ricky. By this time, others were piling out of the building. She fought desperately, angry with the fate that had allowed them to come so close, only to crash and burn. For several moments, she was all arms and legs and shouting, but then there was the prick of a needle. The last thing she saw was that Allison had stopped moving.

And then, blackness.

144

PART TWO

KINGDOM OF THE CROCODILE

CHAPTER 12

The world came back suddenly, even though she tried to will it away. Ricky had not felt as hung-over since waking in the back room of The Edsel, a dive bar in Chicago, where she had taken her first drink in six years. Or, more accurately, after she had taken her many first drinks in six years. But this was not The Edsel. She was not sure it was Tessero's compound either. It smelled...different. The language was garbled, mostly unfamiliar, but then the man spoke in English.

"Wake up!"

Ricky opened her eyes. She was outside. The blue-gray with pink-tinged sky suggested it was early morning. Details of the previous day flooded back to her, the failed escape attempt. She felt a slight chill and wondered whether they had left her to sleep the night in the compound's walled yard as punishment.

"Goddamn it!"

The man spoke again in the foreign, vaguely Coptic tongue. She recognized a few words. "*Meryt...danger...cobra...*"

She sat up, recognized the man as Masud, but he was dressed in the fine threads that an Egyptian nobleman would have worn in the distant past. Around his waist and down over his knees was a white, linen shenti, a kilt-like wrap. A pleated robe was draped around his shoulders. He wore several metal bracelets and an amulet hung around his neck. However, to Ricky, the most unusual feature of all was the black, Buster Brown-style wig.

"What the hell!"

She could tell that her reaction frustrated him, and he leaned close, speaking softly and in English. "You're needed. Quickly. Remember, you are Panya. Say as little as possible."

He grasped her left elbow to pull her to her feet, but she shook him off in horror as she realized she was naked from the waist up.

"Holy damn, you pervert! What the—"

Masud endeavored to silence her, spoke softly again in English. "In this place, I am not Masud. I am Zosar. We are in Egypt approximately 3,000 B.C."

As the meaning of what he was saying struck home, she bolted to her feet, shouting. "What? No! That's not possible, you son of a bitch!"

"Stop," urged Masud, "you must control yourself and remember you are Panya in this place!"

"I'm not anything!" cried Ricky, her heart now racing. "Get me out of here, wherever it is!"

"Do not speak!" hissed Masud, growing angry. "You will ruin everything! Remember your training!"

She wrapped her arms across her breasts, noticed several mud brick huts and a handful of people who, against the sunrise, were only shadows. "Go to hell! Get me my clothes! My real clothes! I don't want to participate in your little Egyptian concubine fantasy! Tell all your little actors to go on home!"

Masud endeavored to control his voice. "These are not actors. This is not a simulation. And you are not a concubine. You are dressed as a slave servant. Say little or nothing. If you must speak, address Luja as Meryt and me as Zosar. Now you must come, and quickly, or the one you know as Luja will die— if she's not dead already."

Masud took a step toward one of the dwellings. Ricky looked around, hugging herself more for concealment than for warmth. She saw that she had been sleeping in a ditch near a mud brick house. The sun had just crept over the horizon, and she could make out several people standing across a path packed hard by human feet and animal hooves, probably a main road in the region. She was about to scream something terrible at Masud when his words finally registered. "What's wrong with Luja?"

"She needs your help," said Masud evasively.

Three onlookers stood a good twenty feet or more from where Luja lay near the dwelling. Two of the group appeared to be women, both wearing the rough, off-white linen of peasants, the younger bare to the waist. The male wore only a shenti and a wrap to secure it. All three stared at Luja as if she might explode at any moment, and as Ricky got closer, she could see why.

"Shit! Shit!"

Luja lay flat on her back, her arms at her sides, her eyes open, staring toward the heavens. She moved not a muscle. A cobra rested on her stomach, its tail trailing off into the sand.

Masud began to speak in the ancient language again, but quickly realized the futility of this in the current circumstances and whispered in English. "We arrived here, at this place. You two were tranquilized, asleep. The cobra, being cold-blooded, was likely attracted by the warmth of Luja's body and snuggled up. Thankfully, when Luja awoke, she immediately recognized the danger and has not moved a muscle. Gotta be pretty goddamn difficult for her."

"You bastard! What are you even doing here? I thought Allison was supposed to...!" Her voice trailed off as she remembered.

"Allison's dead. Now shut the hell up and help your friend."

"You and Tessero got us into this mess!"

"And you're going to have to get Luja out of it," whispered Masud.

Ricky's eyes shot open wide. "What?" And after a silent second or two, an even louder "What?"

Again, Masud tried to shush her. "Remember where you are! Look, we'll find a basket or something! Then you can grab the snake and stuff it inside."

Ricky looked at him as if he were a salmon smoking a cigar. "Are you out of your mind? Why me?"

Now it was Masud's turn to express incredulity. "You're immortal!"

And there it was. She got a sick feeling in her stomach, very nearly vomited. She had no wish to ever come within a mile of a cobra, typically one of the deadliest and most feared snakes. The fact that it could not kill her did not change her feelings. She remembered the pain she had endured in pulling her hands through the manacles in Aruba. Being bitten by a cobra would definitely be painful. She was certain that the monster would fight her with every ounce of its strength.

Yet, no one else was coming to Luja's aid.

She moved a careful half step closer to her friend. For a moment, the world seemed to tilt sideways and then she steadied herself. Was this a dream, she wondered? Had she really traveled five thousand years back in time? The sunrise looked no different than ever. The air? It smelled of something. A slight whiff of human ordure, perhaps from wherever the residents of the mud brick house emptied their clay pots of excrement. Having awakened in a ditch, she hoped that she had not been sleeping in a portion of their sewage chain.

A shitty nap and a cobra. Welcome to Predynastic Egypt!

"I need something. Like you said, a...a basket!"

Masud cupped his hands, whispered the correct words to her. She repeated her request to the onlookers in Ancient Egyptian. *"A basket! With a cover!"*

The older woman said something and the young male hurried into the mud brick hut, returning moments later with a wide-mouthed basket, but with no cover. Instead, he had brought a towel-sized woven cloth, which he eagerly pushed into Ricky's hands, muttering. She understood the words for *"Horus"* and *"courage"* and realized that he must have said something like, *"May Horus grant you courage."*

I wish Horus would grant me a goddamn snake charmer.

She edged forward another step. It seemed as long as Luja remained motionless, the snake had no desire to disturb its comfy little nesting. She slid forward another step and realized that she was now clearly closer to Luja than any of the others. The cobra seemed to notice as well, bringing its black head up several inches.

She thought again of snake charmers. Ricky knew that snakes were, for all practical purposes, deaf. Those who called themselves snake charmers did not tame the creatures with music. The snake gyrated back and forth in response to similar motions by the charmer, trying to match the human's position in case a threat was imminent. Snake charmers in the modern era also frequently removed the cobra's fangs and mutilated their venom pouches. Sometimes they even sewed the snake's mouth shut. Because of these cruelties, snake charming was illegal in most parts of the modern world.

At the moment, however, Ricky had no interest in observing any prohibitions against animal cruelty. If she had possessed a cobra-seeking flame thrower, she would have turned the snake into Egyptian bacon. But she had no weapons. Only a basket and a rag.

She began to weave back and forth, rhythmically, the way she had seen snake charmers do it on television. The cobra did not appear interested in copying Ricky's movements. The creature shifted its position, and while Luja did not move at all, Ricky detected a look of grave concern in her eyes.

Ricky continued to sway back and forth, bobbing to some unheard beat. She slid another foot forward and the cobra's head came up a foot, its tongue testing the air. She so wanted to run. The fear was a great, dizzying force. But, if Masud was correct, she was five thousand years out of her own time. Where would she go?

Back and forth, back and forth to silent music. She choked back a laugh that was more a gasp as she recognized the song in her head as *Saturday Night Special* by Lynyrd Skynyrd, a band she had no interest in until a few months ago. They had been one of Crockett's favorites. He would have busted a rib laughing if he could see her now, in this fantastic situation, knowing what music she was using to attempt to coax a cobra to dance.

And then, incredibly, the cobra did seem to sway very slightly, left, right. She set down the woven basket, slid a few inches closer still. Her next move would take her inside the imaginary circle she had drawn around the snake, the one that seemed to define its striking distance. No one spoke behind her, although she could hear their breathing. Slowly she moved the fabric in her hands, stretching it out close to her torso like a matador's muleta, swaying, swaying. The cobra moved more noticeably now, and Ricky dared to hope that her rhythmic gyrations had indeed cast a sort of docile spell over the creature.

She was now fully inside the coffin circle. If the cobra should choose to strike, it could easily reach her, and there was little likelihood that she could step back in time. Back and forth. If she could purchase another twelve inches from whatever Fates oversaw this drama, she might be able to throw the cloth over the snake's head and then grab it. A low, chanted monotone arose from behind, which sounded to Ricky as if the family who had gifted her the cloth was praying.

Six more inches. The cobra continued to sway, but now its hood extended, confirming that it felt threatened and was trying to make itself appear larger, more menacing.

Mission accomplished.

The creature did not strike. It seemed to Ricky that the cobra was intelligent enough to know that committing itself carried some risk. She slid another inch, but something told her that she had reached her limit. The cobra would tolerate no closer an approach. Ricky's next move had to be lightning fast, covering the snake's head with the fabric while grabbing the serpent and shoving it into the basket.

Just do it! Now! Or you'll lose your nerve! Lose the window of opportunity!

For years, living with her sister in Chicago, Ricky had gone to a health club that had once been an old gym where boxers were trained. An old timer had taught her how to punch the bag without injuring herself, and over the years, she had grown lean, strong, and quick. Her jabs were themselves as swift as cobra strikes. And so she struck, wrapping the fabric over the cobra's head and sliding her hands down to grab the neck, simultaneously pulling the creature off Luja.

Got you!

Ricky backed away, step by step, and Luja quickly sprang to her feet. However, as the snake's head thrashed blindly, it slipped from beneath a loose corner of the fabric and the cobra got a clear view of its captor. Although its movement was limited, it lunged toward Ricky's right arm, sinking its teeth in deeply. Ricky cried out in pain but did not drop the snake, fearing that in its agitated state, it would lash out at Luja or the family bunched behind. The pain seemed to be exacerbated by the circumstances, for seeing the horrid black head with its shining obsidian eyes clamped onto her arm was so terrible that it made her dizzy. She took a deep breath, stumbled away from the group, away from the road.

"Ricky! Panya!" The voice was Luja's, her own panic causing her to forget their agreed-upon aliases for an instant. But there was nothing Luja could do. The family from the hut was shouting as well, and Ricky got the impression that others stood nearby, crying out in shock or watching in mute horror. Ricky tried to run, but the cobra kept attempting to coil around her arm, her torso, trying to give itself leverage. Then it released its grip, lunged for her face, missing by the barest of margins before whipping back and plunging into a new location on her arm at the wrist. The pain was so intense that Ricky almost dropped the creature. It seemed she could feel the poison coursing into her arm, although she wondered whether this was an imagined sensation, the sort of thing the mind does when it is mad with fear. The snake released again, ready for a third strike, but Ricky threw the creature, the fabric still covering a portion of it. The writing coils caught against her and the result was poor. The snake fell near her feet, lunged again and bit her left ankle. However, this time it released immediately, reared back, and Ricky stumbled backwards. With a parting hiss, the cobra slithered off into the shadows of the morning.

Ricky turned back toward the others. The family and several neighbors stood chattering, wide-eyed. Luja ran to Ricky and embraced her, her soft words punctuated by sobs. "I can never repay you! May the gods grant you reward!"

Her right arm and wrist and her left calf burned as if punctured with a red-hot poker. "I don't feel well."

"Come! Sit!" Then Luja turned to the family, speaking in their language. *"Water!"*

The young girl raced off. The others continued to watch Ricky with a mixture of pity and amazement. Ricky sank to a sitting position, found that she was having trouble catching her breath. She would bet any takers that in its three strikes the cobra had injected her with enough toxins to paralyze and kill a hippo. The family and neighbors formed a ring around Ricky and Luja. A moment later, the young girl appeared with a jiggling animal bladder.

Ricky drank. The water helped. She tried to remember the ancient words. *"Thank you!"* She could see that Masud was concerned with this development, that he wished to speak with the two of them, urgently, but because of the small crowd, he could not. *"Thank you!"* she said again, and then there was a cry from the onlookers, a man's voice. She recognized the words *"see"* and *"cobra,"* and for a moment, wondered whether the snake had returned. Then she realized that he was referring to her injuries.

She raised her right arm, noticing that it wasn't as painful as it had been even a minute ago. The redness and swelling were nearly gone, and the bright, red indentations where the fangs had penetrated had disappeared. She noticed the same was true of her ankle. A cry went up from the crowd, and then all were on their knees, their noses pressed to the sand. The same man spoke, using her Egyptian name. Ricky looked uncomprehending at Luja.

"He says, 'Hail, Panya, the mouse who roars at snakes'!"

The woman rescued Ricky from the unwelcome adoration and shepherded her into the mud brick hut. Luja followed, and Masud kept to the rear, continuing to employ his cloak as a hood. A dozen or more who lived nearby, most of whom had witnessed the miracle of the one-eyed woman who had survived a cobra's attack, trailed behind, stopping outside and prostrating themselves in prayer. Mr. Fathi's crash course in ancient Egyptian had been inadequate for Ricky to speak fluently; however, she found that she could understand much of a conversation if the words were spoken by others.

"The gods favor you," said the woman whose name, Ricky discovered after some awkward inquiry, was Masika.

Ricky wondered if "favor" was the appropriate word, given the many horrors she had suffered. Nonetheless, she thanked the woman.

The house was small and seemed to be divided into three doorless rooms. The floor was dirt except for a woven rug in the center of the largest room. There was a mud brick hearth in the wall and several clay pots of varying sizes, along with a couple of woven baskets. Masika bid her guests sit and had her son,

Sadaki, bring small pots filled with frothy liquid. Ricky recognized the aroma as similar to the beer that Tessero had brewed for them. Since beer was valued both as a part of the diet and as currency, Ricky understood this was a significant courtesy extended to the guests. Perhaps Masika hoped a gracious treatment of the visitors would allow some of the gods' favor to extend to her humble family. Or perhaps she was merely a decent, caring human being. A sip suggested that Masika's brew had a higher alcohol content than Tessero's.

"We beg your pardon," said Masika, *"that our home is not more welcoming to such great ones as yourselves."*

"We are only travelers," said Luja, while Masud preferred to remain silent, his head bowed in the shadows.

"More than travelers," said Masika. *"No one has ever been bitten by the Hooded One and lived."*

The woman's daughter, Hafsah, brought bread, which Masika broke pieces from and offered to her three visitors.

"Perhaps the snake was old," suggested Luja. *"Its poison used up."*

Masika bowed to the floor. *"The blessing of Wadjet is on our house. May we feel the peace of her protection."*

Ricky knew of Wadjet, one of the earliest Egyptian divinities. She often appeared with the head of a cobra and was considered the protector of Egypt who helped rescue the infant Horus from the evil god Set.

Masika rose to a sitting position. *"How may we help you good travelers? Our beds are yours. It is our shame that we slept on mats of papyrus while you huddled in ditches."*

"We cannot stay," said Luja.

Ricky knew she was right. Word of the miracle would circulate. If a governor or vizier sent men to investigate, the three of them might be detained or worse. What had been viewed as a blessing by Masika might easily be viewed as dark magic and a potentially seditious threat to power by others.

"Your voices are...strange," said Masika. *"Do you come from across the Great Green?"*

"We come from far away," Luja answered evasively.

Masika thought for a moment. *"And to where do you travel?"*

Ricky could tell that Luja was weighing whether to answer directly. Finally, she said, *"We travel to Menat Khufu."*

Masika smiled. *"Then you still have a long journey before you. Before you depart, rest in our village. Many labor in the necropolis, preparing the burial places. Others of us here are farmers. And the marketplace is quite active."*

"Then we must trouble you no longer," said Masud, the first time he had addressed the woman. He stood, but Ricky shouted "Wait!" in English, which startled everyone. Then she leaned toward Masud.

"I'm not parading around Egypt like...*this*!" Her gesture was an obvious reference to the fact that she was naked from the waist up. "In this century or any other!" Masud seemed about to object, but Luja spoke first.

"The brave Panya is still feeling a chill as a result of the morning's dangers."

Masika nodded and disappeared into one of the other rooms. She emerged moments later with a tan smock that might be worn by an artisan or baker. Ricky slipped into it and secured it in such a way that she would look neither too odd to the Egyptians nor too immodest, Masud removed several bronze rings from the pouch he carried and tossed them onto the rug. Masika's eyes went wide at this unexpected windfall and offered profuse gratitude. However, Masud was already out the door, and the others followed.

When they emerged from the house, they saw that at least two dozen people stood or knelt in the sand. Those standing now dropped to their knees, uttering blessings.

"The gods are great!"

"Wadjet the protector!"

"The power of Horus!"

As Ricky, Luja and Masud began to move away, the crowd stood to follow. Masud pulled Luja close, whispered something in her ear. Then she turned to face the group.

"To please the gods, return to your fields and labors! The Great Ones decree that we must journey alone."

Bowing, they fell behind. After what many of them had seen with the cobra, there was no hesitation. Their belief was strong, and they had witnessed the work of the gods firsthand. If this was what the gods wished, so be it.

After several minutes, the witnesses were out of sight. The time travelers did not pause. When the date palms and grasses increased somewhat in density, Masud spoke. "What shitty luck. Instead of blending in, that damned story of a *miracle* will spread like wildfire. It will put a target on our backs, make it more difficult to accomplish our mission. We'll have to be careful."

Ricky took this opportunity to grab Masud's elbow, swing him around, latch onto the front of his tunic with both hands and slam his back against a palm trunk. Although Masud was bigger, he was caught completely off guard.

"Why? Why are we here? What the hell happened? This is... this is..." She quickly lost steam, having no idea what to say in the face of this monumental turn of events.

Masud pushed her away. "Get ahold of yourself!"

"Get ahold of myself? Are you kidding me? If this is real..." A hand went to her forehead and she slumped into a sitting position beneath a palm.

"Yeah, we're really here. After the shit you two pulled in the yard, Tessero figured he couldn't wait any longer. You couldn't be trusted."

"But it was supposed to be Allison," said Luja. Ricky realized that Luja had not seen the lethal encounter in the yard, as she had been wrestling with Mr. Fathi. And she had not overheard her conversation with Masud shortly after she had awakened in this time.

"Allison is dead."

Luja said nothing to this. Ricky knew she would put two and two together, realize that something had happened during the chaos of their ill-fated escape attempt.

"Why are you here?" Luja asked Masud.

"I'm the backup plan. I sat through every hour of prep that Allison did with that old gargoyle Fathi."

"But *why* are you here?" Luja persisted. "Surely you know this is a one-way trip. Yet you willingly traveled to a primitive time from which you can never return. The reason cannot be money. Tessero could promise you a million dollars and there's no way for you to ever spend it."

Ricky, sitting with her head in her hands, wanted to scream, to hit something, to break bones. None of that would do any good. So she lashed out. "Because he's stupid!" she growled, simply aiming to enrage Masud.

Masud looked like he wanted to break her neck, but then she saw the anger ebb. "Yeah, it's possible I'm stupid. That can be argued. What cannot be argued is that I'm not a very nice guy."

"You're working for Tessero. This isn't exactly shocking news."

Masud shook his head. "Even before Tessero. I did some very bad things. Pissed off the wrong people. Lots of the wrong people. Put a target on my back. Anywhere I go in the world, only a matter of time before they find me."

"Traveling back in time is your escape hatch," said Luja.

"Yeah. Once I finish the job for Tessero, I can find a wife, maybe become a farmer, live a quiet life for as long as...well, for as long as the Fates allow. Better than I deserve."

Ricky laughed coarsely. "All you have to do is make sure we kill Cessair and then you destroy the scroll."

Masud stared at her coolly. "Yeah, something like that."

Ricky got the impression that Masud wasn't telling them everything. Instead of destroying the scroll, was he planning on dipping a toe in the waters of immortality?

"Wait," she said, her head coming out of her hands. "You speak the ancient language pretty well. But I never once saw you do anything back at Tessero's compound except stand around, looking like someone had put a t-shirt on a vending machine."

"Tessero has been planning this for years. You two weren't part of the plan until maybe six months ago. After what happened at An Tsuil, Tessero got this idea that someone who had already beaten Cessair and who knew how she thought needed to be on board." He pointed to Ricky. "After reading the rumors online about your immortality, he was convinced he had to have you. That changed my role a little." He laughed humorlessly. "A lot. I went from primary assassin to insurance, just in case something happened to Allison. And you happened to Allison."

"What was she to get from this?" asked Luja. "Your motivation was to have a simple, peaceful life in the end. But what of her?"

Masud shook his head. "I have no clue what Tessero offered her to do this. But she had to either be running from something big or want something big. Being former MI6, I'd guess she had plenty to run from."

Again, Ricky felt Masud seemed to know more than he was telling.

"You do not seem sad that Allison is gone," said Luja.

"She wasn't exactly the friendliest person in the world. Went out of her way to make you feel like a fuck-up. Let me tell you, taking classes with her was shit. So, no, I don't miss her. But I would rather have her here right now than you two." He looked back in the direction from which they had come. "Jesus, what a dumpster fire!"

"Yeah, it would have been a lot better with Allison," said Ricky contemptuously. "Allison would have woken up with a cobra on her chest, you would have tried to get it off, and Masika and her family would be burying you both in their garden right now."

Masud said nothing to this, and Ricky wondered if this was really how he felt. Or was it a smokescreen? Had Allison's death given Masud an opportunity to put the scroll directly into his own hands? Or maybe he had other plans.

"Okay, riddle me this," said Ricky, her tone mocking. "Your job is to destroy the scroll. That's going to be dangerous. Mr. Fathi, that bastard, told us the Crocodile King would have some sort of palace in Tarkhan. The scroll is probably hidden inside and closely guarded. So what's to keep an enterprising young hoodlum like yourself from saying, 'Screw Tessero! Forget about the scroll!' And then going off to find that pretty Egyptian wife and homestead? You get everything you want, but you don't have to put your life on the line."

Masud let out a long breath. "Tessero has a mole."

Ricky blinked several times. "How is that possible?"

"Months before Allison or I arrived at the compound, Tessero had Fathi prepping someone else. Don't know who. Only that the mole was already in Predynastic Egypt by the time I got to the compound. Tessero's ultimate fail safe. Someone to correct our mistakes or make us pay the price if we fuck up."

Ricky appeared thunderstruck. "You mean it could be anyone?"

"Anyone. Could be a guy we see herding goats along the road. Could have been that lady back there in the mud brick hut. Assuming those weren't her kids. If I decide I'm not willing to go after the scroll, I could get a knife in the gut some night in a dark alley. Or I could guzzle a jar of beer and drop over dead from poison."

"Okay, I get that," said Ricky. "But Tessero's mole can't go back to the twenty-first century any more than we can. How would Tessero convince someone to come back here and play undercover sheriff?"

"Above my pay grade."

"Will you need our help to get the scroll?" asked Luja.

"That will be my task," said Masud. "Let us walk." They set off again following a path along one of the irrigation channels that, in this season, grew full and brought water to the farms farther from the Nile. As they walked, Masud continued.

"Tarkhan is ruled by Crocodile, although he has other names as well. One of his titles is The Subduer. A more common name is Shendjw. Little is known about him, and archaeologists who excavated one of his alleged tombs found no body. In the tomb, however, there were markings to suggest that Shendjw was involved in dark doings and had established a shrine to the god Sobek, an angry and vindictive deity who is pictured with the head of a crocodile and whose powerful magic was feared. However, as with many who possess power, Sobek's intentions may have been misunderstood at the time."

"Just like poor Tessero, right?" She made an insincere sad face.

Masud glowered at her but continued. "Shendjw—Crocodile —is the likely possessor of the scroll. I should be able to bribe my way into a position of influence in his court, although it will take some time. Weeks. Months, even. Eventually, though, relying on bribes, subterfuge and their trust, I will gain access to the scroll and destroy it. Then I will disappear."

The little speech sounded rehearsed, Ricky thought. Or was she reading too much into it?

"But who created the scroll?" asked Luja. "Shendjw? Or did a sorcerer loyal to him do so? Whoever is responsible for the scroll would be able to create a new one or to pass along the secrets written upon it."

"Leave that to me," said Masud. "Whoever is responsible will be dealt with."

Ricky spoke up. "While you're cozying up to the king for weeks or months, what about Luja and me?"

"You know your task. You will find Cessair and gain her trust, just as Tessero had planned. And when the opportunity presents itself, you will eliminate her. Remember, the mole is not here to watch only me. We will all be under surveillance."

"But why must we kill her?" asked Luja. "If you destroy the scroll and its maker, Cessair will never become immortal, will never threaten the world."

"When Cessair returns from the land of the Hatti, she will be distraught," Masud explained. "The legends say that Noah is her step-grandfather. Whether or not the boat is ever finished, or whether a great flood actually occurs, she will believe that her grandfather has condemned her to death for denying her a place on the ark, and she will plot her revenge. That will mean setting her sights on the scroll. If we do nothing to stop her, she could thwart all of our plans. Imagine if she should get to the scroll before I do? You must not let that happen!"

Ricky remembered the viciousness Cessair had demonstrated in dealing with her enemies. She still felt the panic from when Cessair had her lackeys throw her and Crockett into a pit in Frankfurt and then proceed to fill it with concrete.

She also remembered with undiminished bitterness how Cessair had killed a dozen climate scientists—her sister among them—for simply knowing that a clue to the scroll's whereabouts existed. Even Cessair's most loyal followers had fared no better. She had slaughtered fifty of them in horrifying fashion at An Tsuil to send a message of power and fear. For the sorrow she would sow for fifty centuries, Cessair deserved death.

"The royal palace of Shendjw overlooks the Nile," said Masud. "It is nowhere near as grand as the palaces that will be built later in Cairo and Memphis, but it is impressive still. One of our earlier travelers told us there is an open-air porch on the river side that connects to a throne room. If it is like other palaces of the period, there are rooms for food preparation, and quarters for Shendjw's servants and wives. But you will not find Cessair there. She lives in the hills to the west of the village where she is a priestess of Ma'at."

Ricky knew of Ma'at, who Egyptians believed was responsible for creating balance in the universe. Her dedication to truth, justice and fairness gave Egyptians their moral compass. This was reinforced by the fact that Ma'at was said to judge the souls of the dead. Ancient Egyptians had believed that, when the body died, one's soul passed through the Hall of Judgment, where Ma'at would weigh one's heart against her magic feather. If there was balance, the soul passed on into the bliss of the afterlife. If not, the individual's soul was devoured by the most terrifying of Egyptian deities, Ammit, a fearsome creature with the head of a crocodile.

However, this information conflicted with what Ricky knew to be true. Beneath the passage tomb at Newgrange in Ireland, pictographs had associated Cessair only with the terror of Ammit, never with the justice of Ma'at. At least some of Tessero's hastily retrieved intel about this age was in error, and so they would have to be careful observers and listeners.

They paused on a rise. Ahead, mud-brick huts and structures increased in number and density to form a small city. Slightly above these in the distance rose the flat-roofed palace, and just beyond, the shimmering, green waters of the Nile. A sledge carrying grain pulled by donkeys scraped past them, and they waited until it was well ahead before they resumed their journey. Luja's eyes darted around the landscape as if she were the first visitor to a foreign planet. "This is so difficult to process! We are in an Egypt where Cleopatra will not be born for three thousand years."

They walked on. Ricky had to fight waves of nausea that resurfaced every time she acknowledged the reality that they were five thousand years in the past—and that they could not go back.

"When we reach the marketplace, we will part ways," said Masud. "I have no doubt that you will find your way to Cessair and, when opportunity presents itself, do what must be done."

"And what then?" asked Ricky. "We just go native?"

"First, you must be very careful," said Masud. "Egypt has strict laws, and the penalty for murder is terrible. While it varies from region to region, in Tarkhan it is impalement. And not the good kind."

Ricky scowled. "There's a good kind?"

"The Persians practiced a form of impalement where the victim would be tossed onto a sharpened pole, which would penetrate your torso so you would bleed to death quickly," explained Masud. "They considered themselves quite humane. Here in Egypt, the process is much more grim, designed to drag out the suffering of the convicted. The pole—which might be as big around as a baseball bat or more—is inserted in the backside, sometimes into the anus, other times into an incision just in front. The opening is heavily greased to staunch bleeding, for that would end the suffering too quickly. While the condemned is held down, a heavy mallet is used to drive the stake into the body, stopping just short of the heart and liver. Then the pole is set upright and the real suffering begins. It might go on for hours. Even days, in some cases."

Ricky's eye widened. "Or in my case, forever. Fuck."

"Yes," said Masud, with a pained smile, "you would present a unique case to the Egyptians. Perhaps they would eventually remove the pike and revere you as a goddess."

Ricky had no desire to take that route to deification. And she knew that Luja would not survive the process.

"Thus, Cessair's demise must be artfully carried out," said Masud. "In the hide pouch around Luja's waist in a small container is a poison that the Egyptians would be unable to trace or detect. You'll also find a number of copper, gold and silver debens which you can barter for food and lodging. Since there will soon be stories circulating of a one-eyed goddess who survived the bite of a cobra, it might be a good idea for Ricky to wear a cloak or shroud to conceal her face."

"And you expect us to just do your bidding?" asked Ricky.

"It is not my bidding," replied Masud. "And remember, you are being watched by Tessero's secret one."

"What if we need to communicate with you?" asked Luja.

"There will be no need. And if there is, don't try. You'll have to figure things out on your own."

"You still haven't answered my question," said Ricky. "After Cessair, then what?"

"If you're lucky enough to emerge without drawing suspicion to yourselves, think of it as a do-over. How many people get the chance to completely remake their lives in a new place? Especially a place as beautiful and fascinating as ancient Egypt."

Ricky ground her teeth. "It's not fair!"

Masud grunted. "Life rarely is. Whether one's existence is a single year or ten thousand."

CHAPTER 13

As he had promised, Masud parted ways with them once they reached the market, which was busy but only modestly crowded. Five streets intersected to form the wide-open area where market stalls were set up and shop doors stood open. Bakers hawked bread, painted pots stood at the ready, and farmers displayed cabbages, lentils, beans and garlic. One vendor sold dried meat on a stick, which might have been chicken, but more likely was rat. Luja used one of her debens and arranged an awkward exchange that gave them bread and a skin of beer. They sat in shadow against a mud plastered wall off the main street and refreshed themselves as the sun climbed to midday.

"We could just leave," said Ricky as they rested. "With Masud off on his own, we can do whatever we want."

"What about Tessero's mole? Do you not believe he would hunt us down?"

"We just got here. Do you think the mole has locked onto us already?"

Luja tilted her head towards a shirtless man making swift, well-practiced cuts at a table in the marketplace. "He could be anyone. He could be that man right there. Or any of the others we passed on the streets of Tarkhan."

Ricky shook her head. "Not long after we moved to the states, mum took Sasha and me to Milwaukee on the train. We got off and walked a few blocks to the museum. It was amazing. I loved the dioramas of ancient cultures—the Golden Age of

Egypt, the Mayans, Native Americans, the Greeks and Romans. Some of the dioramas were tiny, but they were beautifully constructed. And there were some life-size ones that made you feel like you had stepped into that age in history. I would have gone back every week if we'd had the money. It made me wish I could close my eyes, go back in time and really walk those streets or wooded trails or desert paths. And now, here I am, and it feels so crappy. I'm barely holding it together."

"Is that what you want to do, then?" asked Luja. "Just get out of here and take our chances?"

"No. I mean, yes, that would be the best possible outcome. Like Masud, start over in a new place."

"Far from here," added Luja.

Ricky smiled sadly. "Right. And I'd do it right now except…"

"Cessair."

"We're here. We can't undo that. And I've never hated anyone as much as I hate Cessair. The least we can do is give Crockett, Sasha and the others a chance."

Luja was silent for a bit. "I did not wish to come to this time period either. Being here is dangerous. But you are right; being here is a fact, and it is beyond our control. We can go someplace and attempt to live quietly. By doing so, we would hopefully not have too great an effect on coming generations. But Masud is putting wheels in motion that will leave deep ruts in the clay of time, even if we do nothing. Destroying the scroll will prevent Cessair's five thousand-year reign of sin."

Ricky nodded, but Luja was not finished.

"However, five thousand years is a long time. It is possible that Cessair eliminated an enemy along the way who would have killed millions of people, or invented a doomsday weapon, or a terrible plague. There is a chance that, in expunging Cessair from the timeline, we may unleash something worse."

Ricky opened her mouth to speak, but Luja held up a finger.

"But a *chance* that something will happen is not the same as a *certainty*. We know with one hundred percent *certainty* that an unaltered future with Cessair will be a disaster. And there are likely millions of possible futures without Cessair that would be better."

"So what are you saying?" asked Ricky. "That we should go through with this?"

"The wheels are in motion. We did not put them so, but we can help to assure that Cessair's time ends here in a way that creates the fewest ripples across time."

Ricky was silent for a few moments. Then: "What about this?" She pointed to her face. "Masud said the story about the one-eyed woman and the cobra would be repeated all over the city. It's going to be tough to keep a low profile."

"With the eye patch, you are easy to spot," agreed Luja.

"I kind of stand out without it, too," said Ricky.

Luja stood, and after a moment, so did Ricky. "I may have an idea. One of the vendors may be able to help."

Ricky grunted. "Really? You spotted a vendor of glass eyes?"

"Not glass," said Luja, and led the way out of the alley and toward an open door they had passed upon arriving at the market. Carvings in stone and ivory sat on the sills of window openings. The inside was empty, except for a man sitting on a bench at the back of the dimly-lit room, holding a bit of ivory in one hand, working at it with a small, metal tool. The man seemed at least seventy, but Ricky knew one's appearance might be misleading in a time when hard work bent backs before men and women reached the age of thirty, when skin was parched by a relentless sun, and when diseases, for which there were simple cures in the twenty-first century, could leave one crippled. As he worked the ivory, making impressive progress, Ricky noticed that one shoulder seemed to ride up higher than the other, possibly the result of being thrown from a camel or falling off a roof when he was much younger. He was bald and wore a dirty brown wrap.

"Your work is impressive, good craftsman," said Luja, coming to within a couple paces of the man.

The man spoke while continuing to carve. *"Your words are a feast for my ears. But they do not put bread on my table."* Then he stopped working, sighed, and spoke as if to himself. *"You are lower than a dog, and more foolish."* He looked for the first time at his two visitors. *"But... my manners have deserted me. I am Tuta. What new burdens may I take upon my aching back in order to serve you?"*

After a pause, Luja gestured around the small room. *"Tuta creates that which is both useful and beautiful."*

Tuta gave a small bow. *"I would not dare to suggest so, but neither would I question your keen eye."*

"I am Meryt," said Luja, who then pointed to Ricky. *"This is Panya. She has but one eye."*

Tuta stepped from behind his small workbench. His legs, Ricky noticed, were as slender as her forearm. *"Yes, as feeble and slow-witted as Tuta is, he noticed the cloth over part of Panya's face and assumed as much."*

"Considering Tuta's great skill, I wondered whether you might fashion a wooden eye for Panya,"

Tuta looked back and forth between the two women several times, and then said, *"The question need hardly be asked. Why, it would be as easy as breathing for an artist of Tuta's abilities. I have two wooden eyes myself."*

Luja and Ricky exchanged a worried glance. Then Tuta smiled, revealing several missing teeth.

"Please pardon my miserable attempt at humor. It is one of my many grievous faults. I shall have myself flogged when it is convenient."

"Does this mean you are unable to make such a thing?" asked Luja.

"On the contrary," said Tuta. *"I make spheres of many sizes that are popular children's playthings. But I would suggest that you allow me to paint it to resemble the healthy eye and let me coat it with a special glaze that will harden to a smoothness that will limit irritation. And you may choose between ivory and wood. Wood will be lighter, but ivory is a more durable material."*

"So you have done this before."

Tuta smiled. *"No. But I see what needs to be done. And I enjoy a challenge. Of course, it will be costly."*

Ricky pulled Luja to the front of the room, farther from Tuta, and bent to her in a whisper. "What are you doing?"

"Making sure you are not an easy target. A woman with two eyes attracts little undue attention."

Luja stepped away, removed one of the silver rings from her pouch, held it aloft. Tuta's eyebrows initially raised in surprise, but then he frowned.

"Three silver rings!"

"Do you think to cheat a poor woman like me?" asked Luja.

"Yes, I did think it," said Tuta, his face completely free of irony. *"And you are clearly not a poor woman."*

Luja stepped forward, grabbed Tuta's wrist and placed the ring in his hand. *"One now. One when the work is done."*

"Meryt is shrewd," said Tuta with a bow.

"This I doubt," said Luja. *"I am certain that I am paying many times the price that I could have commanded from others."*

"I am ashamed to say that your words are true," said Tuta, *"yet there are many that I have cheated far more egregiously."*

"Then our bargain shall include two additional items. First, it will buy your loyalty."

"By that, you mean my silence."

"Panya's health and appearance are no one's business but hers," said Luja resolutely.

"No explanation is necessary," said Tuta with a wave of his hand. *"Even were it a criminal enterprise, which of course I have no reason to suspect, my lips would not fracture this sacred confidence to which I now bind myself."*

Ricky had rarely seen Luja irritated, but she could see the signs now around her eyes and in the set of her jaw.

"The second item is your assistance in finding someone. Are you familiar with Cessair?"

"The priestess?" Tuta seemed unsurprised by the question, although he did appear interested. *"All in Tarkhan know of her, she being favored of Ma'at. And of the king."* The last of this drew a curve of smile to his lips.

"Where can she be found?"

Tuta considered his answer, his eyes moving back and forth rapidly between the two women. *"She is a goddess who walks amongst insects."*

"That was not my question."

Tuta smiled slyly again. *"The shrine to Ma'at is in the hills to the west. Not far, but a steep climb. She may be there. Or she may be at the palace. Or she may be elsewhere, as I am not privy to her appointments. Gird yourself with caution if she is the object of your journey."*

Now Luja offered a sliver of smile. *"Why, Tuta, it almost sounds like you care."*

"I care about my second silver ring, and possible additional commissions to come, if my work pleases," said Tuta. *"And Tuta always pleases. Now let Panya come forward. I must take some measurements and select pigments."*

***

Two days, Tuta had promised. After measuring, he discovered that he already had a wooden sphere that would suit, one of dozens of various sizes that he had fashioned as "marbles" for children's play. This he would polish with limestone and cattail to achieve perfect smoothness, paint with a white enamel, and bake to harden the coating. Then, Tuta would carefully paint in the iris and pupil prior to applying a clear glaze and baking the prosthetic again.

During at least part of that time, Ricky and Luja planned to be away from the town and the questioning eyes of its citizens. Tuta allowed them to sleep away the afternoon on the dirt floor of a dingy, rank-smelling back room where his own papyrus mat rested.

Whether owing to the general unease they felt over their mission, or the acute unease they felt over the conditions of the bedroom, the two were unable to sleep much. When they finally abandoned the attempt and stepped back into the main room, Tuta was stepping in through the front door of his shop, a glowing ember in one hand. *"A widow of my acquaintance sometimes makes me dinner, if I please her. And Tuta always pleases."*

Ricky shuddered at the implication.

"There is talk in the town," continued Tuta, *"of a miraculous event."* He took a strip of braided linen, dipped it through the small opening in the top of an oil lamp sitting on a shelf, waited for the linen to saturate itself, used the ember to light it, then tossed the burning stick onto the nearby hearth.

"I would imagine there is," said Luja, stepping through the doorway. *"Let me see if I can guess it. A one-eyed woman, bitten by a cobra, survives."*

Tuta nodded. *"A miracle of the highest order. They say the woman was bitten several times, on the arm and on one leg."*

"Except nothing of the sort occurred," replied Luja. *"Superstitious people see what they want to see, rather than what really happened."* She pulled Ricky forward, lifted her arms to Tuta. *"Do you see any bite marks? Look carefully. Not even a scratch. The same is true of her legs."*

Tuta made a thorough examination. Far more thorough than Ricky felt was necessary.

"We have important business," continued Luja. *"We do not wish to be followed by crowds and their supplications, or by those who would seek to harm us because they might think the dark gods guide our actions."*

"Tuta understands completely," said the misshapen old man. *"A young woman with one eye is not...anonymous. And Tuta has heard descriptions of your clothing as well."*

Ricky and Luja looked down at themselves.

"There is little we can do about that," said Luja.

Tuta raised an index finger. *"Perhaps not. But... I have some clothes."*

"You wish to make us woodworker apprentices?"

Tuta shuffled toward the bedroom. *"I was, at one time, a young gentleman with handsome features. And I had a wife. Just one. She was, of course, a great beauty. I have kept her clothes, sentimental fool that I am."*

He disappeared inside, and Ricky had a sinking feeling. The clothes in question were likely rags, infested with silverfish and moths. However, when Tuta produced them a minute later, they looked as fresh as if they had been folded and put away yesterday. Ricky smelled the aroma of cedar, which helped explain this.

He handed them to Ricky and stepped back. *"They should fit well enough."* He stood as if waiting. Ricky realized, then, that he intended for them to try the garments on right there, as he watched. From their studies with Mr. Fathi and from her observations of life in Tarkhan over the past day, it was clear that the people of ancient Egypt were less modest than those in their own century. As they disrobed, the old man's expression did not change, although Ricky would have bet every deben in Luja's pouch that he was enjoying the spectacle. To her surprise, the clothing did fit well, and while not royal garments, they were a cut above the typical peasant fare—and covered both women from neck to mid-thigh. Ornate designs trimmed the clothing, likely done by Tuta's wife.

"Splendid!" pronounced Tuta as he viewed the results. *"Of course, the clothing was not included in the original bargain."* With a sigh, Luja reached into her pouch and produced a copper deben.

"It is a wonder you do not live in a palace yourself," said Luja as she deposited the coin into his palm.

Tuta shrugged. *"My neighbors are too poor to cheat. Thus am I reduced to cheating only the occasional stranger."*

As the sun's last rays glowed above the horizon, Ricky and Luja set off, weaving their way through the maze of side streets and, once the houses fell away, found a well-worn path winding up through rocks and scrub brush. By the time the sun disappeared completely, they saw the flicker of torches above, and this helped guide them through the final turns.

Ricky had expected Cessair's shrine to Ma'at to be perhaps a shallow cave with oil lamps and a stone bowl where animals might be sacrificed and burned or their blood collected. What they encountered was a temple built into the hillside, its smooth, limestone front filled with pictographs representing Ma'at and her feather ceremony. On each side of the doorless, square entrance, a guttering oil lamp rested atop a copper basket fastened to the stone. The temple had likely been built by many hands years before Cessair's birth and had been tended by several generations of priestesses loyal to Ma'at. Still, the soft stone, while impressive today, would not survive the millennia the way granite or quartz might have.

"It is marvelous!" said Luja, running a hand over a section of wall.

Ricky stepped in front of the entrance. The smooth stone seemed to continue inside for several yards, but then the walls became rough, more like a natural cave. Light flickered from the depths.

"Is Cessair here?" she wondered aloud.

"Someone has been tending the lamps," replied Luja reasonably.

Ricky took a step inside the doorway and, hearing no objection from Luja, took another. As the natural cave walls began, they noticed the path was flanked every five or six feet by identical, plain stone pedestals upon which rested pottery vases containing ostrich feathers. Then the cave opened into a room-sized viewing area. Oil lamps at intervals along the far wall illuminated a stone slab upon which a six-foot-tall picture of Ma'at had been etched and painted, showing the goddess and her scales, with an ostrich feather waving from a headband. In front of this was a stone bench stained with ash.

"No one home," said Ricky at a whisper.

"Except, perhaps, the goddess."

"So what do we do now? Go back to Tuta's shop?"

"I must admit," said Luja, gliding close to the picture, "that the idea of staying at Tuta's is not appealing."

"Especially since, this time, Tuta would be in the room as well," said Ricky. "And 'Tuta always pleases.'"

"Perhaps someone comes in the evening to light the lamps, and then returns in the morning to put them out," suggested Luja.

"That sounds like an invitation to me," said Ricky, dropping into a sit. After a battle with a cobra, a trek through the oppressive heat, and a climb to the temple of Ma'at, she was exhausted. "This floor is smooth enough. And it's cooler in here than outside. Plus, I don't see any snakes." She tipped into a fetal position. Reluctantly, it seemed, Luja lowered herself to the floor.

"Let us hope Ma'at is asleep. Or in no mood to judge."

***

When Ricky woke, a young woman stood over her. She pushed herself quickly into a sitting position, saw that another young woman stood over a seated Luja. Due to the eyeliner, ceremonial wigs and jewelry, the two had initially seemed older; but as Ricky looked closer, it was likely they were fifteen or sixteen years of age. Their slenderness, makeup and similar dress suggested they could be sisters, perhaps twins.

"You must come from the temple," said the woman standing above Ricky.

Ricky muttered an apology in the ancient language as well as she was able.

"We meant no insult," added Luja. *"We are travelers and wished to pay our respects to wise Ma'at. We did not intend to stay. Our weariness overcame us."*

"Please," said the second woman, stepping into the narrow part of the cave and heading toward the entrance. Ricky and Luja scrambled up and followed, their eyes moving, uncertain about what waited for them outside.

The morning was uncomfortably warm, even though the sun had only just climbed above the horizon. Ricky had imagined all sorts of awful fates waiting outside the cave, most involving companies of men with swords or bows who would execute them in gruesome fashion—or in her case, attempt to—for their unforgivable trespass. However, no one waited at the entrance, and the sharp slant of sun's rays lit the city below in a way that made it beautiful.

"Please," repeated the second woman, and Ricky saw that they were being directed to the left of the temple toward a set of rough, stone steps that had gone unnoticed in the darkness. They climbed, though not especially far. Set back from the front of the temple, they now saw, was a small building of mortared stone. Four square-sided pillars marked the front, between which stood limestone panels into which peacock feathers had

been etched. They passed between the pillars and into a small portico with stone columns supporting a roof of cedar beams. The floor was tightly fitted stone tiles. A wall at the back of this contained a hearth. Ricky estimated that it might be situated almost directly above the Ma'at inner temple.

"Wait," ordered the first young woman, as they arrived at the approximate center of the room. Ricky expected them to exit, but instead, they walked to opposite corners of the hearth, turned, faced back toward the center of the room, and stood as if at attention.

Ricky looked to Luja. "The Tarkhanians didn't do human sacrifices, did they?"

Before Luja could respond, a woman strode casually in from behind the hearth wall. *"Wise and just is the goddess Ma'at. We who serve in humility welcome you to her temple at Tarkhan."*

Ricky's gasped, and hatred streamed through her veins. There, in flowing white temple robes, stood Cessair, the architect of fifty centuries of misery, cruelty and death. It was all she could do to keep from rushing upon the woman and choking the life from her. Once again, she thought of the men sent to kill every research scientist at ZERO Station in Greenland, including Ricky's sister. She thought of the thugs who had murdered Crockett's friend Bash, his beautiful wife, and their infant daughter. She remembered her own beloved Grandma Neve. How many thousands of others mourned friends and loved ones slaughtered under Cessair's decree?

Ricky's first reaction, in fact, had been a stab of terror. When the soulless harpy recognized Ricky, Cessair would surely attack. Then she fought back her fears. Cessair in *this* time period had lived twenty-five years, perhaps a bit longer. She had not yet become immortal, not yet begun her bloody campaign. In this temple stood Panya, a servant girl. Cessair would not meet Ricky Crowe for another fifty centuries.

Indeed, this Cessair was different. Her hair, which had hung dark and loose in the twenty-first century, was tightly braided and glistened with some fragrant wax or oil. She wore a feathered crown of sorts and her eyes were painted with charcoal liners as well as alluring purples. Her beauty was magnified here in the time of her origin. Her arms and face appeared more slender than the twenty-first century Cessair, though her flowing robes made it difficult to tell whether her gauntness extended to the rest of her body. Tuta had referred to Cessair as a goddess who walked among insects, and as she stood before them now, this seemed an apt description. Yet, in five thousand years, Cessair would make her transition from goddess to twenty-first century CEO, the head of TROVE. To Ricky, this was unsurprising, for she knew Cessair to be an actress who could adopt a new persona with relative ease.

"That language you spoke," began Cessair, *"it was very strange. What is it? Do you know our tongue?"*

Ricky realized that Cessair had heard but not understood her comment about human sacrifices. It would be millenia before she learned English.

"We do, oh great Cessair, priestess of Ma'at the true judge," said Luja. *"We are travelers. Please forgive us if our trespass has offended."*

"I beg you, speak your names."

"I am Meryt, a scribe. This is my servant, Panya."

Cessair fixed her gaze on Ricky for several moments. *"Good Panya, you have been hurt. How did you lose the eye?"*

Ricky hardly trusted herself to speak, her anger was so white-hot. Cessair's own henchman, Koehne, had gouged Ricky's eye out with a pocketknife. Because it had occurred before Ricky had worked the magic of the scroll, it was damage that could not be undone. Ricky finally choked out the words in the old language as best she could. *"A cruel man."*

Cessair nodded. *"Wise Ma'at will judge him accordingly. The hearts of the cruel weigh heavily on her scales."* Then she turned so as to address them both. *"The lamps are lit throughout the night so that all will know Ma'at does not sleep. Her justice and protection do not waver under sun or moon. Followers and those who love justice are welcome here. Sit on the mat before my hearth and we will eat."*

They sat, and the two young women, who Cessair introduced as Bennu and Kissa, brought boiled grain in a bowl, sweetened with honey, as well as dried, spiced lamb and clay pots of wine. Ricky wondered whether this would be the right time to try and slip the poison into Cessair's drink. However, she was reluctant to speak the idea to Luja even in a whispered language that Cessair supposedly did not understand. What if Cessair was only pretending to not understand? No, that was impossible. In this time, Cessair had no knowledge of the twenty-first century; the Angles, Jutes, and Saxons wouldn't birth the English language for another two and a half millennia. Even so, Ricky could not bring herself to chance it. This woman was still Cessair, alive, bringer of pain, betrayal, and death.

"The ostrich feathers with which you decorate the temple and shrine are beautiful," said Luja.

"A woman, Sisa, brings them. The birds come from Nubia and are becoming abundant in our land. They are popular with hunters."

Although he lived much later, Ricky recalled learning that King Tutankhamen had been an enthusiastic ostrich hunter.

"Have you come far?" asked Cessair as they ate.

You could say that, thought Ricky.

"We have come from lands in the north that few in this region know," said Luja.

"That would explain the unusual sound of your voice," said Cessair, *"although you do not look like ones from the north. Your skin is dark, like those who make their homes along the*

life-giving river. I have a curiosity about lands in the north. We will have to talk of this later. May I inquire as to your destination?"

"It is Tarkhan," said Luja.

Cessair smiled wryly. *"Tarkhan? If one is free to travel the world, I would think there might be more interesting destinations. Uruk, perhaps, for their splendid pottery, or across The Great Green in the land of the cicada-wearers."*

"Cicada-wearers?" Ricky recalled from Mr. Fathi's teachings that "The Great Green" or Wadj-wr referred to the Mediterranean, but she had not heard the term "cicada-wearers" used before.

"The land of olives and music," clarified Cessair. *"The people there wear golden cicadas as jewelry because the creatures are musician insects."*

Olives and music across the Mediterranean suggested to Ricky that Cessair might be referring to ancient Attica, where the city of Athens would later be founded.

"You are too modest, Priestess. We are not high-born travelers. You see before you a servant and one who wishes to learn of the great Iteru and the Two Lands, a wondrous corridor connecting many civilizations. These stories will spark great interest among our people in the north and hopefully lead to fruitful alliances." Ricky noticed Luja used the ancient name of the Nile River and an early name of Egypt itself. The modern names would not evolve for twenty centuries. *"Being strangers, we sought the temple of Ma'at, hoping for fair treatment. The reputation of this temple has traveled far."*

"And you have come with no expectations except fairness?"

Luja smiled, bowed her head slightly. *"I am a scribe, priestess, and during our time in Tarkhan, I thought to offer my services."*

Cessair beamed a genuine smile, but then her expression faltered. *"It is a generous offer, Meryt. I am inclined to accept it eagerly. But I cannot give you an answer just yet. And you may find my reasons troubling."*

"You owe us no explanation, Priestess."

"I wish to tell the story," said Cessair. *"I will be interested to hear your view of the matter."* Cessair took a sip of wine, closed her eyes for several moments as if composing herself, and then began. *"I am the daughter of Bith and Birren in the land of the Hatti. To satisfy a debt, my father was compelled to sell me to a wealthy governor before the Iteru had flooded thirteen times. But that very night, before the governor called me to his bed, I escaped and bribed my way across many miles to the Black Lands, where it was said women were the equals of men."*

"Black Lands?" questioned Ricky.

"This land that connects many peoples goes by many names. In my homeland, we called it the Black Lands because of the fertile soil left behind by each flooding. Many in Tarkhan refer to it as the Two Lands. When I arrived in Tarkhan, I begged for something other than work in the fields. Showing myself to be a quick learner, I was apprenticed to an elderly physician, although some called him a priest, or even a magician. I now believe he is all three."

Ricky could not help but recall Cessair's recollection of some of these same events, under very different circumstances in the twenty-first century. The memory made her seethe with renewed rage, but she endeavored to keep this from showing on her face.

"There was much anger in me. I felt betrayed by my family, and it made me hot to think that the woman must always bear the humiliation of men's mistakes. I wished to lead, not to follow or be used as barter. So I worked and studied, taking it all in like a parched root, surpassing the

others who sat at the master's knee. I learned that the gods of the Black Land were different from the unnamed god worshipped by my people. In the Black Land, there are many deities, each named, each dedicated to different aspects of life and death. For my parents, there was worship of one, a god of everything. Yet I did not wish to give up the god of my people, for I knew of the power and promises made manifest. That may be what drew me to wise Ma'at. The same promise of justice and eternal reward for the good."

This was not the Cessair Ricky knew—a cruel villain who had nothing but disdain for God. Who cared not for justice, but for power. It was as if she were facing a different woman. Or, she wondered again, was this an act? She recalled how easily Cessair had assumed the Rio Armstrong personna in the twenty-first century.

"Perhaps," said Luja as Cessair paused, *"the gods are not so different. Perhaps they simply wear different faces for different tribes."*

"That may be so," said Cessair. *"But it seems the gods sometimes speak different truths. And if I did not speak this truth to you, I would be guilty of a great deceit. The god with no name has spoken to my grandfather. The nameless god has predicted a terrible flood. The rains will come and all land will be covered."*

Although Luja knew the answer already, Cessair did not realize this, and so she responded as if she was ignorant of the implications.

"Why should a god cover all the land? Where will the people go?"

Cessair spoke somberly. *"The nameless god seeks to drown all."*

"But why?"

"The nameless god has spoken with displeasure to my grandfather of the widespread evil everywhere men walk,"

continued Cessair. *"A flood will wash the world clean. But the nameless god has charged my grandfather with building a wondrous boat, an ark to carry and save enough people and animals so that the world can be reborn when the floodwaters recede."*

"Perhaps the nameless god is wrong," suggested Luja. *"The gods of the Black Lands do not always predict the rains or the droughts accurately. More than once I have heard men speak of a god's promise, but then it failed to come to pass."*

"My grandfather is a man of sincere belief," said Cessair. *"His life has been guided by this nameless spirit. It seems a fearful thing to me that he might be wrong. And Shendjw says the stars do portend some calamity."*

"Shendjw is the elderly sorcerer with whom you study?" asked Luja.

Cessair offered a thin smile. "Elderly, yes. But still a man of great knowledge."

Ricky considered this, recalling what she knew of Cessair's history. If Shendjw—Crocodile—was the sorcerer who had created the Scroll of Life and Death, that meant Cessair would go to him after her grandfather's refusal. And Shendjw would refuse her as well.

"If this prediction of a flood is true," said Luja, *"then we are all in great danger."*

"It is true that many will die," said Cessair, *"but there may be room on the ark for some."* She nodded to her two guests. *"I am recently returned from the long journey to my see my grandfather where I supplicated myself to him, begged him to ask the unnamed god to spare the people. My grandfather would not be moved, would not question the unnamed god's wisdom. Seeing that his heart was set, I asked for safe passage for myself alongside his sons and their wives. Perhaps there would be something I could contribute to the reborn world. He was angry, despite the passage of so many years. 'Why should*

I help you who shamed our family?' Yet he marveled at my learning. He told me that he would pray to the unnamed god and send his answer to me in Tarkhan."

"When do you expect your answer?" Luja asked.

Cessair laughed. *"Who am I to know the timetable of the gods? But my grandfather will send word promptly. It is only two weeks' journey across the Great Green to Meroe."*

Ricky was unfamiliar with Meroe but surmised it must be a port city in the region known in modern times as Turkey, for this would be the likeliest route to the region in which Cessair's grandfather lived.

"Once one reaches Meroe, it is several more days into the hills to the site of the ark."

Ricky took in a sharp breath. *"You have seen it?"*

Cessair raised an eyebrow. *"It is difficult to not see it."*

For a moment, Ricky felt faint. Even though she had read the stories of the ark in the mythical history of Ireland, *Labor Gabala Erenn*, which seemed inspired by the Biblical tale of Noah in Genesis, she had considered the vessel a bit of mythology, a sort of bedtime story for the faithful. In her dangerous encounters with Cessair a year earlier, she had even wondered whether her great adversary's references to Noah and an ark were metaphorical. It rocked her to the core to learn that something she had considered a fairy tale was a real, tangible thing, like suddenly being introduced to the Tooth Fairy. Yet, if she had learned anything from the previous year's experiences, it was that behind almost all myth lies a grain of truth. And sometimes many grains.

Of course, none of this meant that there would really be a flood that covered the entire planet. Or that the voice Noah had heard was anything other than his own imagination. She reminded herself that this just might be some eccentric guy building a big boat. Yet, even if there was nothing else to it, the undertaking's importance was beyond calculation. Here was something that had inspired stories that had endured for fifty centuries and would continue to endure far beyond the twenty-first century. It was hard to wrap her head around.

"*Are you unwell?*" asked Cessair, noticing that Ricky had gone pale.

Ricky nodded. "*Yes. Forgive me. Such a story is...a great thing.*"

"*Yes,*" said Cessair. "*My grandfather says that unshakeable faith allows one to accomplish great things.*"

Luja nodded, directed a question at Cessair. "*And when your grandfather replies, what if the answer is no?*"

Cessair smiled. "*He is my grandfather. How can it be no? And it will be helpful to have a scribe along to keep a record that can be passed down from generation to generation.*" She turned to Ricky. "*And the scribe's attendant. My grandfather will certainly see the wisdom in that.*"

"*Your kindness is great, Priestess,*" said Luja.

Ricky searched for the right words. She settled for "*Thank you.*"

"*Do you have business in Tarkhan?*"

"*We have a business transaction to conclude with Tuta, the carver,*" said Luja. "*But not until tomorrow.*"

Cessair laughed. "*Tuta! That old cheat! You are lucky to have escaped his shop with your shendyts!*"

Now Luja smiled. "*We did not! Tuta sold us the ones we now wear!*"

This brought laughter to them all.

"*I will have Bennu and Kissa prepare mats for you for tonight,*" said Cessair. "*There are many responsibilities here that you may help with. And you can tell me of your journey from the north.*"

CHAPTER 14

Cessair's routine became apparent over the next two days. Visitors to the temple were rare, but if they came, it was usually early in the morning or at dusk. Usually it was those who had lost a loved one, or were about to. They wished to pray to Ma'at that the deceased would be welcomed into the afterlife. How such lobbying could add to or subtract from the weight of one's heart, Ricky did not know.

In the morning, Tarkhan's faithful would stop by with food and drink. *"Ma'at will eventually greet all,"* explained Cessair. *"And so, many are happy to contribute their excess to our temple. Not all do so, and there is no requirement. It is simply a reflection of the respect for Ma'at."*

Cessair also spent two hours each day tutoring Bennu and Kissa.

"To chart a strong course, they must know language and numbers," Cessair told her visitors. Once again, Ricky had difficulty reconciling this generous and giving incarnation of Cessair with the cruel and self-serving Cessair she had known. Yet, they were the same person.

"Perhaps we have changed the future already," said Luja as she and Ricky carried water to Cessair's small hilltop garden. "Perhaps by befriending the priestess, we have altered her actions and so altered all of the events that would have occurred over the next five thousand years."

"So hold off on the poison?" asked Ricky.

Luja nodded. "We must know more. Hopefully, we can learn whether Masud has been successful in destroying the scroll. Unless…"

"Unless what?"

"Unless he decides to use it to make himself immortal."

Ricky scowled. "I don't know. Masud sounds like he's just interested in finding peace.

Luja considered this for a moment. "Yes, this is how it seems. Assuming he has been truthful with us. We must continue to think for ourselves, to be cautious observers. With both Tessero and Masud, there remains the possibility that we have not been told everything. And even if Masud is dedicated to fulfilling his promise to Tessero at this time, the temptation of the scroll is great. We have seen it poison the minds of many others."

On the second day, Sisa arrived, climbing the steep path to the temple carrying ostrich feathers like a bouquet. She seemed surprised to see Ricky and Luja in the outer room of the temple instead of Cessair. The woman was no more than five feet tall, slim but well-muscled, with carbon skin, wearing a light-colored kilt that left her naked on top. Luja made simple introductions and reiterated her praise of the feathers.

"I care for the ostriches of Benek. The feathers are easy to get."

"Are you from Nubia?" asked Luja.

Sisa nodded. *"I was brought here when I was nine. But I already knew much about ostriches by then."*

Ricky estimated that must have been a decade ago, but age in this time period was difficult to assess.

"Caring for them was easy. Learning the language of the Two Lands was hard." She smiled broadly.

"We are getting used to the new language as well," said Luja. She then proceeded to fill in Sisa on the highlights of their

travel cover story. Sisa listened like one who desperately wished to travel herself.

"How often do you visit Cessair?" asked Ricky after Luja finished.

"Usually twice every moon cycle," said Sisa. *"I wish to make sure she does not run out."*

"Run out?"

"Of ostrich feathers. Cessair encourages her visitors and followers to take a plume. It is a reminder of Ma'at's desire for our lives to be in balance."

Cessair entered from the direction of the garden, carrying a basket filled with onions. *"Sisa! I always look forward to your visits!"*

"Priestess!" said Sisa with a bow. *"I did not mean to disturb your guests."*

"I am certain they have enjoyed your company, Sisa, as I always do." She moved through an archway and returned moments later without the basket. *"Have you news, Sisa?"*

"King Crocodile has developed a taste for ostrich eggs. We send so many to the palace he must be feeding them to his soldiers as well."

"That is the best gossip you have for me?" asked Cessair, feigning offense. Then she smiled. *"What of the strong farm boy you spoke of?"*

Sisa threw up her hands, though she continued to hold onto the feathers. *"He is young and wishes to copulate whenever there is a moment! But I have been firm with him! He has agreed that we will not copulate in any way that might produce a child."*

Ricky could not help but smile, recalling that premarital sex in ancient Egypt was socially acceptable, regardless of the number of partners one had. However, once married, an extramarital affair could be punished by death.

After several minutes of chat, Sisa excused herself to place the feathers in the shrine. When she had left, Cessair's expression became wistful.

"So many good people in the world. And not only in the Two Lands. It makes me wonder…"

Luja intuited what Cessair was thinking. *"Are you wondering about the flood?"*

Cessair nodded. *"I wonder what the god of my grandfather sees that I do not. Am I so naïve? One day, a woman arrives with ostrich feathers to honor Ma'at, a kind and humble gesture with no malice. Vendors in the market slip pieces of fruit to orphans and the crippled. Even Tuta, bless his heart, the old cheat! But there is no evil bone in his body! And so many more in Tarkhan. And if in Tarkhan, then why not in other cities? Why not in the north and the east? Why must everyone die?"*

"Perhaps there will be no flood," said Ricky.

"But if there is, what of Sisa? I cannot ask my grandfather to save everyone!"

She turned and disappeared through the archway.

After midday, Ricky and Luja headed down the trail to the city and Tuta's shop. Cessair, who seemed enthusiastic about this diversion, accompanied them. This was another departure from the twenty-first century Cessair, who Ricky had observed was a lone wolf. In this ancient setting, Cessair seemed to enjoy camaraderie. The heat was oppressive, and the light breeze modified it little. Even so, Cessair nattered on as if she had known Ricky and Luja for years.

"Tuta, for all his warts, is quite skilled. He created the figurines that adorn Ma'at's temple. I stop at his shop occasionally to collect his wood scraps for fire. Of course, he is completely irreverent. He pesters me constantly to let Bennu and Kissa apprentice in his shop."

Luja smiled gently. *"You have taught the girls numbers and measurements. They might do quite well in a carver's shop."*

Cessair laughed. *"I think we can all imagine what Tutu would have them measuring! The old jackal! The girls' interests are much better served in the temple."* Then she grew pensive. "I hope there will be room to take them on the ark."

Ricky shot Luja a knowing glance but said nothing.

They reached the edge of the city and wove through the narrow side streets, Cessair leading them on a more direct route than they had taken when Ricky and Luja had set off to find Ma'at's temple. Tuta displayed no surprise at seeing the three together, although he bombarded them with flattery.

"What man is more blessed than Tuta?" he exclaimed. *"Tuta should expect no greater reward in the Field of Reeds."*

"Do not be surprised if Anubis does not have the Field of Reeds in mind as your final destination," said Cessair. *"What have you for this woman, old soul?"*

"Always my best," said Tuta, bending beneath his bench and bringing up a small basket. *"But better than my best for friends of the priestess."* From the basket he withdrew a parchment wrap, set it on the bench, and slowly unwrapped the object within. A perfect human eyeball stared up at them.

Cessair gasped. *"My reason tells me this is your work, Tuta, but my eyes say it is real."*

"As always, wise priestess, your reason is infallible," said Tuta. Then he gestured to Ricky. *"The eye is yours, good Panya. But wait."* Tuta turned, shuffled into his sleep area, returned a moment later with a polished copper disk that served as a mirror. *"To aid you in placing the eye. The mirror belonged to Tuta's wife."*

He held it. Ricky hesitated a moment, then reached for the eyeball as if she were trying not to disturb a sleeping scorpion. She held it carefully with her fingertips, examining it. The details were exquisite. The care Tuta had exercised had resulted in the creation of a work of art. She knew that prosthetic eyes had been discovered in Egyptian tombs, but none that she recalled had looked as beautiful as the work produced by this ancient gargoyle. Then again, the eyes found in tombs were thousands of years old. After several millennia, Tuta's wooden creation would probably be just as decrepit and worm-eaten.

"Dip the eye into the crock of salted water on my bench," directed Tuta. *"It will slip in more easily, and the salt will prevent the red evil."*

Ricky realized he meant infection. Carefully, she dipped the orb. Then she removed her eye patch and, bending to the mirror, worked the prosthetic into place. It was not as easy as she had hoped. After more than a year, the socket was mostly dry and the muscles had atrophied. However, she eventually succeeded. There was a feeling of fullness and irritation that she hoped would subside or that she would get used to. While her left eyelid drooped slightly, and the faux eye would not move in coordination with her real eye or provide any improvement in her vision, it was startling for her to see her face look so normal.

"It will not move like your real eye," noted Tuta, echoing her thoughts. *"When you look at someone, instead of moving just your right eye, turn your whole head toward them. The lack of movement in the left eye will be less noticeable."*

"Thank you," said Ricky, her voice almost a whisper.

"Tuta is humbled, but Panya need bid him no thanks. Her pleasure is worth many rings of silver."

"Even I, who know your work well, am impressed by this orb," said Cessair. *"It is as if the gods guided your hands."*

Tuta bent slightly in a bow made awkward by his uneven shoulders. *"Your praise is life-giving sunlight that warms this ancient and broken body. And while Tuta is reluctant to acknowledge the breadth of his talent, which may run as deep and as wide as the Iteru itself, it saddens Tuta to think that his craftsmanship will bring joy to the earth for perhaps only a few seasons more, withered and wrung-out as he is. How Tuta's spirits would soar if only he knew he could pass his craft along to a young apprentice or, in the case of sisters, two. Tuta could then smile, knowing that when at last Anubis came to guide him across the dark waters, his legacy would live on!"*

Cessair made a sound of disgust. *"You old scoundrel! Your slippery tongue could talk a cobra into biting itself! Before I would allow Bennu and Kissa to stay an hour in this shop, I would see your manhood grilled over hot coals and served on sticks in the marketplace!"*

Tuta smiled devilishly, still half bowed. *"On such a day, it is certain there would be no hunger in Tarkhan."*

Even Cessair had to crack a smile at this.

***

With their change of clothes, scarves covering their hair, and Ricky no longer wearing an eye patch, they found they could wander the streets of Tarkhan without attracting undue notice. Mentions of the miraculous survival seemed to have subsided, which they attributed to telling Marika, the woman they had met upon their arrival, that they were journeying to Meant Khufu. This would hopefully have the effect of sending any who might seek the pair to villages far south of Tarkhan. Nonetheless, they continued to avoid crowds and conversations, but they gradually got a feel for the city. They estimated the population at five to ten thousand, and while small by twenty-first century standards, it was a significant hub in prehistoric Egypt. Ricky knew that even Memphis, the "city of white walls" that was Egypt's shining center of commerce and innovation was only thirty thousand.

Tarkhan lay on the west bank of the Nile, which was where most of Egypt's necropolises could be found. The city's extensive cemetery stretched to the west and north, half of it in a valley, the other half—for the wealthier occupants—up the hill farther. It seemed to Ricky and Luja that there must be a thousand graves, most of them no more than holes dug into the ground. There were, however, a number of larger crypts and mastabas—usually shallow, multi-room tombs. One of the principal occupations in the city was building, maintaining, and guarding tombs in the sprawling necropolis.

A long canal had been excavated north of the city and ran roughly parallel to the Nile, creating a narrow island between the river and the city proper. During flood season, the canal would usually protect Tarkhan from the rising waters and redirect them inland via additional, narrower canals. At the river, an extensive dock that ran along the west bank had been built mostly of stone, due to the scarcity of suitable forests from which lumber could be harvested. Trade vessels could load and unload here, as well as passenger boats. A short, wide road led from the dock to the marketplace. The palace stood north of here, along the shore but elevated slightly on a rock plateau.

Ricky knew that, over the next two millennia, Tarkhan's role as a cemetery would decline. Its population would relocate north toward Cairo and Memphis. The mud brick homes would melt back into the desert and the palace would be taken apart, stone by stone, to be used in the construction of other buildings and monuments near the new hubs of commerce. The cemetery with its well-built, well-cared for tombs would be the city's most enduring feature, one that would intrigue archaeologists fifty centuries later.

Those archaeologists would also be intrigued by Shendjw— the Crocodile. As Mr. Fathi had told them, this was a period before a unifying of Egypt under one pharaoh. Crocodile was the last of these regional pharaohs before Narmer began the Dynastic Period. Or was he? Because of the scarcity of historical evidence, and the mystery surrounding Crocodile's reign, some archaeologists doubted his existence. Ricky now had the answer for them, although she had no way to deliver it.

Their walks through the city were usually conducted without Cessair, for their goal was anonymity, and Cessair was so well-known that citizens of all classes were drawn to her. Part of the reason was her generosity, which perplexed Ricky to no end. How could the murderous, power-mad Cessair she knew from the twenty-first century be the same Cessair who, in Predynastic Egypt, brought cabbages, leeks, figs and other items from her own garden and put them into the hands of the city's poorest?

"This is Ma'at's will," Cessair had explained to them. *"When there is more than enough, where is the justice in hunger?"*

In return for the food and lodging, Luja and Ricky helped in Cessair's garden, whose abundance was impressive. The major disadvantage of having it high on the hillside was having to transport water to it. As Cessair had no camel to carry the water-filled bladders from the well or the river up the winding path to the garden, her temple attendants, and Cessair herself, had to carry the bladders using an animal hide harness that hung upon the shoulders. She was grateful when Ricky and Luja volunteered to help.

One morning, as Ricky walked beside Cessair, carrying two of the bulky bladders, Cessair stumbled slightly but recovered. *"Oof! I wish the builders of the shrine had cut steps into the hillside!"*

Ricky offered a commiserative chuckle. *"I wish you had a—"* She stopped herself. She had intended to say "horse," but even though she had not been the most attentive pupil, she recalled Mr. Fathi noting that the Egyptians in their destination time period had never seen a horse. The animals would not be brought to Egypt for another 1,400 years. She was reminded of the acute necessity to avoid such blunders if she wished to continue a credible deception.

Cessair turned toward her. *"What is it you wish?"*

"I... I wish you had a garden closer to the river."

Cessair nodded, smiled. *"Its location is the work of one of my predecessors. And now, much of the good land by the river has been claimed by others."*

Ricky's gut unclenched. *"Perhaps you could get a donkey."*

"Perhaps," agreed the priestess as they walked on. *"However, they are greatly valued and not within the means of all. What grows in the garden is destined for our plates and for those in need. There is little left with which to barter for such extravagances."*

The climb continued, leaving Ricky with conflicting emotions. For just a few moments, talking with Cessair had seemed as natural and pleasant as a conversation with Luja. Yet, such a thing was unimaginable. Again, the memories threatened to overwhelm her. This was Sasha's killer. And Leo's betrayer. Ricky knew she must be blind to some dire truth. Or to some dreadful, world-changing event that was yet to transpire.

They had been in Tarkhan for a week when, following their breakfast of beer, dates, and cheese, Cessair asked them to accompany her to a dwelling on the edge of the city. Each of the women carried baskets, although Ricky and Luja had no idea what was inside. *"It is the home of a reed cutter's family. Cutting reeds is a dangerous job. Papyrus grows along the Iteru. Crocodiles can hide in the thick growth."*

"Was the man hurt?" asked Ricky.

"A leg and part of one hand were torn off," said Cessair. *"This is what I have been told. He was pulled from the water but died."*

Ricky uttered a curse in a language Cessair would not have understood.

"It will be difficult for his wife and the seven children."

Ricky blinked. *"Seven?"*

"The oldest two, a boy and a girl, are eleven and nine years of age; they are also reed cutters."

Ricky knew that children often followed the same career paths as their parents in ancient Egypt. Depending on circumstances, children could begin working as young as four. Poor families sometimes sold their children into a form of bonded labor. She also understood that, with the father gone, fewer papyrus reeds would be cut. While debens were valued, most transactions were bartered. The papyrus reeds would be traded for meat, fruit and beer. But now there would be less to trade, and this would mean less food and fewer household supplies. To make up for this shortfall, a third, even younger child might be chosen to take the father's place in the shallow waters. The thought sickened her, but this was life for these people. And while she found it appalling, none of the poor of Tarkhan would give it a thought.

Their destination was another in a procession of mud brick dwellings that shared side walls. Cessair led them through a walled yard hardly bigger than a motel room and into a single roofed chamber. Papyrus mats covered the window spaces to discourage the heat and dust. A small hearth occupied one corner. Pots, sacks, useful sticks, and clay jars huddled near the hearth. Narrow steps built along the right wall led to the roof, which was where most of the family slept to escape the heat. Ricky had noticed a small canopy atop the structure when they arrived, typical of those used to shield the sun during afternoon rest. Out the open rear door, she observed another walled courtyard containing a vegetable garden. Two young children played there, oblivious, it seemed, to the tragedy that had befallen their family. Two older children sat on the dirt floor inside the one main room, silent. The three other children were nowhere to be seen. Ricky wondered if they might be napping above.

Cessair bent to a kneeling woman, Tiye, who was probably thirty but looked fifty, for several teeth were missing, and her hair was streaked with gray above intelligent eyes. Beside her was the body of her husband, partially covered with a papyrus mat. It was not enough to completely conceal the horrific mutilations, the blue-black blotchiness of the skin, or a faint odor of decay. Ricky felt bile rise in her throat and had to turn toward the door, the sunlight, the fresh air to keep herself from losing her breakfast. The wife wailed her sadness to the world. They had no money for a decent burial. Would her husband be admitted to the Field of Reeds?

"Min was a rough man," said Tiye. *"He told me of things he had done before we came together. Awful things. But he was different after. A good husband and provider. But...his heart may be too heavy with old evil for Ma'at's scale."*

Cessair rested a hand on the woman's shoulder. *"A quarry barge floats higher in the river when the stones have been unloaded. Ma'at will weigh his heart as it is now, not as it was when heavy darkness filled it."*

The woman's gratitude at this statement, from a priestess of Ma'at, was immense, and Ricky felt a surge of unexpected emotion in herself.

"They were going to take Min immediately to the cemetery, bury him in hot sand. We can afford no better. I told them he is not prepared. He must be dressed for the journey! He has nothing to sustain him! I made them bring him here, but we have so little."

"You were right to do so," said Cessair. She reached into her basket and removed a folded sheet of white linen, opened it and spread it on the floor. Then she signaled Ricky and Luja. The three of them moved to the body. Luja seemed unfazed by it all. Ricky had seen death many times in many gruesome forms. Somehow, this was different. She knew the condition of the body had something to do with it, as did the fact that this was

not an enemy. This was someone who did not deserve his fate, someone who was loved, whose family grieved for him right here, right now. And they could see how horribly he had died. She could tell they felt a keen sense of inadequacy, that their poverty left them unable to prepare him for the world of the dead.

Bleeding was no longer a significant issue. If the trauma itself had not killed Min, he had died of massive blood loss at the river. The floor beneath the body showed some additional pooling, but it was merely sticky now, and the blood had congealed at his wounds. They lifted him onto the linen. Then Cessair knelt, motioned for Luja's basket. From it she took a jar containing wine, poured this onto Min's body. Using her bare hands and a cloth, she washed every inch of the corpse. Again, the gratitude in Tiye's eyes was immense and heart-rending.

From another jar, Cessair rubbed Min's body with a watery, pale-yellow oil that smelled of pine needles, which she later identified as juniper berry oil. She placed onion skins over his eyes and onions and garlic under armpits and in body cavities. Then she sprinkled a peppery substance over him. At each new step of the process, she would utter a humble prayer to an appropriate Egyptian deity. All of this Cessair did with such loving care that it brought tears.

She signaled for Ricky's basket next, removing a loaf of bread, which she tucked beneath Min's left forearm. At his right side, she placed a bladder filled with beer—something that could be used for sustenance or currency on a long journey. The oldest girl stepped forward with an alabaster disk somewhat larger than an open hand. Its surface was carved to resemble a coiled snake. Ricky guessed this was a game Min had enjoyed in life.

Now Cessair gently wrapped the linen around the body, securing it in several places with belts made from the same linen. This was not the full embalming process that would have been enjoyed by the wealthy, Ricky realized, but it would be sufficient for Tiye and her family to send poor Min on his way with dignity. In finishing, Cessair uttered additional prayers and pleas for mercy and a fortunate journey.

At a word from the mother, the three absent children descended the stairs from the roof. Cessair, Ricky, and Luja carried Min to the cemetery, Tiye and all seven children following. There was no pyramid, mausoleum, or mastaba waiting for him. His body would go into a pit in the sand. Now, however, he was ready for the journey. Ricky noticed Tiye held her head as high as if she had been queen of Egypt.

As sand was shoveled atop the mortal remains of Min, Cessair raised a hand in farewell. *"Peace, finally, to one who will be missed."*

After they returned to the Temple of Ma'at, Ricky pulled Luja into the garden. "This is wrong. This is so totally wrong!"

"It is very strange," Luja agreed.

"The Cessair in our time sent thousands to their deaths! She ordered executions of innocent people! She was obsessed with power and immortality! I just don't see anything that's going to turn our Cessair here into Supervillain Cessair. Even the ark thing! When she gets the bad news, she's more likely to send her grandfather a loaf of date bread with a note that says, 'Thanks anyway, love, Cessair'."

"I am feeling very conflicted about this," said Luja. "Although I did not meet Cessair in the future, as you did, I know what she became. But like you, I cannot foresee any event that would lead her in such a direction. Unless..."

Ricky prompted her. "Unless what?"

Luja shook her head. "Unless there is some terrifying truth we are blinded to. And I shudder to think that such a truth might exist."

CHAPTER 15

A day did not pass without them waking in the morning and wondering whether it had all been a dream.

Perhaps *hoping* was a better characterization.

A day did not pass without them watching people in the market, looking for eyes that seemed too curious. Had they seen Tessero's mole without knowing? Had they spoken? Was the mole growing impatient with them for not having eliminated Cessair yet? If so, were they in danger?

A day did not pass without them wondering how Masud fared at the palace of Crocodile. In Tarkhan, rumors about life at the palace were commonplace. Some even contained a wisp of truth. There was nothing, however, about the disappearance of a magical document.

Or the execution of a spy.

As Ricky and Luja journeyed alone to the river to fill the bladders on their ninth day in ancient Egypt, they intentionally took a path that brought them closer to the palace.

"The palace is enormous," observed Ricky. "It's hard to believe that this will all be gone someday."

"The desert is relentless," said Luja. "There is no monument so large that the sands will not one day reclaim it. No mortal so great that the sands will not one day cover them."

They walked along the south perimeter of the palace grounds, although at a distance.

"I was hoping we might see Masud—"

"You mean Zohar," corrected Luja, using Masud's alias.

"Yeah, him. Was hoping we might spot him on one of the balconies or strolling across the long portico that faces the river. It's driving me nuts, not knowing what's going on. Is he succeeding? Has he become buddies with Shendjw? Or did Crocodile smell a rat and toss Masud– I mean Zohar–to the actual crocs?"

"He said that it might take weeks. Perhaps longer. We have been here just nine days."

Ricky shook her head. "Call it a gut feeling, but I'm just not seeing it. Masud said he worked with Fathi for months to learn about ancient Egypt and the language. That still doesn't dramatically improve his chances of blending in. He's still a twenty-first century transplant."

"As are we."

"But we're supposedly from some northern land. And it's not like Cessair has anything worth stealing. Well, unless you're using ostrich feathers for currency. So she's probably not going to be as suspicious of newcomers. On the other hand, Shendjw has the scroll and probably all sorts of other secret crap that require a watchful eye. Yet the plan is for Masud to become such a trusted fixture that he'll be able to slip around the palace without raising suspicion and somehow discover the location of the scroll. Something just doesn't sound right about this."

"Perhaps Masud has skills we know nothing about," suggested Luja. "The only times we saw him at the compound were at meals. Who knows how he occupied the remaining hours of the day? And unknown to us, he may have brought technology with him that could improve his chances."

"I don't trust him. Gut feeling. I think he's up to something. Something he has kept from us."

"Is this why we haven't carried out our part of the plan?" Luja asked. Ricky knew she meant the killing of Cessair.

"Partly. But there's other reasons. For instance, what if Masud fails to get the scroll? Cessair has some sort of relationship with the Crocodile. She was his apprentice. She might know where it is. Maybe she could even get it for us if Masud can't."

"Why would she do that?"

Ricky shrugged. "Hey, we're regular pals now. B-F-Fs. Or maybe we can trick her."

"The feeling you have about Masud. You call it a gut feeling. I have a feeling like that, too, about him. Maybe not in my gut so much. And there is also something about Cessair."

"You don't trust her?" asked Ricky.

"That is the strange part," said Luja. "I do trust her. I did not expect this. But even so, I feel...something dark. I cannot tell if it is something within her, or whether it is something from outside with which she will rendezvous later."

"She's nothing like the Cessair I knew in our time. She's kind. She has no aspirations to rule the world. No cruelty. But will that change when she gets the bad news from her grandfather?"

"I think anyone would be devastated to think that they would be abandoned by family and that their own death might be imminent," said Luja. "But it seems that something more than the threat of death would be required to turn her into a villain. She seems...content."

They reached the river and began to unfasten the bladders.

"Maybe..." Ricky hesitated.

Luja looked up from her work. "What is it?"

"Maybe it's just the passage of time," Ricky continued. "Maybe the human brain—even an immortal one—isn't designed to handle so many years. Centuries and centuries. Maybe the price of immortality is ultimately insanity. Maybe that's what happened to Cessair." She shuddered. Luja understood this was because Ricky was imagining the same possible fate for herself.

"One of many prices the scroll exacts," added Luja.

They completed the arduous climb to the garden where they found Cessair waiting. The look on her face told them what had happened without a word being uttered.

The reply had come from her grandfather.

*****

What struck Ricky as significant was that Cessair seemed more frightened than angry in response to the rebuff.

She asked for time alone in the garden, and so Ricky and Luja retreated to the temple.

"Not the reaction I expected," said Ricky once they were alone.

"Perhaps there will be a stronger reaction later," Luja replied. "She feels shock."

"But...can't we end this by simply getting Cessair to wait?"

"Wait for what?"

"The flood," Ricky replied. "I mean, it's not going to happen, right? If you examine the global geologic record going back more than ten thousand years, there's no evidence of a flood that covered the planet. Once she realizes that, there will be no need for her to go to Ireland. Or use the scroll! Which means everything from this point in time will be different!"

"Not necessarily," countered Luja. "While there may not be a global event, it's possible there will be local floods that will cause great damage, cover huge areas of land, and lead to significant deaths. This might drive her to seek safety elsewhere."

"Yeah, she seems really desperate to stay alive. You'd think she wouldn't be that freaked out about death, being a priestess to Ma'at. Based on what I've seen, she's got nothing to worry about when she gets to that feather test."

"Which buttresses our thinking that something else is amiss," Luja reminded her.

"But what? She gives food to the poor. She encourages literacy. She's nicer than Albus Dumbledore. If she's got some deep, dark secret that's going to cancel all that out, it has to be something pretty bad."

"Maybe it is something simpler than that," suggested Luja. "People often claim to be resigned to the idea that they will die. They say things like, 'Oh, it is just a part of life. It happens to everyone.' But when faced with a terminal illness or life-threatening situation, their perspective changes. Death was romantic when it was a mere academic concept, but when it becomes real, they find it terrifying."

As Luja concluded, Cessair appeared in the doorway.

"Please forgive me for neglecting you," said Cessair as she stepped into the room. *"You may have guessed my reason for wishing time alone."*

"Your grandfather's message," said Luja.

Cessair stared toward one of the window openings, her eyes focused on some indefinite point in the distance. She shivered suddenly. Luja moved to her, embraced her in a hug. Cessair allowed it.

"Your grandfather may be wrong," said Luja soothingly.

"That may be so," Cessair replied, pulling away, wringing her hands helplessly. *"But I cannot take that chance. I must go to Shendjw. He is wise and will know what I must do."*

Cessair normally presented herself as confident and able. At the moment, she seemed ready to fall apart. Ricky wondered whether this visit to Shendjw would provide the opportunity for Cessair to steal the Scroll of Life and Death. On one hand, this might solve all of their problems, for they could seize it from Cessair and destroy it. On the other hand, Cessair might use the scroll ritual quickly and become immortal. That had to be avoided at any cost, for it would make their journey into the past irrelevant. The events they were here to prevent would unfold over the next five thousand years. Luja apparently sensed this too and attempted to sway her from going after the scroll.

"*Certainly Cessair has wisdom sufficient to surmount any obstacle.*"

Cessair looked to the window once again. "*There is much you do not know.*"

"*Our services are yours to command,*" said Luja. "*We have traveled far, learned much, and know many things. If there is some private concern that adds to your distress, perhaps we can help you to deal with this burden.*"

Cessair returned a bitter smile. "*Burden.*" She considered the offer silently for several moments, then turned. "*Come.*" She led them out of the temple and up the stone steps to the garden path. They passed between rock piles that formed a gateway and, as they reached the center, Cessair motioned for them to sit on stone benches. Around them, bushes, vines, and rows of gourds provided a lush oasis.

"*I feel that the gods have guided you to my home,*" said Cessair sincerely. "*I sense goodness in both of you. Aside from Bennu and Kissa, I have few people with whom I can share my greatest concerns. And there are some things I have not told them.*"

"*It is kind of you to say such things, Cessair,*" said Luja.

"*You are not the first visitors I have encountered from the north,*" said Cessair. "*Our vessels sail far, and most of our trade is with the cities that touch the Great Green. There have been excursions that dared to seek the edges of the world. And occasionally, the cities at the edge have come seeking trade with us. So it was three seasons ago.*"

The three Egyptian seasons. Ricky recalled Mr. Fathi's teachings. *A year.*

"*Men arrived seeking audience with Shendjw. They shared stories, maps, gifts of gold and strange animal furs. The men were curious and remained to learn of our customs, foods, and language. The last of these I endeavored to teach them. One of the visitors, Fintan, began to help in the garden and we spent much time sharing stories of our homes."*

Cessair paused, seemingly searching for the right words to continue the narration. Luja spared her the necessity.

"And now you are with child."

Cessair's eyes widened. *"You know?"*

Luja smiled kindly. *"It is well concealed beneath your robes, slender as you are. But in my own land, I practiced divination with some degree of success. I could tell right away that you carried a great secret. Its nature became clear when I embraced you just now. And this explains your fear about the threatened flood."*

Cessair nodded, and her voice shook as she replied. *"My life is unimportant. The gods—even the unnamed one—may do with me as they wish. But my child must live."*

"Where is Fintan?" asked Luja.

"He has traveled south to Amarna with Ladra, his navigator. They will return soon. He is a good man. But he is an explorer. He will not have a solution for me."

"Shouldn't you warn the people of Tarkhan?" asked Ricky. *"Let them know there will be a flood? Let them prepare?"*

Cessair shook her head. *"They would not listen. The unnamed god of my grandfather is not their god. The gods of Egypt promise health and prosperity."*

"When will your child be born?" asked Luja.

"In less than three cycles of the moon," replied Cessair. *"But I cannot wait until new rain or new life arrives to seek counsel. I must visit Shendjw now. However, I will not visit him alone."* She gave a meaningful look to Luja and Ricky.

"You wish for us to accompany you?" asked Luja.

The priestess smiled coyly. *"I have heard it said that a warrior stands a better chance in battle if she stands beside a friend. I shall be standing beside two."*

THE BOOK OF DEVILS

CHAPTER 16

A gravel pathway led to the main entrance of the palace. Chiseled crocodile glyphs trimmed the archway through which the three passed. The soldiers standing on either side of the entrance wore only a loincloth and belt into which was tucked a short sword. Each held a long spear vertically. After Cessair spoke to one, he disappeared inside, requiring them to wait. He returned a short time later with one of Shendjw's petty functionaries, a slim, squinting man in a kilt who requested that they follow him.

They passed through a large courtyard paved with smooth granite, passed beneath another guarded archway into a beautifully kept garden with an enormous circular fountain at its center. Several closed doors were set into the walls on either side, likely leading to a kitchen and quarters for servants or concubines. Beyond this garden stood a towering door with posted guards who nodded obsequiously to Cessair before pushing them open.

And now they were in the throne room.

Ricky looked to Luja, whose expression indicated exactly what both of them were thinking. Where was Masud? They had not seen him in any of the areas they had passed through. Of course, it was a large complex, and he might be whiling away his time with the concubines, or perhaps completing minor tasks that would allow him to ingratiate himself to Shendjw.

In the throne room, a roof blocked the sun, requiring lit lamps on ornate stands along the walls. Ahead of them rose twenty-seven steps, which Ricky realized was a multiple of nine.

The Egyptians have really gone all-in on this lucky number thing.

The steps extended twenty feet on either side, to the outer walls of the chamber. Something about the dim lightning and grim architecture reminded Ricky of Dorothy's frightening first visit to the Wizard's throne room in the film *The Wizard of Oz.*

All we need is flying monkeys!

As they neared the top of the steps, a sight more gruesome than flying monkeys greeted them. Thirty feet ahead was a slightly raised dais with a black wall at its back, but to either side was a floor-to-ceiling opening onto a veranda that overlooked the Nile. Centered on the dais was a golden throne, empty. And hanging from the ceiling rafters, about a dozen on each side, were crocodiles, suspended from their tails. Each one represented one of the giants of the species. It seemed to Ricky that Shendjw wished to strike terror into those who dared visit.

Mission accomplished!

Few other ornaments graced the throne room, and perhaps this was by design, so as not to take the focus off the Crocodile King or his grisly trophies. The only other features were two identical doors on opposite sides of the room, each with a single guard.

"The royal apartment," said Cessair, following Ricky's gaze to the right. *"The royal pool is through the door on the opposite wall."*

"This place gives me the creeps," said Ricky. Then she realized the fearful environment had distracted her, and she had spoken this in English. She spoke again, this time in the ancient tongue. *"This palace is terrifying and does not seem like a friendly place."*

"Shendjw practices arts both dark and bright," said Cessair. *"It is the nature of sorcery."*

They stood before the empty throne for several minutes. Then the door to the royal apartment opened and a young man followed by a somewhat older individual emerged, strode toward the dais. The younger man wore a black deshret and kilt with a wide belt striped in gold. A gold usekh hung from his neck, covering a portion of his strong, bare chest, vertical slivers of it glittering like golden piano keys. His eyes were darkened by a thin liner of charcoal and he wore a wig of tight curls that hung down past his ears. The man held in his hand a scepter bearing a small, carved crocodile head. He ascended the dais without speaking or acknowledging anyone in the room. When he sat, the other man began to speak.

"Bow and tremble before Shendjw the great, the Crocodile, King of Tarkhan, protector and consort with the living and the dead."

As they followed Cessair's lead and inclined their heads, Ricky whispered to Luja. "I feel like we're about to see a pro wrestling bout."

However, she now saw that her friend was trembling. Luja whispered a reply. "Something is wrong. Something is very wrong."

As she took in the scene more carefully, Ricky understood. Shendjw was young, no more than twenty-five, she guessed. She leaned toward Cessair. *"I thought you said that Shendjw was an elderly man. Ancient."*

Cessair responded while keeping her gaze on the seated man. *"Shendjw? Elderly? Of course not. Yet, he possesses the wisdom of the ancients."*

Ricky drew back, perplexed. She was sure that was not what Cessair had meant previously. Before she could inquire further, Shendjw stood.

"Cessair!" he called in a strong voice, stepping casually to within a few feet of them. *"You have avoided my company for*

too long. And I see that on this occasion, you have brought guests."

"I have, my king." She made introductions. *"They are visitors from the north."*

"A place of mystery, one that interests me greatly," said Shendjw. *"Perhaps we shall have a chance to talk of those lands. Or might that be the subject of today's visit?"*

"Nothing would give me greater pleasure than to talk of things of little consequence. However, today I come seeking advice."

"Crocodile shall have an answer for you! Speak!"

Cessair nodded, looked to Ricky and Luja as if for encouragement, and then began. *"I have spoken previously of my grandfather."*

"You have," acknowledged Shendjw. *"By all accounts, a man of great faith."*

"He has abandoned me, my king."

Ricky saw that Luja still trembled, sensing wrongness.

In response to Cessair's confession, Shendjw rubbed his shaven chin. *"By your own word, you admitted you were abandoned many years ago."*

"True, my king, but I recently traveled to the land of the Hatti to speak with my grandfather."

"And to what end?"

Cessair took a deep breath. *"You have heard the prophecy of a great flood."*

"I have."

"My grandfather says that the god with no name charged him with building a giant vessel that will survive the coming storm. All else will be flooded and lost. I asked my grandfather for sanctuary, and he refused. I am desperate, my king. What am I to do?"

Shendjw assessed Cessair silently for several long moments. *"And you believe the unnamed god will do this?"*

"I believe in the goodness and justice of Ma'at," replied Cessair. *"I obey the laws set forth by the gods of our ancestors. But my family has strong belief in the unnamed god. It may be possible that ours are not the only deities who hold sway over the lives of mortals."*

Crocodile nodded, seeming to consider the matter carefully. Ricky saw that Luja's trembling had not abated. Suddenly, Ricky felt cold, afraid. She trusted Luja's sixth sense. It was clear that she sensed something now. And whatever it was, it was something to be feared.

"What is it you wish from me?" asked Shendjw.

"Hope," Cessair replied, desperation in her voice. *"A shield against the flood, should it come."*

Shendjw looked her in the eye. *"And why should I help you?"*

Cessair appeared stricken. *"My king, you have been my teacher. More than that. My guide in many ways. Twenty times the Iteru has risen since I first came to you, friendless and adrift. Together, we have dared to look behind the veils that hide the workings of the natural world."*

Ricky stifled a gasp. If Cessair had known Shendjw for twenty years, he must have been a boy himself when she first arrived in Tarkhan. Yet, she could not shake the memory of Cessair saying that she had worked with an elderly magician.

Luja spoke to her in a whispered, nearly inaudible hiss. "It is worse than we could have imagined."

"Friendship demands loyalty, yes?" asked Shendjw. *"Yet, some part of this is missing. You have always been a brave woman. A woman who would face any challenge without whimpering or begging. In many ways, a warrior. But here you are, like a child afraid of the dark. This is not right. You are Ma'at's priestess. Death should not frighten you."*

"My own death does not."

"Whose then?"

Cessair lifted her chin. *"My child."*

Shendjw took a long look at her, and for Ricky, it was difficult to read his reaction to this. Then he smiled kindly. *"I should have guessed. Cessair the protector. Who is the father of this child?"*

"Fintan Mac. A traveler from the north."

Shendjw pointed toward Ricky and Luja. *"Is he a countryman of these two?"*

Cessair shook her head. *"He travels again. But he will return soon."*

Again, Shendjw stood silent in thought. Then he fixed his stare on Cessair. *"When?"*

"The child's birth? Perhaps two cycles of the moon. Or a bit more."

Shendjw turned away, facing the golden throne, clasping his hands behind him as he considered the situation. After a minute, he turned back.

"The child is important to you."

"Yes."

He narrowed his gaze on her. *"What is it you want for this child?"*

Without hesitation, Cessair replied, *"Kindness. And to not perish in the flood promised by the unnamed god."*

Shendjw nodded. *"Will the child be an explorer like its father? Or like its mother, will it seek the dark secrets?"*

"It will seek what it will. And..." She hesitated. *"...I never pursued the darkness, my king."*

Shendjw laughed. *"Oh? Have you not listened to the whispers about your own small garden? How it can produce such bounty? Or the potions you gift to grieving peasants who wish a night of dreamless sleep? Or how, with enough emmer wheat for one loaf of bread, you are able to produce two?"*

"My king, whether these things are the work of magic or not, it is certainly not dark workings."

"You are what you are, Cessair. A witch."

"I am surely many things, oh my king, who has also been my friend for these long years."

"It seems you have many friends now, Cessair."

"This does not diminish our bond. But I will admit that, during our explorations, I did come to fear the intoxicating effects of the dark arts."

"But now you desire my help."

"There must be some way!" Cessair pleaded.

"There is always a way," stated Shendjw. He placed a forefinger on his lips, slowly paced back and forth in front of the dais. Then he stopped directly in front of Cessair, put a hand gently on each of her shoulders. *"We have much history together. You have always been an eager pupil, thirsty for knowledge. Thirsty for...life."* Now he brought his right hand to her cheek, gently stroked it. *"I will help you resolve your problem, my little flower."*

He turned and strode to the door on the right, disappearing inside the royal apartment.

Ricky noticed a tear had left its trail on Cessair's cheek. Luja's voice was low but insistent.

"We must leave this place now."

Cessair turned to her, shocked. *"We cannot! In only a few heartbeats, the Master will arrive bearing freedom from the curse of the unnamed god!"*

"We must leave!" repeated Luja. *"There is so much darkness! So much danger! The circle tightens around us! Don't you feel it?"*

"Shendjw bends the forces of both light and darkness," said Cessair. *"What you feel is surely the agents of dark magic bowing beneath his strong hand, compelled to do his will!"*

Ricky wondered whether she and Luja should simply grab Cessair and run. However, soldiers with grim-looking weapons blocked the way behind them through the throne room and the two chambers beyond.

Moments later, Shendjw emerged from his chambers, carrying four small, clay vessels upon a wooden board. Cessair's eyes took on a feverish brightness as he neared.

"A potion?"

Shendjw smiled. *"One that will not fail. Yours is the nearest."*

"Powerful magic?"

Shendjw inclined his head slightly. *"Indeed."*

Luja spoke out desperately. *"Good Cessair, I beg you—"*

But Cessair had the near vessel in her hands, had removed its stopper, and drank it down in one greedy swallow. She returned the empty container to Shendjw. An attendant took two of the remaining flasks from atop the board and disappeared.

"Thank you, my king! The unnamed god is defeated?"

Shendjw nodded slightly. *"You will have nothing to fear from the flood. Nor will your child."*

Then her smile faltered. *"But what of you, my king? And Meryt and Panya? And the unfortunate citizens of Tarkhan? If only I am saved..."*

"Do not worry," said Shendjw. Then he smiled. *"Still the protector, even with your own fate decided. But do not worry. All have received consideration in my plans."*

"Will there be no flood?" asked Cessair.

"I cannot say," Shendjw replied. *"Perhaps the unnamed god will bring a flood. Perhaps the gods of Egypt will decree otherwise."*

The light went out of Cessair's face. *"But...the potion. What did it do?"*

"What you asked. Your child will not die in the flood. I have done it a great kindness."

"You speak in riddles, my king."

"Then you must see for yourself." With a hand motion, he directed the three women to the door on the left wall. The guard tendered a salute and then stood aside, allowing Shendjw to open the door. A pungent, swampy aroma assaulted them as they stepped through onto a balcony that bordered the south and east sides of a large chamber and overlooked a shimmering pool at least ten feet below. To their right, the east balcony was also open to the outside and offered a wide view of the Nile.

They did not follow the balcony in either direction. Instead, Shendjw bade them step forward to the low wall that allowed them to observe the green pool surrounded by white tile. Despite her meager attention to her studies, Ricky recognized statues of Neith, Khentekhtai, Kherty, Nephthys, and others along the perimeter of the roofless chamber. Yet it was the pool that commanded their attention. Its outer edge was defined by steps, allowing one to enter gradually from any side. At the center of the pool, a circular stone platform resting on the pool bottom supported an island no more than a couple feet across. Atop this stood a column roughly ten feet tall, and upon its flat top rested a stone chest.

None of these features arrested the gaze as readily as did the forty or so crocodiles floating in the pool or lounging on the white tile beside it.

That explains the smell, thought Ricky as they observed the dozing giants, the silence broken only by an occasional splash as a tail was flicked or a snout was repositioned. *This guy is really embracing the crocodile branding.*

Cessair's face reflected her confusion. *"This pool has changed."*

"Yes," agreed Shendjw. *"I remember when, many years ago, you and I, after studying the universal mysteries for hours, would disrobe and bathe ourselves in the cool, blue waters."*

"Beautiful memories. But the waters are green now, and..."

"In recent times, I have found fewer opportunities to admire the beautiful, and more to confound enemies. The crocodile is feared throughout the Two Lands, and fear can keep many enemies at bay. Or it can punish them."

As if they had been listening for his words, someone opened a door on a smaller balcony at the same level as theirs, but on the left side of the pool chamber. Three soldiers pushed two young women onto this balcony.

Cessair cried out. *"Bennu! Kissa!"* She turned to Shendjw. *"What is the meaning of this?"*

"I am doing what I promised! You will see this as a great kindness!"

"More riddles!" Cessair was no longer holding her anger in check.

Shendjw pointed to the other balcony. *"You have been deceived! The two you know as Bennu and Kissa are spies! They were sent from very far away."*

"For what purpose?"

"To make certain that you are killed."

Cessair's eyes opened wide. *"But... I have taught them. Fed them."*

"It is of no consequence."

"Why would they wish to kill me?"

"Their task was not to kill you," said Shendjw. *"It was to punish the would-be assassins should they fail."*

Ricky felt weak. Bennu and Kissa were the moles? While the revelation was shocking, they had known the mole could be anyone, and so she had little doubt that this was the case. But how did Shendjw know this?

Cessair stared across the expanse between the balconies, her eyes glazing for a moment. *"Why?"*

"They were offered something of immense value," said Shendjw. *"Eternal life!"*

"How is this possible? I thought you controlled the scroll!"

"That shall be explained." He snapped his fingers and the soldier standing behind him reached forward with a book-sized wooden plank. *"Bennu and Kissa are immortal now. They have been since the first day you encountered them. And so punishing them for their betrayal would be quite useless. However, the scroll ritual gives us the power to take away this gift. And so we begin. Their names are already written on the cedar board I hold! Earth!"*

Ricky stared. The cedar tree was of the earth.

At a signal from Shendjw—*"Water!"*—soldiers splashed the twins with a small amount of liquid from two of the vessels that Crocodile had brought with him from his chambers. The scroll contained the secret to create two elixirs, and this was certainly the one that would bring death.

Shendjw now pivoted away from the Nile and faced the west, the direction of the setting sun. Whenever immortality had been bestowed upon the twins, they—or whoever had assisted them—had faced the east to speak the necessary incantation. East brought dawn and was symbolic of awakening, birth, renewal, and blossoming. East meant life, or in the case of the scroll ritual, a mightily enhanced life. But the encore performance would be different. West meant light leaving the world and the chill of darkness as the sun disappeared. West meant death.

"Please help us, oh good Cessair!" came Bennu's frantic cry.

But there was no time. As the twins struggled futilely against the strong hands of the guards, Shendjw performed the final parts that would bring air and fire into play. *"May our lives follow the light!"*

His pronouncement: air. The setting sun: fire.

Even though thirty feet away, Ricky heard a clear gasp from both girls.

The two had felt the change. The fifth of the elements, akash, had not altered their appearances, yet it had transformed everything about them except their souls. Even from halfway across the room, it was easy to see how a new, even greater fear had widened their eyes. The fear was also wringing higher-pitched cries for mercy. They wept, they called upon the gods of the Two Lands, they offered to perform the most unspeakable acts, things that even the concubines would not be asked to do.

Ricky knew that, had they not been immortal before the scroll ritual, they would have already crumbled to ash. She could not understand who would have made them immortal. It was clear that Cessair had not done it. Nor had Shendjw. Whatever its source, that gift or curse had been lifted, and at the next sunrise, the twins would be corpses.

Only they would not make it to the next sunrise.

A flattened hand across Shendjw's own throat and his whistle signaled the soldiers to execute the final part of the task. One guard lifted Bennu and tossed her over the balcony wall like a doll. A short cry ended abruptly when she hit the stone, ten feet below, her left shoulder and chest taking the worst of it.

"Bennu!" screamed the twin remaining on the balcony. Terrified beyond reason, she forgot herself and pleaded with her captors in English, removing any doubt of her role as a spy. "Please! It's my sister! Get her out of there!" Cessair cried out in horror as well, begged Shendjw to stop what was surely to come.

How did Shendjw discover the twins? Ricky asked herself, her heart pounding, a terror within her metastasizing. Could Masud have told Shendjw? But no, Masud had not known the identity of the moles.

Bennu stirred on the floor, coughed, attempted to push up with her right hand. But the crocs had seen her. Before she could rise, one lurched at her from behind, latching onto her useless left arm just above the elbow. Bennu emitted a nightmare wail as she was jerked into the pool. She tried to cry out again but was pulled under. Moments later her head surfaced for a gasping scream, and then, as she was wrenched beneath the surface, several additional crocs joined the party.

"This is wrong!" Cessair cried hoarsely to Shendjw. *"This is not what I want!"*

He ignored her, gave the sign, and Kissa was thrown from the same balcony. She tried to land on her feet, but one leg twisted awkwardly and she hit the floor hard. Still, she pushed up to her hands and knees instantly, ready to run. But the crocs were even quicker. They knew it was feeding time, and three of them played tug of war, pulling her under the roiling green waters. Then it was silent except for Cessair's sobbing.

Ricky stood nearly paralyzed with the shock of it all. There was nothing she could have done. Shendjw's soldiers would have stopped her. Her efforts would only have delayed the outcome by a couple minutes. She wondered what Crocodile's next move would be. Did he plan to feed Cessair and Luja to the crocodiles as well? Did he realize that Ricky was immortal, and would he steal this away from her as he had done with Bennu and Kissa?

Cessair now looked away from the pool and her angry eyes flashed lightning at Shendjw. *"Why?"*

"Bennu and Kissa posed a problem," said Shendjw. *"They were immortal and needed to be dealt with. Since I have not aged in all the time you have known me, it must not surprise you to know that I have done the ritual. As long as there were other immortals, they posed a threat to my power."*

Cessair's voice was hoarse, thick with emotion. "I came to you for help!"

"I have already told you, I have provided for you."

"What have you done?" asked Cessair desperately. *"That elixir I drank... Did you grant me immortality?"*

Cessair suddenly doubled over, clutching her stomach, emitting a sharp cry. As she straightened, Shendjw placed a hand gently on the side of her face and smiled.

"No, my sweet henna flower. Your elixir was different. I poisoned you."

CHAPTER 17

Ricky felt herself sway, and Luja reached out to steady her.

My sweet henna flower.

Nothing made sense.

Tessero had told them his wife's name was Henna.

Masud was missing.

Shendjw was not an old man, and Ricky was certain Cessair had described him as such.

Or perhaps everything was swirling into focus, and she did not like the emerging picture.

"*My child!*" cried Cessair as another wave of cramps wracked her.

"*Help her!*" cried Luja, rushing to lower Cessair gently to a kneeling position.

"*There is no help for any of you,*" said Shendjw. "*The poison is beginning to take effect. In an hour, my sweet henna flower will greet Ma'at and see how her own soul is judged.*" He turned to Luja and Ricky. "*You two will not have to wait so long.*"

"*Why?*" screamed Cessair, on her knees, leaning against Luja, who cradled her. "*Why would you end my life and that of my child?*"

"*Ask your friends,*" said Shendjw. "*They have been keeping secrets from you.*"

Cessair had difficulty getting the words out. "*No...I...they have been helping.*"

Shendjw looked to Luja, then Ricky, *"Do you wish to tell it, or must I?"* When he received only acid stares in reply, he laughed.

"Bastard!" Ricky spoke the curse in English, for her command of the old language was insufficient to express her rage. She lunged forward, her hands reaching for Shendjw's throat. Two soldiers coming from behind grabbed her arms before she succeeded. *"Give her the antidote! Do you think your trained monkeys can hurt me? I'll rip your* fucking *face off!"*

"You are Panya, the immortal one," said Shendjw.

Ricky stopped struggling. So he *did* know. *"How...?"*

Shendjw laughed. *"Let me tell you a story."*

"I don't want to hear a story!" cried Ricky. *"I want you to help Cessair!"*

"You will wish to hear this one. It is the story of an old man. A great king and even greater sorcerer. A young girl comes to him. She is quick of mind and radiant like a jewel. The old king becomes her teacher, and she is an apt pupil. But the teacher does not share all. Ah, but what teacher ever does? He must keep some secrets to maintain the illusion of superior knowledge. In the case of our ancient friend, it is the elements. Their potential fascinates him. They seem to hold the promise of great power, and what king can turn away from an offer of greater power? Years pass, and he and the young girl explore secrets that have been difficult to wrest from the jealous grip of the gods. But the sorcerer's most ambitious experiments? These he has guarded, laboring often into the new day. Many years pass. And his efforts are rewarded. The secret of immortality! Of course, he uses the power for himself. While it is a wonderful gift, it does not have the power to make him young. He will live forever—as an old man. It is better than death. Perhaps."

Cessair's cries of anguish interrupted the tale. These were followed by curses uttered by Ricky. At a nod from Shendjw, his soldiers released her to kneel beside Cessair.

"Then one day, the old king receives a visitor. The king does not normally speak to supplicants, but the guards are quite agitated. The visitor has shown them something disturbing. In private, the visitor begs the old king's indulgence and hands him what seems to be a sheaf of parchment, only this parchment is stiffer and very smooth. There is a picture of the old king on it. Of course, the old king's likeness has been carved and painted onto many things, Yet, this is quite different. It is not a simple line drawing or stoic representation of the king. It is the old king himself in every detail. It is more exact than seeing his reflection on the surface of a pond. The old king is fascinated but wary. He asks what sort of magic this is. The visitor calls it a 'photograph'."

Ricky's gaze met Luja's. *Masud.* Shendjw continued.

"The visitor produces more of these photographs, showing the old king in places that seem foreign and magical. There are strange objects that carry people, like boats, but they move smoothly across the land as if they were gliding upon the waters. There are shining monuments made of silver and gold and jewels of value beyond known numbers that rise high into the heavens. There are people sailing through the air in giant birds powered by storms. And in each of these photographs is the old king himself. It can be no other. Just as astonishing, the visitor tells him things that only the old king himself would know. The old king is certain, now, that this is sorcery, and that this magic may be more powerful than his own. The old king nearly summons his guards to slay the visitor on the spot, but two things stop him. First, he is afraid the visitor's magic may protect him from harm, and that an attack might anger him. It is the first time in many years that the old king has felt

fear. Second, in spite of this fear, the old king remains curious. The visitor has not yet spoken of his intentions,"

Shendjw was apparently describing the old king's meeting with Masud. And he was implying, it seemed, that the old king and Tessero were the same person. But Masud was to have made contact with Shendjw. Did this mean that the old king and Sendjw were one and the same? How was that possible? The Shendjw speaking to them now was young. The scroll had no power to restore youth. Ricky held Cessair close as Shendjw continued the narration.

"The visitor claims to know that the old king has used the life ritual to make himself immortal. The photographs, he says, are of the old king in a distant future time. It is a time of great miracles, he says, and tells the old king he will see it when the Nile floods five thousand times. The old king senses that this visiting sorcerer does not wish to harm him, and so he finally asks the visitor why he has come."

"Oh, no!" breathed Luja, who seemed to have understood what was coming before Ricky. *"Tessero's plan was never to destroy the scroll!"* At the mention of the scroll, Shendjw's eyes moved quickly, involuntarily it seemed, to the pool. Then he continued.

"The visitor acknowledges that immortality is a wonderful gift, but would it not be more wonderful still if one were both immortal and young? And so the visitor reveals that he can travel from one age to another, and he desires to bring the secret of life and death to the old king's younger self, forty years in his own past. The young king can then use the power to make himself immortal so that he will not be forced to endure the centuries ahead as a wretched human corpse, undesirable to all but hags. He is persuasive. Convinced by what he has heard and eager for youth, the old king allows the traveler to bring the knowledge to his younger self. And so the future is changed. Now, when the young girl comes to him, the

king is youthful, vigorous. He would have her...except now he knows what must be done. The visitor has told him how the years will unfold, how Cessair will try to steal the secret, betray him. That she will wage battle for the soul of the world. He should kill her while she is young, innocent. Before she has reason to hate the world or acquire power. But...he cannot do it. He..."

"You are in love with her!" cried Luja. *"How can you do this?"*

"Do you think this is easy?" roared Shendjw. *"The visitor implored me to kill her as soon as she arrived in Tarkhan. But I could not. I gave her every chance over the years to forget the ways of her people, the superstitions of her grandfather, to fully accept the destiny of the Kingdom of the Crocodile."*

"To love you," added Ricky derisively.

Cessair cried out in pain again before speaking with some effort. *"My king, love must happen of its own accord."*

Shendjw darkened. *"Love, like all treasures, must be claimed by the powerful. And treasures that cannot be claimed are buried. When Cessair traveled to petition her grandfather, I knew it was time. My future self was aware of my feelings for Cessair, was afraid I would not be able to bring myself to do what was necessary, and so you were sent to slaughter the lamb. But as you can see, I am now an able wolf."*

"Able wolf!" spat Luja. *"You would never have been able to kill Cessair. Your future self knew this! But something changed that turned you into the wolf! Something your future self did not know."*

"Cessair's child!" hissed Ricky. *"That is what changed things! You're jealous! You can't bear that she could love someone else and not you!"*

Shendjw's features twisted in fury. He stepped swiftly forward and delivered a vicious backhand across her face. Ricky snapped backwards, and her head rebounded off the stone floor.

"Panya! My king! No!"

"Soon, my lovely henna flower will die. It is unfortunate, but once she is gone and I have no rival, then the power of the scroll will allow me to expand my kingdom. There are no borders that cannot be crossed, no army that will stop my chosen warriors."

Ricky raised herself onto an elbow. Shendjw's continued use of 'henna flower' to refer to Cessair underscored another deception. The story Tessero had told of a loving wife and children slain by Cessair, all of it fiction calculated to weaken their resistance to his plan. Her anger grew and she cried out as she pushed herself to her knees.

"You're no different than the evil that we encountered in our time! Just another villain, drunk with power who fools himself into thinking that he's using that power to bring order and peace, that he's saving the world from itself!"

Shendjw laughed again. *"You are wrong! I have no dream of saving the world! I intend to claim the world's treasures! Its land, its resources, its gold, its physical pleasures! Those who stand in my way or refuse to submit will be buried! And now, with Cessair gone to dust, I will not have to hide in the shadows or play the role of the respected man of commerce. I alone will know the secrets of life and death. I will fear no one."*

Ricky feared she knew the answer, but asked the question nonetheless. *"What of Zohar, your 'visitor'? He knows many of Shendjw's secrets!"*

"And he shall keep them! His reward for giving me eternal youth was great. What an honor to rest for forty years now as part of the foundation of this very palace!"

Shendjw smiled and Ricky felt a wave of hopelessness, knowing that once Cessair, Luja and she were gone, Crocodile's power would indeed be limitless.

"Five thousand years from now, I will still be young, and in those years, I will have made the world my plaything."

Cessair cried out again, twisted forward so that her forehead almost touched the floor.

Ricky realized that Shendjw's awful vision was worse even than what the Cessair of her own time had planned. She remembered the final vessel that Shendjw had brought from the royal chambers. *"King Shendjw! Cessair is intelligent and reasonable! Now that you have shown her the grim future possibilities, she will chart a different course! There will be no need for you to fear her interference! So I beg of you...the other container! It contains the antidote! Please give it to her!"*

"Ah! Now the lioness squeaks like the mouse she is!" He offered a twisted grin. *"The remaining flask contains no antidote. It is for you, Panya!"*

She suddenly understood. The final flask contained the same mix of herbs, extracts and minerals that had been splashed upon Bennu and Kissa, an elixir that would restore her own mortality during the ritual. All Shendjw needed to do was scratch her name into the wooden plank upon which the flask rested. It might be written there already. A drop of the liquid upon her skin would be enough. Then he would complete the rest of the ritual. Ricky would become immediately mortal and would crumble to dust with the next sunrise. However, once she was mortal, she knew Shendjw would not allow her to live that long. The crocodiles below were still hungry.

"Don't you long to have your mortality back?" asked Shendjw in a mocking tone. *"In a few minutes, you will have it. Just in time to watch my henna flower cross the river of death. Then you, Panya, and you, Meryt, will join her. After which I will truly be free. Then begins the Kingdom of the Crocodile."*

Cessair's spasms were now coming more frequently, and her skin had taken on an ashen hue.

Ricky and Luja had been sent into the past to kill Cessair, to keep her from becoming a monster that would threaten the world. Ricky had not imagined a generous and kind Cessair. She had not imagined such a grand betrayal by Tessero. And she had not imagined that her efforts would lead to an even darker future for the world.

Her thoughts went to Crockett. *Guess I fucked up that whole 'saving your life' thing.*

As Ricky and Luja knelt, one on each side of Cessair, Shendjw unsheathed his knife, began carving figures into the surface of the plank.

My name.

They were out of time. In a minute, Shendjw would be ready to perform the ritual. Cessair was fading. Ricky and Luja could not escape. Guards stood behind them, blocking the doorway back into the throne room, and more guards behind those blocked the way they had entered the palace. There was no way for them to get past those sentries. And in front of them, only a pit of vicious crocodiles. Shendjw would shortly send all three across the river of the dead.

The river!

There were no guards to their right where the balcony stood open. There was no time to consider whether the course she was now considering was inspired or foolhardy. All she could do was act and hope. Shendjw chanted as he worked the knife. Ricky whispered to Luja.

"When I say go, grab Cessair's arm and run!"

Luja's eyes widened. "Run where?"

"The balcony overlooking the river. Then we jump."

"It was twenty-seven steps to the throne room," said Luja. "And the river is lower still. That is a drop of three or four stories."

"Then we'd better hope the balcony overhangs the river rather than the stone walkway."

To Cessair, Ricky said, *"Will your legs work?"*

Panting, Cessair replied. *"The pain is in my stomach and chest. And tingling in my arms has begun."*

"Will your legs work?" Ricky repeated.

"I will do what I can."

A moment of silence and then:

"Go!"

Wrenching Cessair to her feet, they sprang up and ran, half dragging her along the narrow balcony. Shendjw's men were so stunned by this unexpected and futile effort that it took a couple of beats before they reacted. When they did, it was to look to Shendjw for guidance.

"Bring them back! There is no place they can go!"

The guards charged after the three women, but stopped moments later, astonished to see them disappear over the parapet.

***

As the guards rushed to the edge and peered over, they spied three flailing bodies being swept north by the current.

In the river, Luja and Ricky struggled to keep Cessair afloat, for her strength was mostly gone. Somehow, they made it to a reedy spot on the western shore and dragged Cessair from the Nile.

"It's too much!" cried Ricky. "We can't carry her all the way through the city and then up the hill to her temple."

"And what if we did?" replied Luja. "Nothing there can help her! And Shendjw's men would soon come!" Then she leaned close to the suffering woman. *"Where can we take you, great friend? Who can help you?"*

"Tuta!" moaned Cessair weakly. *"Take me to Tuta!"*

Ricky looked to Luja. "She must be delirious."

"Where else can we go?" asked Luja. "Perhaps he *can* help."

Cessair now needed to be carried and her breathing was rapid. Thankfully, Tuta's shop was not far. The old man looked up from his workbench, startled as they shambled in and gently lowered Cessair to the floor.

"What is this?"

"Shendjw has poisoned her!" cried Luja.

Tuta looked to his left, then his right as if seeking an escape route. Then he shifted on his feet, knelt beside Cessair, feeling her limbs, touching her forehead, examining her eyes. He rested his hand on her swollen belly for several seconds.

He rose, grasped Luja roughly by the elbow. *"In her garden there is rue."*

Luja nodded. *"I have seen it."*

"Go! Bring the leaves! Run! And bring back Bennu and Kissa! They will be helpful!"

Luja placed a steadying hand on the old man's shoulder. *"Oh, Tuta! Shendjw brought the two girls to the palace and murdered them!"*

Tuta gasped. *"Murder?"* For a moment, he looked broken. Then his features radiated anger. "We will speak of this later! Go!"

Luja clawed her way out of the shop. Then Tuta turned his attention to Ricky. *"Run to the common well. Take the pot beside my bench. Fill it with water. Go!"*

Miraculously, there was no line at the well, and Ricky returned with the water in minutes. Cessair had grown too weak to moan; her chest still rose and fell with frightening rapidity. Tuta moved to the hearth and set the clay pot on stones in the fire.

"What will you do?" Ricky asked.

Tuta retrieved a cup from near the hearth. *"Tuta will try to undo this great evil."* From a hanging sack, he removed several dried figs, tearing them into small bits in the cup. From a clay receptacle, he gathered walnuts, cracked them with his bare hands, and dropped the meat into the cup as well. He added a small amount of water and then mashed the mixture thoroughly with a stone pestle. When satisfied with his work, he knelt with the cup beside Cessair, lifted her head from the ground.

"Drink, my friend."

Ricky doubted Cessair had the strength to do so, or that she had even heard him, but then her lips moved and she choked down a bit of the concoction.

"What did you give her?"

Tuta sat holding Cessair's head even though she had stopped drinking. *"A mixture of walnuts, figs and rue is a curative for many poisons."*

"But Meryt hasn't brought the rue."

"We will add it when she does."

"Does it always work?" Ricky asked.

"Mostly. Sometimes no. It depends on the poison. How much was consumed. How long ago she drank it. And the mood of the gods."

They waited. From outside came the sound of hurried footsteps. Luja plunged through the doorway, followed by two bearded men with lighter complexions and the clothing of foreign travelers. The taller wore a grayish wrap-around tunic, belted at the waist. He carried a small pack over which he had draped a short, collarless, fur-trimmed coat. The other wore a brown, belted tunic with a hood. Luja hurried to place the rue into Tuta's hands, and he returned to the cup and pestle to add it to the antidote. The shorter stranger, a worried look on his face, knelt beside Cessair.

"What is this, my beautiful butterfly? Fintan is here. Gather strength from our reunion."

His voice did seem to give her strength, for a moment later, Cessair opened her eyes and the ghost of a smile passed upon her lips.

"My great wish is fulfilled. To see your face again. Now I need no strength."

If this man was Fintan, the father of Cessair's child, then based on Ricky's knowledge of his travels described in *Lebor Gabala Erenn*, the other was almost surely Ladra, his navigator.

Luja settled next to Ricky. "They were at the temple when I arrived. Once they told me who they were, I revealed as much as I could on the way."

Tuta wedged himself along her other side, holding the cup. *"Drink. It will taste worse than the last."*

She managed to drink several good swallows.

"She will live?" asked Fintan.

"I will follow the setting sun to the place of the dead," said Cessair, her voice almost a whisper.

Fintan stroked her cheek gently. *"Fever clouds her reason."*

"Her reason, alas, is as sharp as ever," said Tuta woefully.

"No!" cried Ricky. The world seemed to have turned upside down. She knelt beside the woman who had, in a different world, brought unthinkable tragedy into Ricky's life, tears cascading down her face, praying that Cessair would live.

Fintan shook his head. *"We must give the cure time to work!"*

Cessair moaned in a way that frightened them all and then grasped Fintan's hand with unexpected intensity and spoke.

"Listen! Know that my last thoughts will be of you! But you must keep her safe. That is my only—"

Cessair expelled a long breath and was silent. Ricky found it difficult to believe what she was seeing. The great Cessair, feared across the centuries, would-be tyrant ruler of the world, dead on the dirt floor of a poor artisan's shop.

A tear slid down Fintan's cheek. *"This cannot be!"*

Tuta pulled Luja aside and whispered into her ear. When he had finished, she darted from the shop.

"I have failed her!" cried Fintan.

"Only if you fail to keep her child from harm," said Tuta, turning to his workbench. *"Although Tuta supposes it must be your child as well."*

"I have no child," said Fintan, his wet face contorted in confusion.

Tuta turned from the workbench holding a glistening blade, knelt next to Cessair. *"That will not be so in a few moments. If Taweret, goddess of childbirth, guides my hand."*

Luja returned with a small girl, no more than six, apparently the daughter of the merchant next door. Still holding the blade, Tuta went to the girl, spoke a few words, placed something in her hand, and received a nod in reply. Then the girl was off again. He returned to Cessair, and his intentions were clear.

"I don't know if I can watch this," Ricky whispered to Luja. "I didn't think they started doing these things until...well, until Caesar. And that would be what? Like three thousand years from now?"

"There are records of babies being surgically removed from the mother centuries earlier," said Luja. "Typically, this was after the mother had died. The first record of a mother surviving such a procedure didn't occur until the sixteenth century A.D."

Tuta worked quickly. In short order, a small, bloodied form was in his gnarled hands. He sliced and tied off the cord as if he had been delivering babies for decades. The tiny creature uttered a feeble gasp and made some mewling cries. He produced a woven blanket into which the infant was placed and used a wet cloth to begin washing it. "A girl," he said simply.

"She's so small," said Ricky.

Luja nodded. "Remember that Cessair said the baby would be born in less than three cycles of the moon."

"Jesus! So the baby was less than seven months!"

"It will be a challenge for the infant to survive," said Luja as Tuta finished washing the tiny figure, rewrapped the blanket, and thrust the writhing bundle into Fintan's arms.

The small girl arrived in the doorway at this point, accompanied by a stout woman whose age was difficult to determine except to say that she was not young. An ornate kilt covered her lower half, but her full breasts were barely concealed by a thin wrap. Tuta, just now wiping the last of the blood from his hands, smiled at the woman, who was easily a foot taller than he, and stepped forward, placing an arm on her elbow. *"Beautiful Marwa! Thanks be to the gods."*

Marwa looked around the room as if it was not unusual to see a dead woman lying on the floor, her abdomen sliced open, and strangers standing or kneeling over her with anguish written on their faces. And perhaps it was not. *"Where is the child?"*

Fintan moved a step out of the shadows at this point and Marwa pushed forward, scooping the infant into her arms and moving the wrap away from one breast. Crooning a low, rhythmic song, she gently guided the infant's tiny mouth to the nipple, which, Ricky noticed, was surprisingly small, compared to the milk-engorged breast. Then the woman moved through the open doorway into Tuta's bedchamber and out of sight.

"The child will suckle and, if the gods allow, gain strength," said Tuta. *"Marwa's services are used by many. The death of a mother is not rare, and so Marwa has not been dry in twenty years!"*

The small girl from next door reappeared in Tuta's doorway. *"Soldiers from the palace are looking for the three women. They approach."* Then she disappeared.

Fintan took a step toward the door, his face full of hurt and anger.

"Are these soldiers the ones who did this?" He placed his hand on the hilt of his knife. *"They will taste my blade!"*

"There will be at least a dozen of them, and after the first tastes your blade, the rest will rip you to pieces," said Tuta. *"Then they will kill the rest of us and destroy my shop. And your daughter will die. I have a better idea. Drag the human remnants of Cessair into the bedroom and join her there yourself. Meryt and Panya as well."* As they moved into the room, Ricky saw Tuta pick up his own knife and make a four-inch cut down his calf, although not overly deep. Then he stepped into the next room and spoke quietly to Marwa.

The room contained Tuta's sleeping mat and a rumpled woven blanket, but there were also covered baskets, a covered clay basin, and an oil lamp. A tiny window up high let in a bit of light, but the room was largely bathed in shadows. When he had finished with Marwa, Tuta addressed the others.

"Press your backs against the walls, into the darkness so that you cannot be seen from the shop. And say nothing. Tuta does not wish to have Shendjw's soldiers play seker-hemat with his testicles."

"But we must avenge Cessair!" said Ladra, his voice like gravel.

"These men are not your enemy," replied Tuta levelly. *"Once I have dealt with them, we can decide what must be done."* He stepped back into the main room. The newborn was attached to Marwa's left breast and looked to be asleep. Moments later, Ricky heard footsteps—many footsteps— outside the shop and the rustling sounds of several men entering. She saw Fintan's hand move to his dagger, but he remained quiet.

"Old man!" came a voice from the other room. *"We seek enemies of Crocodile!"*

Tuta, who, based on the clinking and scraping sounds they heard, was tinkering at his workbench, replied, *"Fierce and terrifying as it is, a crocodile cannot have many enemies."*

"Withered fool!" responded the soldier. *"You are known to do business with the priestess Cessair."*

"Tuta does business with most of Tarkhan," the carver replied. *"But Tuta of course recalls the priestess well. He showers her with flattery at every opportunity, for who among us does not wish to make a favorable impression with Ma'at?"*

"We must find her!"

"She resides near the shrine on the hill above the city," said Tuta.

"Worm! The priestess has fled the palace with two others!"

It was a moment before he replied. *"The priestess's crimes against the powerful and much revered Crocodile must have been great indeed for such a search to be mounted,"* said Tuta. *"A helper of the poor, a teacher who guided all toward goodness. Little darkness seemed to weigh upon her soul."*

"It is your soul that you will need to worry about if we discover that you are harboring her."

"Tuta can assure you that he has no knowledge of where Cessair's soul might be. However, you may search here as you wish."

The soldier coughed and spat, likely not in the street. *"We do not need your permission."*

Suddenly, Marwa thrust the shriveled infant into Ricky's arms, removed her upper wrap so that she was naked from the waist up. She ambled sleepily to the doorway and yawned as she faced the outer room.

"Tuta, you scoundrel! When will you be coming back to your bed?"

"Soon, my lotus! The business of soldiers is important."

No one in the outer room said anything for several moments. Then the soldier spoke again. *"Perhaps we will look elsewhere."* After another pause, the soldier spoke again, this time his voice tinged with suspicion. *"There is blood on your floor. And it is fresh."*

Without hesitation, Tuta spoke apologetically. *"Ah, Tuta's age and clumsiness will be his undoing! Between our voyages of amorous exploration, Tuta retreated to his workbench to prepare some sliced pomegranate and radishes, foods that are well known to more quickly rekindle the fires in one's loins. As Tuta crossed the room to reach the honey jar, the blade slipped from Tuta's twisted and unreliable fingers and..."*

He paused here, and Ricky guessed he was pulling aside his wrap to reveal the cut he had deliberately placed on his leg.

Now, the soldier's voice took on a more whimsical tone. *"Perhaps after we have found these traitors and relieved them of their lives, we will return and assist Tuta in his 'amorous explorations'!"*

"If you are not of this house, be prepared to pay handsomely for the privilege," said Marwa haughtily.

"What can Tuta say?" said the old artisan. *"Marwa is devoted to me. But then, Tuta always pleases!"*

There were shuffling sounds and, in a minute, the outer shop was empty except for its owner. As the group, minus Marwa and the infant, crept cautiously back into the workshop, it was clear that Fintan had been seething the whole time.

"The one known as Crocodile did this, yes?"

"Yes," said Tuta. *"But rashness will only bring death to you. Shendjw is well protected."*

"More so than you might think," said Luja. *"He possesses a scroll that can call forth powerful magic."*

"We shall hear of this," said Tuta. *"But first we must say our final goodbyes to the priestess."*

PART THREE

THE WOMAN WHO WOULD RULE THE WORLD

CHAPTER 18

They dressed Cessair in a fine wrap that had once been worn by Tuta's wife. Tuta also contributed an ostrich feather, which he knew the priestess would have deemed appropriate. Cessair was then wrapped in linen and, as twilight deepened, Tuta shuttered his shop and secured the door with a plank. He had brought in palm fronds to cover the dirt floor and traces of blood. There had not been much, since Cessair's heart had been stopped by the time Tuta had begun his surgery, and most had been absorbed by the robe she had been wearing. As the somber group convened, only Tuta sat on the single bench in the shop. Marwa rested on Tuta's mat, facing out into the shop, cuddling the infant, which had cried little. Whether this was a good or bad sign, Ricky did not know. The two men stood near the door while Ricky and Luja knelt facing their grieving elderly friend.

The episode had brought back some memories of a year ago when Ricky and Crockett had been trapped with a group of tourists in a hitherto undiscovered tunnel beneath Newgrange passage tomb in Ireland. There, too, she had been witness to the birth of a child under extraordinary circumstances. However, in that case, the mother had survived.

In the hour since the soldiers had left, Luja and Ricky had stepped out of the shop to discuss what they must—and must not—tell the others when they were called upon to explain the circumstances that had led to Cessair's demise.

"Are we really going to tell them we're from fifty centuries in the future?" Ricky had asked. "Do the people in this time even have the context to understand something like time travel?"

"They understand magic," Luja had responded.

"We should also probably skip the part about us planning to kill Cessair," Ricky had added. Unexpected emotion welled up in her as she made this statement. An emotion that, two weeks ago, would have seemed impossible.

Now, as they all faced each other in the guttering light of the shop's oil lamps, Tuta's eyes carried a heavy sadness, but the set of his jaw was angry.

"Tuta is trying to understand. How could Shendjw do this? For years he was Cessair's teacher. Perhaps her closest friend."

"Shendjw is a powerful sorcerer," Luja replied.

"This is widely known," said Tuta. *"The Crocodile defies death. He ages not. He and Tuta were both young men at one time. Now, only one is ancient."*

This proclamation reminded Ricky of the malleability of the timeline. Cessair, Tuta, and others in this age had no memory of an elderly Shendjw. But Ricky and Luja, who had stepped into this age from elsewhere, were able to recall the elderly Tessero of their own time. Whether this would fade as additional years passed and they were fully assimilated into the new age, she did not know. Or maybe they would forever be a grain of sand on the mantle of time's oyster as the universe attempted to smooth over whatever maverick influence they might have on the world.

"Shendjw will bleed at my feet!" growled Fintan.

Tuta sadly shook his head. *"Even if the ageless king can bleed, vengeance makes a poor general. What other miracles he can perform, one may only guess."*

"Meryt is a worker of miracles as well," said Ricky, sensing a cue to reveal one of the details she and Luja had agreed upon. *"She has the gift of foresight."*

All eyes turned to Luja whose expression suggested that this abrupt transition was not quite how she had wanted to be drawn into the discussion. However, she saw now that there was no other way to proceed.

"Is this true, Meryt?" asked Tuta.

"I have such a gift," said Luja. *"And it is the true reason that Panya and I traveled to Tarkhan."*

Tuta seemed lost in thought for a moment and then pointed a finger at Ricky. *"You are the one Tuta has heard of. The woman who was bitten by the cobra. Yes! Tuta thought this to be a story of the naïve and ignorant who observed events poorly and believed what they wished to believe, for when Tuta first met you, you denied it, you carried no marks. Your health was not compromised. But now, Tuta believes the story is true! Panya and Meryt are favored and empowered by the gods!"*

Ricky said nothing.

"Foresight," grunted Fintan, turning from Tuta to Luja. *"You can see tomorrow."*

"I can see many thousands of tomorrows," said Luja.

"Yet you did not see what would happen to my Cessair."

Luja sighed wearily. *"I do not see everything. I see what the gods see fit to reveal to me. I saw the trouble between Cessair and Shendjw. And I feared where it would lead."*

"Yes, it led to Cessair's death," said Ladra angrily.

"Shendjw can also see many thousands of tomorrows," said Luja. *"He saw that Cessair would grow powerful and challenge him for supremacy. His love for power was greater than his love for her."*

"What did Shendjw see?" asked Fintan. *"In his thousand tomorrows."*

"Cessair was afraid for her child," said Luja. *"Her grandfather believes a nameless god will send a great flood. When he refused to help Cessair by giving her a place on his boat, she went to Shendjw."*

"But why should this cause Shendjw to harm Cessair?" asked Tuta.

Luja took a steadying breath. *"Great magic preserves Shendjw's youth and keeps him from harm. Crocodile feared that Cessair would attempt to steal it and use it to save herself and her child."*

"I still do not understand why this should matter so much to Shendjw," said Ladra. *"Would it not be desirable to have another who would remain young as the ages crept past? Particularly one who has long been a friend?"*

"Shendjw's foresight showed that Cessair would threaten not only his empire, but also his life," explained Luja. *"The scroll that carries the secret of eternal life also carries the secret to take it away."*

Tuta stroked his whiskered chin. *"And this is what Shendjw saw?"*

"It is," said Luja. *"And I see that Shendjw will grow more powerful and more dangerous as the years pass."*

Fintan looked from Ricky to Luja. *"And Shendjw will keep looking for both of you."*

Luja nodded.

No one spoke until Fintan turned to Ladra. *"We must think on these things."*

***

Under cover of darkness, Ricky and Luja carried Cessair north of the city to one of the cemeteries indicated by Tuta. There they met a man, Bes, with whom Tuta had made hasty, clandestine arrangements, and who directed them to an open grave. They lowered the body gently into the ground.

"This feels wrong," said Ricky, as they stood staring down at the bundle. The circumstances of one's burial were largely dictated by wealth; only wealthy Egyptians received the careful attention of embalmers, who removed organs, dried the corpse with salts for two months, filled the empty cavities with cloth or sand, and then wrapped it in strips of linen–after which it was placed in a sarcophagus and interred in a hidden tomb of stone, along with valued objects that would assist one in the next world. Those who had little or no wealth were consigned to poorly marked or unmarked graves that were no more than narrow pits in the sand. In Cessair's case, an unmarked grave was desirable, for Shendjw would not know with certainty whether his poison had succeeded.

As Luja reflected on the white bundle, which looked so small in its inglorious resting place, she expressed her agreement. "The woman who would rule the world, buried in an unmarked grave."

There was more to it. Ricky tried to put it into words. "I felt different than I expected bringing Cessair here. Jesus, she tried to kill me. More than once. Her people killed my grandmother. It's crazy, but...I feel heavy. Like I've lost someone important."

"I, too, must admit to feelings I did not expect."

They were silent for a bit.

"Is the future changed?" asked Ricky. "Since Cessair will never become a powerful woman, create an empire and inspire a cult, everything should be different, right?"

"How can we know?" Luja responded.

"What do you believe?"

Luja thought several moments before answering. "I believe that there can be changes. But nature being what nature is, the timeline will try to heal itself. We've spoken of this already."

"The self-healing timeline."

"If this is how the universe works its magic, it may restore itself to as close as it can come to its original state. Like bark growing over the area of a removed tree branch until, years later, the shape of the tree appears little different.”

“So what we did, it’s all for nothing?”

“Consider this. In the original timeline, Cessair made herself immortal, but then the scroll was stolen from her and hidden. Cessair could not begin building her empire until she controlled the scroll, for if she emerged too soon, an enemy who might come into possession of the scroll’s secrets could destroy her.”

Ricky saw what Luja was getting at. “But Shendjw doesn’t have to worry. He’s immortal and he has the scroll. No one can stop him.”

“Not exactly,” said Luja. “With Cessair dead, Shendjw will believe himself invincible and untouchable because he will believe no one else will know what is written on the scroll.”

Ricky understood. “But you do!”

“Yes. If we can work the counter-spell on Shendjw, we can make him mortal,” said Luja.

“And then he’ll die with the next sunrise.”

Luja nodded. “But if we fail, the future could be worse, for with no one to stop him and no one to fear, Shendjw can begin building an empire not five thousand years from now, but tomorrow!”

Ricky shuddered. Under those circumstances, what the world might look like fifty centuries from now, she did not care to imagine.

Seeing that Bes waited, they decided to end their reflections. Ricky stood above the grave one final time. She uttered a farewell in the ancient language.

“Peace, finally, to one who will be missed.”

***

It was not an especially long walk back from the cemetery, but the skies were clear and the night warm. Moonlight fractured itself upon the surface of the Nile. Ricky was reminded of a similar evening in twentieth century Cairo a year ago when she, Crockett, Dr. Campion, Leo Brenner, and Cessair —in her Rio Armstrong persona—had dined at a restaurant along the river. Afterwards, she and Crockett had taken a walk. And argued. God, she wished she could argue with that stupid hick again. His Carolina drawl had irritated her when they had first met; now, she would give anything to hear it.

Was it possible that they had done enough already so that, five thousand years in the future, Crockett had not been pushed out of a helicopter?

It was maddening to know that they could only speculate on this.

After walking in silence for a spell, Ricky spoke softly. "Tuta and the rest did not seem surprised to hear that you could look into the future."

"Belief in magic is the way of Egypt," said Luja. "And in Tarkhan, they've seen evidence of it. Their king hasn't aged in forty years."

"The timeline smoothing things over," said Ricky.

"But...things are still not right. I can feel it. Part of it is the scroll. Until that's resolved, the future may remain unsettled, or even unchanged entirely. We must find a way to get it."

"Why?" asked Ricky. "We already know how to reverse-curse Shendjw."

"If Shendjw dies and the scroll still exists, the danger to the world remains. One of his subordinates could come into possession of it, realize its awful potential, and become a tyrant as terrible as the Crocodile.

"Shit."

"And...there is something else. Fintan and Ladra."

"According to the legend, they were on the side of the good guys," recalled Ricky.

"Yes," agreed Luja, "but I am sensing something... unexpected. Something that makes me uneasy."

"What?"

Luja shook her head. "It is unclear. It is not evil, just… chaotic."

Ricky sighed. "Yeah, chaotic is not particularly comforting."

"My senses rarely give me specific messages," said Luja. "But they're never wrong."

"After the terrible battles we waged a year ago, I just have a hard time accepting it. Of believing it. That Cessair is dead." She wiped at her eye.

"It cannot be undone. The scroll has the ability to grant immortality, but not to restore life."

"And…aarrgh! It's like a year ago all over again, just like in Ireland! We've got to find a way to get close to this power-crazed psycho, make him mortal, and keep him from taking over the world."

"I hesitate to bring this up, but what if Shendjw has performed the scroll's life ritual on himself a second time? If he has done that, then he is forever immortal. Even the power of the counter-ritual cannot hurt him."

"No," said Ricky. "Shendjw will never do that."

"What makes you so certain?"

"Something he said back in our time when he was using the Tessero name. He went on this big rant about how awful it would be to truly exist forever. I think the idea scares the hell out of him. The scroll gives him an escape hatch."

"At which time he may face eternal judgment."

"What was it Tessero said? He talked about how Cessair hadn't thought it all through. The long-term consequences. Something about meeting one's maker with blood on your hands is better than immortality that can't be undone. He wasn't selling us on the project at that point. That was something that just came out. Like maybe he's terrified of irreversible immortality."

"If you're right, that gives us a tiny bit of hope."

Ricky raised her hands to the wide universe. "Why? Why? I feel like goddamn Sisyphus. I push the damn boulder up the hill last year, then the gods knock it out of my hands and tell me I have to push an even bigger boulder! I wish I could go back in time to..."

"To the time before this all began? When you were a frightened mouse sitting alone in the dark in front of a computer screen playing games of no consequence?"

Ricky said nothing to this.

"Perhaps this is not the curse you think it is," Luja continued. "When the map came into your life, you emerged from seclusion. You found things in the real world that mattered more than the virtual world. People that mattered. And you found purpose."

"But Sasha died," said Ricky, her voice thick with emotion. "Crockett died. They all died."

"It is both the blessing and the curse of mortality that we will love others and ultimately lose them," said Luja. "The weight of none of those deaths falls upon your soul. Great evil took them from the world. I believe you are better for having known and loved others. You have changed because of them. You are no longer the mouse. You have become the lion. And where, before, you were inconsequential, you may now be the most important person in the world."

Ricky chuckled humorlessly. "Shit. I think you just activated my Imposter Syndrome."

"You are no imposter. You will succeed."

"But how?"

"When we return to Tuta's shop, we will speak with the others. All are threatened by Crocodile. Together, we will rid the world of this evil."

"But how?" Ricky asked again.

This question went unanswered, and the walk grew quiet as they re-entered the city and made their way back to Tuta's shop.

CHAPTER 19

The craftsman sat at this bench, partially illuminated by the guttering oil lamp. Otherwise, the workshop was empty.

"It is done," said Luja.

Tuta nodded.

"The others are asleep?" asked Ricky.

Tuta made a tired motion with his head toward the other room. *"Fintan is asleep."*

Ricky stiffened. *"Where are the others?"*

"Gone," said Fintan, who was not asleep after all, and now stood in the doorway to the back room. *"The danger to the child was too great for them to remain."*

"Where?" asked Ricky.

"They travel north tonight with Ladra, the faithful and faultless navigator. Tomorrow, they will board a boat."

"Ladra has the baby?" asked Ricky, trying to process this unexpected turn.

"Ladra fends for them all," said Fintan. *"Marwa accompanies him to care for the infant. Another woman travels with them as well."*

"Marwa's sister," said Tuta. *"And all of my debens!"*

Ricky glared at Fintan, astonished. *"So you're the only one left."*

"The child must be protected. She is my daughter. And it was Cessair's final request."

Ricky shook her head. While the infant and Marwa needed protection, she had assumed Ladra would be able to help in finding the scroll and outwitting Shendjw.

"Where did you send them?" asked Luja, but Ricky guessed she already knew the answer.

"A distant island in the north," replied Fintan.

Ricky met Luja's gaze. "Ireland!"

"It is likely that Shendjw believes the child died with Cessair," said Luja.

"But he will continue to pursue both of you," said Tuta wearily. *"Until your bones lie crushed beneath his sandals, Shendjw will not relent."*

"What a delightful thought," said Ricky.

"No, it is a terrible thought," said Tuta, horrified. *"And he will use every means of excruciating torture to assure himself that your words ring true, that Cessair and her child are truly dead."*

"Which means we must stop Shendjw," said Luja.

"Yes," agreed Fintan. *"To avenge Cessair."*

"Crocodile cannot be stopped," said Tuta. *"He lives forever."*

"There is an enchantment that will restore Shendhw's mortality," said Luja. *"We must find a way to use this against him. And he possesses a scroll upon which the magic is inscribed. This we must also find—and destroy, so that no other may repeat his evil."*

Tuta raised a clenched fist. *"I would speak the enchantment myself and then choke him upon his own testicles to avenge Bennu and Kissa."*

Ricky and Luja had not spoken to any of them of Bennu and Kissa's betrayal of Cessair. They had decided such a disclosure might do more harm than good, for it might lead to revelations about their own roles as would-be assassins.

"I will battle any mortal enemy," growled Fintan. *"But magic is not intended for mortals. Do we dare challenge the powers of the gods?"*

"Shendjw is no god," Luja responded. *"He has insulted the gods by stealing secrets never meant for humans."*

"If what you say is true, Shendjw will have hidden this scroll in a place where it can be fiercely protected," said Tuta. *"And where none would think to look."*

"When we met Shendjw in the palace, there were many guards," said Luja. *"But where the scroll is hidden no guards are needed."*

"You know its location?" asked Tuta incredulously.

"We believe so," said Ricky.

"In the palace, Shendjw has a pool filled with crocodiles," explained Luja. *"A column rises out of its middle, and atop it, a stone chest."*

"It's almost like he's daring his enemies to try and get it," said Ricky.

"And there are guards at the entrance to the palace that must be overcome," noted Tuta.

"And also inside, as one passes from chamber to chamber," added Luja.

Finton ran his fingers over his chin. *"So one must defeat several groups of guards, a crocodile, swim to the middle of a pool and scale a tower."*

"Not a crocodile," Ricky corrected. *"At least forty."*

The hope seemed to drain from Fintan. *"Forty crocodiles! There are not nearly enough of us!"*

"What else do you know of the palace?" asked Tuta.

"There are two chambers that lead off the throne room," explained Ricky. *"On the right, the royal chambers. Behind the door on the left, the crocodile pool."*

"If Tuta recalls correctly, you mentioned your escape was off the balcony. Could the throne room or pool be reached from this direction?"

"The balcony is too high," replied Luja, recalling her long drop into the Nile.

"What else can you tell?"

"Shendjw wishes to intimidate visitors," said Luja. She described the hanging crocodiles on each side of the throne.

"You are certain the scroll is in the pool room?" asked Tuta.

"How certain can one be of anything when one is dealing with a wicked deceiver like Shendjw?" asked Luja. *"Yet there seems to be no other purpose for the stone box on the pillar. Or for turning the pool, which was once a pleasant bath, into a crocodile pit."*

"There is another thing," said Ricky. *"When we stood on the balcony and mentioned the scroll, Shendjw's eyes went to the pool, just for an instant."*

Fintan regarded her gravely. *"If Crocodile is as clever as you have suggested, he may have done this intentionally to deceive you."*

"You could be wrong," agreed Tuta, addressing the two women. *"Builders in the Two Lands put many things on pillars. A pity to waste your lives on mere supposition."*

"All lives in all futures will be wasted if we do nothing," said Luja.

"Even if you are correct, the palace's defenses are no easier to pierce," said Fintan. *"If I had Ladra and my men, the palace guards would enjoy the points of our spears."*

"But you are without them, and so if we are to pursue this course, we must find another way to breach those walls," said Tuta.

"We?" Ricky laughed. *"Does this mean Tuta has decided to risk his life to avenge Cessair?"*

"As little wick remains in the candle that is Tuta, it is a small risk," said the old man. *"And even if Tuta does nothing, he is already endangered. How long before Shendjw realizes Tuta's role in his deception? Better to poke a pointed stick at one's enemies than to let the enemies spill all of the blood."*

"But this is not the time to scheme," said Luja. *"Our minds are clouded from emotion and lack of sleep. In a few hours, the sun will rise. Let us sleep now, and in the morning, with our wits sharpened by rest, make plans."*

***

"We must hunt a crocodile," Tuta proclaimed the following morning. *"A large one. A giant, if possible. A true monster will help us reach the scroll."*

"Agreed," said Luja. *"Shendjw uses the preserved beasts as fearsome reminders of his power. A giant would most certainly excite his interest."*

Ricky rubbed the sleep out of her bleary eyes. *"Are you all insane?"*

"We cannot defeat Shendjw's soldiers," said Luja reasonably. *"The palace walls are impregnable and closely guarded. This limits the methods that we might use to gain entry."*

"We could build a hang glider," grunted Ricky to Luja. "They're not guarding the roof. And that sounds a helluva lot safer than hunting crocodiles."

"We have neither the knowledge to build such a craft nor the experience to safely pilot it from the surrounding limestone cliffs. Attempting to land on the roof of the palace would be suicide."

Ricky laughed humorlessly. "Funny. I was thinking trying to catch a croc was suicide."

"It will be dangerous," admitted Luja, "but our chances of success are greater than is our chance of inventing the airplane." She returned her attention to the others, smiled contritely, and spoke in the old language. *"Please forgive us. Talk of crocodiles is... upsetting."*

"But talk of them we must," said Tuta. *"We will go south of the city to a shallows along the river where the creatures feed and sun themselves. We must travel stealthily. It is daylight and Shendjw's soldiers are about."*

Knowing that more talk would only allow doubt to flourish, they gathered the necessary supplies and set out. An hour later, the four found themselves south of the mud huts where Ricky and Luja had first awakened in a new age. Fintan carried two long poles, while a foul-smelling sack filled with the entrails of a freshly butchered goat was slung over Tuta's shoulder.

"The more detestable it is, the more they will like it," said Tuta, smiling as he hobbled along.

The Nile flowed wide with occasional groves of date palms along the banks. The terrain was rocky and uneven, yet a path was discernible. The rooftop of even the palace was soon lost behind them and Ricky felt less anxious about Shendjw's soldiers. However, her concerns about what lay ahead grew exponentially.

They drank water from bladders that each carried and occasionally gnawed on flatbread that Tuta had made them tuck into their robes that morning. The sun scorched the life out of everything as the shadows disappeared. Then the trail angled toward the river and Ricky grew more alert.

"Ah!" said Tuta as they drew closer. *"Seven. No, nine sunning themselves! Sleeping babies!"*

Well, shit, thought Ricky. And then, *Shit! Shit! Shit!* Egyptians revered the crocodile, as evidenced in their art and their inclusion in myth, but they also feared them greatly, and it was no secret why. Families like the reed cutter Min's suffered frequent reminders of their lethal ferocity. And Bennu and Kissa's cries would forever echo in her ears. She imagined the pain even she would feel as the beast's powerful jaws clamped shut upon an arm or leg and rolled her over and over beneath the green waters, the horror of being trapped below the surface, perhaps unable to rescue herself. Would she remain conscious under such circumstances, choking ceaseless on muddy water that filled her lungs? Luja noticed her discomfort.

"It will be all right. Tuta and Fintan have lived in this time period and know its dangers well. They will be careful."

Ricky snorted derisively, remembering that Tessero had pointed out the average life expectancy for men in this time was only twenty-five years. Thinking of Tessero made her wonder: Now that Shendjw had been made immortal as a young man, that meant some things in the distant future were surely changed. It was too tempting to not think of what form these changes might take. Would Shendjw still use the Tessero name fifty centuries from now? With Cessair dead, was Crockett now alive? And with no immortal competitor to fear, had Shendjw transformed the world into a dystopian hell? Or would the self-healing timeline that Luja frequently spoke of reveal a world virtually unchanged from the one they had left—no matter what the outcome of their efforts to stop the corrupt sorcerer? When she had questioned the need to battle Cessair in the twenty-first century, she had been able to gain an answer by confirming the powers of the scroll. It was legit, and so Cessair had to be defeated. She had no such test she could administer here in Predynastic Egypt to determine the exigency of challenging the immortal Shendjw. Win or lose, they would never know what transpired in the centuries ahead.

As they approached the shore, five of the basking crocodiles made a slow retreat into the river. One of those that remained was significantly larger than the others.

A damn monster!

"If I believed in the gods of the Two Lands, I would believe that this is one of them, unleashed upon the world!" said Tuta, his voice full of awe.

"That is the one!" exclaimed Fintan, tossing his two poles to the ground and fashioning a rope loop at the end of each.

"He will definitely get Shendjw's attention," added Luja.

Ricky felt her stomach go queasy. *"He's got my attention."*

"Now listen carefully," said Tuta, heaving the bag off his shoulder and onto the ground. *"Tuta will lure the brute by throwing a few scraps in his direction. Once he comes away from the water and is separated from the others, Luja and Fintan can slip a rope loop around the crawling mountain's neck, one on each side."*

"What will I do?" asked Ricky.

"As Meryt and Fintan work to subdue the mountain, you will toss some of the entrails to the remaining demons on the left. Tuta will do the right. Toss it toward the water or off to the side so that they move farther away from Fintan and Luja."

Tuta then hoisted the bag a few feet toward the river, reached inside and brought forth a handful of stinking meat and guts. He heaved this toward the giant who, without a sound, lurched forward to gulp it down like a linebacker inhaling sushi. Then, before Tuta could react, the beast vaulted ahead with deer-like speed, swallowing the entire bag whole. Whether from surprise or contact, Tuta fell onto his backside, just a few feet from the croc who, having dispensed with the hors d'oeuvres, eyed the old man as the main course. Lying on his back, partially propped on an elbow, there was no way Tuta could escape. A single, reluctant thought flashed into Ricky's mind.

Well, shit. Only one of us is immortal.

Before the croc could open its jaws again, she dived over the old man's head and landed on the croc's snout, looking directly into its eyes. Somewhere, she recalled reading that the muscles that closed a croc's jaws were far stronger than those that opened them. Or was it alligators? She clamped her arms around the snout and clasped her hands in a vice grip underneath, as if giving a dinosaur a bear hug. The monster attempted to open its mouth. Instead, it let out a snort that reminded Ricky of the snuffling of a horse. But her grip just held.

Damn! Thought Ricky, both repulsed by where she was and pleased that her plan appeared to have worked. She heard the scrape of Tuta's elbows, hips, and sandals against the ground as he scrambled away, and the shouts of the others, but she could not make out exact words. She also realized that, with her clinging to the beast's snout as she was, they could not loop the ropes around its head.

Then the nightmare got worse.

The monster tried to lift its head, then thrashed it savagely from side to side, causing Ricky to nearly lose her grip. It thrashed again, then tried to use its stubby front legs to claw at her. Ricky cried out, but the croc was unable to muster the leverage necessary to do much damage. It immediately executed a barrel roll, twisting itself as it turned, slamming Ricky against the ground. Still she held, although she felt herself slipping.

If I let go, it'll be on me in a second!

She wondered whether the others would try to jump onto the body of the giant and attempt to bind it. As she caught bits of activity with her peripheral vision, she saw Luja and Fintan using the long poles to try and keep the other crocs from joining the mayhem. If they failed, Ricky knew she would find herself in the midst of a feeding frenzy. The croc rolled again, demonstrating the agility of an Olympic gymnast. *Can't hold on much longer!*

Fintan and Luja were both some distance from her now, and she felt her grip loosening again. The monster, seemingly frustrated with its lack of success, rose up on its squat legs and began backing toward the river. This sent a renewed stab of panic through Ricky, as her grim imaginings of being pulled underwater returned.

"No!" she wailed.

The croc ignored her cries of distress, was perhaps encouraged by them, and seemed to pick up speed. Once in the Nile, Ricky knew no one would be able to help her.

She felt a spray as the croc's tail slapped the water, and she cried out again, even louder.

"No!"

And then, the croc did stop. She readjusted her grip, waiting for it to start again, but the beast merely sat there. Ricky noticed that its jaws no longer flexed, its legs had relaxed, and in fact, it felt like it had fallen asleep. Yet she was reluctant to release her grip. What if the croc was trying to trick her? She wondered whether such creatures were capable of that sort of subterfuge.

A moment later, Luja was helping her up.

"Come! We must get it away from the water before the other monsters come again!"

Fintan had a grip under one of the beast's front legs and Luja grasped the other. Ricky joined in beside her.

"What happened?"

"It is asleep."

"How?"

Tuta shuffled over to the two, dusting himself off. *"The goat entrails were laced with herbs and shoots Tuta had prepared for the purpose of soothing the creature into a state of endless sleep. It required a few minutes to take effect."*

Ricky required several seconds to suppress her anger before she could speak. *"Why didn't you tell me this beforehand?"*

Tuta grinned sheepishly. *"On a creature so big? Tuta was not sure it would work!"*

CHAPTER 20

With bare hands, the men and women of antiquity built edifices that still stand after millennia. The Dolmen of Menga in Spain, Newgrange Passage Tomb in Ireland, the Gigantija—translation: giantess—on the Island of Gozo in Malta, the Tumulus of St. Michel in France, the Tower of Jericho on the West Bank, the Gobekli Tepe in Turkey. Each of these buildings, groups of buildings, or monuments stands today after at least five thousand years. There are some whose ages approach twice that.

The great skyscrapers of the twentieth and twenty-first centuries were built not with bare hands, but with massive and powerful steam and diesel and electric machines that pushed them to miraculous heights. But does anyone expect the Empire State Building or the Shanghai Tower to survive even a single millennium?

Of course, not every great building from antiquity has survived, and it has not been monsters, but rather bare hands that erased them and muddied the waters of history. The great capital of Egypt was once Memphis, a revered city of white walls and impressive buildings, fitting for overseeing one of the world's most powerful and advanced civilizations. Then the Romans arrived, and with their victories, moved the Egyptian capital to Alexandria. The stones from buildings and monuments in Memphis were carried away to create new buildings in the new capital. Where once stood formidable edifices in the old capital, now stood a barren landscape.

So it would be with Tarkhan.

When the usefulness of the necropolis was exhausted, the city would slowly die. The palace of Shendjw, a stone fortress, would be no match for the bare hands that would arrive to carry away its already quarried and cut stones to become someone else's fortress. Eventually, nothing would remain to attest to the fact that a great king had enjoyed vibrant gardens, sparkling pools, pillowed comforts, and the fear of his subjects, all within the high walls that rose beside the Nile.

And while bare hands would ultimately level the palace of Crocodile, there was some irony in considering that bare hands were useless against the palace walls that must be breached by Ricky, Luja and the others. At more than thirty feet in height, they could not be surmounted by ladder. Guards were posted at both entry points and upon raised, stone watch platforms at each of the four corners. Torches illuminated the ground around the palace's outer walls at night, spoiling any thoughts of an assault under cover of darkness. Inside were more guards at each junction.

An army might be able to initiate a sudden attack on the palace and, by virtue of far greater numbers, overcome Crocodile's defenses. They could then break through the heavy entry door, where they would confront more soldiers. It is likely they would sustain heavy losses, but if their numbers were sufficient, they could prevail and gain access to the palace interior and whatever secrets it held.

But what chance was there for an army composed of a grieving explorer, an old artisan, a fortune teller, and a one-eyed woman?

CHAPTER 21

Crocodiles hung upside down, suspended from ropes, twelve on one side of Shendjw's throne, thirteen on the other. The throne room was dark at this hour and, like the surrounding city, tomb quiet. The sound of the wind and the lapping of the Nile against its western shore wafted in from outside. Three small oil lamps lit the areas around the three guards who, at this hour, remained on watch. Each guard could see the other two, and so if one encountered trouble, an alarm would be sent up by the others. This would bring reinforcements in seconds. But with additional guards on night duty outside the castle and at the entrance to the throne room, what intruder would have a chance of making it this far?

One guard stood outside the closed door leading to the Royal Chamber of Shendjw. This was a reasonable precaution, for he could otherwise be surprised in his sleep and taken captive, immortality notwithstanding. The occult ritual had granted him no superpowers aside from subtracting death from the burdens that he, as a human, must otherwise carry.

A second guard stood all the way across the wide room outside the closed door to the terrible pool. Having eyes on both sides of the room and at its entrance door—which was where the third guard stood—afforded Shendjw's defenses a view of the entire floor area. The lamplight did struggle to illuminate the middle of the room in front of the throne platform, although the outline of the throne itself was visible, and its polished surface would frequently reflect a flicker from one of the lamps. No light reached the high ceiling above the gruesome trophies. But what of that? No invader could swoop in from the skies.

In that darkness, one of the hanging crocodiles moved.

The knife she carried was razor sharp and easily sliced through the stitches that closed the incisions Tuta had made after removing the croc's guts and having Ricky climb inside. They had all agreed—Ricky reluctantly—that she had the only chance of surviving being sewn into the dead creature. She was also the smallest among them, aside from Tuta, who was not a good candidate for what would need to be done. And so there had been little discussion, for it appeared to be their only chance of getting someone into the palace.

"Tuta has an acquaintance who has dealt crocodiles to the palace," the old man had told them as they had dragged the enormous creature back to Tarkhan, lashed to Fintan's poles. *"When he presents this giant, they will not refuse."*

And so she had been sewn into darkness, like being sealed into a tight-fitting body bag. Then there were periods of waiting and being carried, and jostled, and muffled conversations, and eventually being lifted into the air.

And more waiting.

Now the wait was over.

Breathing cool, fresh air for the first time in two days was such a pleasure and relief that Ricky had to exercise care not to suck in her first breaths too loudly. She sliced away several additional stitches. Too many and her weight would rip out the rest and she would plummet to the floor, where the soldiers would make her their prisoner. She recalled Mr. Fathi's nauseating description of torture on a sharpened stake. Now more than ever, she had no desire to experience this aspect of the ancient culture. Now more than ever, she wished to avenge an unexpected friend.

Carefully, she worked her head and right arm out of the opening in the croc's abdomen. Moving quickly was unimportant. Silence was paramount. The river and breeze would conceal some sounds of movement. And because the soldiers stood near their lamps, it would take their eyes some time to adjust if they felt the need to investigate the darkness near the ceiling. Ricky's goal was to give them no reason to.

A hook had been inserted into the lizard to catch its ilium, part of the pelvis. A taut rope extended from this to a rafter configuration near the ceiling. Ricky slowly pushed herself farther out of the giant, using the rope now with both hands to make progress inch by inch. She paused frequently to check on the guards, but they stood as silent and still as statues.

Despite her cautious efforts, her croc swayed slightly from side to side. Ricky hoped they would not notice. Slowly she slid her body out of the carcass until she could partially support her weight on the croc's pelvis. She had stripped to only her essentials in order to be packed into the croc. This meant a light, tan smock. As the cooler air brought out goosebumps on her body, she smiled, again recalling Crockett's long-ago joke about going commando. Her dark wig was gone, too, and her shoulder-length hair had grown out enough for the red to be noticeable. Since red hair was somewhat rare in ancient Egypt and often associated with the deity Set, Ricky wondered whether its seemingly sudden appearance would give her some leverage if she was discovered. Set was, after all, the god of storms, chaos, and violence. Whether or not this cosmetic oddity would provide an advantage, it seemed to her that Set possessed the appropriate qualities to be her patron deity.

After resting for several minutes, she moved both hands up the rope and gripped hard in preparation for the climb just a few feet to the ceiling. As she pulled herself off the croc, the thin knife that had been tucked into the hemp belt encircling her waist slipped free. She stifled a gasp and pinched shut her eyes. A moment later, the knife clattered onto the stone floor.

Ricky opened her eyes, her mind racing to scheme a way out of this dilemma. She could think of nothing. If she jumped to the floor, even if she avoided temporary injury, the guards would have her easily. And if she frantically continued her climb, she would be discovered and find herself trapped on the roof of the palace. She closed her eyes again, attempted to slow her breathing and to steady the rope and croc as best she could.

From the sound of things, at least two of the guards were cautiously making their way toward the center. Any moment, Ricky expected to hear the shouts of alarm and to be forced from her perch, but their progress seemed to take an eternity. Then, from directly below, one of them kicked the knife and sent it skidding a foot or two. After another pause, she heard laughter.

"The sloppy mud-breather who gutted and stuffed the new demon left his knife in the stitches!"

The other guard laughed. *"A nice one, too. Too bad for him!"*

"No smarter than the sheep they sleep with," said the first.

Then each man ambled back toward his post.

They couldn't see me. It was too dark near the roof.

She wasted no time, knowing that the two returning guards would provide a visual distraction for the third, and that their movement would camouflage any small sounds she might make. As they walked, she carefully worked her way up the rope to the rafters, pulling herself on top and then resting uncomfortably on her stomach. After a moment she was on the move in the dark, carefully crossing to the roof vents that allowed breezes to cool the throne room on blisteringly hot days.

In seconds, she lay on the flat roof, panting.

After allowing herself to recover for several minutes, she stood, crouching, cautious. She noticed that people must occasionally use the roof during daylight hours either to surveil the city or to take a break from the repressive routines below. She saw the rinds of fruit or melons and an empty, discarded animal bladder that might have contained water, beer, wine, or tisanes—not tea proper, but brewed herbs laced with ephedra. It was possible that palace guards or servants snuck to the roof to consume some of these the way people in the twenty-first century slipped out to balconies, rooftops, or alleys to grab a cigarette, smoke a joint, or do a line of coke.

After satisfying herself that she was alone and unobserved, Ricky strode lightly to the northeast corner of the building. The roof did not cover this area, and the space below was cloaked in shadow. Just enough ambient light, most of it supplied by stars, allowed her to see a ripple in the pool's surface.

The smell wafting out of the darkness below brought back the awful memories of three days earlier. The stench had a fishy, animal quality to it. And something rotten, like spoiled meat. She tried to push away memories of the horrors she had witnessed.

Sick bastard.

She stared into the opening, waiting for her pupil to dilate more fully, waiting to see more. Finally, she detected movement. Her ears caught it, too. Something heavy sliding over stone. Then more movement and the faint glint of starlight reflected off eyes in the dark.

Golden eyes. At least a dozen pairs.

She wondered if they could see her. Maybe they had smelled her.

Or maybe they could sense her fear.

She settled onto her stomach and remained perfectly still. As the minutes ticked by, more details of the dark hell below revealed themselves. Her observations confirmed that the pool was round with several concentric steps leading down to the water and continuing beneath the surface, giving the pool a deep center. From this center the stone island arose, upon which sat the round pillar, taller than a person. At the top, a rectangular stone chest. From her rooftop vantage point, she could see a figure carved into the top of the chest, a figure that had not been visible to her on the balcony. An ankh, the Egyptian symbol for life, death, and immortality.

There was no doubt. The scroll was on an island guarded by crocs.

She surveyed the scene more carefully. Most of the crocodiles rested on the stone tiles surrounding the pool. Only a few crocs floated in the dark water. Had she missed anything? Once she felt confident, she could put her plan into action.

Perhaps "Once she felt confident" was an inappropriate phrase. Perhaps "Once she had seen all the potential horrors that must be avoided."

Fintan, Luja, Tuta, and she had discussed and discarded various plans which might be employed after she reached the roof. They had agreed that there seemed to be no way for one to reach the island from the edge of the pool without encountering crocodiles. And crocs would easily be able to pull someone off the narrow island ledge surrounding the pillar. Of course, the pool, the island ledge, and the crocs could be avoided by leaping onto the top of the pillar. She calculated that one only needed to be a world-class long jumper to cover that distance from the roof edge. And a world-class gymnast to stick the landing atop the pillar. And immortal to survive any injuries incurred by the fifteen-foot fall from the rooftop onto the column of stone. *At least I've got the immortality thing nailed,* she had thought. They had also confronted the problem of egress. After grabbing the scroll, how would she escape? The door into the throne room was secured. The only way out was through the open roof. They had spent hours discarding one impossible plan after the other. And then, they had settled on one that was barely possible.

Ricky pushed herself to her feet, returned to the vent opening she had crawled through. The throne room below was as silent and dark as before. Leaning down through the opening, she was just able to reach one of the ropes woven from papyrus leaves that held one of the crocs. Because this one was much older and smaller than the croc she had hidden inside, it had dried to a point where it was also lighter. However, it was still like pulling a sack of wet flour toward the roof. She pulled slowly, due both to the difficulty and her desire not to alert the soldiers in the throne room. Once again, she was grateful they could see nothing near the ceiling. Sweat drenched her by the time she pulled the croc carcass onto the rooftop.

Due to the loss of her knife, it took some time for Ricky, hanging over the opening, to unfasten the rope from its ceiling hook. Then she went to work detaching it from the crock itself. When this was accomplished, she unwound the many coils of hemp belt from around her smock and added this length to the papyrus leaf rope. Finishing quickly, she carried her trophies back to the opening over the pool.

For the plan to have any chance at working, she needed two things: a rope and a distraction. Ricky now hoped she possessed both.

She did not stop to rest or think about what she was doing. This would have only raised more serious doubts about her current path. Instead, she secured one end of her borrowed rope to a hole in the low, decorative parapet and tossed the remainder into the pool room. Then, because she had no knife, she gashed her arm against the stone wall and, wincing in pain, rubbed the blood on the croc carcass. However, the wound healed quickly, and so she had to do it twice more.

Despite the simplicity of the plan, it required precise timing —and luck. She would toss the carcass into the far end of the pool, which would hopefully distract the crocs and perhaps, because of the blood, make them think that an early breakfast had arrived. The fact that it was croc would make no difference. Tuta had explained that crocodiles were known to eat other crocs, that they harbored no taboos against cannibalism. She would then sprint back to the rope, shimmy down to the floor, quickly swim to the island while the crocs were moving toward the other end—it was only twenty feet or so—climb the pillar, grab the scroll, descend, swim, back up the rope, and then another leap into the Nile to escape the palace. This time from nearly double the height.

What could go wrong?

In truth, she had already calculated a lengthy list of things that could go wrong. And each of the many variables on that list was complicated by the fact that she had heard that crocs were smart. Some would even set out twigs as bait to catch birds who were looking for nest building material. If these crocs outsmarted her, or if something else went wrong with her plan, she could scarcely imagine a worse way to die.

Correction. She would not die. And that might make it a thousand times worse.

Ricky picked up the carcass, hauled it along the opening to the far end of the pool, held it over the edge and whispered. "Hey! Pretty boys! You hungry? Come and get it!"

She tossed the old croc down the opening and it splashed unceremoniously. Almost immediately, there was movement. Pretty soon, dozens of dark forms were moving toward the decoy.

Ricky wasted no time in congratulating herself. She was on the move too, sliding down the rope in an instant, wading into the croc-free end of the pool to the island. She pulled herself onto the narrow edge and assessed the column. While the stone had been polished, figures and images had been cut into it that afforded her the kinds of wedges and footholds that would accommodate rock climbers. She climbed. The chest at the top had no locking mechanism. *Why would it need one? Who would ever get past an army of hungry crocodiles? Who would be foolish enough to even try?* All that remained was grabbing the scroll and making her getaway. Ricky pried off the lid and tossed it into the pool. She squinted into the dark enclosure.

Empty.

No!

She ran her hand over the inside of the box to make sure. Perhaps there was a secret door. But she found nothing.

There was no time to search elsewhere and nowhere to search. Ricky slid down to the ledge and something heavy slammed into her left leg. The crocs were back. No time to think. Only time to leap into the pool, flail, punch, make it back to the other side. Try to get to the rope. The missing scroll was a puzzle for another moment.

She felt the first bite but wriggled away. A second on her other side was more painful, but again, the creature had not gotten enough of her for a good hold. She found the steps, started crawling up, kicked away another croc. But now one came fast from her blind side. A second followed it. She felt the excruciating pain of jaws closing on the left leg and the beast began pulling her back into deeper water. She twisted, kicked, cried out.

Then there was nothing.

CHAPTER 22

It was well past midnight. If Luja had been required to guess, she would have said one o'clock in the morning as time was measured in the twenty-first century, but she had no way of knowing. She knew that Ricky had been gone a long time, and each minute had been torture.

Almost two days ago, they had sewn her inside the crocodile carcass. Then Tuta had made arrangements with a vendor. Word had come that the croc had been eagerly procured for display in Shendjw's throne room.

Then the waiting had begun.

She had not slept well the previous night, imagining the hell that Ricky endured inside the croc. Tonight, she and Tuta were awake by design. They anticipated that Ricky would arrive at the shop some time before sunrise.

With the scroll.

Unless something went wrong. And there were a thousand things that could go wrong.

Luja had disliked the plan from its inception. But they had come up with no others. Perhaps there existed a better, safer way to secure the scroll, but any such plans would likely require weeks or more to evolve. They did not possess that luxury of time. Shendjw's soldiers were looking for them. The noose would tighten quickly. Consequently, they needed to strike even more rapidly.

A single lamp near Tuta's workbench offered a flame that would be barely visible from outside. The gnarled artisan sat on a bench, carving a bit of ivory. Luja sat on the floor with her back against the opposite wall, her eyes closed. They had not spoken for two hours. Tuta broke the silence.

"Tuta's existence previously allowed for more naps."

"Previously?"

"In the days before the coming of the scribe and her one-eyed attendant."

Luja smiled. *"We brought much tumult into your life, good Tuta. We beg your forgiveness."*

"You shall not have it!" exclaimed Tuta. *"When one has nothing to look forward to except sleep, death may be preferable. When you and the other are gone, Tuta shall miss the chaos that defined his hours. And reminded him that he was alive."*

"You could come with us," suggested Luja.

Tuta raised a hand in protest. *"Like an image carved on the palace walls, Tuta has become a part of the scenery in Tarkhan. The shock to the city would be too great if Tuta's bench was suddenly empty."*

"Is that a way of saying that you dislike change?"

"Perhaps," said Tuta with a wry smile. *"But Tuta is a realist. He is an old man who would slow you down. And while Tuta is both charming and knowledgeable on many subjects, he realizes that Panya and Meryt may soon tire of him and wish he had been left behind. Better for Tuta to recall you both as if you were the daughters he always wished he had been able to bring upon the earth."*

"That is sweet, Tuta."

"Daughters whose oddities and adventures he could recall fondly in his declining years, even though they never came to visit."

Luja rose, walked to the other side of the room, knelt beside Tuta. *"You make me laugh and hurt my heart at the same time, old one,"* confessed Luja. *"For I have enjoyed our* friendship. Yet, it hurts to know that, once Panya and I leave, it is unlikely we will see you again."

"Tuta feels this hurt as well. Perhaps you will grant him a small kindness before this unhappy hour arrives."

"What do you wish?"

"To know the truth of who you are, Meryt. You have said you are from the north. You have the gift of foresight. But you have not told all, have you? Your knowledge of Cessair and Shendjw was...quite detailed. It is interesting that the gods should choose to give such knowledge to one who must travel from the far end of the world, rather than to simply reveal it to one who already resides in the Two Lands."

Luja smiled. "It may be that Tuta sees more than Luja."

"Tuta often sees more than he should, it seems."

"You are quite clever, my unexpected friend. And you have risked your life for us. Were I your daughter, I would deem it an honor." She took a deep breath. "You are correct. There is more than we have told you. I was born in the Two Lands. I later went to live in the north. Panya was born in the far north but spent much of her life in a new land across a great sea."

"The priests tell us that the land of the dead is across the great sea."

"There is much the priests do not know. Would it surprise you to know that the world is not flat, like bread, but round like a melon?"

"Tuta is easily amazed, yet not surprised."

"Great magic brought Panya and me here from a place too distant to understand. We did not wish to make the journey, but when we arrived, we resolved to keep Shendjw from working great evil upon the world."

"The place you come from...a place too distant to understand...what is it like?"

"In many ways, it is like the Two Lands. There is art and music. There are the rich and the poor. Some are cruel and *some are kind. Most have the skills of scribes. People who wish to be free struggle against those who wish to enslave them. In other ways, it is different. Travel from one land to another is swift. One can reach any land in a day inside a great metal bird. One can send a message to any land in a moment."*

"A place of wonders to be sure!"

"Yet, I have seen no artisan whose skills are the equal of Tuta's."

For the first time, the old man seemed at a loss for words. He turned away from Luja for a moment. When he returned his gaze, the rims of his eyes were bright with unshed tears.

"Will you return to this place that is too distant to understand?"

Luja shook her head. *"It is not possible."*

They sat silently for several minutes. Then footsteps sounded outside. The small child from the nearby shop poked her head through the doorway.

"Soldiers in the marketplace!"

Tuta quickly snuffed the lamp.

"Shendjw will not relent. When Panya returns, you must leave tonight." He secured the entrance door with a palm wood crosspiece. *"Cover yourself on my mat. I will do what I must to send them away."*

Luja felt her way to the back room in the dark as several heavy blows were delivered onto the door.

"Shopkeeper! Give us entrance upon order of Crocodile!"

Tuta paused a few moments to give the impression that he had just been roused from slumber and was making his way blearily to the door. As a second round of blows began, he spoke.

"Tuta is coming! The dark is an obstacle, as is the age of Tuta's bones!"

He removed the crosspiece and opened the door, whereupon several soldiers pushed into the shop, one carrying a lantern.

"Tuta gladly opens his shop to the great Crocodile's soldiers, even if this intrusion has interrupted the dream of a much younger Tuta in the arms of several enthusiastic concubines!"

"Silence, fool!" shouted the leader. Then he signaled two of the others. *"Get the woman!"*

Tuta's face fell as Luja was dragged from the back room.

"As we suspected," said the leader with a malicious chuckle. *"Harboring an enemy of Crocodile, old fool? Your bones shall surely know pain as never before."*

"An enemy of Crocodile?" Tuta wore a look of shock. *"Tuta took the woman for a homeless wanderer in need of lodging for the evening. Tuta would never think to betray he who provides land for farms and shops, who breathes life into the city, who protects—"*

"Enough, maggot! Tonight we discovered the other woman had entered the palace inside a crocodile skin! Not long ago, we disturbed the sleep of the dealer. He was reluctant to tell us who supplied the creature. However, we were persuasive."

The soldiers hustled their two captives into the street. Overhead, starry skies bore witness.

"What of Panya?" asked Luja.

The leader's smile was just visible. *"Let us say she did not fare well!"*

"What does that mean?"

"You shall see for yourselves!"

She expected that they would be going to the palace, but it quickly became apparent their destination was elsewhere. As they reached the edge of the city, she whispered to Tuta.

"What lies ahead?"

"Nothing good," he replied. *"Only the cemeteries of Tarkhan."*

***

Ricky awoke shivering. Remembering the crocodiles, she jerked in startle, but quickly realized she was no longer in the pool. Her hands were bound and rested upon her stomach. Her feet were bound as well. She lay uncomfortably on her back on a hollowed-out slab. The flicker of oil lamps lit the windowless room, which appeared to have cut stone walls. She struggled to sit up, but a voice stopped her.

"Stay."

Shendjw.

She stopped struggling, endeavored to assess her situation. After a few silent moments, Shendjw spoke.

"You are wondering why you were saved from the crocodiles."

She said nothing. Turning her head to the side, she saw that on this occasion, the sorcerer was dressed in what appeared to be a sleeveless black robe, belted, and wearing a wide, segmented gold neckpiece. His eyes were again outlined in black.

"It was a simple matter. The guards heard your cries. A few thumps on the snout with the butt of their spears. A few scraps of meat tossed away from you. The guards pulled you free. The brutes would not have killed you, of course, immortal as you are. The wounds you had already sustained healed quickly. And my plans for you call for something else."

Ricky did not respond to this at first but eventually asked, *"Where am I?"*

"Not as comfortable as my palace, is it?"

"I didn't find your palace all that comfortable," said Ricky. *"Must have been all those monsters hanging from the ceiling. Oh yeah...and our host."*

275

Shendjw laughed. *"Ah, Panya, you amuse me! If only you could be coerced into joining me!"*

"I'd feel safer joining the real crocodiles."

Again, he laughed. *"And you would be right about that!"*

"You knew I was coming."

Shendjw nodded. *"Yes. When Zohar visited me long ago, he warned me of your coming after forty years had elapsed. He did not know exactly when or how, only that you would come."*

"You created the crocodile pool to protect the scroll."

Shendjw said nothing for a moment. Then he smiled. *"You wonder why the scroll was not where you expected it to be."*

Their conversation was interrupted by scuffling footsteps on the stone stairs. Ricky strained to see over the edge of the odd bed upon which she had been placed. Through a narrow opening into an adjacent room, she saw a thin figure shamble down the last of a flight of steps. He went down on one knee, then raised himself to stand again. Two palace guards followed closely behind him. As the flickering light illuminated his deeply lined face, Ricky's heart skipped as she recognized Tuta.

"Surely the Crocodile's guards have better things to do than harass an old merchant," said Tuta, as one of the soldiers gave him a push forward. *"And to pull Tuta from his bed so deep into the night. Crocodile must desire some great service that only the master carver Tuta can provide."*

Behind Tuta's guards was a sight even more disheartening. Luja followed stoically. Unlike Tuta, her hands were bound. Two more soldiers trailed her.

No! This can't be happening!

Tuta and Luja were directed to stand against the wall at Ricky's left, a soldier on each side of the pair. The other two soldiers hung back by the entrance.

"Luja!"

"Did you get the scroll?" Luja asked in English, her eyes pleading.

Ricky shook her head. "It wasn't there!"

"Ah, Great Crocodile!" Tuta began again. *"Magnificent Crocodile! How may I be of service? A carving to grace your temple? I can do stone, ivory, wood. Just—"*

"Shut up, old man!" Shendjw raised a finger accusingly. *"You are here because of your association with these traitors."*

"These?" asked Tuta in feigned disbelief, inclining his head toward Luja and then Ricky. *"Tuta has never seen them before tonight. But yes, they look shrewd and dangerous."*

"I should cut out your incessant tongue and feed it to the jackals," said Shendjw. He reached into a fold in his garment and withdrew a small object. Straining to lift her head, Ricky recognized it as the wooden eye that Tuta had carved for her. She had not even felt it was missing, but now realized Shendjw must have removed it while she was unconscious.

"When I saw this up close, I knew there was only one man in Tarkhan who could have created it," said Shendjw. *"And when my men discovered that you had supplied the crocodile that had concealed Panya, it confirmed that you were concealing the other traitor as well."*

"Traitors they may be, Wondrous Crocodile," replied Tuta. *"To Tuta, they were merely customers who paid for shelter and Tuta's carving talents."*

Shendjw glared at him. *"Be quiet, fool! And what of Cessair? She cannot live! The poison was too strong. What has become of her?"*

No one replied to this. After a long silence, Shendjw smiled again.

"I have heard that I will see many miracles in the future. Carts faster than a cheetah that will move without being pushed. Weapons that can be held in one's hand and strike down a distant enemy. People able to fly inside metal wings. Pictures that travel invisibly through the air and appear in a box."

"Wait until you hear the part about people getting to choose their leaders," said Ricky. *"You're really going to love that."*

Shendjw smiled while grinding his teeth. *"The changes I shall make over the centuries shall result in a different outcome. One pharaoh, one king, forever! With Cessair gone, there are none who can challenge me."*

Now it was Ricky's turn to smile. *"Someone will stop you! Even if we failed, some day, someone will discover the Scroll of Life and Death. You'll screw up. Or some group of rebels a thousand years from now who are tired of living under your thumb will figure out where you've got the scroll hidden. No one can keep a secret forever."*

"Unless..." Luja stared at Shendjw, horrified. And suddenly, Ricky understood.

"There was never a scroll to find!" The implications of this were staggering and drained the remaining hope from her. *"You don't need a scroll. You created the enchantment. You have it in your brain."*

"My heart," Shendjw corrected her, and Ricky recalled that the Egyptians of this time period considered the brain a worthless organ, believing that the heart was the source of all thought and emotion.

"So it was all a game," said Ricky, her eyes flashing with unconcealed disgust.

"The unfortunate Zohar, he brought you to this age to deal with Cessair," said Shendjw. *"Instead, you befriended her. But in the end, the result was the same. Because of Zohar's words, I am now able to still the hearts of all my enemies. Once he brought the scroll to my younger self forty years ago, I used its magic and then destroyed it."*

"In the end, you're just another drunk-with-power barbarian, surrendering to his most vulgar desires," taunted Ricky.

Shendjw smiled. *"Words make weak swords."*

"History will regard you as the foulest of tyrants."

"It is the pharaohs who determine what scribes chisel onto the temple columns!" roared Shendjw. *"What will be immortalized in stone and plaster will not be the opinions of rebellious vermin. It will be stories of terrible power and warnings that inspire fear. So vast will be my rule, and so swift my vengeance that none will cry 'tyrant' or dare stand against me!"*

"You underestimate the human spirit and the desire for freedom," retorted Ricky.

"Spirit and desire are mere words that will die on the lips of my vanquished enemies. Cessair is gone. And once you and Meryt are gone, there will be none to oppose me! I will take what I want, rule as I see fit!"

Luja laughed, an act so out of place it startled Ricky.

"Knowledge turns the slave into a king," said Luja. *"Ignorance turns the king into a slave."*

"Your words mean nothing to me, witch!"

"They will mean everything to you! For you are wrong!"

Shendjw regarded her darkly. *"Cessair was mortal. She might have opposed me, if she had learned the secrets of life and death. If she had become immortal herself. But your interference doomed her. Now she resides among the dead. You know the secret of the scroll, witch, but you also will be dead soon."*

"Tuta is ignorant of all of this sorcery!" said the old man, waving his hands about as if confused. *"Perhaps he should return to his shop and sequester himself in prayer to the gods of the Two Lands."* He took a step toward the next room but was pushed back roughly by one of the soldiers.

Shendjw laughed. *"Ignorance may be a slave's salvation."* Then he turned to Ricky and his mood darkened again. *"You are immortal. Very curious. That, too, will change. And when you are no longer among the living, no force shall threaten my rule. I alone will possess the secret!"*

"No!" cried Luja. *"There is another!"*

"If you think to delay your death, witch, you will be disappointed."

"It is you who shall taste disappointment, mighty Crocodile! And fear!"

Shendjw glared at Luja. "Crocodile fears no one!"

"Crocodile shall come to fear Cessair!"

Shendjw laughed. "Cessair is dead!"

"Yes. Cessair is dead. And Cessair lives."

Shendjw glowered. *"Pretending madness will not save you, witch."*

"Look into my eyes, King of Crocodiles, and you will know that I am speaking truth!"

The king narrowed his gaze on Luja. *"Empty words may buy you a moment, witch, but they will not buy you your life or alter my destiny!"*

There is another, Luja had said. Was she simply trying to confuse Shendjw? It seemed to Ricky that only Fintan knew of the magic, and he was likely in hiding somewhere outside of Tarkhan. Otherwise, he would have been taken prisoner along with Luja and Tuta. But Fintan certainly posed no threat to Shendjw, since he did not know the ritual. Was Luja planning to give up Fintan in an attempt to bargain for their freedom by suggesting he knew more than he actually did?

"Luja, say no more!" Ricky gasped.

Luja turned to her friend. *"It must be told. Shendjw must know that his power is not absolute!"* She returned her icy stare to Crocodile. *"Fintan Mac is the father of Cessair's child. He is a great explorer and warrior."*

"And why should I be afraid of this Fintan Mac?"

"You should be afraid of Cessair!"

"Cessair is dead!" bellowed Shendjw, whose voice reverberated off the stone walls.

"Hear me!" Luja cried. *"Fintan has left Tarkhan. He is beyond your reach. And he has taken the child with him."*

Shendjw's eyes widened noticeably. *"Child? You have already said that Cessair is dead. Her unborn child died with her!"*

Luja's countenance brightened as if bathed in the light of Hathor, the sun goddess. She spoke with the vitality of one who has emerged from a great battle, victorious. *"Although your poison killed the priestess, the infant survived."*

For a few moments, Shendjw seemed unable to respond to this revelation, but then be gathered himself. *"Of what interest is this to me? All people, whether farmers or warriors, withered crones or children will soon bow down to me."*

"This child has something no other has. The Scroll of Life and Death!"

Now it was Shendjw's turn to laugh. *"Foolish woman! There is no scroll!"*

"But there was at one time."

"I destroyed it!"

"In our time, in the mists of distant future, the story was recorded in Lebor Gabála Érenn. Cessair stole the scroll. It was brought out of the Two Lands and hidden in a secret place for thousands of years. Cessair assumed a different name and searched relentlessly for it. And what were you doing during these many centuries?"

"He was hiding!" goaded Ricky, hoping that she could somehow provoke Shendjw into making a mistake that might provide them an opportunity to escape. *"The brave and powerful Crocodile was hiding!"*

Shendjw burned with hatred, but it was Luja who continued speaking.

"You were an old man. You assumed an alias of your own and awaited your chance, not wishing to reveal yourself, knowing that you could be destroyed by Cessair if she recovered the scroll first and stole away your immortality."

"That is the old story," said Shendjw with a thin smile. *"I am changed, and a new story is being written. Cessair will not be stealing any scrolls this time,*

"She did not need to," continued Luja. *"In the far-away future time, I was asked to translate the ancient scroll. And I do not forget what I read!"*

Shendjw took a spear from one of his soldiers, and his eyes darkened. *"Death will make you forget!"*

"I am not the one you must fear!" said Luja. *"You must fear Cessair!"*

"Cessair is dead!"

"Yes! And Cessair lives!"

"You speak nonsense!" roared Shendjw. *"You may have come from a time when Cessair existed and I was ancient. But you have helped to change what will come to pass in seasons too great to count. In that distant time, I will be young and powerful! And there will be no Cessair!"*

Ricky's head was spinning. They had buried Cessair. Had her friend's mind snapped as she found herself facing what were likely her last moments in the world?

Shendjw shouted at Luja, *"And if you are thinking of a resurrection, you are certainly aware that the scroll enchantment cannot bring the dead back to life!"*

The blaze of torches flickered in Luja's eyes. *"I do not forget what I read! Panya hoped to find the scroll in the palace. But if she failed, what then? We gave much thought to this. Something must be done to keep a balance of power so that Shendjw cannot sack the world with impunity. And so, as we schemed in Tuta's shop, I told what I remembered. I remembered it all. Tutu wrote it onto goatskin parchment.*

And that scroll was sent with Fintan when he left tonight. In time, he will be reunited with Cessair."

"That is true," said Shendjw. *"They will be reunited when I have hunted him down and ripped out his bowels!"*

Luja shook her head. *"No. He will meet up with Ladra, with whom Cessair travels."*

Ricky shook her head. *"But Ladra is traveling with..."* Then she understood. Luja saw the truth wash across her friend's face and smiled. And Luja spoke this truth triumphantly.

"Fintan has said he will name the child 'Cessair,' to honor her mother and her sacrifice."

CHAPTER 23

Ricky began to shake as the puzzle pieces fell into place and she understood. Cessair's daughter would grow into a young woman and then use the scroll to become immortal. Raised on the stories of her mother's murder by Shendjw, she would grow bitter and embark upon her own campaign for vengeance. Alarmed by the changes in his daughter, Fintan would hide the scroll. Five thousand years later, Ricky and Crockett would find it in a passage tomb. And they would fight for their lives against Cessair—not the priestess that they had befriended, but rather her daughter of the same name.

This was why the Cessair that she and Luja had met in Ma'at's temple seemed so different from the Cessair they had battled.

A prolonged, primal cry from Shendjw indicated he now understood as well. Not the details of what would transpire in Ireland. But he now knew that the Kingdom of the Crocodile could not begin until after Cessair's daughter had been vanquished. If he reached for the brass ring too soon, Cessair's daughter would realize he was the murderer of her mother. And that would put a target on his back. If she discovered Fintan's hiding place for the scroll, she might be able to strip him of his immortality and, before he could restore it, send him to Ma'at. And he knew how his soul would fare against Ma'at's feather.

"Nothing we did mattered," said Ricky to Luja in English, her voice cracking. "Nothing will change. The timeline found a way to repair itself." She had harbored such hopes. Leo

Brenner, Doc Campion, her sister. She had hoped there would be a way to change the past so that they would enjoy better fates.

And Crockett.

His chance to live again was gone.

"Where?" roared Shendjw. *"Where did Fintan go?"*

"To the land of the Hatti, of course," said Luja. *"Perhaps there will be space on the ark for a child, once they understand what has happened to her mother."*

"You are lying!"

"Then perhaps they journey through the great mountains to the east, to the mysterious lands beyond—where they will never be found."

"I have methods that will make you talk!"

"Oh, I am sure of it," said Luja. *"In fact, we will tell you many stories of Fintan's whereabouts. Which of them is true? Or are any of them?"*

Shendjw ground his teeth, clenched his free hand tightly and stared at the ground. Then he seemed to come to a decision, turned and spoke with one of the soldiers, who then disappeared up the stairs.

"He will summon my best trackers. They will find Fintan and the Scroll of Life and Death you have created. And there is no reason for me to delay my plans for the three of you."

"Three?" interjected Tuta. *"Certainly Generous Crocodile has no quarrel with Tuta, whose memory, made unreliable by age, will cause him to forget everything he has seen and heard on this night before the sun rises."*

"And rise it shall, Tuta," said Shendjw. *"Soon. And so there is important business to conclude."*

***

Shendjw handed the spear he had been clutching back to its owner. *"Suffer our company a bit longer, Tuta, before you are put on your way. Few people have seen the wonder that you will now have the privilege to witness."*

He turned to a man standing just behind him and accepted a cedar tablet. Then he turned back to Ricky. *"Your name is here written!"* He held the tablet above his head.

Ricky gasped. *The elements! Earth!*

Now Shendjw exchanged the tablet for an unadorned bowl and stepped beside Ricky. From the bowl, he withdrew a feathered brush and flicked a mist of liquid onto her.

Water! No! The deadly elixir!

As it had with Benna and Kissu, this version of the scroll ceremony would bestow death. Once her mortality was restored, a grim fate would follow at sunrise. At An Tsuil last year, she had watched fifty of Cessair's followers become disoriented, begin to age, and crumble to dust and bones as the process accelerated.

Shendjw handed the bowl to one of the soldiers, faced Ricky, raised both hands above his head as if beseeching a deity. *"Let our lives follow the light!"*

Wind!

He then turned immediately to his right, which could only be the west, the direction of the setting sun.

Fire!

She suddenly felt a chill, a sickly weakness.

"You feel it already, don't you?" said Shendjw, smiling darkly. *"Your return to the world of mortals."*

Ricky had nothing to say. Her lips trembled. Suddenly, her thoughts seemed to make no sense. She could not tell whether it was panic or something else.

"Now my embalmers will help you on your next journey!"

Real terror now enveloped her as she understood where she was. This was not a room in Shendjw's palace. This was a tomb in one of Tarkhan's cemeteries. The recessed surface she was lying on was part of a stone sarcophagus.

Two men stepped forward and began to wrap Ricky tightly in the burial linens used in mummification. When she struggled, several soldiers stepped in to hold her still.

"This tomb was constructed for me when I was a barely a man. My name is inscribed in its walls. My history painted upon stone. But I have no need of it now. When my embalmers are finished, you will be sealed into the stone sarcophagus once intended for me. You will be sealed inside, alive for now. Then I will leave this place, bury the entrance. When the sun rises, you will turn to dust. Perhaps someday you will be found —only dust and wrappings. It could be that the hunter of treasures will believe he has found the remains of Crocodile!"

Ricky ceased struggling. The wrappings had made it difficult to move at all. It was truly hopeless. She heard Luja's laughter. Her friend, knowing this was the end, must have succumbed to madness. Only Ricky's eye was unwrapped, and she could see Tuta looking at her with the greatest sadness as he stood near the wall beside her friend.

Shendjw again took up the spear and walked to within a few feet of where Luja and Tuta stood. Luja laughed once more, and Ricky saw Shendjw's shoulders tense. The fortune teller spoke to him glibly. *"My life has been well lived. I shall only be sorry that I will not live to see you humbled and destroyed. Such a waste. The good you could do with your power. The evil you will do."*

"For a witch and a seer, your view of the future is quite cloudy," said Shendjw, speaking slowly, deliberately. *"I will be neither humbled nor destroyed. But you are right about the other. You will not live."*

Luja turned to Ricky and began to speak. "Remem—" She got no further. Shendjw's spear tip shot forward lightning fast, the lance piercing Luja's chest, the tip sparking on the stone wall behind her.

Ricky's cry was muffled by the wraps. Luja made not a sound, but turned toward Tuta, her eyes flickering. The old man cried out as if *he* had been struck by the spear. He clutched at her, tried to lower her gently. It seemed to Ricky that Luja's lips moved near his ear. Tears suddenly streamed down the old man's face as he lay the now motionless form on the floor of the mastaba.

Shendjw glowered at Tuta. *"You show such sorrow for a stranger and an enemy of Crocodile?"*

"Forgive Tuta, Merciful Crocodile," said the old man, coughing, standing, his voice, while halting and shaky, quickly recovering some of the tone of a sycophant. *"Even in his old age, Tuta is distressed by the death of a beautiful young woman...who is the same age as Tuta's own daughter. Tuta's own... my own daughter. A daughter who often brought the blessing of chaos into Tuta's life to remind Tuta that he was alive. If such a fate were to befall her... it would tear Tuta's heart from his chest."*

Shendjw laughed. *"Enough, old fool! It is time for you to leave this place."*

"As you wish, for Tuta always..." He seemed unable to finish the sentence. An instant later, Tuta seemed to regain some of his self-assurance, pointed to Ricky. *"This one, this Panya attempted to ensnare Tuta in her evil plan. May I speak a curse to her?"*

"Anything you wish. She is already cursed, and there is none who can undo it. But be quick about it!"

Tuta lurched to Ricky's side, bent close to her ear, spoke in the faintest of whispers.

"Ricky...Mars Library of Unforgivable Sins."

Ricky's eye widened. Tuta straightened, began walking toward the anteroom. After only a few steps, Shendjw pulled his knife, stepped behind Tuta and slit his throat. The old man gasped, scrabbled at his neck, made a gurgling sound and collapsed onto the floor. Shendjw stood over him until he stopped moving.

"That, old man, is for creating the scroll for my enemies!"

***

All that remained of her life was reduced to twisting against and screaming muffled noises from beneath the bindings, an impotent show of defiance against her captors. With Luja dead, the last of her allies was gone. And Luja had been the only person other than Shendjw who could possibly do the life enchantment that would save her. Even if she were to escape, death would follow shortly, for it was now surely just minutes until the sun would rise. No one else knew the secrets of the scroll. At least no one who would reveal them to her.

As the embalmers lifted the lid of the stone sarcophagus, Ricky began to weep and moan uncontrollably. She wept for Luja, for Tuta, and for gentle Cessair. She wept for their failure. Five thousand years from now, the world would face unimaginable peril. All their efforts, their sacrifices, for nothing.

She wept for Crockett.

Was there a place beyond the physical world where they would come together again? She doubted it. More likely, in a few minutes, there would be...nothing. This terrified her in a way she did not understand. Death had always seemed an academic concept, something that happened to others. It seemed impossible to wrap one's head around the idea that it would all be gone, every thought, memory and sensation. That she would just cease.

On the other hand, perhaps this existence was not the end. Cessair—whether the woman they had befriended in Tarkhan or her daughter—had flouted God by conducting her scroll ceremony at the Irish abbey known as An Tsuil—the Eye of God. Had an angry God retaliated by setting in motion the events that had led Ricky, Brenner and Crockett to destroy her? At the time, their success had seemed to favor the existence of some divine providence. If so, where was that same God now?

Shendjw came to stand over the coffin.

"Before I leave you, Panya, I return what is yours." He produced the prosthetic eye that Tuta had so meticulously created, held it aloft for her to see. Then he reached forward and, with surprising gentleness, lifted her lid and slid the eye into place. Then he stepped back. "There may be other worlds that follow this one. That is uncertain. What is certain is that you shall see this world no more."

In response to a slight motion of his hand, the embalmers lifted the heavy lid onto the sarcophagus and Ricky found herself in complete darkness.

She tried to slow her breathing. There was nothing to do. Luja and Tuta lay dead in the now dark tomb and could not help her. Fintan was far away, journeying to a rendezvous with Ladra and his daughter on the island that would one day be called Ireland.

The thought of Luja struck down by Shendjw was unbearable. If she and Crockett had never gone to the fortune teller's shop in Dublin, she would still be alive, living a life at peace with the universe, helping people navigate their lives' convoluted pathways, and enjoying a steaming cup of tea. Then again, without Luja's help, they would have never been able to defeat Cessair. Perhaps it was all pre-ordained. Maybe everything was connected and, no matter what choices had been made, Luja was slated to die.

Maybe this was the timeline, healing itself.

But if everything was connected, part of some great master plan that, when complete, would prove to be a masterpiece on every level, what was the significance of Luja's final words? Ricky had suspected Luja had whispered something to Tuta with her last breath, her punctured lung unable to muster enough force to shout across the tomb. Tuta had delivered the message to Ricky, whispering it in English, and using the name Ricky. Tuta could not have known that name or contrived those words on his own.

Ricky...Mars Library of Unforgivable Sins.

This message seemed nonsense. And useless to one who was about to die.

Everything seemed so useless.

She closed her eyelids.

Just like everything in her life, it seemed to make no difference. And despite this, she knew that her last thought in this world would be a question to which she would never know the answer. Words spoken from a dead woman to a dead woman. An unresolved question she would take with her into the eternal.

Why?

CHAPTER 24

Shendjw mounted the last of the stone steps and emerged into the retreating night. The sky was lightening in the east and, in moments, the sun would send its first rays over the horizon. His laborers were finishing the anteroom wall. After that, the tomb entrance would be sealed, and they would immediately begin shoveling earth into the pit. In minutes, tons of sand would cover the stone door that blocked entry into the mastaba. Even if an army arrived to aid Panya, they would not be able to reach her before sunrise.

He had no doubt his men would find Fintan, the Scroll of Life and Death, and the child. The Kingdom of the Crocodile would rise soon. He was immortal. He had nothing to fear.

Yet, the witch's words echoed.

I shall only be sorry that I will not live to see you humbled and destroyed.

Why should this bother him? He was immortal, the most powerful being in the world. And she was a corpse. He smiled toward the rising sun, which had just now spilled its first rays over the arid landscape.

"Goodbye, Panya."

Flanked by soldiers, he began the walk back toward the palace.

THE END

AUTHOR'S NOTES

That wide 'no man's land' that exists between what we *think* we know, and what we *actually* know, is my playground as an author. It's where I get to dig around and get messy and learn things. I spent much time in that playground writing *The Book of Devils*.

No ancient civilization has perhaps captured the popular imagination as have the Egyptians, from films to traveling exhibitions to mythology. When people think of ancient Egypt, the first things that often come to mind are racing horse-drawn chariots, the Great Pyramid (as well as the lesser ones) at Giza, the Sphinx, and Pharaohs like Tutankhamun.

And that makes sense. Films like The Ten Commandments, The Mummy, and Cleopatra have reinforced these images. But Egypt is an old civilization whose language, art, architecture, and stories go back much farther.

And because of this, writing not merely about ancient Egypt, but about *ancient*, ancient Egypt poses some challenges.

A good portion of *The Book of Devils* is set approximately five thousand years in the past. Egypt at that time was already a thriving culture, but it would have looked quite different than the movie depictions that have become so popular. For instance, there was no, single, powerful pharaoh uniting all of Egypt. Ramses? Cleopatra? Seti? Nefertiti? All of these came much later. If you showed up in Egypt right around 3000 B.C. looking for Cleopatra, well, bring a couple of good books to occupy your time, because you'd have to wait almost thirty centuries for her to ascend the throne. Instead of a united Egypt, you'd discover lots of regional rulers, although Egypt was already trending toward a single king, which began the Dynastic Period. Setting an exact date for when this occurred is difficult, and even the best guesses could be centuries off.

So there was no single, all-powerful pharaoh. And, five thousand-ish years ago, there were no pyramids at Giza. The Great Pyramid and others would not be built on that site for at least another five centuries.

And no chariot races. Egyptians didn't discover the wheel until about the time the pyramids were built, and it was another seven hundred years before they decided to slap them onto chariots. No horses either until around 1700 B.C.

The reason I mention these differences is because their absence makes it more difficult to write about ancient Egypt. It's easy to paint a picture of Egypt using the familiar tropes. Without them, one must look elsewhere to create a convincing and relatively accurate environment for the reader. What were their houses like? Their temples? How did they dress? Did they call Egypt "Egypt"? We know or have a sense of these things if we're imagining Ramses' or Cleopatra's time, but centuries earlier? Our knowledge of truly ancient times is limited. And even finding the answers can be difficult, for clues become scarcer the farther back one digs. On top of this, the evidence that does survive may be the subject of conjecture and debate. As a result, my construction—or anyone's, for that matter—of Egyptian civilization five thousand years ago, while supported by some evidence, is still colored with guesswork. Still, doing the digging into the past and arriving at that place where one can make those guesses and create a credible, ancient Egypt for readers is where the fun comes in for a writer.

What complicates the study of that era in a different way is the language. Even if you had studied the ancient language before traveling far into the past, you might not be understood by the Egyptians of five thousand years ago. Ancient Egyptian written language is an abjad language, which means without vowels. As a result, we have to guess what sound they intended when trying to pronounce the words. There are no recordings to guide us. So if you were going to ancient Egypt, it would probably be a good idea for you to sit back once you arrived and listen for a while.

The aforementioned language issues created another hurdle in writing this book. I couldn't just send my time travelers into the past, since they would be unable to communicate. The Doctor (as in *Doctor Who*) might have the Tardis and possibly telepathy to provide instantaneous back-and-forth translations anywhere in time and space, but my characters were not Time Lords. Nor did they possess Douglas Adams' Babel Fish which, once inserted into the ear, accomplished the same thing. My characters are human beings thrust into extraordinary situations. Thus, a portion of the story had to include their preparation for a journey to a culture very different from their own, and which included giving them training in the language specific to that period.

Consequently, most of the time I spent in that no man's land mentioned earlier was devoted to creating a credible Predynastic Egypt and creating credible paths for my characters to navigate the various hurdles placed in their way. To be honest, both of these have been a great deal of fun for me. To be sure, I took a bit of artistic license in building my ancient Egypt, but I hope that none of this diminished your enjoyment of the finished product.

With respect to the stumbling blocks with which I confronted my characters, in both The *Book of Invasions* and *The Book of Devils*, I have enjoyed painting my characters into corners—places and situation from which it was seemingly impossible for them to extricate themselves, and then finding reasonable solutions for them. A columnist for the review giant Kirkus recently likened *The Book of Invasions* to Indiana Jones and *The Girl with the Dragon Tattoo* for the characters' harrowing and inventive escapes. That brought a smile to my face.

Ultimately, I hope my readers have as much fun with it all as I do.

—Rod Vick
www.rodvick.com

ABOUT THE AUTHOR

ROD VICK

Award-winning author Rod Vick writes mysteries and thrillers. *The Book of Invasions*, the first book in the Five Ancient Elements Series from Penmore Press, was the recipient of an elite Kirkus Reviews starred review. In the nineteen and a half waking minutes of the day when he's not writing or giving foot rubs to his Lovely Wife Marsha, Rod runs half marathons, travels by train, and daydreams of alternate dimensions where lawns mow themselves. He lives in Wisconsin where cheese is a religion, and you're never far from something that might go "moo."

IF YOU ENJOYED THIS BOOK VISIT

PENMORE PRESS

www.penmorepress.com

All Penmore Press books are available directly through our website.

The Book Of
Invasions
By
Rod Vick

The Book of Invasions is a globe-spanning adventure, a romp through history and mythology, a grudging love story, and an all-in battle against an evil hidden in plain sight. The world is stunned by the inexplicable murder of a dozen climate scientists at a remote research station in Greenland. When twenty-six-year-old Ricky Crowe, sister of a slain researcher, unexpectedly comes into possession of a parchment map found in Greenland's 5,000-year-old ice, she attempts to set aside the demons of her own grief and alcoholism—and a terrifying past that has left her with an eight-inch facial scar—in order to determine whether the map holds a key to her sister's fate. Bringing it to experts at the foundation that funded her sister's research, she sets in motion a race with her new allies to unravel puzzles hidden in tombs in Egypt and Ireland, and in an obscure book of Celtic myth—The Book of Invasions—before the secrets are lost to the ruthless cult that has searched relentlessly for the world-changing evil the map promises since before the pyramids were built.

FENMORE PRESS
www.fenmorepress.com

DEADLY VISION

BY

T.D. SEVERIN

A revolutionary medical breakthrough. A technology, so advanced, people will kill to prevent its discovery. Dr. Taylor Abrahms, rising above his troubled past, is an expert in the burgeoning field of Medical Virtual Reality. A gifted researcher, he's created an experimental fusion of virtual reality, artificial intelligence, and microsurgery that will revolutionize the way surgery is performed. With the Virtual Heart Project (VHP), Taylor can enter a virtual recreation of his patient's beating heart and perform critical, life-saving surgery entirely within the realm of virtual reality. But in the political war zone of San Francisco University Medical Center, not everyone is thrilled. With a health care crisis threatening to bankrupt the nation, advanced biotechnology is a flashpoint in health care reform. Taylor's research is scapegoated and he finds himself caught between warring factions in medicine and politics that will do anything to shut his project down, a battle that rages all the way to an upcoming Presidential election.

PENMORE PRESS
www.penmorepress.com

Blossom In The Ashes
By
Ron Singerton

1941: Two Brothers, One Woman, One War

Tad, elder son of Russian-born political refugee Alexei and Japanese-born Kimi, flies planes for the U.S. Navy; his brother, Koizumi, is a fighter pilot in the Imperial Navy of Japan. When Koizumi visits his family in Hawaii, he is accompanied by the beautiful Sayuri. To Koizumi's dismay, she and Tad begin a passionate romance, only to be torn apart when she and Koizumi are ordered back to Tokyo.

All too soon, Tad discovers that, if being estranged from a brother for 25 years is bad, seeing him in your gun sights is worse. And as American bombs fall on Japan, Tad fears that he will never see Sayuri again.

Commitment, terror, compassion and unswerving loyalty comprise *A Blossom in the Ashes*, a story of unyielding nations in a world gone mad.

"A riveting novel that is a new twist on family relationships during World War II. Singeron's characters are interesting, the story engrossing and fast-paced. It's a must read for those who like this genre." — Marc Liebman, author of award-winning novels *Forgotten* and *Inner Look*, and *Big Mother 40*, a top 50 war novel.

The sequel to award-winning *A Cherry Blossom in Winter*

A Congress of Kings
BY
James Boschert

The Year 1191

Under the vigilant protection of Lord Talon and his companions, the land of Kantara enjoys peace even as the tyrant Isaac Komnenos continues to plunder the rest of Cyprus. However, dark clouds are gathering and great storms bring with them unwelcome Norman visitors. Soon Talon is embroiled in the invasion of Cyprus, assisting King Richard of England who, en route to Acre for the Third Crusade, must save his royal sister, Queen Joanna, from Isaac's clutches.

Talon is forced to accompany Richard I to the besieged city of Acre—a city which holds painful memories for Talon. There, quarreling kings, men who once were kings, and men who want to be kings form the leadership of the Crusading armies. Their lust for power blinds them to the threat posed by Salah ad Din, the skilled general who fights on the Arab side, continuing the tragedy that started with the terrible defeat at Hattin.

And lurking out of sight is yet another implacable foe who prepares his own assassins for a mission of revenge. Talon has eluded the *Fidai* of The Master Rashid ad Din for nearly twenty years, but his luck may be running out.

PENMORE PRESS
www.penmorepress.com